DATE DUE

NOV 2 9 1988		
OCT 2 4 1990		

DEMCO 38-297

SECOND
HOEING

HOPE WILLIAMS SYKES

Introduction by Timothy J. Kloberdanz

University of Nebraska Press
Lincoln • London

First Bison Book edition: December 1982
Most recent printing indicated by the first digit below:
2   3   4   5   6   7   8   9   10

Library of Congess Cataloging in Publication Data
Sykes, Hope Williams, 1901-73
    Second hoeing.
    Reprint. Originally published: New York: Putnam, c1935.
    I. Title.
PS3537.Y52S4 1982   813'.52   82-8424
ISBN 0-8032-4136-4   AACR2
ISBN 0-8032-9129-9 (pbk.)

This edition is reprinted from a copy of the first edition graciously
loaned to the publisher by Charlene Tresner, Fort Collins, Colorado.

Introduction to the Bison Book Edition
by Timothy J. Kloberdanz

When *Second Hoeing* first appeared in the spring of 1935, it provoked a curious mixture of critical acclaim and bitter controversy. The accolades came largely from book reviewers, writing for both national and regional publications, who warmly praised the novel's "obvious authenticity" as well as its engrossing "power and beauty." Disapproval came primarily from members of the ethnic group who inspired most of the characters in *Second Hoeing*, German-Russian farmers and laborers in the sugar beet country of northern Colorado. Negative reactions to *Second Hoeing* were so strong among German-Russians of the 1930s that heated feelings persist even today, though greatly cooled by nearly half a century of detachment and reevaluation.

Despite the flickering controversy that still surrounds *Second Hoeing*, Hope Williams Sykes's first novel fully warrants reissue in a form that will make it readily available to potential readers. Until now, copies of *Second Hoeing* have been difficult to obtain outside of major libraries and special collections. (In German-Russian communities throughout the western United States, the few hardbound copies of the

---

Born and reared on a sugar beet farm in northeastern Colorado, Timothy J. Kloberdanz is now an assistant professor of anthropology at North Dakota State University. He is author of more than a dozen articles dealing with German-Russian emigration.

book that continue to circulate often are dog-eared and thumb-worn.)

While *Second Hoeing* is foremost a work of fiction, its importance as a regional portrait and as social commentary is accentuated by the book's faithful depiction of the Colorado sugar beet country during the 1920s and 1930s, the problem of child labor in the beet fields, and the experience of German-Russian immigrants and their children at a time when many of the familiar ways and values of the Old Country were yielding to the inevitable lure of the New. The fact that Hope Williams Sykes was able to integrate all of the above into a compelling story that focuses on a central character—young Hannah Schreissmiller—helps explain the novel's broad-based appeal.

Upon its release, literary critics hailed the "new and fresh view" that *Second Hoeing* offered, largely because of its detailed representation of a then little-known area in the American West: the sugar-producing farmlands of northern Colorado. A reviewer for the *New York Herald Tribune* commented on the day that the novel went on sale (May 13, 1935): "*Second Hoeing* cultivates soil hitherto untilled in American fiction and reaps a rich harvest from it." The well-known novelist and essayist Hal Borland (who had grown up on a homestead in eastern Colorado) praised *Second Hoeing* in a May 10, 1935, issue of the *Philadelphia Ledger* as "excellent human drama" and added: "Any one who knows the Colorado beet fields can vouch for the truth of Miss Sykes' characters and her background."

In the early decades of this century, Colorado was the leading producer of sugar beets in the United States, yet relatively little was known about the people associated with such an important industry until the appearance of *Second Hoeing*. The novel's lucid description of sugar beet culture and the lives of those whose chief source of livelihood depended on it—immigrant families, tenant farmers, factory workers, and landowners—remains unparalleled even today.

Hope Williams Sykes's grim picture of small German-Russian children working long hours in the beet fields aided in fanning the fires of protest sparked by reformist groups of the 1930s such as the National Child Labor Committee. Rose C. Feld, a reviewer for the *New York Times*, considered *Second Hoeing* a significant work because of its unforgettable depiction of the child labor problem in an agricultural context. Feld commented in a May 12, 1935, issue of the *Times*:

> It may be that Hope Williams Sykes, when she was writing "Second Hoeing" . . . was not consciously inspired by a desire to write a propagandistic book about this phase of child labor in America. . . . The fact remains that "Second Hoeing" takes on the stature of a powerful proletarian drama of the American soil, with children the main protagonists upon whom the bitter impact of economic struggle is spent.

Just as John Steinbeck's well-known classic *The Grapes of Wrath* (1939) brought the plight of rural migrants in California to national attention, *Second Hoeing* contributed to increased public awareness of the child labor problem in Colorado. Two years after the appearance of *Second Hoeing*, effective legislation was implemented that helped curb the callous exploitation of children in the sugar beet fields. The extent to which Hope Williams Sykes's novel may have influenced such child labor legislation remains to be investigated by scholars. (Among the pieces of congratulatory fan mail Hope Williams Sykes received following the publication of *Second Hoeing* was a letter from the political reformer and then First Lady Eleanor Roosevelt.)

Besides acquainting readers with the sugar-producing region of Colorado and the severity of the child labor problem in the beet fields, *Second Hoeing* also introduced readers to a relatively unknown group of rural immigrants who were in the throes of Americanization: the German-Russians. A reviewer for the May 19, 1935, issue of the

Denver Rocky Mountain News enthusiastically praised *Second Hoeing* and commented: "A better subject for a novel of people living on the soil than the German-Russians . . . would be hard to find. Until now astonishingly little has been written of them, yet they present some of the richest fiction material in the West."

The German-Russians in *Second Hoeing* are all Volga Germans, not "Volga Russians," as one character in the novel erroneously speaks of the group. The Volga Germans, who traditionally refer to themselves as *unser Leit* (German dialect for "our people"), are the descendants of some twenty-seven thousand German peasants and craftsmen who emigrated to the steppes of Russia during the years 1764–67. The early settlers established more than one hundred settlements on both sides of the lower Volga River (between the present-day Russian cities of Kuibyshev and Volgograd). For more than a century, the Volga-German colonists enjoyed free land, exemption from military service, religious liberty, and numerous other privileges on the isolated steppes. Then, prompted by Russification measures, economic distress, and overpopulation, thousands of Volga Germans began a second great migration, this time to the New World. From the mid-1870s until the outbreak of the First World War, Volga-German families traveled to the wheat-growing areas of the western United States and Canada, the fertile pampas of South America, and the beet-growing districts of Colorado, Nebraska, Wyoming, Montana, Idaho, Minnesota, Iowa, and Michigan.

In Colorado, most of the early Volga-German immigrants worked as "stoop laborers," thinning, hoeing, and harvesting sugar beets by hand. Their extremely large families, Old Country work ethic, and agricultural expertise won them begrudging acceptance by Anglo-American beet growers. A majority of the Volga Germans, however, were determined to remain in the "stoop laborer" class as briefly as possible. Soon the Volga Germans were renting and eventually buying sugar beet farms of their own. By the 1930s, the sugar industry in Colorado and in neighboring western states was dominated by beet growers of Volga-German ancestry.

The Schreissmillers in *Second Hoeing* are in many ways typical of a Protestant Volga-German family in the Colorado beet country of the 1920s and 1930s. Hannah Schreissmiller is the fourth oldest daughter in a beet-worker household of twelve children. Hannah's early years, so sensitively described by Hope Williams Sykes, mesh well with the pain-filled recollections of grizzled Volga German–Americans living today: at the age of four, Hannah watches over her younger brothers and sisters at the end of a beet field in which the other family members toil; at six years of age, Hannah crawls behind her hoe-wielding parents to thin the lettuce-thick beet plants; by the time she reaches sixteen, Hannah has been exposed to every facet of the sugar beet cycle, however laborious or harsh.

Second Hoeing opens with Hannah's domineering father, Adam Schreissmiller, announcing that the family will soon leave its three-room shack in the beet worker community of Shag Town to move into a larger farmhouse as renters. This economic and social transition was indeed a big step in the lives of Volga-German immigrants, for it meant that they were on the way to becoming not only independent farmers, but also Americans.

Many of the background settings described in *Second Hoeing* were inspired by locations intimately familiar to the book's author: Valley City is Fort Collins, Colorado, during the 1920s and early 1930s, while Shag Town was inspired by "The Jungles," an immigrant hamlet located northeast of Fort Collins across the Cache la Poudre River. Some of the dramatic events that figure so prominently in *Second Hoeing* were based on actual happenings in northern Colorado, such as the incident in which hundreds of freshly dipped feeder lambs perish in a sudden January snowstorm (pp. 157–62). Undoubtedly, such firsthand knowledge on the writer's part explains why *Second Hoeing* was praised for its unsparing realism by reviewers and simultaneously derided by less appreciative German-Russian readers.

Born Iris Hope Williams in a sodhouse near Kanorado, Kansas, on November 2, 1901, the author of *Second Hoeing* knew early the unsentimental side of rural life. "Times were hard in those days," she later wrote of her childhood on the Great Plains, "but from them came my understanding of the land and the ever real problem of the farmer's battle with the elements."[1] After moving from western Kansas to Colorado during her teenage years, she enrolled at Colorado Agricultural College (now Colorado State University) and taught elementary school near Fort Collins. The two-story brick schoolhouse in which Hope Williams did most of her early teaching was located only a short distance from "The Jungles." Here, for the first time, she came into daily contact with struggling German-Russian families who unashamedly kept their children out of school to work during the spring beet thinning and the fall harvest.

After marrying in 1925, Hope Williams Sykes began writing her beet field saga while living at a combination service station–home built by her husband. The Sykeses' rural business was an ideal observatory, overlooking the tall gray smokestack of the Fort Collins sugar factory and the outlying beet fields. The actual writing of *Second Hoeing*, however, proved to be a prolonged and painstaking task, as Mrs. Sykes later recalled in a letter to a Colorado women's club:

> I wrote "Second Hoeing" completely three different times during a five-year period. I kept notes for two years on the conversations of the [German-Russians], jotting down tricks of speech here at the station. I spent a year keeping notes on all the work that was done in a beet field which joins our small half-acre of ground. I kept notes on all the activity of the beet dump from early morning until night. For seven years I just absorbed the feeling and undercurrent of the beet industry and these people.

Even before the publication of *Second Hoeing*, Hope Williams Sykes began to receive official recognition for her writing. She won the prestigious Bonfils award (presented by *The Denver Post*) on two separate occasions for stories about Colorado's sugar beet industry. Following the critical acclaim that greeted *Second Hoeing* on its release in the spring of 1935, Mrs. Sykes received a fellowship to the Bread Loaf Writers' Conference in Vermont, where she made the acquaintance of several nationally known writers and literary critics. In 1937, G. P. Putnam's Sons published her second novel, *The Joppa Door*, which was based on the life story of a German immigrant woman in northern Utah who had met and married a German-Russian pietist in Palestine. Hope Williams Sykes later drew a distinction between her two novels about the German-Russians by noting that the writing of *Second Hoeing* was "a physical thing, a tangible, material thing," while *The Joppa Door*, in sharp contrast, was "spiritual . . . . The forces back of it cannot be explained, or seen." In 1940, the Sykeses left Colorado and moved to southern California, where Mrs. Sykes continued to pursue a variety of creative endeavors until her death at the age of seventy-one.

Although Hope William Sykes's portrayal of the life of Volga-German beet workers and farmers in *Second Hoeing* is a convincing one, the novel initially drew stinging criticism from German-Russian readers. Exactly why the novel offended the sensibilities of so many Volga Germans remained something of a puzzle to the book's champions. To complicate matters, Volga-German critics were reluctant to discuss openly their objections to the book with outsiders for many years, fearing that their trust would be violated or misrepresented.

What upset so many Volga-German readers of *Second Hoeing* was not what non-German-Russian readers today might expect: the harshness of a tyrannical immigrant father who sometimes beats his recalcitrant children with a horse whip; youngsters who are kept home from school to work in the sugar beets from dawn to dusk; or the seriously ill who are pressured by family members to labor in the fields, sometimes to the point of physical collapse. Such incidents—however disturbing or unflattering—are readily admitted by present-day Volga German–Americans to have occurred in real life.

German-Russian readers of *Second Hoeing* were disturbed primarily by references in the book to members of the Volga-German minority as being dishonest and dirty. Upon reading the novel, one does find a seemingly unbalanced number of characters who fit these ethnocentric views of German-Russians so popular in the early-day beet growing districts of Colorado. All of the German-Russian house maids in *Second Hoeing*, for example, turn out to be thieves—with the sole exception of Hannah. Even Hannah's father and the youngest member of the Schreissmiller family—a small child—are caught stealing. At one point in the novel, Hannah sadly concludes that "stealing must be a common trait among her people" (p. 203). This specific passage angered many Volga-German readers, some of whom recalled that even during difficult times in their peasant past, the theft of a cupful of lard was so unconscienable as to be immortalized in folk song.

Volga-German critics of *Second Hoeing* during the 1930s also felt that the constant references in the book to the filthy homes and uncleanliness of the German-Russians were exaggerated or taken out of context. This was an extremely touchy topic at the time the novel appeared, for the epithet "dirty Rooshun" frequently was hurled at self-conscious Volga-German immigrants regardless of their physical appearance. It is wholly conceivable, of course, that the work clothes and crowded houses of many Volga-German families rarely met the sanitary standards of their more affluent American neighbors. Yet within the tightly knit Volga-German communities (where ridicule was an effective means of informal social control), dirt—like theft—was anathema. The allegation that German-Russians were dirty was viewed by more astute members of the group as a way for American landowners to justify the chicken coops, box-cars, and sordid tarpaper shacks that had been given large Volga-German families as living quarters. Furthermore, the prejudice of some Americans that the Volga Germans—whether farm laborers or house maids—were thieves, was interpreted by the immigrants as a subtle rationale for less subjective realities: low wages, discrimination, and seques-tration.

Some German-Russian readers also found the English spoken by the Schreissmillers and other Volga-German characters in Second Hoeing to be unnecessarily awkward and unnatural. Hannah's parents, for example, would have used German dialect when conversing with each other or with their children, not broken English. Hope Williams Sykes undoubtedly resorted to English speech patterns for the immigrant characters in her novel out of courtesy to read-ers. Nonetheless, the German-Russian dialogue in Second Hoeing occasionally smacks not so much of the broken En-glish spoken by early Volga-German immigrants in Col-orado, but rather of the contrived and thus intentionally humorous folk speech of the Pennsylvania Dutch (as, for example, when Adam Schreissmiller orders his oldest son to "got out und throw the horses over some hay" [p. 90]).

Despite the criticism that Second Hoeing received from German-Russians who found it condescending and prejudi-cial, the novel does treat most aspects of the Volga-German experience in the beet country accurately and sympatheti-cally. There seems little doubt that Hope Williams Sykes tried to describe the harsh life of the German-Russians in northern Colorado as forcefully and yet as honestly as a single observer could. Mrs. Sykes herself later offered a succinct and surprisingly warmhearted explanation as to why many German Russians reacted so negatively to her novel: "In the sugar beet sections [of Colorado] the people say 'Second Hoeing' is not fiction but non-fiction. Perhaps this is true, for too many German-Russian families whom I have never met see themselves in the book."

In *Second Hoeing*, Hope Williams Sykes presents an unusually rich and perceptive picture of the church-oriented round of German-Russian ceremonial life—christening, confirmation, marriage, and the funeral—which is matched only by her expert description of the sugar beet farming cycle. In addition, *Second Hoeing* is sprinkled with a generous sampling of Volga-German cultural symbols and traditions that figured so importantly in the everyday life of the immigrants: bloodletting; ribboned canes; black head shawls; sunflower seeds; the preparation of butterball soup, sugar beet syrup, and garlic-flavored sausage; shower dances; and weather lore.

While gathering the background material for her novel about German Russians in the Colorado beet country, Hope Williams Sykes had developed two indispensable qualities: a meticulous memory and an inestimable amount of patience. In describing how she obtained some of the information for the vivid account of the German-Russian marriage celebration in Part I of *Second Hoeing*, Mrs. Sykes remembered:

I attended a wedding at the church [in Fort Collins], and then went to the home. I stood among the people, I sat at the bride's table to eat the splendid food, and through it all I set my mind to memorize every detail for I could do no writing of notes there. Late in the afternoon my husband and I came home. I was mentally exhausted but I sat right down to my typewriter and wrote out the notes. But I did not know the meaning of all that had taken place. . . . So I asked an old German Russian who had managed the wedding what it all meant. Mr. Sykes and I went to his home. There I sat at the kitchen table writing in the light of a kerosene lamp while the old man talked. . . . For three hours we sat and listened.

The fact that two of the novel's strongest characters are both women—Hannah and her mother, Ana—deserves special mention. Volga-German families in Russia and in the New World settlements included similar female members who, while visibly submissive, actually wielded much subtle power and considerable influence. It is to Hope Williams Sykes's credit that she understood something of the complex dynamics of German-Russian family life. Unlike less discerning observers, she was not misled by certain Old Country customs and mores that seemed to insinuate an unwavering patriarchy.

The description of Volga-German attitudes toward work in *Second Hoeing* also is supported by ethnographic data. Industriousness was such an integral part of the traditional Volga-German value system that hard work sometimes was glorified as an end in itself. In the beet country of Colorado particularly, Volga-German immigrants frequently gulped down their food at mealtime and exclaimed as they hurried to the outlying fields: *"Die Arweit schmeckt besser als Esse' "* (Work tastes better than food). Only after many seasons of back-straining labor in the sugar beets did even work-hungry Volga Germans admit the truth of a new proverb: *"Die Riewe sein siess, awer die Arweit is' bitter"* (The beets are sweet, but the work is bitter).

The arduous agricultural lifestyle of German-Russians in the sugar beet country did not, however, completely erode the Volga-Germans' family structure or their identity as a distinct people. Ironically, perhaps, the pressures that Volga Germans faced for so many years—both economic and social—often led to greater family loyalty and increased ethnic consciousness.

Today a significant number of "Hannah's people" are still concentrated in their original areas of settlement. Their prosperous, cottonwood-studded farms now cover thousands of acres in the sugar-producing valleys of the American West. Innumerable changes have taken place since the early 1900s, when sun-blackened Volga-German children crawled up and down long rows of sugar beets in the dizzying heat of summer. Much of the culture that the first German-Russian immigrants brought with them to the beet fields has disappeared or has been modified to fit comfortably within a modern context. Yet Volga-German Americans continue to gather for huge wedding celebrations where many of the Old Country customs described in *Second Hoeing* are faithfully enacted: smiling guests still pin paper money to the bride's dress and dance to the gentle waltz music of the hammered dulcimer or to fast-paced tunes such as the "Onion Lizzie Hop" and the "Beet Toppers' Polka." At Volga German–American ethnic festivities, church picnics, and family reunions, conversations inevitably turn to the familiar topics of sugar beets and earlier beet field days.

For many present-day Volga-German Americans, *Second Hoeing* helps fill an already widening gap; it will satiate the curiosity of younger members and future descendants of this ethnic group who will wonder what the sugar beet industry meant to their German-Russian ancestors in the early decades of the twentieth century. With time, the controversial novel *Second Hoeing* may well become—like the bittersweet beet field experience that inspired it—a powerful symbol of Volga-German American pride and achievement.

Yet, despite the focus of *Second Hoeing* on one facet of the Euro-American immigrant experience and the book's unusually rich geographical setting, *Second Hoeing* transcends the status of either social commentary or mere regional portrait. The story of Hannah Schreissmiller's struggle—though steeped in the vernacular of the Colorado sugar beet country and colored by the pervasiveness of German-Russian folk life—is one that will continue to strike a medley of responsive chords in readers everywhere.

1. Biographical details about Hope Williams Sykes and quotations from her personal correspondence were provided by her family, and used with its permission.

PART I
PLANTING

CHAPTER I

WITH her back defiantly against the wall of the crowded kitchen, sixteen-year-old Hannah Schreissmiller looked through tear-blurred blue eyes at Fritz.

"You coulda just as well took me. You're mean like dirt!"

Fritz shrugged his work-thickened shoulders. "Kids don't go to shower dances, Sis."

"Yeah! 'Just a kid!' That's what you all say. I'm taller'n Olinda and she gets to go every place."

"Oh, can it!" Olinda snapped as she pressed the waves deeper in her brown hair and smoothed the tight pink satin dress over her short pudgy hips.

"Yeah! You get your hair all marcelled and I gotta wear mine in braids. *Braids!* I gotta wear short dresses and old cotton stockin's and you get to have silk and you're only two years older. I'm sick of it!"

"Wait till you're confirmed. You can knock 'em all cold." Fritz grinned.

"I don't wanta wait. I—"

"GOTT IM HIMMEL! SHUT DER MOUTH!"

Adam Schreissmiller pounded his bony knuckles on the worn oilcloth-covered table until the kerosene lamp danced and smoked the chimney.

"Got out und go mit the dance!"

"We was waiting for Henry Goelzer," Fritz muttered, turning his back on his father.

"GOELZER! You don't go mit him! Worth nothing like one

3

nematode beet, he is! Bah, got out so we have some peace mit ourselves, oncet!"

An icy blast of late February air rushed in as Olinda and Fritz hastily left. Hannah shivered. Adam, still muttering against Henry Goelzer, dragged a battered chair closer to the stove.

"Move oncet, Tabia," he ordered when his foot accidentally struck a thin girl lying on a sheep-lined coat.

"It's cold," grunted the fourteen-year-old Tabia.

"Yah, sure it cold, und snows, he is deep. Eight, might ten feet high in the back mountains. Much waters we have so we irrigate beets next summer. Yah, good." Adam picked up his newspaper from Russia.

Hannah sat drearily down into a chair at the table and buried her face in her arms. She never got to go no place, never got to do *nothing*. Cooped up in this cubbyhole of a kitchen stinking of dung from the cowbarn and kids underfoot so you couldn't move.

"Weine nicht! Make no cry." Her mother's low guttural voice came softly to her ears. A hard hand smoothed her shoulder gently. "Be glad, Hannah, you is young und not growed up."

"I wanta be grown up. I wanta go places. I wanta have swell clothes."

"Yah, yah. Sure, Hannah. This Easter you is confirmed. Your hair we curl. Young woman's clothes we buy for you. Yah, und I think on how once again, you will wish sometime you is a child."

"I won't ever," Hannah denied, raising her head to brush her golden hair back from her forehead. She smiled in the midst of her tears into her mother's calm round face, with the brown hair pulled into a tight knot on the back of her head; the thick body full two hundred pounds; the stubby, workworn hands.

"Can I have my dress long, and silk?"

"Yah, yah yah."

"Mamma, high-heeled slippers, too? Me and Katie Heist seen some just like we want. And silk stockin's, an' silk underwear, an' silk everything?"

4

"Yah."

"Ooh!" Hannah breathed and little tingles ran down her back. "And Mamma, Katie says she wants her dress just like mine. She's fatter'n me. You s'pose we can get them different sizes?"

"Yah, might."

"Mamma, Katie says her old man's gonna get her a pearl necklace to wear. You think Papa'll—" Hannah saw her mother's warning hand. She looked quickly to where Adam sat hunched, his mustache moving as he read half aloud to himself.

"Mamma," Hannah's voice was a mere breath, "Katie says her brother Jake says he's gonna ask me for a date right after confirmation. Ooh, I wisht Easter was here now instead of six weeks away."

"Better you not listen so much to that Katie Heist, und better you think on what confirmation mean. White you wear from the skin out; white it is to show how you is clean und holy; clean inside und clean outside; und that you walk mit God, und keep always His words mit you. Better you think on that und not on dates und how you is looking. That Katie Heist, she has not one brain in her head. Better you study good your catechism for Saturday School tomorrow, or you don't get confirm."

The fire crackled. Adam rustled his paper. Marble snapped against marble where Alec and Solly played on the splintery floor.

"Ouch! You quit kickin' me!" Tabia's shrill voice rent the stillness. "I'll show you to keep kickin' me in the back! Take that! And that!"

"Kick *me?* You think you're smart!" Alec shouted. "You ain't smart so you get invited to no birthday party! 'Cause you're a Russian! A Russian!" Alec kicked at Tabia but she dodged away, and fell back against her father.

Adam's gnarled hand struck Tabia's face a smacking blow. "Gott im Himmel! Stop him!" he roared, getting up from his chair. He caught Solly by the back of his overalls, setting him down smartly on a fifty-pound lard can.

"What you mean, 'Russian,' Alec?"

5

"Nothin'. I don't mean nothin'." Alec shrank against the wall, half raising his arm to ward off the expected blow.

"Answer or I beat you so you don't can set!"

"Yes, sir, yes, sir," Alec stuttered, "Alice Wetherington says her mother don't let her invite no Russians by her party, and she says Tabia's a Russian, so she don't invite her, yet."

"So-o. We Russian, huh? Russian! Gott! We don't been Russian. We German!" Adam shook his fist at Tabia.

"I did tell her that." Tabia rubbed her smarting cheek. "And she said we come out of Russia so we gotta be Russian."

"Gott im Himmel! We German! *German!*" Adam shrieked the words, shaking both fists.

"Yah, Adam," Ana stopped sewing, her round face calm. "You got right. Remember the minister say just last Sunday how we is Volga Russians und the Volga Russians is German."

"Tabia," Adam broke in, "you tell that Alice the Germans come into Russia when Catherine the Great is rule. Und for one hundred year the German peoples live in Russia—"

"The Germans," Ana interrupted, "they stay so long as Catherine the Great und the rulers after keep the promise. Catherine, she promise if the German peoples come into Russia they can still been German und not have to been Russian—"

"Gott, und I die before I carry a gun for Russia, so I come into America." Adam pounded his fist on his knee. "I remember how the first German peoples come into the wheat country of Kansas."

"The minister, he say 1880," Ana put in.

"Into Kansas they come first, und then they come into the sugar beet country of Colorado—"

"Being of the land, und knowing how to work beets in Russia," Ana finished complacently.

"Sure, we is German und not Russian." Adam threw back his skinny shoulders.

"Yah, und we hold mit the German ways, not marrying even the Russians." In and out Ana wove her needle. "Your papa got right, Tabia. Go in bed. Ach Gott, Solly, Alec, go

6

in bed." Heavily, Ana rose and shook two small boys, slumped with heads on folded arms, fast asleep at the table.

"Chris, Coonie. Wake, so you go in bed." Stripping their shoes, shirts, and overalls from them, she sent them to bed in their underwear.

"We all go in bed," Adam ordered, cleaning carefully between his bony toes with his fingers.

"I gotta finish my lesson for tomorrow," Hannah protested. "The minister scolded last Saturday."

"Gott, always it take kerosene in the lamp." Adam slammed the bedroom door after him.

"Hurry, Hannah. It grows late," Ana puffed as she bent to pick up the two-year-old Reinie from the floor.

"Mamma, you all right?" Hannah asked anxiously.

"Yah, Hannah, make not the worry."

"But I do. The doctor said you shouldn't have no more kids, and now this one's coming."

"Such talk! Shame!" Ana walked stolidly across the floor with the small, silly Reinie.

Hannah heard the springs creak under her mother's weight. Heard her father grunt, then silence.

Cold air whistled in around the loose casings. She moved to the cookstove, propping her feet in the oven, book open on her knees.

It was hard to learn these lessons of the Bible in German when for five days a week she went to school learning her eighth grade lessons in American. But her mother had wished her to take her confirmation in German as had both of Hannah's older married sisters, Lizzie and Mary, as well as Fritz and Olinda. It was easier for Ana to understand her own language.

Katie Heist was taking her confirmation in American. Hannah wondered if she'd get pearls like Katie. Her father hated so to let old man Heist get ahead of him. Maybe she would get the pearls.

A fierce gust of wind swept the kitchen. A bunch of rags came tumbling out of a broken pane. The lamp went out. Hannah hurriedly searched in the darkness for the bundle. It was icy with snow. The chill bit into her hand as she stuffed the rags back into place. She blew on her cold fingers and reached for a match. The box was empty. Feeling her way to the wood box, she searched for a sliver to light at the stove.

"Ooh." A mouse went running over her hand and escaped.

"Ana."

Hannah became motionless at the sound of her father's voice.

"Yah, Adam," her mother answered.

"Ana, I make today the deal. I am renter now. Next week we make the move."

Hannah drew in her breath sharply. Renters! This was news! Not to be contract beet-workers living in Shag Town during the winter, moving each spring to some farmer's unpainted two-room shack to live during the summer while they worked his beets. But renters!

"One hundred sixty acre, the Boswell farm is. So big he is, Ana, I think on how I don't farm him, sometimes. So much moneys it take for buy all the beet machineries, und horses, und everythings. Ach, one million little things! So many big things! Ana, never do I boss mineself. Might, I can't do it now?"

"Yah, yah yah, sure you done it, Adam. Make not the worry on your head."

"Sure, I done him, Ana. Don't I ask the minister und he say I do right? Heist und all of them look high on your old man, now, Ana! I guess they bug their eye. Remember, Ana, how it is twenty-two year since we come into this country mit only a pack by our back und one feather bed? Gott, how I am work them first year."

"Good you done, Adam."

"Yah, I make the succeed."

Hannah, sitting cramped by the wood box, heard her father turn over in bed, but she dared not move until he was asleep. He never told the children any of his business. They would not know until the day of moving.

At last she heard Adam's loud whistling snore. Softly she crept to the bedroom on the opposite side of the kitchen. Putting her hands on the two beds she steered her way down

8

the bare, cold lane of floor. Leaving her stockings on for warmth, she got in beside Tabia. Olinda would come in late, nearly frozen from sitting outside with Henry Goelzer. Fritz would snuggle up to the two boys in the other bed.

Warmed, Hannah lay thinking. Moving! It was too good to be true. Renters! And this year she was being confirmed. She'd be grown up, and have dates, and now—moving! Moving to the Boswell place where they had worked beets when she was nine. She could remember how thirteen-year-old Jim Boswell came down to the tar-paper shack to let her ride his pony; remember eating angel cake on the back steps of the Boswells' big cream-colored brick house, and Jim getting mad at Fritz and kicking him on the shin, hard. Hannah smiled into the darkness. Jim, black-haired, hot tempered. He'd be twenty now. And the Schreissmillers were renters. No longer just beetworkers.

CHAPTER II

"TABIA! Hannah! Come. You ride the furnitures on top!"
Adam shouted excitedly as he stuffed a squawking chicken
into the slatted coop fastened at the back of the wide beet-
bed wagon.

"The old man acts like he was crazy," grunted Fritz, who
was helping Hannah boost the big iron soap kettle on top the
crate.

"Oh, but I feel the same way! I can hardly wait."

"Hey! Head her off!" Tabia shrieked as she pounded the
rump of a cow with a broken broomstick.

With a whoop Hannah waved her arms and ran to head
off the calf. She herded it back with the two cows, the goat
and her little one. With a "Hey yuh, hey yuh," she drove
them out into the narrow dirt street.

"Gee, Tabia, ain't yuh thrilled? We're moving!" Hannah
whirled Tabia off her feet.

"Tabia! Get the wagon on. Alec, Solly, take the cows."

"Solly an' me's gonna drive the cows. Alec can go help
unload." Tabia swung her stick at the frolicsome calf.

"All she wants is to get outa work. She's—"

"Shut the face, Hannah. Tabia got right." Adam tossed
a chair up to Fritz.

"Baa," Tabia sneered. She stuck out her tongue, wiggled
it and thumbed her nose.

"Baa, yourself!" Hannah turned impatiently into the
house. Her mother was standing before the pantry door
running her stubby hand along the casing.

"Ach, Hannah, good times we have. Ten winters we live

10

here und you kids grow up high so. See, the marks is here."

"Aw, Mamma, you don't hate to leave here? Three dinky rooms. Dirt yard! Neighbors so close they can look in the windows. And the roof leaks. The floor is splinters. Just think! We'll have five rooms. Renters! Oh, it's fine!" Hannah hugged her mother.

"Yah, but Hannah, this is home."

"Crying! Silly! You ought to be laughing because you're leaving Shag Town and the dirt and squalling kids. You should sing and dance like this—"

"Ana! Gott im Himmel! Come, or I drive the car off und leave you so you ride mit the furnitures."

On top of the slowly moving wagon, Hannah lay on her stomach on a feather bed beside Olinda and looked through the rungs of an upturned chair.

"Look, Olinda, there's old lady Goelzer sweeping her dooryard." Hannah pointed to a fat big-boned woman. A smile wreathed the leathery face framed by a once-white 'kerchief. She waved her broom, then came to lean against the sagging wire fence.

"Hm, you s'pose she ever washes? Peuw! Look at them windows. I bet they ain't never been washed. An' Gotfried in that shack in the back yard ain't any cleaner." Hannah wrinkled her nose.

"You'd stink, too, if you had five kids and lived in two rooms," Olinda sniffed.

"Dave's just as dirty and he's only got one kid."

"Yeah, and one room."

"Three shacks, a hog pen, chicken house, and barn, all in one dinky yard. When you and Henry get married you'll have to roost with the chickens or sleep with the cow," Hannah giggled.

"Shut your face! You think you're so damned smart!"

"Can't you take a joke? I know you ain't gonna marry Henry. Papa wouldn't let you. Him hating old man Goelzer the way he does. I don't blame him. Them big pop eyes and round head pulled down into them bony shoulders gives me the creeps."

11

"Oh, shut up!" Olinda turned her back and pillowed her head in her arms.

Hannah rejoiced as she watched Shag Town—one-room shacks with stove pipe chimneys sticking out of the flat roofs at crazy angles, their weathered sides hugging the dirt yards, sagging fences hemming in dirty faced children— slowly slide behind her. All drab, colorless, with here and there a brightly painted house, a good fence, only adding to the sordidness of the scene.

Separated from Shag Town by a dirt road were the stinking pulp pits adjoining the many-windowed red-brick sugar factory—gray, fermenting noodles of shredded sugar beets from which all the sweetness had been taken. Beyond was a high gray smokestack and the black water tower on its four spraddling legs.

"Gee, Olinda, just think, we're leaving it all."

Hannah turned her face to the east and the fertile valleys, the sugar beet country of Northern Colorado; the farmhouses with gaunt cottonwoods sheltering the big red barns, high silos, outbuildings clustering close. Small fields were cut by irrigation ditches, with cottonwoods following the larger canals that curved over the level countryside.

"There's Tabia and Solly," Alec shouted.

"You kids get a move on," Fritz yelled, "it's gonna storm."

"I don't see no storm," Tabia argued.

"Me neither," Solly agreed. "It's too hot to storm."

Hannah looked toward the west in search of clouds. Long's Peak reared its snow white head, and small bits of far peaks stood out clear as crystal behind the range of blue-black Rockies which stretched from south to north. At the north a dark haze hovered.

"That ain't storm, Fritz," Hannah spoke softly and kept looking toward Valley City nestling at the foot of the mountains, the windows glinting in the morning sun, and Shag Town crowding close.

"A storm's coming." Fritz spoke sharply to the horses.

It was five miles to the beet dump and its long inclines, up which the wagons, in the fall, went to dump beets into railroad cars below. A little red, one-room scale house where the loads were weighed, squatted at the foot of the incline.

"Boswell beet dump," Fritz spoke. "That's the Boswell house over there."

"Ooh, Fritz, ain't it swell? Two stories, and cream brick. Where's our place?"

"Across the road in them trees."

"I'm so excited." Eagerly, Hannah crawled up beside Fritz to get a better view.

"Huh, we gotta work just the same as ever."

"Oh, but we won't. I bet Papa hires the beets worked. And I'm getting confirmed and graduating and going to high school next year. Oh, gee!"

"I hope you do, Hannah. All us older kids worked an' helped him make his money so he could rent, an' he didn't spend none on extra schoolin'."

"Cheer up, Fritz. The world ain't so bad."

"You ain't tied hand and foot. You ain't worked your fingers to the bone for the old man. But I'm leavin' the day I'm twenty-one. A year from this July."

"Why don't you go now, if you feel that way?"

"An' have the old man take my wages? I stay till I'm twenty-one." Fritz turned the team into a lane opposite the Boswells'.

Hannah looked at the dun-colored house that seemed too high for its narrow base, the unpainted buildings, sagging fences, straggly trees.

"I thought Papa said it was a swell place," she whispered.

"It's the land that's swell," Fritz corrected.

Hannah's throat ached as she saw the dingy barns, sheep pens along one side near the dilapidated back door, a weedy irrigation ditch cutting across the cluttered back yard. She shivered though the sun was hot.

Ana rose stiffly from the back step. "Got the soap kettle, und soap, und brooms. Dirt, he is everywhere."

Climbing slowly down, Hannah went toward the house. She yanked the torn, rusted screen door open, stepped over a back porch full of rubbish, and opened the sagging kitchen door. She put her hand to her nose to fend off the sickening stench. Dirt and filth! Rubbish in corners, and blood stains

13

mingled with grime and grease. In one corner an old sheep pelt. Dead sheep had been skinned there.

"Ach, Hannah, it bad, but he look good when we get him cleaned."

"It'll never look good. It's awful."

"Make not the cry. Mit tears it don't do no good. Fritz, start the fire under the soap kettle. Alec, pump water mit the cistern. Hannah get the scoop shovel." Ana spoke calmly as she dumped a can of lye into the black soap kettle.

Hannah listlessly pushed the big scoop across the kitchen floor and carried the heaping shovel to the bonfire outside.

"You'll never get the dirt off the woodwork. It ain't never been clean."

"Mit lye he come off. Better no paint, *als* dirt." Ana swished her yellowed broom over the baseboard.

"Hannah, go see mit the boys."

Alec, Coonie, Chris, and little Reinie were down on their knees in one corner of a bedroom, shouting and looking at something.

"I betcha mine beats!"

"Aw, mine's bigger. I bet he runs away from all the rest!"

"Little ones run faster. Mine'll skin all yours!"

"Mine's fattest. I bet he beats. Come on, bug!"

Hannah stood over them. Bedbugs! Racing bedbugs!

"Get them bugs outa here! Right now! Clean 'em all out! Shame! Shame! Playin' with them dirty things!"

"Aw, gee, Hannah, they're so thick we can just scoop um up by the shovelful. Why can't we play with just four of um?"

"Get 'em out of here! Every one!"

"Hannah, what is?" Ana called.

"This is the dirtiest hole I ever saw! Bedbugs! And them dark stairs is slick with dirt, and the two bedrooms upstairs. They stink! I never—" Hannah stopped at sight of a thick-set, gray-haired man standing in the kitchen doorway.

"I'm Mr. Boswell," he said, looking around the room. "To make up for this, I'll furnish paint and paper for the rooms if you will have it put on."

14

"Yah, yah yah. We clean him good for paper und paint," Ana smiled and nodded her head.

"Let me know when you are ready for it." Mr. Boswell smiled and departed.

"Well, think of that?" said Olinda.

"Yah, new paper und paint. I save mine moneys und buy new furnitures, brown mit brown leathers for the front room und slick linoleums so he clean easy." Ana was pleased.

"I hope he keeps his word. I'd be ashamed to bring my high school friends to this dump," Hannah said.

"You won't go to high school," Olinda snapped.

"Papa promised, didn't he, Mamma?"

"Yah, Hannah, he promise."

"His promises ain't worth the air it takes to say 'em," Olinda muttered.

"Hey! Everybody come help! The storm's come!" Fritz bellowed from outdoors.

"Take everything in the kitchen," Ana ordered.

Before half the furniture was unloaded, snow was spitting out of the north. By the time the stove was carried into the house, the wind had become a rush and sweep of sleet.

"My ear's froze! I can't wiggle it," Alec complained as he and Hannah dumped the coop of chickens down inside the barn. They went crashing into the house, sending little Reinie tumbling against the table.

"Mamma, Mamma, he's gonna have a fit. I didn't mean to hit him," Hannah cried.

"Ach, Gott, here, Mutter take him. Reinie, stop him. Fritz, hurry mit the fire so I get him in hot water. Reinie, come." Ana chafed his small hands and blew her breath into his rigid face. The small child was chewing his lips; his eyes rolled in their sockets involuntarily from side to side.

"Yah, yah. Make the cry und you been all right. Next time, Hannah, you look where you go. You und Tabia always —Gott! Tabia und Solly!"

Fritz dropped his wood and threw on his heavy sheep-lined coat. Hannah, yanking Alec's coat from a chair, followed. Standing in the wagon, she caught hold of Fritz's arm to keep from falling as the wagon careened out of the lane. She beat her mittened hands together and turned her face away from the driving snow, but it crawled beneath her clothes and chilled her down to the toes.

They found Tabia and Solly crying and futilely trying to head the cows into the storm. The calf had lain down in the fast drifting snow.

"Get in the wagon," Fritz ordered as he unfastened the chains that held the sideboard in place. "Cover up with quilts."

Hannah strained to help Fritz boost the calf into the wagon. It was heavy, awkward, and all legs.

"What's the trouble?"

A strange voice spoke from out the storm.

"Hello, Jim. Can you put these kids in your car and take them home? Hannah, you go along, too. It's Jim Boswell."

In the coupé Tabia kept up a low moaning; Solly silently shivered, and when Hannah put her arm around the two children, her fingers brushed Jim's shoulder. She felt him shrink. She looked at his thin face, the lips set in distaste, eyes looking straight ahead.

"Well, here we are," he announced briefly, opening the door.

Hannah turned to thank him but the car shot away into the storm.

"I s'pose it woulda cracked his high-upty face if he'd smiled once," she thought as she ran to the kitchen, warm and fragrant with coffee fumes.

Ana vigorously rubbed snow on Solly's nose and ears. "He freeze," she said sternly. "Next time I guess you hurry."

Adam came in beating his hands against his sides. "One million dollars this storm makes. Snow, he puts in the high mountains so the ditches run full next summer. But the sale —the snow no good for him. Gott, the stuff go cheap. I buy mine beet drill for one-third a new one. Und I buy a swell couch. Long, so I sleep on him after supper. Green velvets mit roses, und no back und sides to get in a feller's way." He chafed his hands above the cookstove.

16

Hannah looked in dismay at her mother.

"Yah, und I buy a puffy rocker so I read in him, und one carpet. Red mit fancy pictures in him. One bargain he was. Fritz, tomorrow, you go und bring him home on the wagon."

"Yeah, but—" Hannah stopped seeing her mother's shaking head.

"Yah, Adam. Der front room, he look fine. Yah."

Hannah just looked at her mother. "She won't fight for nothing she wants. Not even a brown leather couch."

CHAPTER III

BY Saturday every inch of wood in the entire house had been scrubbed with lye water. The furniture had been installed in the front room.

Hannah, coming in from hauling manure to the fields, stood and surveyed it. "You sorry, Mamma, you didn't get the brown leather?"

"Ach, not, Hannah."

"If we just had some new paper and the woodwork painted, it would be swell."

"Next winter we fix him, Hannah. After the beets is out we have time to done him, und Mr. Boswell, he promise to buy the paper und paint." Ana calmly kneaded bread dough. "Better we think on your confirmation, now, und not the house."

"Mamma, when am I gonna get my things? If Katie and me get our dresses just alike we better be getting them."

"Yah. Your papa say we go this afternoon, might."

"Ooh, swell! I'll go telephone Katie right now!" Hannah went running to the long box of a telephone hanging on the wall. It had belonged to the former tenants and Adam, feeling his importance as a renter, had retained it.

"Hello, Katie," Hannah shouted, "Papa's gonna take me and Mamma into town this afternoon to look for my confirmation things. You think you can go? Huh? Sure. Swell!

"Mamma, what time'll we go?"

"Two o'clock, might. Und I like not the word, 'swell,' Hannah. That Katie sounds smart mit using it."

18

"Oh, but it is swell." Hannah laughed joyously, and began to dance.

Ana's eyes twinkled. "Ach, Hannah, mein liebling, make done the foolishness. Quiet mit folded hands I am walk when I am confirm, und let not one smile come on mine face."

"Oh, but Mamma, America's different from Russia."

"Ach, might. I don't know." Ana deftly molded a light puffy loaf of dough.

Adam came in groaning as he slid into his chair at the dinner table. "Gott, it dry. Too many beets I sign up to raise. Forty acre. Gott, und no snow und no rain!"

"Aw, it always rains, always has," Fritz said.

"Ach, shut the face." Adam speared a piece of bread with his fork.

"Olinda, you und Fritz clean the barn. Tabia und Solly, clean mit the chicken house. Alec, und Chris, pick off the tin cans in the yard. Hannah, you go in town so we buy the confirmation things."

"Heists are going, too," Hannah laughed as she hurried from the table.

"Heist! Gott im Himmel! Drag him mit the confirmations!"

"Katie and me wants our things just alike," Hannah said and went running upstairs, singing.

In Valley City they met old man Heist, fat and shrewd with his fatter wife and the chunky Katie.

"How's the renter?" Heist pounded Adam's skinny back. "Smart in the head, ain't you, huh?"

"Yah, sure. Them renters before me is so dirty they rot, but I get rich on their dirt. The sheep pens is full mit manure. Gott, it make mine land rich. Twenty ton beets I raise, I bet." Adam spat to the side of the curb.

Hannah looked at Katie. Katie shrugged her shoulders and twisted her mouth. She shifted her weight from one foot to the other. "Papa, me'n Hannah'll go ahead and look around."

"Ach, Heist, better we keep an eye on. They buy the town," Adam laughed. "Shoes, we buy first."

19

Hannah looked covetously at a white kid slipper with straps crossed in fancy design.

"Katie, lookit! Leather! Mamma ain't this swell?"

"Yah."

"Take him away. Too **much** mit straps. Und too high mit price," Adam declared.

"Yah. Right," Heist agreed.

"Here's a good number in white canvas." The clerk held up a pump.

"More better," Adam grunted.

Reluctantly, Hannah pushed her foot into the slipper. It looked queer with her black cotton stockings.

"They hurt my feet," she lied. "The white kid ones fit better."

"Come. We go." Adam walked away.

At three shoe stores they tried on slippers, pricing them, discarding, arguing.

"We go back und get the canvas ones by the first store," Heist suggested.

"We ain't been to that big store," Adam pointed.

"Ach, crazy mit renter moneys, you got," Heist grumbled.

"All afternoon we chase and don't get even to look at dresses," Katie complained.

"Yeah, but it's fun." Hannah smiled.

"A sale!" Adam crowed turning in at the store.

"These white kids are half price. All odd sizes. Then we have a special sale on canvas slippers at the same price." The clerk was courteous.

"Let me see the kid slippers."

"Me too," Katie echoed.

Hannah wiggled her toes as she walked on the strip of carpet. "Ooh, I like them," she breathed delightedly, then she saw Katie's face.

"What's the matter, Katie?"

"They ain't got my size."

"Let me try on a canvas one. We want to be just alike." Reluctantly, Hannah took off the kid slipper.

Adam reached over and felt of it. Next he examined a canvas one.

20

"Gott im Himmel! We don't leave one bargain like this. We take these." He shoved the slippers at the clerk and dug out his money pocket.

Heist snorted. "Canvas is good enough for mine girl. Crazy-headed notions I don't got mit mine brain."

"Gee, Katie, I'm sorry."

"Aw, it's all right. Nobody sees nothin' but the bottoms of your shoes when we're kneeling nohow."

"We'll get everything else just alike," Hannah whispered as they went to look for silk stockings, silk bloomers, and vests.

"We go home," Adam stated at last.

"But we ain't got our dresses," Hannah and Katie wailed.

"We come back tonight. It Saturday."

Adam was chuckling as he drove home. "Hah, that Heist mit his fat Katie. I guess mine Hannah look more better yet."

That night, as soon as Adam parked the car next the curb, Hannah went to join Katie. Tabia saw a group of her friends and was gone like a streak. The smaller boys waited beside their mother.

"Mamma, you goin' with Katie and me?"

"I buy the groceries first."

At a half-run, arms linked, Katie and Hannah dodged in and out of the crowds of people.

"Gee, Katie, I'm so excited I can't even think!"

"Me too. Let's go to Gundstroms' first."

Lights streamed from the store windows filled with attractive articles but Katie and Hannah did not stop. They hurried across street traffic, passed the Salvation Army on the corner in front of the drug store. The rattle of the tambourine and the beating of the drum mingled with the tooting auto horns.

"Don't you just love Saturday nights, Katie? The crowds of people standing on the corners, and—ooh, there's Fritz and Jake!"

They halted in front of the boys. "We're huntin' for our confirmation dresses." Hannah's voice was high and excited because of the way Jake looked at her. He was going to ask her for a date. Right after confirmation. Gee, he looked swell. Gray suit. Gray felt hat. Of course he was working by the month, now. Had his own money.

"Come on, Hannah, let's go." Katie pulled at her arm.

They left the boys leaning against the store building, and swung along at their former fast gait.

"Jake's sure crazy about you, Hannah. And he's got a Ford roadster, now."

"Really, Katie?"

"Yeah, and after confirmation, Fritz and me, and you and Jake can go places." Katie giggled.

At Gundstroms' they looked at two white dresses with silk rosebuds around the neck.

"This one fits me swell," Katie preened in front of the long mirror.

"I think I look funny in mine. Let's go some place else, Katie."

They were held up at a street corner by a traffic jam. A big black coupé stopped in front of them. Hannah drew in her breath sharply. She started to speak but the man gave no sign of recognition.

"The sign's changed," a girl's voice said. The car moved forward. Hannah felt queerly sick.

"That's the way we'll go in Jake's car. Four of us," Katie was rattling. "Course Jake's car ain't so swell—and say, wasn't that guy a looker. That thin face—say, what's the matter? You know him?"

"Jim Boswell," Hannah said dully.

"The guy that lives across the road from you? God, ain't he got the come-hither eyes! And them lips! Wouldn't you just die if he ever kissed yuh?"

"Shut up, Katie. Everybody'll hear you. We gotta get us a dress."

"That rosebud one at Gundstroms' is the only one that fit me good, and we've been every place," Katie complained.

"There's the little new store on Main Street," Hannah suggested.

As they passed a group of older women on a corner, Katie's mother called to her.

"I'll meet you at the new store," Katie said.

In the window of the dress shop Hannah saw the dress! Softest white georgette! The round neck was low with a deep cape collar. Small rosettes of white satin ribbon adorning it were whirls of light. A larger whirl decorated the left hip where the full skirt joined the tight fitting waist. Hannah visioned herself in that dress—golden hair waved, blue eyes shining, white kid slippers peeping beneath the softly gathered skirt.

"So we'd like to have a new dress." A deep voice broke in upon her thoughts.

"Oh, Fred, I just gotta have it." Hannah smiled at the tall broad-shouldered man with the twinkling brown eyes.

"That's right. Buy the nice dresses while you're young, then when you're old you are glad you had the good time."

"You talk like you was fifty instead of twenty-eight, Fred. Don't you think I'd look swell in that dress?"

"Sure, you look damn fine in it. My dad says you look just like your mother when she came from Russia on the same boat with me and my mother and dad, and your dad and the older girls."

"I can't remember that far back," Hannah grinned impishly. "Where's Frieda?"

"She went to buy some face powders. She worries about her looks with this new baby coming." Fred smiled.

"What you two talking about?" Frieda Hergenboch came up with a small boy who looked like Fred.

"Oh, we're buying Hannah this dress."

"Your old man won't let you have that dress. Even to be confirmed in. How's your mother?"

"I'm worried about her, Frieda. That awful dirty house. She worked till she was near sick."

"She don't look right. This having kids is hell. I tell you I don't have no more. You hear that, Fred?"

"There's Papa and Mamma with Mr. and Mrs. Heist and Katie."

"You find the dress you like, Hannah?"

"In the window, Mamma. Lookit, Katie!"

"God, that's swell. I betcha, Hannah, that dress wouldn't make me look so fat."

"Let's try it on," Fred suggested. "Come on, Adam, see how your girl looks in a fine dress."

Ana and Mrs. Heist sat down carefully on spindly chairs, while the men stood stolidly waiting.

"Size 34," the clerk held up the dress.

"I can wear it." Hannah followed into the dressing room.

"You have size 36 for mine Katie?" Mrs. Heist inquired of a second clerk.

"We have size 36 but it is in blue."

"Ach, white it must be."

"We could order it in white if the blue one fits."

"Try the blue on." Heist spoke loudly.

"Ooh!" Hannah whispered, not taking her eyes away from this vision of herself. Why, she was pretty!

"I just gotta have this. I just gotta." Tears came into her eyes.

She walked slowly into the main room. Ana's face remained stolid, without expression. Adam walked forward to pinch the skirt between thumb and fingers.

"Thin like one veil. He don't hold together for oncet, even."

"I assure you georgette wears well," the clerk defended. "And this is an excellent piece of material."

"It's beautiful," Frieda exclaimed.

Hannah turned round and round before the mirror. The white satin rosettes shimmered like silver. Her hair was pure gold, her eyes bluer than ever. "I just gotta have it." She looked at her father, her mother, Fred.

Katie came out in the blue dress. It looked nice but Katie could never look like Hannah.

"Adam, that's Hannah's dress," Frieda spoke up.

"Gott, it ain't. Fourteen dollar for one spider web! Gott im Himmel! Not crazy in the head, am I. Take him off!"

Hannah's lips trembled. Tears filled her eyes. She turned her back.

"Adam, that dress, it makes of Hannah a most beautiful person." Fred's voice was low, courteous. "I am think-

24

ing how at confirmation all the people will say, 'That Adam Schreissmiller not only is smart in the head and a renter but he makes the most beautiful girl ever confirmed.' "

Adam threw back his shoulders. Squared his chin. "Yah, Fred, right you got. What is fourteen dollar when I am a renter mit a girl like Hannah?"

Old lady Heist spoke. "I take a dress for mine Katie if you get him in white."

"Crazy mit the head," old Heist shouted.

"Katie so good as that Hannah. Such a good dress she gets, too."

"She don't!"

"I handle the moneys." Mrs. Heist fished into a deep pocket inside her black wool skirt, bringing forth a roll of bills.

With the precious dress in a box, Hannah caught hold of Fred's arm. "Fred, you're swell. I'd never of got it without you."

"You have to know how to manage these old men. They think this is still Russia."

CHAPTER IV

"MÄCH! Hurry!" Ana ordered. "Late you been for Sunday School und this is Hannah's confirmation. Ach!"

"Huh, old Heist bug his eye I bet when he sees this!" Adam crowed as he fondled a string of pearl beads.

"They're just swell, Papa. I never had anything so pretty in my life." Hannah's eyes shone.

"Yah, sure. One dollar twenty-five cent pearls these. Heist, he buys only one dollar pearls for his Katie.

"Adam, after nine he is. You und the children have to go." Ana set a cap on Coonie's head.

"Hannah, you got your ears washed clean? Und your teeths? You bath good last night? Ach, let me see?"

"I'm clean, Mamma. Ooh, this silk feels so good. I betcha I stub my toe or fall down when I walk up the aisle in these high heels. I'm all goose-fleshy."

"Ach, Hannah, you rattle like one empty brain." Ana shook her head.

"But Mamma, you don't know how I feel! All in white silk and the swellest dress to be confirmed in."

"Ach, not," Ana agreed. "Confirmation, he is different from when I am confirm. Black, I am wear, mit long sleeves, und skirt sweeping the ground, und head shawl covering mine hair slicked plain mit mine face. That head shawl was beauty. Black silk ball fringe, und black silk embroidered rose where the back of mine head is. I remember him good. Black cashmere, he was." Ana smiled.

"I'd rather have silk." Hannah gently smoothed her bloomers. "I can't believe it, Mamma. Confirmation, graduating

26

from the eighth grade, and next year—high school. Reinie, don't you touch me!" Hannah pushed two-year-old Reinie away from her.

"Lizzie und Mary, they both wear mine head shawl when they is confirm. But they.wear white muslin dresses mit high black shoes. Und now you wear white complete. Ach, so change." Ana sighed.

Hannah smiled into the mirror as she pushed the waves deeper into her hair. Ana, on her knees, pulled the soft folds of white georgette into place.

"Mamma, what you crying for?"

"I am cry because you is no more mine baby but a woman, mit all a woman's troubles. Many things you do now. You sing in the choir. You can hold babies to been baptized. Und from now, you think on marriage. Ach, Gott. You is a member of the church, now, und you must pay your dues. Remember always, Hannah, the church, he come first. Go often to the Communion und take of the Lord's Supper so you don't backslide."

"I will, Mamma."

"Wait, oncet!" Ana went to her bedroom, returning with two books.

"I buy you a song book wrote in German, Hannah. When I am confirm, I have learn the songs from cover to cover. Und I buy you a Bible mit the German words. Hannah, mein liebling, it give you peace in time of troubles."

"I got so much, Mamma. My pearls, my dress, and now these." Hannah laid the books down and picked up her beads.

"Ach, Hannah, I remember, this day, mine own confirmation. Mine father und mother, they so poor they don't can buy me one Bible. When I am older und working, I save mine moneys und buy mine own Bible."

"There's the Heists, Mamma." Hannah stood impatiently while her mother combed the back of her hair.

"Mamma, how'd you make Papa get me the pearls?"

"Your papa, he good. He—"

"Come in, Katie, Mrs. Heist," Hannah called loudly.

"Gee, Hannah, you look swell!" Katie's voice was envious. "Oh, gee! If I just looked half so good."

"You do. You look swell. Twice as thin." Hannah's smile faded. "Mamma, Reinie's trying to catch hold of my dress with his dirty fingers! Reinie! Get out!" Hannah pushed Reinie away. He went tumbling.

"Don't you make a fit! You hear, Reinie!" Ana picked the baby up. "That's it. Make shut the cry, und we take you to see Hannah confirmed." Ana carried him into the bedroom.

"Which side do I pin my flower on?" Hannah held up the pink carnation with its spray of green fern.

"Over the heart." Mrs. Heist placed the flower. "Up high on the left—so."

"Ach, these confirmations, they cost like hell," old lady Heist shouted to Ana in the bedroom. "That old man of mine, he don't belong mit the church so we have pay ten dollar on top everything elses for Katie. She better marry one good man, quick. See you done it, Katie!"

Katie giggled. Hannah winked at her. Ana came out adjusting her black lace head shawl, folding it back at the temples, tying it snugly under her chin.

"Ach, mine coat, he don't meet no more in the middle." Ana looked at her bulging figure.

"Ana Schreissmiller, I don't see why you don't get a good black hat. My Katie, she tells me long ago how she is shamed mit mine head shawl." Mrs. Heist complacently settled her hat more firmly.

"Yes, Mamma, why don't you get you a hat?" Hannah appraised her mother. She *did* look old fashioned with her smooth comfortable slippers, her long black skirts, and that shawl over her head. Hannah looked from her own whiteness to her mother.

"Hey, you gonna be late. It's after ten already," Heist called, tooting his horn furiously.

There was a hushed stillness in the church as the confirmation class followed the black-robed minister down the long center aisle to the altar.

Hannah, first in the line of girls, set one high-heeled, white-clad foot before the other, timing her step to the slow

28

stately march. She was acutely conscious of her golden hair framing her face, of her pearls gleaming against her throat, of her pink carnation with its shield of green over her heart, of her long white dress of softest silk. There was a singing inside herself but she kept her eyes lowered and watched only the movement of the black robe of the minister.

She was aware of the older men sitting in the pews on her right, of the older women row on row to her left, of the young people upstairs, all watching, admiring.

She felt a breathless waiting filling the church as the procession of nine girls all in white followed by the ten boys each with a white carnation, symbol of purity, in his dark lapel, slowly made its way to the seats before the altar. Hannah watched the minister mount to the white and gold pulpit. A deep reverence filled her. Never before had the church held such beauty.

Through the stained glass windows curving back of the chancel the golden sunlight rested like a benediction on the dark palm in each window sill. Flowers banked the altar table at the foot of the standing figure of Jesus. The air was heavy with the fragrance of carnations and sweetpeas. An ache came into Hannah's throat as she looked at the Christ standing with hands outstretched in blessing.

Pale yellow paper roses were intertwined on the gold and white baptismal font. Purest white velvet deeply fringed with gold covered the pulpit railing. A banner of white velvet fringed in gold with the lamb of God in the center radiated golden light. Everything was white and gold. Pure, holy, and beautiful! Even as she, Hannah, in white, her golden hair, with that holy feeling flooding her with its radiance.

Hannah saw Fred Hergenboch's father, bent and old, take down the long-handled candle lighter with the snuffer. Walking with dignity to the altar, he carefully set aflame each of the tall white tapers in the slanting gold candelabra. Seven candles in the first, seven candles in the second, their flames glowing like deep yellow balls of light. It seemed to Hannah that the tapers reflected her own inner feeling of shining happiness.

29

"I therefore ask you, each and all alike, do you renounce the devil, and all his works, and all his ways?"

The minister's voice was deep, reverent, and forceful, asking question after question which they answered in unison.

"Yes, I renounce," they answered as one.

"Will you continue steadfast in the true Christian belief?" The words seemed to stand out before Hannah.

"I will," she vowed silently even as her voice joined the others. "Yes, I will by the help of God."

The minister faced them with raised hand, his words ringing clear.

"Our help is in the name of the Lord."

"Who hath made heaven and earth," replied the class.

"Blessed be the name of the Lord."

"Henceforth, world without end," came the answer.

"Lord, hear our prayer."

"And let our cry come unto Thee."

"Let us pray."

The minister raised both hands.

A devout sincerity filled Hannah. She would follow, reverently, the path set before her. All through high school, and in all life afterward. She would make her life as beautiful as this the most beautiful day of her life.

"Thy will be done," she repeated softly.

Slowly the girls went forward to kneel at the altar. Hannah felt the minister's firm hand laid upon her bowed head, heard his deep voice giving the words of blessing.

"Hannah Marie Schreissmiller.... Defend, O Lord, this Thy servant with Thy heavenly grace, that she may continue Thine forever, and daily increase in Thy Holy Spirit more and more, until she comes unto Thine everlasting Kingdom, Amen."

Then the hand lifted, the voice stilled. Once more Hannah felt the gentle pressure upon her head while forcefully and clearly, the minister repeated the words of her life verse.

"Seid frölich in Hoffnung,
Geduldig in truebsal,
Haltet an am Gebet."

"Rejoicing in hope." Oh, she was rejoicing. Before her stretched high school, college maybe! Life was happiness, and laughter, and rejoicing.

"Patient in tribulation." When trouble came, she would hold fast to her faith.

"Continuing instant in Prayer." "I will, I will," she promised as with bowed head she accepted the confirmation certificate from the minister.

The golden light from the window shone upon the picture of Jesus surrounded by angels. It made the trailing flowers and grapes shine. A ray of pure gold struck the picture of the Lord's Supper. Hannah thought of her mother's words, "Go often to Communion und take of the Lord's Supper so you don't backslide."

"I will," she whispered, rising from the altar to lead the way to the seats.

The boys went forward to kneel and receive their certificates. When they returned to their seats, their faces sober and serious, all the children rose to sing the closing hymn. It seemed to Hannah that the words and music became a song of freedom, of happiness, of life that was to be a triumph.

Outside the church, Katie caught Hannah's arm. "Gee, Hannah, wasn't it just swell?"

"I can't talk about it, Katie. I feel all different inside. Holy or something."

"Yeah, me too. Say, Fritz told Jake your old man said he could have the sedan to take us into town this afternoon when we all get our pictures took. Ain't that swell? I ain't never had my picture took. I s'pose I'll look cross-eyed or something."

"You look nice." Hannah smiled and went to join her mother and father who were visiting with neighbors.

"I tells you, we got have rain or them beets don't come themselves up! Got im Himmel, I don't sleep come night!" Adam twisted his straggly mustache.

Hannah sat in the back seat of Adam's sedan with Jake. Fritz drove with Katie beside him.

"Gee, Hannah, I always knew you was a swell looker, but

31

you take my breath. I want one of your pictures when they are finished. You look different somehow."

"I feel different, Jake. Like I wanted to be good all the rest of my life. I feel like I could just love everybody, and never stop smiling, ever. I'm all choked up inside. I want to pinch myself to see if it's really me. Me, that's confirmed, that's finishing the eighth grade, and going on to high school in September."

"Aw, you don't want to go to high school," Jake grumbled, putting his arm around Hannah.

"Oh, but I do, Jake. I want it more than anything in the world. I think I'd die if I didn't go."

"Aw, just when you can have dates, and fun, and go places, you wanta go away. Listen, no matter what happens or where you go, just remember, you're my girl. And you're gonna begin by going to church with me tonight. Ain't yuh?"

"I guess." Hannah dared not look higher than Jake's full lips. Would he kiss her tonight? At the thought the strange tingle ran through her.

"Jake, don't. We're home."

"Just one kiss, Hannah."

"You're too bossy," Hannah laughed happily as she left the car.

"Tonight, then," Jake called.

Hannah went skipping to the house. "Hello, everybody," she called happily, standing in the doorway, her hands on the casings, smiling.

A smell of roasting meat and browning vegetables filled the air with a savory goodness. The kitchen table was extended to its full length, snowy white with the best tablecloth. Oh, home was a good place, Hannah thought. And she had the best family in the world—her sister Mary, with all her children playing on the floor around her; Lizzie, dressed so fancy; Fritz, and her younger brothers; and Tabia. Oh, she loved them all. And her mother so short, so fat, but oh, so dear. Her father, holding little Reinie on his lap. He was a grand sort of father to have. He raised Cain lots of times, but he was good to them all.

"Just think," Hannah laughed, "the next time I wear white will be the eighteenth of May when I graduate from the eighth grade. I'm so happy I could cry, almost."

"Oh, yeah," Olinda twitted, "and after that you'll be walking up the aisle to the tune of 'Here comes the bride.'"

"All you think of is love since you been stuck on—you know who." Hannah winked.

"No weddings for me," Hannah said quickly. "I'm going to take me a business course in high school, and then get a job."

"You'll fall like all the rest of us, and be raisin' kids," Mary announced dully. Mary was trying to rear six children on a hired man's salary of seventy-five dollars a month.

"None the rest of us got to go to high school," Lizzie snapped.

"Huh, you should cry. Swell clothes, swell house, just one kid, and a husband that works in a store and gives yuh everything."

"I got it myself. Nobody helped me." Lizzie was mad.

"And don't you know it? Won't speak to your folks on the street. Too good to come home. You wouldn't be here today if it wasn't Hannah's confirmation."

"Hannah don't need no more'n the rest of us. She—"

"Shod op! Everybodies! Hannah stay hame!"

The clock ticked loudly in the stillness. The small children stopped their playing.

"But Papa—you promised! You promised me."

"Shod op! School, he is done! *Done* I say! Sixteen you got. Confirmed you is. Tomorrow, the field you work him."

"But you prom—"

"Let her go, Dad. You're keepin' me till I'm twenty-one. We've all worked for you. Let her—"

"Shod op! All she do is got married und there goes all that money for nothings! Already, that Jake Heist makes eyes on her."

"But you promised," Hannah whispered, her stricken eyes upon her father.

"It took all mine moneys for this rented place. Machinery, he is high like a cat." Adam tilted his chair against the wall

33

while he calmly pressed tobacco into the bowl of his long-stemmed pipe.

"But you promised," Hannah repeated.

"Got out und stop standing like one dumb ox," Adam roared.

Blindly, Hannah ran through the front room, groping her way up the narrow dark stairs, to her bed.

"Hannah, make not the cry." Ana's arms enfolded her.

"He broke his promise! He's a cheat and a liar!"

"Hannah, stop. Don't make mad on your papa. Better we rent this farm over always making the move."

"He told me I could go."

"Stop, Hannah. You make yourself sick. Your papa got right."

"Sure, he's got the right. He can do anything. He keeps Fritz till he's twenty-one, he makes you have another baby, and now he keeps me home to work till I'm old and wrinkled. I won't, I tell you! I won't."

CHAPTER V

"O GOD. O God, I can't stay. I gotta go," Hannah prayed. "Olinda's home. She can help Mamma. And Papa can hire some one. He can hire Jake. He won't, he'll keep me. He can't. I'll get a job in town. He'll take your wages." Round and round went Hannah's thoughts as she rode the harrow across the freshly plowed ground. She braced her rough work shoes more firmly on the wooden cross plank.

The wind tugged and sucked at her blue overalls. It beat against her thin face, whipping loose strands of pale gold hair from under her boy's cap. She gritted her teeth and faced into the chilly blast. The two horses kicked up little puffs of dust as they plodded up the field and the wind blew the dirt back into her grim face.

She looked at her father sitting hunched down on the little beet drill, his straight-sided black cap just showing above his sheepskin collar. Up and down the field he went, driving the black and the gray, seeding the beets.

The factory field man stopped his car at the side of the road; Adam went to the fence, leaning there, talking and gesturing.

"He can rest and visit while he works us kids to death," Hannah thought, even though she knew the field man had stopped to see whether the ground was properly prepared for the beet seed.

Hannah watched her father and the field man walk slowly over the field inspecting the soil. Checking up on her work, she thought savagely. The sugar factory was always sending its men to keep an eye on the crops. The farmers had signed

35

contracts to grow so many acres of beets at a certain price to be paid in the fall of the year. Nothing but work, work, work.

She'd never forgive her father. Never. He coulda just as well let her gone to school to finish her eighth grade.

Every jiggle of the harrow over the freshly plowed beet ground added to her hate and resentment. In her mind she went back over the sixteen years of her life, as far as she could remember, as she fought the wind and dirt.

She'd been just four years old when she was left at the end of a beet field to look after two-year-old Tabia, and two-months-old Alec. There, in the shade of a gunny sack stretched over four upright sticks, she had tried to hush the squalling Tabia, and the wailing Alec, while her mother went up and down the rows of beets chopping with the long-handled hoe. Hannah had cried for her mother who could not stop work. The beets had to be thinned.

"Yeah, an' now he cries about how hard he's worked, and how big a succeed he's made. We all worked an' Mamma worked harder than all of us put together, and he'll work her in the beets this year too!" Hannah savagely yanked the horses around at the end of the field. She slapped the lines smartly across their backs, shouting, "Gid-ap."

She thought of the time when she was six, big enough to crawl behind her father and mother and Lizzie and Mary, who swung their hoes up and down, blocking the tiny sugar beet plants.

On the ground among the dirt and clods, she had crawled on hands and knees, grasping the plants with dirty fingers, pulling the extra ones out so the biggest and strongest would be left to grow.

Her fingers had become stiff and dirt-caked. Sweat had run down her body. There was no rest. Adam eternally yelled that the beets had to be thinned. He got them up before daylight and kept them in the field until it was too dark to see.

It was when she was ten that she'd cut her knee with the bright-bladed beet knife while haggling the top off of a big beet in harvest. She'd been too little to lift the heavy beet;

36

so she'd held it on her knee. Swish, the knife had cut through the beet into her knee. That same fall Fritz had broken his arm when he was thrown by a runaway team. Adam had cursed day and night because Fritz couldn't top beets. It took two good arms and hands to top a sugar beet.

Adam had driven all the rest of them, screeching that the beets would be frozen in the ground.

"Yeah, and he still drives us. He thinks we're cattle that he owns!" Hannah spit the words into the wind. "And he'd buy us gum and break the stick in two pieces so we'd work harder. No wonder he saved money so he could rent!"

Hannah looked bitterly into the south. "Nothin' but a dump," she thought, as she compared their place with the Boswell house across the road. "The Boswells' got it easy." Then she saw Jim's coupé turn on two wheels into the circular driveway.

Hannah went sprawling across the harrow. She got up quickly, yanking at the horses to turn them around. They'd stopped suddenly at the end of the field.

"All I'm good for is to grub in the field," she half cried as she rubbed her barked shins. "I bet the hide's took off," she said aloud. "I'm not gonna stay here. I'll leave. Papa can't keep me till I'm twenty-one!" But even as Hannah spoke she thought how he'd kept Lizzie and Mary, and how he was still keeping Fritz.

It was getting dark. She hurried her horses from the field before Adam could speak to her.

As she came into the barnyard she met Alec and Solly bringing in the two cows. At the same time Ana, white kerchief tied over her head, came out of the house carrying two milk pails.

Hannah called to her. "You go back, Mamma, I'll milk."

"Ach, Hannah, all mine life I am milk the cow."

"All her life," Hannah muttered as she threw hay to the horses. "Papa'll work her till she drops in the field."

At the table, that night, Hannah helped Reinie with his food.

"Drink your milk, Reinie," she coaxed.

"Me want some milk," shouted four-year-old Chris.

37

"Me, too," chimed in six-year-old Coonie.

"Ach, eat the supper. The pigs, he don't got milk enough so he grow good," commanded Adam.

"He even puts the pigs before us!" Hannah thought. She watched her father as he shoveled his food into his mouth. As he chewed, the ends of his straggly mustache moved up and down across his leathery cheek. His sharp beak of a nose wiggled. Industriously, he piled potatoes onto his knife blade using his fork as a pusher. Raising it to his mouth, he stopped the loaded knife in mid-air, and roared:

"Solly! Drop that cat! We don't eat mit cats on the tables!"

"Hannah, tomorrow you drill mit beet seeds, und Olinda, you ride the harrow. Hannah, she got you skinned one mile for work. Gott, I wish it rain, oncet."

Hannah couldn't sleep after she went to bed. She felt gritty and dirty all over from the dust of the field. Her mouth was parched and dry. Dirt-caked. She slid out of bed and crept down the narrow stairs.

Feeling her way to the water bucket, she stopped. Adam was praying in the bedroom off the kitchen.

"Gott, make it rain so mine last beets come themselves up. Gott, you make it rain und next fall I pay twice over mine church dues. Yah, I make him up mit you. Too many acre I think I am farm, und I worry so I don't can think, und I need the rain so I raise good beets. Make him rain und I praise you all mine days, Gott. Sure, I done it."

Grimly Hannah dipped her cup into the water bucket. "Hypocrite," she muttered. "His word don't mean nothin'. He won't keep his word even with God. All he wants is something for himself, and he's scared to death he's gonna make a failure, so he can't crow to everybody how swell he is."

The next morning she started drilling. The factory field man had come in March with the contracts and Adam had signed to grow forty acres of beets. Twenty acres had been planted first week of April, then ten days later, the south field had been planted. Rain had come and the first beets were up in long slender rows of green.

38

It was dry now and there was not enough moisture to bring up beet seed. Adam held up the lid of the drill box for Hannah to empty the gunny sack of beet seeds, and said: "We got make space between time of plantings so we got time to done the thinnings before the plants get too big in the other fields, but Gott, he don't rain, und the beets come themselves up all to oncet."

The big bulky sack sagged against her knees. Adam roughly put a hand under it, watching the brown, curly seed tumble into the narrow red drill box. Hannah grabbed for a firmer hold and lost her grip. The sack slipped sideways and the light, sponge-like tiny seeds scattered on the dry ground.

"Spill seed, will you?" Adam sent her tumbling to the dirt.

Hannah got up, hating him. She stooped and tried to gather up the seeds with her trembling hands.

Adam's foot struck her on the hip. She fell flat in the dirt. She gathered herself up and faced him.

"You hit me again, and I go to the house. I don't work. You ain't in Russia." Hannah shrank away from him, defiant, but also fearful.

"Ach, mein Gott im Himmel! Make shut the mouth." He advanced upon her shaking his fists. "Get the drill on, und get busy! Expenses I got on mine back mitout spilling seeds. Fifteen cents a pound I pay for him!"

Sullenly, Hannah climbed on the drill and clucked to the horses. "I'm goin' to leave. I'm goin' to get out," she declared to herself. "He's made me dig manure out of the sheep pens and ride on the old manure spreader. I've plowed and harrowed. I've rolled his old fields with the roller. And now I'm drilling. He makes us all work, Fritz, and Olinda and me, and he keeps the other boys home whenever he thinks he can get by without the truant officer getting him. He keeps us all till we're twenty-one, but he won't keep me."

Adam's voice roared up the field. *"Hannah! Make them horse go faster! You hear?"*

Hannah paid no attention. "Let him yell," she muttered.

She stopped drilling before noon. She went to the house to hunt for Adam, and found him mending the pig pen. "I'm outa seed."

"Yah, sure, you spill him on the ground!" As Adam spat out each word a sunflower seed came from his mouth.

"I never spilled no hundred pounds of seed. The factory says you gotta plant twenty pound to the acre. It's only half planted."

"Shut the face. Me, I don't plant no more und seventeen pound. Tell Fritz to get more seed."

Hannah found Fritz sharpening blocking hoes in the barn.

"Fritz, he wants another sack of seed. I'm going with you to get it. He knocked me in the dirt, an' he kicked me." Hannah put her hands to her face and the tears trickled through her dirty fingers.

"Come on, let's get seed," Fritz insisted gently.

They turned into the road beside the red factory, going past the main building to the storehouse. The foreman took Adam's card from the files. There was note of the acreage signed up for, the Boswell dump to which he would deliver his topped beets in the fall, and there was note of the amount of seed allotted, with the amount Adam had gotten and planted.

Fritz boosted the huge sack of seed onto the front bumper of the car and headed for home.

"They sure check up on you," Hannah said.

"Yeah, the Sugar Company thinks when you sign the contract to grow beets that they got the right to know how you raise 'em and what you do. I guess it's all right. Kinda good to have your district field man to run to if you have trouble or want some advice. The Sugar Company guarantees the exact price you get so I guess it's all right. Some people think the company don't pay what they should but me, I don't know. The old man'll sure cuss. That field won't take a whole sack and the factory don't take back no broken sack nor one with its seal broken. He'll grumble 'cause he's got some seed left over."

"He thinks he owns the earth." Hannah was bitter.

"God, I wisht it'd rain," Fritz broke the silence. "I just as soon be shot as irrigate beets up. They don't never do good. It makes the ground hard, and you can't get it fine all summer, and beets don't come up good."

"Quit your worryin', Fritz, the old man does enough of that."

"Yeah, I guess." Fritz stopped at the beet drill to unload the seed.

After supper that night, Hannah washed the dishes while Tabia, grumbling, dried them. Olinda had a date with Henry.

When the last dish was put away, Hannah went out onto the front porch. A car came out of the Boswell driveway and turned toward Valley City.

"Jim," Hannah said, watching the bright lights twinkling above the city; large clear red ones, smaller pale yellow ones. Above the little lights there was a soft brightness, like a halo, with the dark mountains behind. In the darkness between the city and where Hannah sat, lay the blackness of Shag Town, the beet-workers' city.

"Jim's got the light, the sunshine, while I got nothing but the darkness. He don't even know I'm on earth. He won't ever know it so long as I work in the field. But I won't stay. Papa can't keep me here." Hannah spoke the words defiantly.

"What you say, Hannah?" Ana sat down heavily on the step.

"I said I wasn't gonna stay here and work on this farm forever! Mamma, I'd think you'd hate the everlasting work and the dirty houses, an' the moving, an' the beets, an' babies comin' all the time?"

"Ach, Hannah, life, he is not hard when you get used to him. We take him like he comes."

"But I don't wanta take it like it comes! I wanta go places! I wanta have swell clothes, and have some fun!"

"Good times we have here, Hannah. Be glad you're not in the Old Country, Russia. We work there, I tell you.

"Up in the morning before day is light, und driving oxen or camels, two, three, might five miles to the fields. We take the tent und stay 'til we get the crop planted und the old man he ride out in the little light cart mit the high stepping horse to see if us kids is working. You think your papa hard, but in Russia the old mens never work. Sons he want so he get more land from the governments. For every son when he is born, the old man gets five or ten acre. Five acre if it been good land. Ten acre if it been hilly und rough.

"You think we crowded here. In the Old Country the houses is full of peoples: aunts, uncles, grandfathers, und grandmutters. Yah, they all live in the towns close by each other, und go out in the country to the farms. The childers have to work over there."

"There's no difference. Papa still thinks he can do like in Russia."

"Stop it, Hannah. Your papa not for blame. Some day you see it, und you will been shamed the way you talk."

A car stopped at the front gate. Katie Heist called, "Hannah, I got the swellest news! You can't guess! I've got a job! A job!"

"Really, Katie? Where?"

"You couldn't guess in a million years! The Boswells! Think of it, right across the road from you. Just think I'll see that swell Jim every day. Boy, won't I make eyes on him!"

"Yah, und lose your job," Adam spoke from the open doorway. "Better you keep your eyes on yourself. That Jim he steps high. If you know him, you don't wipe your feets on him or roll your eyes on him neither. Too much moneys! Too much car! Und too much girls! Bah, Katie Heist, better you leave his kind alone."

"If he was German, you'd think he was swell," Katie laughed. "Well, I gotta be goin'." Katie went running toward the waiting car.

"Nothin' but a sassy piece," Adam muttered.

Nothing further was said for several moments. Then Hannah spoke, tears in her voice.

"Katie's got all the luck."

"Ach not, Hannah, you have luck, too. Today the minister come, und I tell him how you want go in high school und he say you come work for his wife this winter und the next three winters. Adam let you go sure, if the minister ask. Yah, you go. Sure."

Hannah felt stunned. Freedom! No more beets! No more dirt!

"I can't go. I ain't finished the eighth grade."

"Yah, you smart. You take the examinations."

"Oh, Mamma, I can't believe it! I'll get my books from school and I'll study. Ooh, just think, Mamma, in town at the preacher's. Oh, it's the swellest place, thick carpets, big easy chairs, and a bathroom even. Ooh! Just think never havin' to scrooch up in a dinky washtub to take a bath no more; no more kids a-squallin'! But Mamma, can you get along without me?"

"Yah, Olinda, she help good. She eighteen, und Tabia, she help."

"Mamma! Mamma! Reinie's havin' a fit. Coonie pushed him down the stairs."

Ana pulled herself erect by the supporting post and went hastily inside.

As Hannah followed her mother indoors she thought: "And it'll be heaven to have some peace. No kids havin' fits."

CHAPTER VI

IT was long after midnight when Hannah heard Olinda tiptoe into the bedroom, undress and slip into their bed.

She don't want no one to know when she gets home, Hannah thought, but it's after midnight because I just heard the night passenger train. Her and Henry got it bad. Won't papa explode if they wanta get married! Them Goelzers! But she can't get married—not for a year anyway—'cause I'm going to high school. I'll get my books from school and I'll sure study. Only missed a week anyway—it's all review from now on—

"What's that?" Hannah held her breath, listening.

Olinda was crying, softly. Hannah could feel the covers quiver with her shaking body.

"Olinda," Hannah whispered, "what's the matter?"

The crying stopped. The very stillness of the room shouted. A mouse crawled in the wall.

"Nothing," Olinda finally answered.

"What you cryin' for, then?"

Silence.

"You and Henry had a fight?"

"No."

"You sick?"

Olinda cried harder.

"If you don't wanta talk, shut your face and let somebody else sleep!" Hannah bounced over in bed, gave the snoring Tabia a shove, straightened out her knees.

What on earth was the matter with Olinda? Ever since they had moved she had been going around with a sober face.

44

"Come on," Hannah forcibly turned Olinda and cradled her wet cheek against her own face. "Spill it," she commanded.

"Henry and me's gotta get married—right away."

Hannah's breath stuck in her throat. A coldness crept from her head to her feet. A dog howled beneath the window—a long mournful howl that sent prickles running over her body. "Olinda! No!"

"Yes. I been scared for weeks." Olinda cried harder.

"O God. O God," Hannah whispered as her whole world tumbled about her. Gone was the future, gone everything but this terrible reality.

"Olinda, how could you? How could you?"

"I'll never be able to hold my head up again. Never, never, never."

Hannah, though stricken, tried to comfort her. "Don't worry, Olinda, I'll tell Mamma in the morning. You and Henry can get married right away. Quit your cryin' and go to sleep."

But Hannah wept silent tears into her pillow for a long time. If Olinda got married, she'd have to stay. She couldn't leave her mother now. Tabia was too little and too lazy to help with a tiny baby. Her mind went over all the things that high school would have meant, all that staying at home next year would mean. Lugging water from the cistern. The pump handle frozen with ice, and almost taking the skin from her fingers. Water slopping on her shoes with their run-over heels and broken laces. Dirty chicken coops to clean out and brush with oil to keep down the mites. The setting of hens, and broken eggs in the nest all wet and yolky. There would be the tiny baby, its washing to be done, dirty diapers, and the ceaseless squalling. There would be the everlasting baking of bread, bedbugs and the dirt, and the dank smells from the barnyard, and the stinking beet pulp in the winter with the men carrying oodles of it in on their broad-toed rubber boots. There would be the beetwork, the bending, backbreaking work of the thinning with the sun scorching down in the late spring. And in the fall they would top beets in the cold wind and spitting snow in order to get the beets out

45

before freezing. In her bitterness she reviewed it in detail.

"You're tied," a still voice whispered. "You're here for-ever. You'll never get away. This is just the beginning. This will always be your life."

"No! No! I will get away! The devil himself can't keep me here!" Illogically, the words of confirmation came to her, "Do you renounce the devil and all his ways? All his ways?"

Her life verse stood before her, "Rejoicing in hope."

"I have no hope," she murmured.

"Patient in tribulation."

"I can't. I can't."

At last daylight came. Carrying her shoes, she slipped down to the kitchen. Quietly, she started the fire.

"Ach, Hannah. So early. Nice it is to have a fire." Ana smiled as she tied up her stockings with strips of muslin.

"Papa oughta start the fire."

"The womans always start the fire in Russia."

"This ain't Russia. No American women get up and start fires." Hannah was in a vicious mood. She slammed the dishes onto the table, thinking of how she would tell Ana.

She looked at her mother standing at the table by the stove mixing sour milk pancakes. So sure and serene, Ana stood, her face calm, unworried. The dark apron pinned around her made a narrow indented line in the dark bulk of her dress. Her broad feet were planted firmly in their soft comfort slippers; the smoothness of her brown hair pinned in the big knot above the fold of her neck.

I can't tell her. I can't, Hannah thought, clenching her hands, I'd sooner take a beating, but I gotta tell her.

"Mamma—Olinda's gotta get married."

Ana stopped her stirring and stood absolutely motionless.

Hannah looked at the quiet broad back and began to hate Olinda for doing this to her mother.

"Henry Goelzer?" Ana asked.

"Yes. They gotta get married next Sunday, even." Hannah studied the plate in her hand.

"Better I tell Adam." Ana left the kitchen, her face wooden, showing nothing of her feelings.

The children came straggling into the kitchen half-dressed.

46

"Get up to the table," Hannah ordered.

Ana returned. "Eat mit breakfast," she said quietly.

In a moment Adam appeared in the doorway. With his hands braced against the door jambs, he surveyed them, his face dark and threatening. He shook his fist at Olinda.

"So-o! You hussy! You bring disgrace on mine head! Me, Adam Schreissmiller, a renter! Mein Gott im Himmel! What you care, they point the finger und say, 'Ha, Adam Schreissmiller! Ha! He got that girl Olinda what is no good. A fine girl he makes! Lays mit that Henry Goelzer what is no good! She don't can marry in the church! She no can wear the wreath on her head!'

"I tell you! You do marry in the church! You hear?" His face was purple under the tan. He shook both fists at Olinda, then he turned on the rest of the family.

"You hear me? Hear me good! Not one word do you say, or I beat you so you don't can talk. Me, I don't have no girl what can't been married in the church. Gott, I say I don't! You tell that Henry, tonight he come und ask for you. You hear, Olinda? Next Sunday the minister say your names in church. Three weeks then you been married. Just the same like you was a good girl, a virgin. Virgin! Bah! You hear? Hear me good!"

He turned his dark glance upon each in turn, Fritz, Olinda, Hannah, Tabia, Solly, Chris, Coonie, and Reinie. He shook his fist and yanked out his chair.

That evening, Hannah helped her mother clean the front room and kitchen in preparation for old man Goelzer and Henry's godfather.

"One good lunch, we must make," Ana insisted, her face a wooden mask, showing no feeling. "Might they not come till middle-night. Ach, in the Old Country such lunches they make mit whisky und cold meats, und cakes. Ach, Gott."

"I think Papa's crazy to make all this fuss over Olinda. It was all right for Lizzie and Mary, but Olinda— You know how she is, and you make her wait three weeks to get married. Make her go through all this silly business."

"Ach, Hannah, better we hold high the head und not drag ourselves deeper in the dirt. Better we make the good of a

47

bad business. Me, mine heart near break. I think I not know this day should come on me."

"Everybody'll know it sooner or later. They'll whisper behind our backs."

"Yah, but they think better on us for making the best of it, Hannah."

"I wish they'd come and get it over with. It's ten o'clock. Oh, quit your crying, Olinda. You got yourself into this mess. You might at least act like you liked it."

"Hannah, say it not," pleaded Ana.

"Here they come!" Tabia and Solly came running.

"Go mit bed. You hear? Tabia, you, too. Und don't you be peekin' or papa beat you good." Ana waved the smaller children upstairs.

Adam rose from the green couch.

"Well, well, Adam, how is you? Lookin' fine mit yourselfs."

"Yah, fine, fine, Peter Goelzer. Hello, Daniel Kniemer! Hello, George Ochmidt! Henry, Olinda is in the kitchen. Come in. Come in." Adam held high the kerosene lamp.

Daniel Kniemer was Henry's godfather but George Ochmidt did the talking. "Well, Adam, how comes the seeding?"

"Gott, it dry. I never seen such a wind."

"Yah, but I seen snow in this country the last of May already. We plant the beets und the rain come."

"Yah, sure, what else we do?" Adam agreed.

George Ochmidt cleared his throat, shuffled his feet. "Well, Adam, Peter's boy Henry wants that he should marry your girl, Olinda."

"Mein Gott im Himmel! I don't stand for it!" Adam jumped to his feet, shaking his fists.

"Ach, Adam, think on how they is love each other und want it so they live together und raise their own children."

"Yah, George, but think on me. I am rent a big place here. One hundred sixty acre. Forty acre mit beets und alfalfas to irrigate und work und cut. Olinda, I need him so I get mine work finish. No! No! You don't take him away from me." Adam spoke loudly.

48

"Ach, but Adam," Daniel Kniemer pleaded, "Henry, he is good boy, und a good husband he make Olinda. Think on how they is love each other, und want so much to be together in their own little house."

"Yah, might, but I no can harvest mine crop mitout Olinda." Adam gave the appearance of being stubborn.

"It is not good that man should live alone. You know it, Adam. Und Henry, he is of age so he marry. It not good that he waits."

"Yah, but how Henry take care mit Olinda? You don't got no more room in your place for him, Peter."

"Ach, not, but Henry have a job working beets, und a beet shack to live in und might a steady job after beets," Kniemer answered.

"I need mine Olinda. How I get mine work done? How I get all mine beets thinned?" Adam appeared obstinate. The argument became more intense.

At last Ochmidt said, "Yah, sure, Adam, but think on when you was love mit Ana. Think on how you was love her und want been mit her. That way Henry is over Olinda."

Adam threw wide his hands. "Well, I give in. If they want to get together married, let them."

"Adam, you don't been sorry. Henry—Olinda, come," Ochmidt called.

Hannah and her mother stood in the kitchen, watching, while Ochmidt's deep voice boomed, "Henry, take Olinda's hand— Now Henry, do you want this girl, Olinda?"

"Yes, sir, I do."

"Well, you know, Henry, this isn't for one day, or one week, this is forever. No matter what happens, sickness or anything?"

"Yes, sir."

"You have to go out now und make your living yourself."

"Yes, sir."

"Tomorrow, you get your license, you go see the minister, so he will call your names in the church next Sunday. Three weeks, then, you marry."

"Yes, sir."

"Yah, good," Adam grunted. "Come, we eat." He led the way to the kitchen.

"Have a drink, Goelzer. This damn good whisky is. Und you, Kniemer, und you, Ochmidt."

"To Henry und Olinda, might they have lots of kids so they work good beets, ha, ha."

"Adam, you got any beets up? Mine first planting has already come themselves up. That's what comes of planting early."

"Yah, und they get themselves froze off, sure. Too early beets ain't so good. I got mine first twenty acre planted und ten acre what I plant next, und ten acre more I have plant. How I get them all worked mit Olinda gone? Gott."

Yes, Hannah agreed, how were they to get the field work done, and plan for Olinda's wedding, too?

CHAPTER VII

THE next day Hannah and Fritz burned the weeds from the fence rows and cleaned out the irrigation ditches.

Watching the smoke ascend, Hannah thought bitterly, everything's got its freedom but me. She raked the weeds from around the fence posts with head bent to hide her tears.

"I'm sick of it all," she said suddenly. "It's beet work day in and day out in the spring, day in and day out in the fall, and in the winter it's beet pulp, and stink, stink, stink!"

"Aw, Hannah, you make it hard on yourself. You forget thinning only lasts three or four weeks and topping only lasts six weeks or so in the fall." Fritz shrugged his shoulders.

"We spend all the rest of the time thinking of the beets and getting ready for them, and I hate 'em. I hate 'em. I tell you, Fritz, I'm not gonna stay! He can't keep me 'til I'm twenty-one!"

"Huh, he kept Lizzie and Mary. You're no better than them."

"They didn't have any backbone."

"Just try using yours and you'll get it busted for you." Fritz turned his back.

"O God, I can't stay. I gotta go," Hannah said over and over, despairingly, thinking of long ago when Adam had whipped stubborn Fritz with the black-snake whip, thinking of Lizzie's high sharp tongue silenced against Adam's fist, of Mary, crying. He'd kept them all. He'd keep her. O God, he couldn't! He couldn't! I hate Olinda for making such a mess of things!"

When other girls had gotten into trouble, she remembered how the old men smirked and laughed. She shrank at the thought of it. And Adam was going to insist that Goelzers make of this wedding a fine thing, even as when Lizzie and Mary were married.

Hannah remembered those weddings. Joyous occasions of laughter, and happiness, and sly jokes. But there was no happiness here. She thought of her mother's still face, hiding the deep hurt within her. And her mother was sick. There was a puffiness around her face; new lines were drawn tight. Ana kept on working, but she moved more slowly.

"I'm afraid! I'm afraid!" Hannah thought. Her fear quickened that night when she went to the house. Her mother lay on her bed in the tiny bedroom off the kitchen. Even in her pain, Ana seemed to dominate the plain drabness of the room with its worn splintery floor, the old dresser with the wavy mirror, the iron bedstead with its pieced but clean coverlet.

"Mamma, you all right?" Hannah went to her and smoothed the straight brown hair. There was a tightness in her throat.

"Yah, Hannah, I been all right come morning. You and Olinda have finish putting the patches on the overalls. That first field of beets, he soon been ready to thin. You think you can patch, Hannah?"

"We'll get it done. Don't you worry." Hannah patted the broad arm.

In the kitchen she turned on Tabia. "Why don't you help a little more," she whispered hoarsely. "You're always a gettin' outa work. You'd let Mamma kill herself!"

Tabia made a face at her and went on playing jacks on the table.

Olinda came in with a bucket of eggs, her eyes red from crying.

A burning smell filled the kitchen. Hannah ran to rescue the skillet of potatoes. Savagely, she cut off the burnt ones with the spoon and dropped them into the coal bucket.

Olinda started crying.

"Stop it, Olinda! There's other things beside yourself to

52

bawl about. Mamma for one. Set the table. Papa's comin' in."

After supper Hannah left Tabia doing dishes and went into the front room to sew. Olinda was just finishing patching the seat of Solly's overalls. Tears dripped down onto the denim stretched across the sewing machine.

"Go to bed, Olinda. You make me sick with your crying. I'll sew."

Hannah cut the long strips of white dam canvas, measuring so that they would fit along the front of the legs of the boys' overalls. She looked anxiously at her mother lying on the green couch.

"This is one year you don't thin beets," she said firmly.

"Yah, Hannah, I been all right." Her mother's voice stopped, as though to gain strength.

"Und Hannah, I am been thinking how Tabia is fourteen, und she can help mit the work. Next week you take your examinations und when the beets is thin you go by the minister."

Hannah sat still, looking at her mother. "But Mamma, you can't."

"Foolish you is, Hannah. I been this way before und always I work in the field 'til the day comes, und this is no difference. Look at Mis Heist. Her last one come before noon, und she gots up and makes the supper for the men when they come from the field."

Hannah was silent. She couldn't tell her mother that she felt this time was different. There was such a pinched look around Ana's nose and mouth, and Hannah remembered the doctor's words. "There must be no more children, Mr. Schreissmiller."

"Papa's to blame for it all," she declared stubbornly.

"It makes for hurt, Hannah, when you think hard on your papa. Always, he work hard, und he buy good clothes, und we have enough to eat. Hard it is for feed und dress so big family."

"We all work, and we earn our keep. He saved money while he worked us. He couldn't a made so much nor worked so many beets without us."

"Ach, Hannah, some day, you see how your papa ain't for blame. The beets got been worked so we have money so we eat und live. How Adam help that?"

"I know I'm sick of it all!" Hannah took long stitches in the white patches.

From the silence, Ana spoke, her voice low, calm, unruffled. "Hannah, everything fall by you. But you is strong. Some day, the dirt, he don't bother you so much. You do what you is able, und don't worry by what is left. Life, he is not hard when you don't make mad und fight him. But, Hannah, I think on how always you fight mit life und it wear you out und try the heart mit pain. So I tell you, Hannah, when everything go hard und backways, und you think you no can stand it, go by the minister for the help. Und pray to Gott, und He give you peace."

Hannah's needle stopped sewing. Her fingers became still. Unseeing, she stared at the overalls on her knee. God in Heaven! Did her mother know that this time was different? Oh, no, no, no! But why then, was she giving her advice to take through life. It couldn't be! It couldn't be!

"What you want me to do, Mamma?" she asked, her voice thick with unshed tears.

"I ask nothing, Hannah, mein liebling. You will do the right. Always, I know that. You have a strength like none of the rest. I pray for your happiness, not what you do."

"Mamma, you think—"

"Ach, not, Hannah. Come, we go in bed, und tomorrow I been fine, und next week, we thin mit beets, und we have plan by Olinda's wedding. Play once before we go in bed mit the organ, just one hymn. I like it good when you sing low mit the playing. Mine song I like best."

Hannah sat down to the old organ and softly played the hymn and sang the words.

"Thou art my portion, O my God—
The testimonies of Thy grace
I set before mine eyes:
Thence I derive my daily strength, and
there my comfort lies."

The next morning Ana was up and around as usual. Hannah felt reassured. She'd been crazy last night to imagine her mother was worried.

Two nights later she came from the field, too tired to walk, but the house had to be cleaned. Daniel Kniemer and Henry Goelzer's father were coming to talk over wedding plans.

"Yah, I give out the invitations," boomed Kniemer as he came into the front room. "Such good verses I make up, und such a good cane I have so it hold many ribbons, und room I got so I hold much whisky." Kniemer patted his fat stomach, laughing heartily.

"Give us the verses, Kniemer. We see if they listen good," Adam said.

"I do him like when I invite." Kniemer went outside slamming the front door after him. Presently, there came the sound of the tapping cane on the porch, followed by a pounding on the door.

"Hello! Hello, Kniemer!" Adam flung wide the door, acting well his greeting.

Kniemer tapped his cane on the floor as he advanced, reciting the invitation in a deep voice.

"WEDDING GREETING!

"Good evening, my dear people, we come to you with a message of gladness. For God, the Lord, has given you and us a new wedding couple.

"We are sent by the parents and the young people, this you can see by the cane and the ribbons. We invite you to be their wedding guests and go with them into the church to bless them as at the wedding of Cana. And when the church wedding is over, then you will hear wedding music inviting you to the wedding home. There we will have a wedding feast. Therefore, put your knives and forks into your pocket, otherwise, you will have to eat with your fingers.

"Cattle and poultry has been fattened and already cows, calves and hogs have been butchered. Also geese, ducks, chickens and turkeys came flying. We saw a rooster so fat that it looked like a hog. A cow so high a bird couldn't fly over it. A calf of only seven weeks weighed sixteen hundred pounds.

55

"Truly a feast for the gods. In the cellar there are many cases of good strong beer. So herewith we extend the invitation to you. Now because we have given you this invitation, we ask for a ribbon on our cane. If you don't have a ribbon, a drink of whisky will do.

"You have a ribbon?"

Tabia produced a hair ribbon. In silence the bow was tied on the cane.

"Fine! Fine!" Adam and Peter Goelzer pounded their knees in joy.

"One big drink of whisky I give for that, Kniemer. Ana, bring!"

Adam poured himself a drink, taking it at one swallow, smacking his lips. He filled the glass for Kniemer, then for Goelzer.

"One hundred peoples we invite. Ach, mein Gott, we have the big wedding. Next week we have the shower dance in mine barn loft," Adam said with decision. "Tomorrow, Goelzer, we go by town so Henry buy Olinda's wedding clothes."

"Yah," Goelzer agreed, ducking his bullet head deeper into his shoulders.

"Foolishness," Hannah thought, waiting to go to bed. "All for Olinda just to fool people."

The next evening, Adam came home from Valley City storming and raging.

"That Peter Goelzer, he make me sick mit mineself! A lookin' on cheap dresses to buy for Olinda. Gott, me a renter! A renter!"

"Maybe he got as good as he could," Hannah put in. "It takes a lot of money. He's got to buy the bride's dress, two of everything from pants and stockin's to the bride's bouquet and the fancy orange blossoms for her veil."

"Yah, und he want buy cheap ones from the fifteen cents store for one dime. Bah!"

"Henry bought lovely stuff. My dress is just beautiful," Olinda said defensively.

"Sure, he buy good stuff, I don't let him buy no cheap. Me you got to thank." Adam pounded his chest.

56

"Yeah, I was shamed to death! You and old Goelzer a fightin' in all the stores and arguing so all the clerks smirk their faces, and Mamma and old lady Goelzer nodding 'yes,' to everything. You make me sick!"

Olinda stamped out of the kitchen.

"Hah, sick I make you! Gott im Himmel, sicker you make mine belly," Adam roared.

"Make not the fight," Ana chided. "Better we plan by the shower dance, und the wedding."

"I'm so tired," Hannah said. "Work in the field all day. At night fightin' about Olinda. I'm sick of it. We don't need no shower dance."

"Gott, we have make moneys so they fix a house. That Henry, he got nothings! Better she have somethings."

"Yah," Ana said.

"Und Hannah, you been Olinda's best girl, und you smile like you happy! You hear?"

"I'm not gonna do it!" Hannah put her hands to her face.

"Yah, Hannah done him," Ana said.

"Und Jake Heist is Henry's best boy. That Jake, he smart in the head. Already he makes money. You set your head for him, Hannah, und he come und live here und work for me."

"I'm not marryin' Jake." Hannah dashed out of the room.

At the shower dance Hannah danced with a set smile on her face. Even Olinda was all smiles. Friends came from all around. They brought fine presents of curtains, bedspreads, tablecloths, pans, dishes, everything for the house. Good presents, for wasn't Adam Schreissmiller a renter? Standing high in the church and community?

Peter Goelzer had friends, but not so fine nor so numerous as Adam, and Adam crowed openly, drinking glass after glass of good liquor.

After midnight the party became more noisy. Adam went around with a pitcher insisting that every one let him fill his glass. "Good liquor, have some!"

Disgusted, Hannah went to the house and to bed. All too soon morning would arrive. Another day of dirt and dry wind.

Rain fell for two days the next week. Ana rejoiced for it gave them all time to get ready for the wedding.

Ana took dishes to Goelzers' and flour to Heists'. For Adam and Peter Goelzer would split the expense of the wedding. Down to Goelzers' to help clean and fix things. Ask Mrs. Heist to make the noodles for the butterball soup, and the angel food bride's cake.

"The biggest one you ever made, Mis Heist," Adam insisted.

"Yah, yah, sure. I cook him in mine dishpan. Mit the whites I make the cake, mit the yellows I make the noodles. Ach, the fine wedding."

"Yah, fine, six hundred butterballs, it take. Might you better get Mis Ochmidt so she help." Adam rubbed his hands together.

On the Saturday night before the wedding, Hannah went with Ana to Goelzers'. Furniture had been moved out. Long narrow tables were set up in the emptied rooms. Two tables filled the small front room, two more filled the dining room. The bedroom off the dining room held a long table made of planks laid on trestles. There was scarcely room to slide onto the benches lining the walls.

The front bedroom, made up with the best spread, held all of Olinda's shower dance presents. Hannah sniffed. There was the faint smell of rancid dirt and foul air. All the cleaning had failed to remove traces of the dirt that usually filled the house.

Mrs. Ochmidt came with her boiler full of dry hard butterballs, round, cream-colored marbles of a deep richness, made of browned bread crumbs, butter, thick cream, and beaten egg. Two neighbors came in carrying a long clothes basket filled with great slabs of black coffee cake, rich with dried fruit and raisins. Mrs. Heist puffed as she helped carry in great dishpans of finely cut noodles, dried so that each noodle kept its shape.

"Look mit the wedding cake!" Mrs. Goelzer shouted, pointing to Heist, bearing a three-tiered cake frosted in brightest pink with green and blue decorations.

"George, he cook by the bakery, so he decorate him good

for me und puts the bride und her man on top." Mrs. Heist chuckled as the women exclaimed at the beauty of it.

Huge boilers on the cookstove sent forth delicious odors of chicken, ducks, geese, and turkeys.

"Yah, the gooses it makes the rich broth for the butter-ball soup," Mrs. Goelzer laughed deeply, her huge body shaking. She lifted the lid, peering inside. "We cook the meat tonight so we brown him good in the oven mit the potatoes tomorrow. Ach, good he is." She ran her tongue around her lips. Hannah crowded close to see the boiling broth with pieces of fowl floating in its richness.

"All this for Olinda," she thought.

"Hannah, come here. You gotta help me," Jake Heist called.

"You know the best girl and the best boy gotta decorate the bride's car." Jake caught her fingers and held them.

"Don't, Jake. I don't feel like foolin'." Hannah twisted the crêpe paper ribbons and handed the ends to Jake; bright streamers of rose, nile green, and heavenly blue cut three inches wide.

"Gee, I bet this'll be one of the swellest decorated cars," Jake laughed as he twined the ribbons from the fender to the opposite corner of the windshield.

"I feel like I was gettin' ready for *my* funeral instead of a wedding. Olinda's free, but I'll never get away."

"Aw, sure you will. You never wanted really to go to high school. You wait. I got a good job and I'm savin' my money. Maybe by next summer we can get married."

"Don't be a fool, Jake," Hannah snapped. But even as she said the words she became aware of feeling less alone, less trapped.

CHAPTER VIII

OLINDA was married at twelve-thirty on Sunday right after the regular church services.

The entire congregation, it almost seemed, had come to the church, but, instead of entering, quietly lined the sidewalk.

The older women, with black head shawls of delicate lace or cashmere, stood with their dark full skirts spreading wide around them, their weathered faces expressionless, waiting patiently for the bridal party to come from the parsonage. The older men, in black, with small straight-sided black caps on their home cut hair, stood stolidly in the best positions. The younger people, brightly clad, huddled in groups. Their flashy modern clothes looked out of place among the dark foreign garb of their parents.

Through this lane of friends, the minister led the bridal party. Hannah, with head bent, hands holding the ends of Olinda's long bridal veil, stepped slowly. Hatred burned in her heart.

Oh, it seemed holy, reverent, and beautiful. The minister leading, the bride and groom following, then Hannah, the bride's best girl, walking beside Jake, the bride's best boy. Next came the three bride's girls, marching in clashing colors of bright green with ruffles, pink with white lace, and purple with black, each beside a bride's boy. Everything for the bride; the bride who was clean and white as the bridal gown she wore. A virgin.

A virgin! Hannah thought bitterly.

The empty pews jeered "Mockery! Disgrace!" Hannah looked down at the veil she held in outstretched hands. White, the symbol of purity! Purity! God in heaven! There was no purity, no decency, no rightness! Nothing but lust, and shamelessness.

Carefully, and with dignity, she took her place as the bridal party spread on either side of the bride and groom at the altar. She stood quietly, listening as the old women filed into the wooden pews on the left, and thinking that all too soon they would know of this disgrace. And the old men, sitting on the right, would know it sooner. Hannah visioned the sly lowering of an eyelid, the nodding of a round head, the twisting of weathered lips, the whispered words behind sheltering fingers.

The minister's deep voice, commanding and reverent, broke in upon her thoughts. "Dearly beloved." Didn't he know, couldn't he sense, that they were not dear? No, not even beloved? She shut her ears against his voice. The deep purple of the stained glass windows seemed like dark threatening storm clouds with Christ crucified upon the cross. It held her. Fascinated her. Crucified! The ends of Olinda's veil felt as nails piercing her palms. God, why should she be crucified, set forever to drudge in the field? Tied, while Olinda went free. "God have mercy!"

This must be a dream: the four bride's girls, each with a pink carnation pinned to her shoulder; the four bride's boys, each with his white carnation in his lapel. She felt that she had been here before. Confirmation. Rejoicing in Hope. She had stood to be confirmed such a few short weeks before, filled with hope, the future bright. And now this was crucifixion, "Patient in tribulation." Was patience being killed inside oneself? Was patience showing a wooden face to all one's friends while inside hate and fury burned?

The words of the minister beat in upon her, "Premising that there is nothing to hinder your union, or to render your marriage improper."

She felt like screaming the truth from the altar. This marriage was improper! This marriage should not be in this holy church, and it wouldn't be in this church, if the minister knew the truth. Only virgins in all their cleanness and purity

61

could be married here under the benevolent gaze of the Holy Jesus.

Devoutly, to all appearances, Olinda and Henry knelt at the altar. Carefully, Hannah lowered the veil to the steps. With bowed head she stood while the minister blessed the bridal couple, his closing words tolling in her ears:

"And give you peace, amen."

"No peace," she cried to herself as she followed Olinda out of the church. The old women were crying. She saw Tabia put her arms around Ana, who wept unrestrained.

Why should they cry for Olinda? Tightly, Hannah clenched the ends of the wedding veil. Better to cry for Ana whose heart was hurt, for Adam whose pride would be dragged in the dust, for her, Hannah, who must stay home, who must never go to high school.

Out of the church, dodging and shrinking, trying to avoid the rain of barley, corn, and wheat which showered round them from numerous pockets and small sacks, the bridal party ran to the parsonage to get coats and have witnesses sign the marriage license.

Hannah tried to shake the grain from her clothes. Small red spots showed on her throat where the grain had pelted. She tried to dislodge the last of the seeds as she rode with the bridal party to the photographer's.

They waited awkwardly for the photographer to get ready. She looked at Henry Goelzer, small, skinny, and loose jointed. Not much like his huge fat mother, more like his bullet-headed father. He had the same drooping shoulders, the same watery blue eyes. Henry looked simple, ashamed. No wonder he wouldn't meet her glance.

"Well, that's over." Jake Heist took Hannah's arm and led the way to the car. "Now for the wedding eats. I'm starved." He grinned at them all.

Down through the wide streets of Valley City they went, across the river to the narrow streets and little houses of Shag Town, to the dingy home of the Goelzers.

A group of young men held a thick rope stretched across the gateway.

"You gotta pay to get in," they shouted in unison.

"Open that gate, or I get out and throw you away," one of the bride's boys called loudly from the car.

"One dollar you pay before you get in to eat. You know the bride gotta have some money. She don't feed you for nothin'. One dollar."

"We don't! Twenty-five cents is all we pay," Jake replied loudly.

The four bride's boys each threw a quarter to the gate keepers, and the rope was lowered.

As the car came into the yard, three old men standing under a tree started playing, "Jesus, now lead on 'til the peace is won." The bass horn, clarinet and cornet sent a high lilting melody across the yard, the bass horn boomed.

Older women came running out of the house to kiss Olinda and shake Henry's hand.

The bridal party made their way through the crowded Goelzer kitchen. The odor of cooking was thick in the warm air. The old women cooks bustled about in woolen dresses covered by great aprons.

"In the front room," shouted one, motioning.

Stepping sideways, turning and twisting, they made their way.

Hannah stepped over the board seats and slid along until she was beside Olinda at the long bride's table. It was covered with snowy linen and set with thick white dishes.

A cook brought a glass pitcher. "For the bride's flowers," she said, and waited while Olinda soberly placed her pink carnations and sweetpeas within. She placed it in the center of the table directly in front of Olinda, moving the huge bride's cake to one side.

Bowls of butterball soup, with the tin dippers resting in their depths, were brought in by the cooks, and each guest at the bride's table ladled out the delicious yellow butterballs and finely cut noodles into his own individual soup bowl. The great platters of brown and sizzling turkey, goose, and chicken were brought in. The browned potatoes followed with rich dressing, pickles, and homemade bread.

Henry poured a small wine glass of whisky and passed it. The glass was returned, filled again and passed to the next one at the table, and so on until every one had drunk. Soberly, Hannah emptied the glass; stolidly, she set to eating her butterball soup.

Fingers curved around her ankle, then moved on. Hannah felt Olinda move slightly, and sensed that she moved one of her feet backward so that the unseen prowler could not touch it. At the same time, Hannah knew that Olinda put her other foot forward so that her slipper could be taken off, but in such a manner as would give the impression that she didn't want any one to steal her slipper.

One of the cooks came in with her right arm bandaged in a huge white cloth.

"I burn mineself mit the bride's soup," she shouted loudly, holding up her arm for all to see.

"Money, I got have so I pay a doctor. Two, three, might five dollar it take. I take up a collection so I pay him," she shouted.

Hannah watched while the fat cook squeezed around people, reaching her long-handled tin dipper across the table so that the nickels, dimes, and quarters could be tossed in. She slapped some of the men boisterously upon the back, telling them loudly to put in plenty of moneys.

Every one knew the cook's arm wasn't hurt.

As the men sampled the liquor, talk and laughter flowed louder.

Old lady Heist shouted for silence. She elbowed her way to the tables holding a huge white pillow in a fancy embroiddered case. In the center of the pillow was a small paper basket surrounded by great paper roses. Across one corner stood two dolls, dressed as bride and groom.

"Money to buy the bride's bedclothes! The bride und her man got have some covers so they don't freeze when they sleep mit each other." Quarters dropped into the elaborate basket.

Hannah woodenly watched the whole procedure.

Daniel Kniemer held aloft Olinda's white bridal slipper. A great pink bow of crêpe paper and a pink carnation were tied around the instep.

"You're some bride's boys," Kniemer said in mock severity.

64

"Why don't you take care mit the bride more better? There she sit mit cold feets. You want her to catch cold so Henry lose her right away?" He laughed loudly.

"Well, boys, I got the bride's slipper, here. You wasn't smart enough to keep it for her, so now you got to buy it back for her. You know a bride's got to have her slipper or she don't can dance mit you. If you want to dance mit the bride, she's gotta have shoes. You have to pay so you get it back.

"What am I bid for it?"

"Fifty cent," came a call from an adjoining table.

"Just fifty cents for this beautiful bride's slipper? Ach, too cheap. Who'll make it one dollar?"

"Two dollar," came a deep rumbling voice from the other room.

"You make it two dollars?" The auctioneer nodded to the bride's boys. Jake soberly nodded his head answering for all of them. This was serious business for the bride's boys had to chip in and buy the slipper at the highest price bid.

Three dollars, four, five, six, seven. Then it jumped to ten dollars. It sold at twelve dollars. It was too high. It meant that each of the four bride's boys would have to pay three dollars apiece. Resentment boiled up inside of Hannah, but none of the turmoil showed in her face. Then the older women brought out the wedding presents, placing them on the cleared table.

Henry and Olinda stood up, and according to the custom, Henry unwrapped each present, saying aloud to Olinda the name of the giver. Olinda took the present from his hand, held it aloft, and thanked the giver. She passed it around for each to see and feel, to decide whether it was worth much or little.

Expensive gifts: bedspreads, linens, curtains. Cheaper gifts of dishes, cooking utensils, towels and small useful articles from the fifteen cent store. A motto from the minister, "The Lord Is My Shepherd." More suitable, Hannah thought, would have been, "Forgive Us Our Sins." Foolish gifts: a bright pink baby hood in a purple box. Olinda held it up,

65

a faint smile touching her blushing face. The crowd roared, and jokes and suggestive stories began.

Jake pressed Hannah's hand, giving her a slight shove. "Come on, let's get out," he whispered.

Daniel Kniemer blocked her way.

"Have a drink, Hannah," he urged, holding up a pitcher. Hannah shook her head and moved around him.

Old lady Kniemer, unable to get out, slid down and crawled under a table. Hannah helped her to her feet.

Hannah stood on the porch. The cool air blew upon her hot, powder-streaked face. The party was breaking up and some of the young people pushed past her.

"Come on, let's ride around a while before we go on to Schreissmillers'," someone shouted.

In the brightly decorated cars, laughing loudly, with horns honking, they tore down the dirt streets. It was four o'clock in the afternoon when they stopped near the Schreissmiller barn.

"Hurry, you don't wanta miss the dance," Jake shouted, pulling Hannah up the rickety ladder to the barn loft.

Benches were ranged along the walls. In one corner cake, sandwiches, and glasses were piled upon boards laid on trestles. This was for the midnight lunch. On one corner of the table was the wedding cake, waiting to be cut into the smallest pieces possible. Each piece would be auctioned off at midnight. Each piece would probably bring from ten to twenty-five cents.

In a far corner, near the window, were the two violinists, and Fred Hergenboch with his big harpboard, laid on a table in front of him.

Hannah looked at Fred's strong dark face and at his big husky body clad in his best suit. Fred was good looking. No wonder Frieda was proud of him. It was too bad Frieda couldn't be here, her baby had come just a week ago, a puny boy. Fred had had to come. He had the finest harpboard in all the country and played for all the weddings. His harpboard had a six-inch sounding board and was hand-made of solid oak, with many wires strung across its broad surface. In the sunlight streaming through the window the brass bound corners gleamed and the many tightly strung wires glistened like silver.

Daniel Kniemer stepped up and held his hand high for silence.

"Everybody's what dance with the bride will have to pin a dollar bill on her dress, or they have to give one silver dollar. The womens can dance for fifty cents." He turned to Fred. "Go on with the dance," he ordered.

Fred struck the wires with two curled, soft-wood sticks. Instantly the room was filled with sound, as though a dozen violins were wailing in slow mournful tones.

Olinda and Henry stood stiff and straight before the harpboard, faces serious, looking down as Fred played the slow music. This was the bride's music. Fred's strong hands flew faster, the music quickened, and the two Ochmidt boys raised their violins and joined in the fast and joyous tune.

Henry danced this first dance with Olinda. The older men and women crowded around the open doorways and against the walls. Hannah saw her mother crying. Great tears were splashing down her cheeks and she was wiping them away with her broad hands. Tabia was comforting her, and Lizzie and Mary stood near. Lizzie straight as a rod, Mary dumbly patting Ana's shoulder.

This was the groom's dance, the only time during all the wedding dancing that he had to dance. He had it easy, Hannah thought, and Olinda will be sick. For the bride was compelled to dance every dance that was played.

Olinda had sinned but she would pay, Hannah thought grimly. She watched Olinda dance by with her long white veil tied to her arm by a pink satin ribbon. Rice and grain showered around Olinda and Henry. It fell on Olinda's hair, rattled as it hit the worn boards of the bare floor.

Mrs. Hergenboch, Fred's mother, who was Olinda's godmother, wriggled her way through the packed crowd and, raising her arm high, shouted, "Hockzeit!" (Wedding Time) and dashed a large dish to the floor, where it broke into bits. Olinda and Henry kept on dancing, and the scrunch of the broken dish under the soles of their shoes sent shivers racing up Hannah's back. Some of the older women and

67

men stooped down and picked up the largest of the broken pieces. The smaller pieces were left to be ground into the floor.

Henry danced with Olinda for three rounds before the music stopped.

Jake nudged Hannah's arm. "You dance with Olinda next, Hannah. I'll pay for it."

Hannah started to shake her head, but she saw Ana nod and smile at her, so she consented. Jake pinned the dollar bill to Olinda's dress, Fred struck up the music, slow and mournful, and Olinda and Hannah stood side by side, facing the harpboard. When the music quickened Olinda and Hannah went into the dance. Every one watched.

Hannah felt that she dared not look at Olinda. She held the pudgy body lightly, but even so it seemed to her that all who danced with the bride must know. Round and round she danced, three whole rounds. It was the custom to allow members of the wedding party three rounds with the bride; all others paid their dollar for but two rounds. When each of the wedding party had danced with the bride, guests were allowed the privilege of dancing with her.

The old women smiled happily as they watched each man pin a dollar bill upon the bride's dress. Their jiggling feet kept time to the music. Some of the old women danced with each other, their faces wreathed in smiles.

Whenever the musicians stopped to rest the old men, as well as the younger, stamped their feet on the wide boards of the loft until it sounded like the thunder of stampeding cattle.

"Hey, Hannah, I been looking all over for you. Come on, let's dance." Jake caught her by the hand and pulled her out into the middle of the floor.

"Come on, smile a little. I bet you're the next bride in the Schreissmiller family." He laughed at her. Hannah shook her head.

Old man Goelzer cut in on Jake. Already tipsy, he would be dead drunk before midnight. Hannah tried to hold herself away from him but he pulled his round head deeper into his bony shoulders and his popping blue eyes leered at her.

"That's not the way to dance," he muttered. "Up close like this." He pulled her toward him. There was no use fighting. Hannah looked around the crowd, hoping to catch the eye of Jake or some other man. She saw great fat, old lady Goelzer, with her hands on her hips, watching.

It was Fred Hergenboch who came to her rescue. He left his harpboard and cut in.

"Gee, Fred, you saved my life. That old geezer was almost spitting in my face, and I thought he'd squeeze the breath outa me."

"He's got to have some fun. Imagine living with old lady Goelzer all your life, Hannah." Fred laughed.

"Say, this is my dance," Jake cut in.

The harpboard again sent out its volume of music. The violins chimed in. The floor became crowded with dancers.

Katie Heist elbowed her way to Hannah and pulled her arm. "Hannah, I got the swellest news," she whispered. "Jim Boswell's coming over tonight to the dance. Adam invited all the Boswells but the old lady stuck up her nose in the air and said she'd have nothing to do with such riff-raff. She sniffed her high and mighty nose and said we'd all be drunk before morning." Katie giggled.

"Most of them will," Hannah said.

"Yeah, I know, but ain't you excited over Jim coming?"

"How you know he's comin'?"

"Well, I was throwing out some bones to the dog at the kitchen door, an' he went past in his big car, and he leaned out and said, 'See you at the wedding dance,' just like that. Ooh, I'm so excited, I'm simply crazy about him!"

"He won't come," Hannah said, and turned to dance with one of the Kniemer boys.

But she couldn't get Jim out of her mind. It made her feel sick to have Katie be so crazy about him. Jim, so slender, so dark, looking sweet on fat dumpy Katie, his mother's hired girl. It wasn't possible.

Hannah's eyes continually looked toward the hole in the far corner of the barn loft. But Jim's dark head did not make its appearance.

The harpboard beat a dull melancholy into her brain.

69

Bugs flew about the glaring white lights of the gasoline lanterns hanging from the rafters. Men and older women lined the sides of the loft. Fumes of stale beer filled the air. The glasses kept passing. Olinda was beginning to tire. Some one was offering her a drink.

The men were getting louder. Two of them were scuffling in the far corner. Old Lady Ochmidt was tipsy. Leering drunkenly, her back comb sliding to one side of the flat knot on the back of her head, she winked at Hannah as she passed. "You next bride," she laughed and danced on.

Hannah turned away without answering.

"Come on, Jake, let's go down and get some fresh air," Hannah said, and took his arm. They had almost reached the ladder when Hannah stopped.

There was Jim Boswell coming up the ladder. He crowded to the side of the wall and stood, no smile showing on his dark face.

"Come on, Hannah." Jake pulled her arm.

"Let's stay. I'd rather," she said absently, for Jim's black eyes were looking at her. She saw his gaze rest on her golden hair, slide down over her slim whiteness to her white kid slippers, and come back again to her eyes.

She turned her glance away, but she wasn't surprised when she heard Jim's voice addressing Jake.

"Jake, won't you introduce me to the lady?" His eyes were smiling in a still face.

"She's your neighbor, Hannah Schreissmiller. I s'posed you knew each other." Jake's voice was sullen and he pulled Hannah's arm.

"May I have this next dance?" Jim's voice was soft. Hardly waiting for Hannah's nod, he swept her onto the floor into an effortless step.

He held her tight, close, and inside she began to tremble.

She hated it when Jake came to claim a dance. She noticed the awkward juggly way he bumped into every one, but Jim soon cut in and swept her away again.

Hannah knew that the other girls were watching her enviously, but she didn't care. For the first time since her

70

confirmation she was really happy. She heard only Jim's low voice.

"You know, you are very lovely," it said, and his arm tightened. His face bent closer.

"I never see you," he went on. "When school is out I'll have more time."

Hannah did not answer. Did he mean that he would see her after school was out? That he'd ask to take her places?

"Where you been keeping yourself?" Jim asked.

"In the field." Hannah pressed her lips tight. Her hate for her father had flared again. "But I'm going to stay with the minister's wife and go to high school next winter. I'm gonna go just as soon as the beets are thinned." To herself she added, "And as soon as Mamma's baby comes."

"Fine!" Jim pressed her closer. "I'll see you in town."

Everything and everyone was a shadow in a shadowy background. She knew that the violins and harpboard would play on through the night like a phantom orchestra. To her, only Jim was real.

"Come down to the car with me," his voice pleaded.

Down by his car Jim kissed her good night. His lips were soft and demanding, his arms hard. Hannah knew that she shouldn't let him, she tried to stop him, but it was no use.

CHAPTER IX

AS Hannah chopped beets from the rows, she re-lived that breath-taking moment when Jim had held her in his arms.

With a new, grim determination, she set her will upon the future. Some way, regardless of others, she was going to town and to high school. Her mother had had babies before and this would be no different.

Hannah watched her mother hoeing beets near by. The round, sun-browned face beneath the folded white 'kerchief was shining with sweat. The end of the 'kerchief flopped against the dark-clad shoulders. The broad back seemed to droop even though the strong arms continued their up and down motion. The broad-toed, high-topped shoes were stolid and wide apart in the dust of the field. The woolen skirt swished with each dogged motion about the stocking-covered bulges above the shoe tops.

"Mamma, go to the house. You gotta take care of yourself."

"Ach, Hannah, how you worry mit yourself. The beets got be thinned. Late we is mit them."

"Forget the beets. They'll be here after you're gone, and I'm gone, and all of us are gone."

Ana shook her head. "The beets is what we live mit, Hannah. How we eat if we don't got them thinned so we get the moneys in the fall?"

"I'd rather go without eatin' than have you work like this. You know what the doctor said when Reinie was born, and you ain't been near a doctor since."

"Better it been to work und not sit holding mit the hand." Ana's voice was labored.

Hannah hoed faster and decided to meet her father at the end of the field.

Swearing, he pulled his horses to a standstill. "Got to work," he roared. "What you do? Play all the time?"

"Papa, you gotta send Mamma to the house."

Adam twisted around in the iron seat of the cultivator. He looked intently at Ana.

"She's sick. She oughta see a doctor," Hannah insisted.

Adam snorted. "Got to work! Crazy mit the head you is! Your mother don't look no difference from what she look mit all you kids. Got to work! We don't never get the beets done!"

"But Papa, you can't let—"

"Shod op! You is a fine one to talk nice by your mother. You, what makes her work mit the field while you sit mit the school house und write examinations. Got to work! Move, or I knock you mit the field!"

Hannah went back to her hoeing. Adam was right. She had let her mother ride the cultivator while she wrote examinations, but she couldn't help herself. Ana had insisted. For two days her mother had worked in the field. But that was two weeks ago, and she was still working in the field. And Adam was to blame. He was keeping her working.

"You've got to stop," Hannah muttered as she came even with where her mother worked.

"Hannah, the jug, he is empty." Ana held out the brown stone water jug. "You go fill him und mix down the bread."

Hannah walked down the road to the house, still worrying. Brakes whined at her back.

"Cinderella in her working clothes," Jim Boswell said, stopping his car.

Hannah felt her face go hot. She looked down at her overalls. Long, dirty-white, canvas patches extended almost the length of the legs.

"Go riding with me, tonight," Jim said softly. "I've got to make a trip for Dad. Twenty miles."

73

"We're in the beets," Hannah answered, digging the toe of her canvas shoe in the dust.

"You can get away," Jim urged.

"I'll try."

"Good girl. Eight-thirty." Jim smiled at her.

The rest of Hannah's day was filled with thoughts of Jim —of Jim's soft lips pressing hers. Tonight.

The sun set behind the purple mountains. Blue and deepest rose, slowly changed to dark gray in the western sky. Would her father never stop work? At last, Hannah heard his shout.

She reached for her mother's hoe. Casually she tucked her hand under Ana's elbow, walking slowly beside her. She felt the weariness of her mother's slow step, sensed the slumping of the heavy body in fatigue.

"Mamma, you gotta stop this work," Hannah said softly.

"Ach, yah, Hannah. I 'fraid you have to get the supper. The pain, he comes und he goes so bad." Suddenly Ana sagged to the ground.

"Papa! Papa! Come!" Hannah screamed in terror. She tried to hold her mother, but could not.

Fritz came running to Hannah's aid. Adam added his puny strength to help Ana to the house. They laid her upon the old green couch.

"Get the doctor," Hannah pleaded.

"We wait. Might, we not need him. Too much he cost. Get out und leave her be." Adam went outdoors to supervise the chores.

Through all the confusion of supper Hannah heard her mother's suppressed groans. Hot grease splashed on her arm as she dropped meat into the skillet. Reinie kept crying for her to take him up. She was glad when supper was over and she could send Tabia upstairs with the children.

Hannah took a plate of food in to her mother but Ana shook her head.

"Mamma, you gotta get a doctor."

"Ach, Hannah, in Russia we don't have a doctor. Might I be all right come morning." Ana was as firm as Adam.

74

"I'm going to telephone Fred Hergenboch's mother to come." Hannah went straight to the telephone and called.

"Gott im Himmel!" Adam roared at her. "Crazy mit the head you is!"

Hannah went to the back door to throw out the dishwater, ignoring him. She saw a car stop at the back gate. It was Jim. She'd forgotten. She set her dishpan on the steps and went out to meet him.

"I can't go, Jim. Mamma's sick."

"We won't be gone long. Come on."

Hannah was silent. She wanted to go with him more than anything in the world. His big car. His knowledge of things. Oh, she had to go.

"Come on. I'll wait for you to get ready."

"I can't, Jim. She might die."

The kitchen door opened and a stream of light flooded the darkness.

"Hannah! Come!" Adam bellowed.

"I gotta go, Jim. I'll go sure, next time." Hannah ran to the house.

"Ha, you think you go mit that smart alec, Jim Boswell! I tell you, you don't! You hear me? Hear me, good! You go mit him und I beat you so you don't can set!" Adam set his bony fingers into Hannah's shoulder.

"I didn't go with him." Hannah wrenched her shoulder free.

"I seen him sparkin' mit you on Olinda's wedding dance, und I don't say nothings, but I say it now! You stay away from him. You hear? No good he means!"

Ana's voice called to them. "Adam, better you call the doctor. I no can stand. Und get Mis Ochmidt so she come."

Mrs. Hergenboch and Mrs. Ochmidt arrived at the same time as the doctor.

"I warned you two years ago," the doctor spoke sadly. "Why haven't you been to see me?"

"Ach, Gott, the moneys!" Adam groaned.

"You have saved no money. She must go to the hospital."

"Gott, she don't!" Adam sputtered. "All the babies is born mit home."

The doctor was firm. Adam had to give in. Hannah helped gather her mother's things into a paper bundle. Small baby clothes were put in a separate package.

Panic filled Hannah as she watched her mother being helped into the doctor's car.

"Hannah, you look after things good," Ana whispered.

"I will, Mamma. Don't you worry one minute." Hannah wanted to cling to the moving car.

All the next day, while Adam stayed at the hospital, Hannah worked in the beet field with the other children.

At noon, she telephoned.

"Mrs. Schreissmiller is doing as well as can be expected," came the crisp answer.

"But I'm Hannah Schreissmiller. I gotta know how my mother is!"

The nurse's voice softened. "You have a fine new baby sister, and your mother seems a little stronger."

"A little stronger." The words didn't mean a thing. Her mother was no better. Tears blurred the long rows of beets. If her mother was all right, her father would have been home long ago.

"He'll let her die, and I'll never get to see her again." Hannah spoke aloud in her bitterness and grief.

Twice that afternoon and again in the evening, she called. "As well as can be expected," was the response.

Adam called at nine o'clock to say that he would spend the night at the hospital. He hung up before Hannah could question him.

All night long Hannah turned and tossed. She was glad when morning came, but it brought no peace. She went to the field with the others, but kept watching the road. Why didn't her father come? Maybe he was telephoning. She sent Tabia to stay at the house.

"O God, just let me see her once again." She prayed and tears wet the handle of her hoe.

Fred Hergenboch, not Adam, came in the middle of the afternoon to take them to the hospital.

Hannah searched his quiet sad face. "She's dead! I know she's dead. I'll never get to see her again." Hannah put her

76

hands to her face and her tears suddenly dried. Fred patted her shoulder.

"No, Hannah, not yet, but I've come to take you all to see her. You must hurry."

Hannah said no word as they rode the five miles to Valley City. She carried Reinie, the other children tiptoed after her down the hall to the closed door.

Ana was lying quiet. Her face wreathed into a welcoming smile as soon as she saw them.

"Ach, mein lieblings. Mine blessed lovelings," she called in her low mother voice. She stretched out a weak hand that did not have strength enough to hold itself up. Her browned, big-knuckled hand dropped limply on the white spread.

Timidly they approached the high hospital bed. The little boys were shy. Never had they seen their mother lying help-less before them like this.

"Ach, go by your Mamma," Adam urged, his voice full of tears. He pushed Chris and Solly forward and lifted Reinie up.

Hannah saw her father's tears. She ached all over, but she couldn't cry. Now that she was faced with the reality of her mother leaving there were no tears.

Hannah watched her mother touch each of the little boys. "God bless you und keep mit you," she said softly to each of them and smoothed his hair. "Tabia make not the cry." With these words the tired eyes closed.

The room was suddenly suffocating. For an instant Han-nah thought the gray walls were pressing in upon her and that the high iron bed had begun to sway.

The nurse hurried the children from the room and mo-tioned to Hannah to follow.

"Hannah."

Hannah bent over her mother. "Mamma. Mamma."

"Hannah, you been good girl. Hard, it been for you. Harder, it got yet to be. Mine baby, Martha, I name her for mine own blessed mother. She sweet, Hannah. You love her good?"

"I will, Mamma."

"Und little Reinie. He a trouble is. You look after him,

Hannah. Und your Papa, he not for blame. Think not hard by him. Promise me, Hannah."

"I won't, Mamma.'

"Hannah, mein liebling, mein blessed, I love mit you und pray for your happiness. Und when you think you no can stand it, pray mit God und he give you help." The slow voice stopped. Only Adam's hoarse sobs tore the silence.

"Mamma, don't die!"

The nurse put strong arms around Hannah and led her from the room.

She walked slowly and alone down the hall.

CHAPTER X

THE quietness of the field filled Hannah with a dull aching. When Reinie, laughing, offered her a bouquet of yellow dandelions, she turned away. He was *laughing* while her mother lay in the mortuary at Valley City. A bitter numbness filled her. Tabia, crawling along on the ground thinning out the blocks of beets, was sobbing, and whenever Hannah heard her she hoed faster.

O God, she *had* to get away from this place where her mother had lived and worked and died.

Hannah tried to keep from thinking but her thoughts accused her, accused Adam, accused them all. At last she cried out to her father.

"If we'd taken care of her she'd be alive. You don't even honor the dead. Here you work while her body lies unburied."

"Gott im Himmel! We take the day of the funeral is all. We got to get the beets thinned! Got to work."

He couldn't be so unfeeling, so hard, if he'd ever loved her mother. But he'd cried at the hospital. Just to make a show. No. He'd wept in the dead of night when he'd thought every one was asleep. Hannah remembered that she had wanted to cry with him and that the tears would not come.

Going to the house to heat milk for the tiny baby, Hannah met Mrs. Boswell on the back steps. Tall, gray-haired, with piercing black eyes, Mrs. Boswell looked severe. She spoke in crisp, decided tones.

"I brought some cake and cookies." She extended a box.

"Thank you," Hannah mumbled and opened the door into the kitchen. The baby was crying in her basket.

"You shouldn't leave a three-day-old baby alone like this." Mrs. Boswell spoke coldly, eying the baby with critical eye.

"We gotta get the beets thinned." Hannah repeated her father's words. She could think of no better excuse.

"We'll be glad to help in any way we can." Mrs. Boswell's words were kindly but her voice was not. Hannah wished that Jim's mother had stayed away.

"We can get along. We take tomorrow off from work. It's the funeral. Lizzie and Mary and Olinda will help, and friends will come. I gotta go back to the field."

The next morning the house was full of friends and relatives. The little boys hung around Hannah, silent, remote, and sober. The baby cried continuously.

"Poor little thing," Frieda Hergenboch crooned, as she held the baby against her shoulder, patting its back.

"That kid ain't gettin' any care," Lizzie snapped.

"S'pose you take it and do for it." Frieda held the baby out.

Lizzie backed away. "God, I don't want no more kids."

"Shut up, and get out, then. All of you get out of this kitchen. I'm going to help Hannah give the baby a bath." Frieda shooed every one outside.

"Fritz, go on outdoors." Gently, Frieda touched Fritz's hunched shoulders.

"A little peace at last." Frieda poured warm water into the washpan. "You look awful, Hannah. It ain't right to bottle it all up inside of you. Makes it all the harder."

"I can't cry, Frieda. It's just like part of me is dead. My head don't think, even."

"Poor kid." Tears filled Frieda's eyes as she undressed the baby.

"Hey, Frieda, your baby's crying. Fred said for you to come feed him."

"Go on, Frieda, I'll wash Martha," Hannah said.

"Yes, better you do it yourself. It keeps the hands busy, and the heart don't hurt so much." Frieda's voice was rich with feeling.

80

The baby's tiny fingers curled around Hannah's thumb. She looked intently into the dark blue eyes, the bald head, the tiny wrinkled face. Did this little Martha look like Ana? Hannah thought of her mother's life. It seemed to Hannah devoid of any ray of light. And yet her mother had been content, yes, *happy*.

Mary and Frieda came in. Mary put her arms around Hannah. "I'll help you all I can. I've got so many kids I know how better'n you."

"Fred and me'll come over, too," Frieda added, picking up the baby. Instantly she murmured, "Oh, you're a nice fat baby!"

Hannah turned her back. She couldn't stand the sight of this baby. It had cost too much.

"I can't love her. I can't stay. Mary can take her." Hannah laid her head wearily on the table.

"Hannah, get her dress. It ain't here."

Hannah rose and opened the door into the front room. Lizzie's loud sharp voice was speaking.

"You can't tell me she cares anything about Mamma. I ain't seen her cry a tear. Mamma's being dead don't mean a thing to her."

"Aw, lay off Hannah, Lizzie. She's keeping it inside and you keep a jawin' her—" Fred stopped talking as Hannah stepped into the room.

Ignoring the awkward silence, Hannah went on upstairs. Let them talk. Lizzie always had to have her say. Grimly, she hunted out the baby's dress, and marched back downstairs.

Jim Boswell was standing in the kitchen holding a basket of flowers. "Mother sent these with her sympathy," he said gently.

"Mamma never had no flowers when she was alive. Only some geraniums in tin cans. She loved them but she never had them. Nothing but work." Hannah turned away.

"Hannah, you must not talk so." Frieda cried openly.

"Hannah! Hannah! Reinie's havin' a fit. Chris hit him and he's makin' a fit!"

Hannah ran outside to receive the stiffened body in her strong arms.

"Get some warm water in the tub," she ordered, beginning to strip the clothes from the child's body, chafing his arms and legs.

A dozen people tried to help at once. Like sheep they were, Hannah thought, seeing them crowding against each other.

"Frieda'll help me. The rest of you go in the other room. He'll come out of it. He always has."

Swiftly, Hannah and Frieda rubbed the small body in the tub of warm water. Hannah had helped her mother so many times, but these fits still frightened her.

At last Reinie started crying. "It's all right, Hannah's here," Hannah said softly, gathering him in her arms, wiping him dry with the towel.

She saw Adam standing in the doorway, watching. At sight of him, all her terror and desolation gathered force. He hadn't called the doctor soon enough. He'd kept Ana in the field. He was to blame for this last baby. He was to blame for her mother's death.

She saw tears in his eyes. Out of her bitterness, she thought, "Yes, you can cry now, but you're to blame. You worked her till she died." Accusingly, she looked at her father.

"Ach, Hannah, look not so. I am love mit your mother." His voice broke. He seemed old, tired. "I no mean to work her so hard mit the field. But what I do? How we eat, how we sleep if we don't got the beets worked? Always, babies, they come, und we don't can do nothing. The Bible says we don't can do nothing, just take them like they come. Ach, Hannah, I don't want it been like this. Me, a renter. I don't plan by this. What I do? What I do, Hannah?"

"I don't know," Hannah spoke sadly. Some way, it hurt her to see her father so broken.

"Get ready. We must go to the church," she said quietly.

In the church, Hannah sat with the black clad women on the left opposite the men in their frayed black. Impassively, she heard the soft low crying around her, heard the minister's voice rising and falling, heard the people giving the responses. The words beat in upon her, but without meaning.

"Lord Have Mercy Upon Us."
"Lord have mercy upon us."
"Christ Have Mercy Upon Us."
"Christ have mercy upon us."
"Lord Have Mercy Upon Us."
"Lord have mercy upon us."

"Have mercy, have mercy," Hannah repeated, holding the baby closer in her arms.

"Out of the depths have I cried unto Thee, O Lord. Lord hear my voice—"

"Hear my voice," Hannah echoed the minister's words. But it seemed that she was petitioning some one who was not real. "Lord hear my voice—"

The words of the minister flowed over her, leaving her without solace. Tearful voices sang the words, "It is not death to die—"

"It is death. It *is* death," Hannah denied. "Mamma is dead."

"Behold how the righteous dieth—and the just are taken away—"

Her mother had been a righteous person and she was gone.

"From the evil to come is she taken away—her memory shall be in peace."

Was it better for her mother to be gone? From the evil to come. "From the evil to come. Her memory shall be in peace."

"Ach, Hannah, mein liebling, always you do the right. For your happiness, I pray."

"Always the right." Hannah looked at the sleeping baby in her lap. She hadn't been planning to do the right. This baby was her mother's. If she denied it, surely, she denied her mother. Other words came back to her.

83

"Make not hard mit your papa, Hannah. He not for blame."

Hannah looked across the aisle to her father. He sat slumped down in his seat, old, beaten, defeated. Hannah thought of her mother's kindness to him. "He good, Hannah."

Yes, Hannah admitted, maybe he was good; as good as he knew how to be. As good as his life would let him be.

She raised her eyes to the figure of Jesus. "Forgive them. They know not what they do." The words seemed so clear —almost as if they were spoken.

The minister's voice spoke reverently, "Jesus saith unto him, 'I am the resurrection and the life; he that believeth in Me, though he were dead, yet shall he live.'"

Her mother had believed. "Though she were dead, yet shall she live." Blessed words of comfort.

Tears slowly slipped down Hannah's cheeks, and with them went all the hate of the past months. The words of her life verse came to her: "Patient in tribulation."

"I'll stay until next spring, until Tabia is through the eighth grade."

She must be patient. Her mother had told her everything would fall upon her. Long ago her mother had known.

Standing at the grave beside her father, with the children clustering close, she slipped her hand under her father's arm. Going to the car, she laid a comforting hand upon Alec's shoulder.

The house was desolate. It didn't seem like home. The rooms were empty, cheerless. In such stillness the purring of the cat was a loud sound. The little boys started to cry. Fritz went to the barn, his shoulders shaking. Adam slumped in a chair, his head in his arms.

Panic filled Hannah. She wanted to run away. Any place was better than here. She felt as helpless as the small boys crying for their mother. Her mother. She would not have wanted them to grieve this way.

Hannah straightened her shoulders. "Come, Papa, start

the fire, and we'll have supper. Chris, stop your crying and I'll make you some cookies."

"Um raisins, too, Hannah? Can we have raisins on top of um?" Solly asked tearfully.

"And raisins, too, loveling. Come, you can all help me."

PART II
THINNING

CHAPTER I

"YES! Yes, I'm getting up," Hannah moaned, shrinking away from the fingers gripping her shoulder.

"Make a move! We never get the beets thinned! Already we lose one day mit the funerals!" Adam's voice was high and demanding.

Hannah jerked away from his cruel fingers and sat up in bed. Moonlight came through the one window, but it must be morning. The morning after her mother's funeral.

"Hannah! Move!" Adam turned and went clattering down the bare stairs.

The echoing footsteps of her father filled Hannah with an unreasoning dread. Desperately she wished for her mother —so strong, so sure, so calm.

Hannah put her face in her hands and sat hunched on the edge of the bed.

"Everything, it fall on you, Hannah, but you is strong like none of us." These words of her mother came back to her. But Hannah knew that she wasn't strong. She was afraid. Afraid of life. Afraid of her father. Afraid of this terrible aloneness. She couldn't stand it!

"Und when you no can stand it, pray mit God und He give you peace." But she couldn't pray. God had taken her mother.

"Hannah! I come mit the whip!" Adam's voice roared up the stairs.

Hannah shivered. She pulled on her clothes and went down to the cold kitchen.

"Got a move on, Hannah, so we have some breakfast!

89

Fritz, got out und throw the horses over some hay so I cultivate." Adam stamped out of the house after Fritz.

Resentfully, Hannah started the fire. She took the empty water bucket out to the cistern. The early morning air was cool and still. She stood a moment absorbing the quietness; sensing the breathless waiting for the sun to rise. To the east the sky was flooded with red and gold; the trees on the banks of the ditch stood out like black silhouettes against the skyline; to the west loomed the black and purple mountains, the towering snow peaks which were tinted pink. The moon was going down and soon would be behind the mountains.

"Hannah! Gott im Himmel!"

Hannah started to pump as fast as she could. The iron handle of the pump worked easily, too easily. She increased the speed, but the water came forth only in jerky spurts. The cistern was empty. There was not enough water even to fill her bucket.

Adam came into the kitchen before she had breakfast half ready. "Got a move on, Hannah!" he nagged. "Und no water's in the teakettle!" He slammed the kettle down on the stove.

"The cistern's empty," Hannah told him. "There's not hardly enough water to get breakfast."

"Gott! I don't go by town mit the water tank today! I finish mine cultivating! Carry water from the Boswells'! Move oncet!"

Hannah dodged Adam's hand and almost dropped the plates on the table.

Tabia came downstairs after repeated callings. Her hair was awry, her temper on edge.

"Finish setting the table," Hannah said.

"I don't feel good. I'm sick in my stomick." Still whining, she lazily began to put the knives and forks on the table.

"Shod op! Got to work or I make you more sick mit your belly," Adam ordered, sitting down to the table and starting to eat.

Before the boys were through eating he said: "Come, we

go mit the field. Und Hannah, you make the lunch und come quick mit the field."

Relieved, Hannah watched Adam, Tabia, and the older boys leave, their hoes on their shoulders.

Summer sausage sandwiches and cake would do for the midmorning lunch. But on the bottom of the tall blue cookie can which served as a bread box lay a single slice of bread. There was no bread for sandwiches.

What on earth should she do? She thought how hard her father's bony hand would slap when he saw nothing but summer sausage and cake. She'd borrow from Mrs. Boswell —she couldn't. It was bad enough to borrow water.

"If I just didn't have to do all the thinking it wouldn't be so hard." She laid her head on her arms and sat slumped at the littered table. "I'm no good at managing," she cried.

She remembered how her father had worried aloud to her mother. "Always, I have a boss. I don't know if I can boss mineself, Ana."

It looks easy but it ain't easy, Hannah thought. Why was it that things seemed so easy when some one else was responsible, and so hard when you had to do your own thinking and planning? It wasn't the work. It was the deciding, and the everlasting managing, and thinking.

She'd have to bake bread today, and there wasn't any potato water, there wasn't even any water. She'd have to go to Boswells'. Before leaving, she combed her hair, powdered her face, and put on a clean housedress.

With the stone jug in one hand and the water bucket in the other she went across the road. Katie Heist answered her knock.

"Hello, Hannah."

"We're out of water." Hannah held out her containers.

"Come on in. I'll fill 'em for you."

Hannah sat on the edge of a high white stool. This was the first time that she'd been in the Boswell house. So clean it was. The pale yellow curtains, the cream-colored woodwork and cupboards, the softly tinted green walls—made her feel ill at ease. She wished she'd put on her good slippers.

"So this is the early bird." Jim Boswell appeared at the

inner door. His face was quiet but his eyes were laughing.

"I come over for water," Hannah stammered, looking away from his intent gaze. All at once she was glad that her hair was shining, her face powdered, her dress clean.

Jim went to the sink and lifted the bucket and jug. "I'll carry them over for you," he said.

"Oh, no! I'm used—"

"Jimmy! Come here just a moment!" Mrs. Boswell's clear voice came from a far room.

"Wait just a sec," he said, setting down the water.

Hannah hesitated, then she picked up her pail and jug and went toward home.

She went swiftly to work: mixed bread sponge, packed cake and sausage in a tin pail, and put on her overalls, blue shirt, and huge straw hat. But all the while she was thinking of Jim's admiring eyes. The terrible despondency of the earlier morning was lifted. Before leaving the house she peeked in at Reinie and Chris, still asleep in Adam's bed, and covered the baby in her basket.

Taking her hoe, she went toward the beet field. She tossed her hat to one side and stood looking over the field a moment before she set to work. The small beet plants, standing three inches high, twenty inches apart, stretched, lush and glossy-leaved, in long narrow rows. The dark earth was like a brown cloth marked with narrow stripes of growing green.

Fritz and Tabia were hoeing halfway up the field, chopping out ten inches of plants, leaving a small clump to be thinned by Alec and Solly, who crawled along on the ground on hands and knees. With dirt-stained fingers they pulled out all the small beet plants and weeds from each clump, leaving the largest and strongest sugar beet plants to grow and flourish.

Adam was riding the cultivator, shouting to his horses, as he went slowly up the field.

He drives us just like he does his horses, Hannah thought, and resentfully struck her hoe into the row of growing beets.

At eight-thirty Hannah brought the baby out to the field in Reinie's old buggy. Chris and Reinie tagged at her heels as she went along the rough road at the end of the beet rows. Already she was tired and the day was hardly begun. The low whine of car brakes startled her.

She looked up to see Jim Boswell stepping out of his coupé. He came to the fence.

"Why didn't you wait this morning?" he asked softly.

"I had to hurry," Hannah spoke slowly. She was ashamed to have him see her dirty and in her work clothes.

"Not afraid of me, are you?" There was a twinkle in his black eyes.

"No—but—"

"Hannah! Got to work!" Adam's voice roared from a third the way up the field.

Hannah saw Adam's team coming down the rows. "Please go," she begged Jim. "He don't like to have me talk to you. Please, I gotta go."

"Listen, tell him my dad wants to see him. He does. Wants to talk to him about lambs. Tell him that." Jim smiled and turned toward his car.

Hannah started pushing the baby buggy, but Adam's voice yelling, "Hannah, stop it," halted her. She waited for him to reach the end of the field.

Adam jumped from the iron seat of the cultivator and came toward her. "Hannah, I beat you so you don't can walk if you make eyes mit that Jim! You hear me good!" Adam shook his bony fist in her face.

Hannah drew back from that menacing fist. "I wasn't making eyes," she stammered, hating him, yet fearing him. "He said his father wanted to see you—about lambs."

"Mine Gott im Himmel! Mit lambs I don't feed! I don't put no moneys in them!" Adam turned to his team, muttering.

Hannah left four-year-old Chris to look after the baby and Reinie in the shade of a cottonwood tree.

As the morning wore on the baby commenced to cry fretfully. Its crying worried Hannah, causing a nervous tension in her whole body. She could see Chris standing near the buggy shaking it gently, then more violently, as little Martha cried harder. Reinie set up a high thin shriek, joining the baby. Chris finally gave up trying to quiet the two younger ones. He sat down on the ground and added his lusty bellow to the others' cries.

Hannah increased the stroke of her hoe. It seemed to her that she could not work with that incessant crying in her ears. She thought of her mother.

It's a wonder she wasn't crazy, Hannah thought. She realized how calm her mother had been. How patient, and gentle, when dealing with them all. Thinking of her, Hannah slowed her mad hoeing and tried consciously to relax. When she reached the end of the field she went running to the children.

"Hush, hush," she softly murmured, lifting the baby from the buggy. She laid it gently against her dusty overalled shoulder and patted its back. She laid her cheek against the baby's soft face and crooned, "Hannah's baby mustn't cry. She must be Hannah's good little girl while Hannah works."

She held the baby away from her shoulder and looked into its tiny wrinkled face. She smiled at it tenderly. Its soft helplessness gripped her heart. "Poor motherless baby," she said softly.

"I want sumpun to eat. I wanta drink," Chris howled.

"Me iss eat, too. Me iss eat," Reinie chanted as he wiped tears from his eyes with his fists.

"Sure, you get somethings to eat. Just look, the graham crackers. Cake, too." Hannah hunted the food from the foot of the baby buggy and held it out to them.

She left the children satisfied and took lunch to the field workers. They gathered at the end of the beet field and hastily washed down their cake and summer sausage with lukewarm water from the stone jug.

"Gott! Hannah! Cake mit sausage!" Adam snorted. "Bread mit sausage it is!" His hand shot out to strike Hannah but she dodged quickly.

"There ain't no bread. I gotta bake it today."

"Lazy! Mit nothings you do! Come, Tabia! Alec! Fritz! Got to work. We never gets done."

The afternoon was hotter than the morning. Adam shouted more often. The baby cried continuously. Reinie shrieked

94

at the least provocation, and Chris sat on the ground and howled whenever Reinie did.

By midafternoon Hannah was worn out traipsing to the house to look after the bread and trying to still the children's crying. She felt as if she could scream if the children cried once again. Her arms ached to the bone, and her back was a solid pain. Chop, chop, up, down, up, down, went her hoe. Only one phrase, going round and round in her brain, gave her comfort: two weeks and you're through thinning. Two weeks. God, how could she keep this up day after day for two whole weeks? She'd thinned beets every spring of her life since she was six years old and it had been tiring work. But nothing like this. Her mother had prepared the meals, had taken care of the children, had planned everything. Hannah had only hoed beets.

Adam stopped his team and came across to inspect the thinning and blocking.

"What you do? Leave doubles. Look by this! Und this! I say you leave one beet by himself!" Adam's hand shot out and sent Alec sprawling in the dirt. Hannah burned with resentment. Alec was only eleven.

"Tabia! What you do! Sleep all the time?" Adam's voice sent a quiver through Hannah. She flinched as Adam booted Tabia who had been resting on her hands and knees.

Tabia went rolling. She gathered her skinny self together and for once in her life worked like fury. Hannah felt sorry for Tabia. She watched her bony body jerking along the row, the set expression on the little white face. Tabia often felt "fainty" in the hot sun. "Next spring I'll be gone, and Tabia'll have everything to do. She's just a kid. It'll be harder on her than it is on me," Hannah thought. With a rush of compassion she decided that she would be easier on Tabia the coming year.

"Hannah! Got to work!"

Hannah started hoeing faster. Adam followed her. "Chop even! You hear? Chop so when you come to a poor stand mit big gaps you leave the beets closer by the end of the spaces. Beets every foot, I want."

Hannah dodged automatically, but Adam instead of threat-

95

ening to strike her had turned to Fritz. She saw Fritz hesitate in his hoeing, saw him turn on Adam with upraised hoe.

"Get on your cultivator and leave be," Fritz growled not giving ground. "We work 'til we near drop. What more you want?" And Adam went, cursing his luck in having such a son.

When evening came, Hannah was trembling. It seemed that she just couldn't push the baby buggy to the house. She had quit an hour earlier than the others so she could bake the bread and have supper ready when they came in.

She hurried and built the fire, for her bread was raised in great puffy loaves, and the rolls were white and round.

"Ha! Mit rolls you feed us," Adam gloated as he sat at the supper table and helped himself to three of the beautifully brown crisp rolls. "One damn fine cook you is make, Hannah." He beamed upon her and his praise seemed to relieve some of her tiredness.

"Here you kids, eat Hannah's good rolls. What's the matter mit you?"

"I ain't hungry. My stomach's sick." Solly's face was sober.

Hannah looked around the table at the sad faces. Sick for their mother, that's what they were. Tabia sat with her head on one upraised palm while she slowly shoveled the food into her mouth. Reinie was asleep with his head resting beside his filled plate. Chris was slowly playing with his knife and fork. Alec, Solly, and Coonie sat with their arms propped on the table just looking at their plates.

"Eat der supper!" Adam roared at them. "Mit dumb oxes like you we never get finished the beets. If you no eat you no can work! Yah, already near crazy I am mit you hoeing out the beets und leaving the roots so they dry out. Sick mit mineself I am—" Adam choked and spat out a half chewed roll.

"Gott, Hannah. Mit slop you feed us!" Adam threw his other two rolls onto the floor.

Hannah took a hasty bite of her own roll. Slowly, she chewed it, savoring its flatness. She'd left out the salt. Tears came to her eyes. It was no use trying to do anything. Everything went wrong and she was so tired.

"It eats good with jelly on it," Fritz broke the silence, trying to console her.

But Hannah laid her head down on the table and cried. "We can't do it all by ourselves," she sobbed. "We can't get it done with Olinda and Mamma gone."

"I want mine Mamma!" Chris cried. "I want mine Mamma!" His voice rose still higher.

"Mamma, Mamma." Reinie waked up and added his voice to Chris's.

"Stop it!" Adam roared and pounded the table with both fists.

"We gotta have help!" Hannah wiped the tears from her eyes with the corner of a dishtowel, and tried to look squarely at Adam. She could not meet his angry eyes.

"Jake Heist ain't busy, we could get him," Fritz added his argument to hers.

"Spend! Spend! Spend! That's all you think on! I'm sick on it! We work mit the beets! We don't hire. You hear?" Adam shook his fist at Hannah and Fritz.

Fritz shrugged his shoulders. "Makes me no difference. But you don't get the beets thinned on time. They'll grow big and then the root is loosened when we do thin 'em, and they die. You won't have no tonnage come fall." Fritz pushed his chair back from the table.

"You save by hiring," tiredly, sullenly, Hannah said.

"Gott im Himmel! Hire Jake! Hire him und we all go broke mit the poorhouse! Call him by the phone, Fritz. What you do? Sit there like one dumb ox? Call him and tell him to come Monday morning."

97

CHAPTER II

AT eight o'clock the next morning Adam went to Valley City for water, leaving the children working in the field.

"I get the water for the cistern," he grumbled. "Und you work when I am gone. I count the rows of beets on you when I am come back." He left to borrow Boswell's long red wooden water tank.

Hannah knew it would take him a full two hours, or more, to make the trip. She rejoiced at her father's absence. Tabia and the boys chattered together and Fritz joked as he hoed along with her.

"We don't have to keep listenin' to the old man yellin', 'Got to work,'" Fritz said in a relieved voice.

The morning sun became hot. There was a sultry, baking stillness in the air. Cotton from the many cottonwood trees drifted about them like giant flakes of snow and settled on the beets and the ground. They seemed to add to the still heat of the morning.

"This is the hottest day yet," Hannah panted. She looked at the small boys and Tabia. Their faces were dirt-streaked, and tired. She dropped her hoe and stooped to help them with the hand thinning. The ground was dry and gritty and the beet plants were wilting and limp. She crawled along the ground on her hands and knees, pulling out the extra plants in each clump. The sugar company wanted the farmers to leave their beets twelve inches apart so as to have a heavier tonnage, but it was hard to do so when there were gaps in the rows from poor sprouting.

Life's not like beets, Hannah thought despairingly as she

pulled the poorest beets and left the largest to grow. Life takes the strongest and leaves the weak to grow as good as they can. Mamma was the strongest of all of us and she's gone. Tears filled her eyes; she let the extra plants fall to one side to wilt and die.

"Hello! Need some help?"

Hannah jerked herself around at the sound of the familiar low voice.

There, leaning on the high woven wire fence, was Jim Boswell.

Hannah got slowly to her feet, brushing the dust from the blue denim overalls which had the soiled white canvas patches sewed along the front of the legs. She wiped the sweat from her face with her grimy hands, and pushed her straggling hair up under the brim of her wide hat. She felt dirty and ashamed. Always she wanted to look her best whenever Jim saw her.

Jim was dressed in the smartest of sweaters and trousers, *and so clean!* She wanted to get down and crawl away and hide. She looked at her feet. Her gaze held, horror-stricken. One big toe, bare and dirty from the dust of the field, peeked out from the end of one canvas shoe. She felt her face go hot and her mouth became dry like the field. In misery, Hannah looked at him. His black eyes were twinkling, his lips half-smiling.

"You don't act as if you were glad to see me," he said softly so that the children a few feet away could not hear.

"You kids get to work," Hannah commanded before answering. "I told you not to stop. It makes Papa mad."

"I saw Papa on the water wagon going to town," Jim grinned. "Listen, go riding with me tonight. Meet me in town. This is Saturday night, you know."

"Papa won't let me go. He don't want me to go with you. He said I couldn't."

"He needn't know," Jim insisted.

"I can't go to town without takin' the baby. I'm gonna stay home." Hannah dug her toe into the dirt. She wished Jim would go. She was embarrassed because she was such a grimy sight.

99

"Fine! I'll be seeing you." Jim smiled at her. "Tonight," he added and turned away.

Hannah stood and watched the car disappear toward the town before she bent to her thinning. Tonight. Tonight. The word sang in her mind.

Fritz came even with her. "Hannah, the old man told you not to have nothin' to do with young Jim," he warned. "And for once, Hannah, the old man's right. Jim don't mean no good by you. He's just runnin' after you for what he can get."

"Mind your own business," Hannah snapped. "I ain't gone any place with him, have I? Did you ever see me go any place with him?"

"What'd he want, then?" Fritz was persistent.

"He wanted to see Papa," Hannah lied, swinging her hoe faster.

She'd wash her hair when she went to the house to get supper. Her father would just think she was primping up to go to town. She'd try some of that lipstick Katie Heist had brought over. She'd— Plans for the evening lightened her heart and made the hoeing easier.

Adam returned around eleven o'clock. Water dripped from the long wagon as he drove up the lane and into the back yard. From a lowered tin trough he let the water run into the empty cistern.

"What you do, lay by the house?" he asked.

"I was fixing the baby's feed," Hannah answered, going on toward the field with the bottle of warmed milk. No use telling him that she'd slipped to the house to iron a clean dress to wear this evening.

Later, Adam came to the field and religiously counted the rows to see if they had worked faithfully while he was gone. He shouted for them to work faster. But his words didn't bother Hannah any more.

She was thinking of Jim's dark eyes looking deeply into hers, of the words, "See you tonight." As she hoed she smiled happily to herself.

They quit half an hour early, for it was Saturday evening. The children hurried through their supper; the older

100

ones searched for their good clothes. They yelled to Hannah, wanting to know where was this shirt, that tie, or some one's else pants.

"Hannah, hurry. We go!" Adam shouted.

"I'm not goin'. Reinie's asleep already, and the baby'll cry all the time. I'm too tired. I'd rather stay home." Hannah sank wearily into a chair. "I won't carry that crying baby up and down them streets," she stated flatly.

"Yah, she near make mine head bust mit her bawling," Adam agreed. "Come, get in the car," he commanded the others, "Hannah stays home."

In the quiet house Hannah quickly undressed Reinie and put him in Adam's bed. For once in her short life the baby was sleeping soundly, and Hannah rejoiced.

She took a washpan of warm water upstairs and gave her whole body a quick sponge bath. She had been afraid to take a bath in the old washtub in the kitchen. Jim might come before she was through washing. She hurried for fear Jim would come before she was ready. She slipped into a clean housedress, and brushed her hair until it shone. She powdered her face, rouged her lips and then stood back holding the old lamp high so she could see herself in the wavy mirror of the dresser. She did look pretty. She smiled at herself and pressed deeper waves in her hair. She wished Katie could have come over and put a finger wave in her hair. Hannah was glad of the slight natural wave. If her father had only let her quit work earlier. For a moment Hannah's conscience hurt her, but she excused herself. "He broke his promise to me. He lied. His word ain't worth nothin'. All he thinks about is how much work I can do for him."

Uneasily, she picked up the scattered clothes in the front room. She kept listening for Jim's car, for his footstep on the porch. She swept the kitchen and stacked the dishes. She filled the teakettle and put water on to heat in the dishpan. She powdered her face again. The house seemed so still. Crickets chirped near the back door. Mice scampered on the back porch. Was that car coming in? No, it had gone on by.

At last she heard the sound of a motor. She went to the

back door and stood looking out into the darkness. Her breath came faster. She smoothed the ruffle on her gingham dress.

"Hello, Hannah."

It was Jake Heist's cheerful voice. "Come on and go to town. I come back for you."

Hannah hated him and his cheeriness. Jake Heist! With his smart alecky ways and his grabbing arms as if he owned her.

"I can't, Jake. Martha and Reinie's in bed and I can't leave them alone." She spoke sharply.

"Aw, Hannah, you're tired. You sure have it like hell." Jake came close and caught her in his strong arms.

"Don't, Jake. Let me alone." Hannah tried unsuccessfully to pull away from him. He set his lips against hers. His lips were hard and cracked. His face moist from recent shaving. The sweat of the field still clung to his body.

"Your lips are all cracked," Hannah spoke cruelly, wishing he would go.

"Yeah, it's the wind and dirt from the field. I been cultivatin'. I'm goin' to get some stuff for 'em at the drug store tonight. Wish you'd go with me, Hannah, 'cause I can't take you to church tomorrow night. I gotta take a bunch of baseball boys down to Factory City and I can't get back in time. Ain't you glad I'm goin' to be workin' here for the old man? I'll be here early Monday morning. Gee, it'll seem good to see you every day. Come on, go with me tonight."

"I can't, Jake." Hannah was firm.

"If you can't, you can't. I'd stay with you but I gotta get me some new work shoes. My feet's on the ground." Reluctantly, he turned to go.

Hannah drew a breath of relief as she heard his car rattle away into the darkness.

She went out onto the front porch and sat down, looking toward the Boswell house. Not a sign of a light anywhere. Jim wasn't coming. His word didn't mean a thing. But even as she decided this she realized it was with sharp disappointment. He was probably in town riding around with some girl. Katie Heist said he was a heart smasher. Hannah felt as

102

if she could cry. "I'm just a darned fool," she thought. She might as well go to bed.

Then she heard his step coming up the path from the front gate. He sat down beside her, not saying anything.

"I thought you wasn't coming." Breathlessly Hannah broke the stillness, watching, as Jim cupped his hands, lighting his cigarette.

"I thought I wasn't either," Jim replied indefinitely. From the silence he spoke again. "Want to go for a ride? I'll get my car."

"I can't. I gotta stay here. Reinie and the baby's asleep. Anyway, Papa'd kill me if I went. I guess he'd kill me if he knew you was here."

"That's about the third time you've said he'd kill you. You aren't scared of him, are you?"

"You don't know him when he gets mad. He's gonna be mad when he comes home and finds I didn't do the dishes, too." Hannah felt as if she were talking just to be saying something. Jim's nearness here in the dark made her unsure of herself. His silence unnerved her.

"Let's do the dishes. I'm one swell dish-drier," Jim chuckled softly.

"Oh, no!" Hannah objected.

"Sure. Come on. Tonight we do dishes, and tomorrow night you go riding with me." Jim caught her hands and pulled her to her feet.

Hannah expected him to put his arms around her but he didn't. Instead he opened the screen door and pulled her toward it.

Half-disappointed, she led the way to the kitchen. She was thankful that she'd cleaned things up and dug out the worst of the dirt.

Laughing and suddenly rested, she tied a dishtowel around Jim and gave him another one with which to dry the dishes.

His nearness made Hannah so happy that her hands trembled. She almost dropped a dish as she started to put it in the draining pan. Jim caught it. Caught her hands and held them tight for a moment before he released them.

The last dish was in the cupboard. Hannah reached up to

103

hang the towel on the line back of the stove. Jim came up behind her and held her tight, her arms upraised.

"Hannah, you're mighty sweet," he whispered softly. "You know your hair is just like gold and you're easy on a fellow's eye."

Hannah couldn't answer. She blinked back quick tears. Her throat ached.

"Listen, Hannah. Meet me somewhere tomorrow night, and we'll go places."

"Oh, that'd be swell—but—I don't know if I can sneak away."

"You can do it." Jim pulled her back against his shoulder and kissed her. His lips were soft, tender, sweet. There was a freshness, a cleanness about him. Hannah touched his cheek. It was velvety and smooth-shaven. She nodded her head, her voice just a whisper saying, "Yes."

She had to go. She knew that in some way she would get away tomorrow night.

"I'll tell him I'm gonna go to church. I better meet you at the corner a block south of the German church."

"Seven-thirty," Jim said softly.

"No, our church starts at seven," Hannah said.

"Seven, it is," Jim repeated, smiling down at her.

The sound of a car coming up the lane jarred upon them. In a sudden panic Hannah pushed Jim away.

"It's Papa. You gotta go," she whispered, fear in her voice.

"Tomorrow," Jim said and slipped through the front door.

Softly, swiftly, Hannah sped up the stairs. She took down her hair as she went. Yanked off her dress. Even as she heard the family come in the back door, she was tumbling into bed, pulling the covers up over her.

She heard Adam stamp into the kitchen; heard the children's sleepy voices; heard Tabia's shrill yell, "Well, for cryin' out loud! Lookit that cigarette on the washstand! I betcha Hannah's had company or maybe she's learnin' to smoke!"

Hannah's body tensed as she heard Tabia's shrill laughter.

104

"Hannah! *Hannah!* Come here!" Adam's bellow almost shook the house.

Hannah pulled on her overalls and went slowly down the stairs. She leaned against the kitchen doorway fighting for time.

"Who been here?" Adam pointed to the cigarette.

"Jake. He wanted to take me to town." Hannah was surprised to find how calm her voice was. She straightened and looked Tabia in the eyes daring her to open her face again.

"Go in bed," Adam grunted, satisfied with her answer.

Tabia followed Hannah upstairs. "You're a liar," she sneered softly, closing the bedroom door. "Jake don't smoke them kind of cigarettes. But I know who does. Katie Heist swiped some one time from Jim's room."

"Listen, here, Tabia, you gotta keep your mouth shut," Hannah pleaded as she looked into Tabia's smirking face.

"Oh, I'm not talkin'," Tabia shrugged her shoulders. "But don't you go to ridin' me too hard about how I work, see? And I don't wash no more dishes. Not a single cup or spoon, even." Tabia rocked on her heels, her hands on her hips.

"I'm not promising you, smarty. But if you even peep, I'll beat you so you can't talk."

"You mean you'll be the one that can't talk," Tabia answered as she crawled into bed.

Hannah couldn't sleep. She kept thinking of Jim. Could she get away? Would Tabia keep her mouth shut? But Tabia didn't know about tomorrow night. Nobody but her and Jim knew. Jim, with his soft lips, his black eyes, twinkling. Tomorrow night.

CHAPTER III

HANNAH slipped stealthily behind a car parked in front of the German church. With this protection between herself and the church she dodged in and out along the cars parked at the curb. She glanced backward to see if any one might be watching, but she saw no one. She had waited in the dim entryway until the church services had commenced.

Now, as she walked rapidly toward the street corner south of the church, she wished that she didn't have on such a conspicuous white dress, but she had nothing nicer than her confirmation dress. And tonight she had wanted to look her very best. Her first date with Jim Boswell.

Half-fearfully, she wondered if he would be waiting. It had taken her so much longer to get away from the church.

She breathed a sigh of thankfulness as she saw Jim's black coupé waiting at the corner. She slipped gratefully into the seat beside him. Her heart was pounding.

"I see you got away."

"Yes, I come with Katie Heist and Fritz. Papa stayed home from church." Still breathing deeply from her haste, Hannah was glad that Jim said no more. The quiet silence gave her a chance to get hold of herself.

"We mustn't go very far. I've got to be back by the time church lets out," she said quickly when she noticed he was driving steadily toward the mountains.

Jim nodded and immediately turned into a tree-bordered side lane. He stopped the car. Without saying any word whatever he put his arm around Hannah.

She stiffened. Jim tried to draw her closer.

106

"Don't be afraid. Just tuck that bright head of yours over here on my shoulder." There was soft laughter in his voice. Hannah felt ashamed of her rigid primness. Half fearfully, she let him draw near.

"Glad you came?"

She nodded her head against his shoulder, content. This was heaven, she thought. The intimate silence, the quiet dusk of evening, Jim with his arm around her. She couldn't really believe it was Jim.

Gently, he moved his arm, and turning her sideways started to pull her over against him. Hannah stiffened, resisting him.

"I'm not going to hurt you," Jim reassured her. "I'm just making you more comfortable. You know, Hannah, I don't believe you've had much real loving in this world."

Hannah laughed shakily, and partly relaxed, letting Jim have his way. She was crazy to be afraid of Jim, she knew, but she felt bewildered as he lifted her and held her against him so that she lay in his arms. Unconsciously, she was braced ready for flight but Jim held her quietly, unmoving, silent.

Hannah could feel her heart pounding. The odor of tobacco came to her from the soft wool of Jim's dark suit, filling her with his nearness. Gradually, she became calm.

"Comfortable?" Jim bent his face to hers. She could feel his breath upon her cheek, warm, faintly tobacco.

"Like me a little?" he questioned. His voice was low, husky. Timidly, Hannah touched his cheek with her fingers. It was smooth, clean shaven. Jim laid his face against hers as he whispered, "So you do like me a little."

"No, I don't like you a little," Hannah's whisper held a tremulous, half-laughing note.

"You little devil!" Jim set his lips full against hers with a slow pressure that increased. He held her even more tightly. She hadn't known he was so strong. She felt that she couldn't stand another minute of that embrace, yet she couldn't pull herself away. At last Jim released her and she slumped against his shoulder, tired.

"Like me a little, now?" Jim's hand touched her cheek, lifted her chin.

"Not a little, a whole lot," Hannah whispered.

107

"You know you're such a little thing." Jim cradled her close in his arms. "When I see you in the field in overalls and blue shirt you look like a husky boy, but now you're all cuddly, soft, and warm. I think you must be two persons, Hannah." He smoothed her cheek with his hand. Hannah caught his fingers and held them tightly.

She felt that she never wanted to move. If she could always rest in Jim's arms, she'd ask no greater happiness. She loved him. She adored him. He was hers; hers alone. There was no world, no time, nothing but Jim, and his soft lips. Hannah pressed his fingers tighter. She suddenly wanted him closer, his lips, his arms. An inward trembling shook her as his lips touched hers.

She could feel the fast beating of his heart. Hear the quickness of his short breaths. Her hand dropped limply from his strong fingers. She must tell him to stop kissing her but she couldn't. His lips were against hers. She'd push his face away but her hand wouldn't move. Her hand didn't want to move. What was the use? He was her Jim. She loved him. His arms held her tightly and she was tired, blessedly tired.

"Hannah." She heard his voice, tender, low. She felt his cheek hot against hers, his lips press hers again, briefly, gently, his muscles tighten. Her body lay as if lifeless, while thoughts flowed swiftly through her suspended mind.

"Whither thou goest, I will go. Thy people shall be my people. No—that can't be. His people are American, mine are German-Russian. No matter."

Her mother's words illogically came to her. "Go often to the Communion and take of the Lord's Supper so you don't backslide. Remember, Hannah, the church comes first." Yes, the church. The church.

Hannah flung herself from Jim's arms. "Jim, Jim, what time is it? I've got to be back at the church by the time it's out."

In the flare from his cigarette lighter, Jim looked at his thin gold watch. "Time we were going," he agreed, reaching forward to turn the switch of the car.

Back on the main highway, he put his arm around Hannah. "You're trembling?" His voice was concerned.

"I feel funny and I can't stop shaking," Hannah stammered.

"Put your head on my shoulder. You'll be all right in a minute." Jim's voice was reassuring. His arm tightened around her shoulders.

When they reached the church, they found the cars still parked along the curbs. From inside the building came the final deep tones of the closing hymn. Jim stopped near Adam's car which Fritz had driven.

Hannah started to move from Jim's encircling arms but he held her a moment and kissed her tenderly.

"All right, honey?"

"Yes, I'm all right." Hannah touched his cheek gently before slipping from the car.

She curled up in the back seat of Adam's car and waited for Fritz and Katie to come from the church.

"Gee, we lost you, I guess," Katie laughed.

"I had a headache and I come out early," Hannah told her.

"Oh, gee, that's too bad." Katie turned to Fritz. "I bet part of her headache is because Jake's not here." She laughed loudly. Hannah didn't answer. She wanted to be alone with her thoughts. As the car bounced over the five miles to the Schreissmiller home, she enfolded the image of Jim close in her arms. But beneath all the breathless wonder of Jim's love, there was fear. Fear of her father finding out. And still another fear she could not have defined, even if she had had the courage to do so.

"Hey, Hannah, get out. We're home. I'm going to take Katie over to her home so she can get some of her things to bring back to Boswells'." Fritz's voice was loud and rather excited.

Hannah thought of Fritz and Katie as she let herself silently into the kitchen. Her own experience with Jim caused her to smile with warmth and good will. It seemed right to her that Fritz would not come home right away.

She made her way on tiptoes to the mirror above the

washstand. She scrutinized her face. Did she look different than ever before? She felt different. It seemed to her that every one could see the new Hannah shining forth from her sparkling eyes, her happy lips. Would her father notice a difference? She glanced quickly toward the closed door that led from the kitchen to his bedroom. He was sound asleep. She had nothing to worry about.

But maybe some one had seen her running down the street from the church. Maybe some one had seen her getting into Jim's car. Maybe some one had seen her getting out of Jim's car and slipping into Adam's to wait for Fritz and Katie. Hannah shivered and looked down at her fragile white dress. Its whiteness would show so plainly in the early evening light. Though she was now safely at home, an acute uneasiness filled her.

The sound of a car coming up the lane startled her. Who would it be at this time of night? It must be Fritz coming back for something. Anxious to do something that would be an excuse for still being in the kitchen, she took a cinnamon roll from the bread box. She took one bite and stood waiting.

"Well, what'd you forget?" she asked as the door opened. But it wasn't Fritz. It was her father who stood framed there.

In the first brief second Hannah took in her father's threatening face, gimlet eyes, thin drawn lips. Little chills ran down her back. Her breath came in short gasps. She shivered, trying to move her gaze from her father's accusing face. But she couldn't. She could only stand and stare into his hard cruel eyes. The cinnamon bun dropped from her trembling fingers as Adam came slowly toward her. As he advanced she began to back away.

"So-o. You sneak mit that Jim Boswell."

The words struck Hannah as if they were blows. This wasn't her father's high pitched shrieking voice. This was a deeper, colder, cruel voice full of hard, condemning hate.

"You go mit that girl-chaser, Jim. Und you lay mit him like that hussy, Olinda, lay mit Henry." Adam's still, accusing face came closer to the girl backed against the wall. Hannah felt as if her throat were paralyzed. She couldn't speak. She couldn't move. She could only look into her father's hating, furious eyes.

"You think that Jim marry you like Henry marry Olinda? You think he marry you? No. He lay mit you but he don't marry mit you. Yah, he lay mit you. You, in your white confirmation dress."

She wanted to run, but she couldn't move. She wanted to scream for help, but her lips wouldn't move. It was as if she were dumb, paralyzed with fear.

"Now, you tell it to me. You tell me how you lay mit Jim Boswell."

She opened her lips but only the sound of her breathing came forth. She couldn't answer, for in her father's eyes she saw death lurking.

"Und I say you tell it." With slow deliberate movement Adam reached for the blacksnake whip which stood in the corner nearest Hannah. Thick at the butt, tapering to a fine flexible thinness at its tip, the whip lay balanced in Adam's horny, work-cracked hands. This was the whip that was used to drive the cows, to lash fractious horses, and sometimes to discipline the older boys.

"You tell it, true." Adam raised the whip. A sharp whistling sound hissed through the room as it snapped on the floor near Hannah's white clad ankles.

"Answer it oncet, or I beat you so you don't can talk. Say how you lay mit him. Say how you sin. Before God you sin. Yah, don't I go by church mit old Heist und I see you running away? Und don't I see you come back mit that landowner's son what don't marry mit you. Yah, he lay mit you but he don't marry mit you. Tell it true."

The whip curled through the air once more. With sure, deadly aim, it circled Hannah's shoulders and flicked across her face.

Hannah screamed.

The baby in its basket in the front room started crying. The door to Adam's room off the kitchen, opened, and showed Reinie's and Chris's heads peeking out. As if by magic Tabia, Alec, Solly and Coonie appeared in the doorway leading to the front room.

III

"Tell it true!" Adam roared at Hannah. But that first lash had released Hannah's fear-bound muscles. She dodged past her father and into the front room. As she brushed past Tabia she spoke, "Call the minister." She tried to reach the front door and the safety of outdoors, but Coonie got in her way. She tripped, and Adam barred her way to escape. The whip struck across her shoulders.

She turned, thinking to wrest the whip from her father's hand but its lash sent her reeling. She was forced to turn her back to protect her face. He was crazy. She knew it by the inhuman gleam in his eyes, by the deep, rasping tones of his voice. She tried to dodge away from him but the whip always met her. At last she broke and sank to the floor beside the old green couch. She covered her face with her arms and crouched.

"You tell it now?" Adam's voice was rising. "Disgrace mit mine head. Better you been in the grave over laying mit one American what don't marry you mit your shame. You tell it now? You tell where that Jim take you. You tell how you lay mit him. Gott, mit shame it bring on mine head! Mit shame it bring on mine head!" Once more the lash fell across Hannah's shoulders.

Hannah could make herself no smaller. He could kill her. He probably would. Nothing she could say would stop him. Pain was beginning to numb her mind.

"Tell it true! Tell...."

"Mr. Schreissmiller! What are you doing!" The minister's deep stern voice broke in upon Adam's fury.

Hannah lifted her head. She saw her father lower his arm.

"Mr. Schreissmiller, no man will mistreat his grown daughter."

"Gott, she lay mit Jim Boswell, und no minister even let mine daughter disgrace me. *Me! Adam Schreissmiller!* In Russia she would been whipped to death. 'Till she die, she would been whip!"

"This is not Russia, Mr. Schreissmiller. In America, people are put in jail and kept there for whipping a person as you are whipping your daughter. No matter what your daughter has done, you must not whip her as you are doing!"

"Hell! Hell! I don't let no minister . . ."

The minister raised his hand. "Stop, Mr. Schreissmiller. If you continue as you are doing, I'll see that you are put where you can never do this again. You hear me?"

Adam's whip dropped from his hands. With a quick motion he turned and went toward the door. "Hell. Hell," he muttered. "I go mit Boswell und I tell him—" The door slammed behind him.

Hannah put her hands to her welted face. Tears began to run down her cheeks. She heard the minister speak gently to the smaller children. Then she felt his firm hand upon her shoulder and heard his deep, kind voice speaking to her.

"Hannah, child, are you all right? Can you stand?"

"I hate him! I hate him!" Hannah brushed the tears from her eyes. "I'll hate him as long as I live."

"Hannah, you must not. In his way he thinks of your happiness."

"Happiness? Him? He don't! He don't think of nothing but himself. I don't have any happiness. I don't have nothing."

"Yes, Hannah, you have God, and if you take your troubles to Him, he will give you peace."

"I don't want peace. I'm young. I want happiness. I want to live, and when I'm happy, he beats me. *He beats me!*"

"Hannah, you must not. No matter what you have done, you still have a friend who believes in you. Will you believe me, Hannah, when I tell you that?"

"You mean you believe I'm all right no matter what I've done?"

"Yes, Hannah. I've known you since you were a little girl. I knew your mother. I know how she taught you. I have faith in you."

Hannah's eyes softened. "You don't know what knowing that means to me. I didn't do anything wrong. We just went riding."

"Why didn't you tell your father?"

"He wouldn't've believed me."

"If he ever lifts his hand against you again, call me, Hannah."

"He won't touch me again."

Hannah got slowly to her feet and followed the minister to the door. She returned to the front room and stood there looking at the overturned chairs, at the baby in her basket. She heard the kitchen door open. She saw her father standing there.

"Go mit bed," he muttered. He did not look at her, and turned away to his own bedroom.

Hannah looked down at her white confirmation dress. The delicate silk was cut and torn. She could never wear it again.

She started slowly for the stairs—quietly, deliberately, she felt her way up the steep darkness to her own bedroom. She lighted the kerosene lamp and, with Tabia lying in bed looking on, she gathered her few gingham dresses from the hooks. She folded her two Sunday dresses—faded and old—and laid them with her few possessions.

She paid no attention to Tabia when she spoke to her. She did not consciously hear the words, "I don't blame you for leavin' the old fool. But where you goin', Hannah? And what's to become of us? You gotta stay, Hannah."

Hannah gathered her belongings and went downstairs, leaving Tabia crying in her bed.

In the front room she took off her torn confirmation dress. For a moment she held its soft folds to her face. The strong fragrance of tobacco came to her from it. Jim. She'd lain in Jim's arms. There'd been beauty and love, and sweetness, and now her father had made it foul. Never again would he have the chance to do it. She put on another dress, slipped her feet into her broad everyday shoes. The five miles to Valley City would be a long walk.

With her bundle in her arms Hannah turned the knob of the front door. At the same moment Martha, in her basket placed on two chairs, let out a thin wail. The sound of that cry halted Hannah. She hesitated. Once more she turned the doorknob. But she could not go and leave the baby crying. It was time for her feeding.

Hannah laid her bundle upon a chair. Through the room, dimly lighted by the low-turned lamp, she went to the kitchen.

When she had put the bottle of milk in its pan of water to warm, she went back and picked up the baby.

She'd feed Martha, *then* she would go. Poor little motherless thing. No one to care for her. The thought startled Hannah from her own deep abstraction.

There was no one to care for Martha. She looked at the helpless baby cuddled in her arms.

Sitting on a battered chair in the kitchen, she knew that she could not abandon this baby. This baby which had been her mother's, which she, Hannah, had cared for since its birth.

Leaving her bundle of clothes lying on the chair, she took the baby to the front room. Lying down on the old couch she cuddled the baby in her arms and tucked an old quilt about them both.

CHAPTER IV

WHEN Hannah wakened the next morning she saw her father standing in the doorway to the kitchen looking at her.

"So-o, you think you run away. I tell you somethings, Hannah. You run away und I beat you more worse over last night."

Hannah rose, fully dressed as she had slept, and faced him. "No, you don't ever beat me again. You beat me last night because I was scared to death of you. I ain't scared of you no more."

"Gott! Mein Gott im Himmel! Gott— I show you!" Adam turned to the kitchen. Hannah's calm hard voice stopped him.

"I'll do like the minister told you. I'll call the sheriff and I'll have you put in jail if you touch me again. I'll tell the minister. I'll tell everybody I see. People will point their fingers at you and say, 'There's Adam Schreissmiller that goes to jail for beating his daughter. Jailbird! Jailbird!' That's what they'll yell at you." Hannah looked steadily at her father as she spoke. Looked into his gimlet eyes until she saw them waver and shift. He seemed to her to shrink, to become but a shell of an old man standing there.

Queer thoughts raced through Hannah's mind. Why, her father was old and skinny. Nothing but a shriveled bag of bones. Last night she had been the one who was afraid. This morning he was the one who looked like a whipped dog. She looked at him with new eyes, as though she had never seen him before, and she knew that even though he had beaten her last night, this morning she was the one who held the victory. She was not afraid of him, and he knew it.

"I stay until Tabia gets through school next spring, but you treat me decent. You buy me some decent clothes, and you keep your hands off of me, or I'll do like I say." Slowly, Hannah turned her back and picked up her clothes.

As usual she built the fire. With stolid deliberate movements she put the breakfast on the table.

Fritz came in. "My God, Hannah!" he exclaimed at sight of her.

"He beat me," she told him flatly.

"What'd you do, Hannah?"

"For going with Jim Boswell last night. I'll go again, too."

"But you went to church with Katie and me!"

"No, I went with Jim Boswell." Hannah left the kitchen and went upstairs with the crying baby.

"You mustn't cry, Martha. Crying don't get you nothin' in this world. You gotta get hard and not care for nothing. Hush, hush, Hannah loves you." Absently, she patted the baby, setting her lips against the tiny velvety cheek.

"Hannah! Come. Eat the breakfasts. We go by the field!"

Hannah went down to the kitchen. "I don't go to the field," she said flatly.

Adam jumped from his chair. Shaking his fist he came toward her. Hannah stood still waiting for him. She looked him in the eyes, daring him to strike her.

Adam stopped short. Indecision was in his face. His hand dropped to his side. "Tabia, Alec, Solly, go by the field! We never gets the beets done," he shouted.

After the family had gone to the field, Hannah left the dishes as they were and lay down on the couch with a magazine Katie Heist had brought over. Her face stung like fire. Her body was a solid pain. She couldn't keep her mind upon her reading. She kept thinking of her father. She felt like a stranger who was seeing him for the first time. Seeing his outward self, proud, overbearing, and blustering, hiding that inward Adam who was afraid. Afraid of what people would say. Afraid of failure. Afraid of disgrace.

Jake Heist drove up to the back gate in his roadster.

117

When he pounded on the back door, Hannah slipped into Adam's room, and stood quietly until Jake left to hunt Adam.

At noon, she had dinner ready. Silently, the family ate. Hannah looked at her plate, not meeting Jake's pitying eyes. Adam hastily shoveled his dinner into his mustached mouth and left the house.

"Gee, Hannah, I could kill that old fool." Jake waited until the others had left the kitchen. "If I just hadn't a gone to Factory City."

"Don't, Jake. Go on to the field." Hannah turned her back.

In the afternoon, she lay down on the couch with the baby beside her. She was awakened from sleep by Katie Heist's high voice.

"Oh, my God! Oh, my God!" Katie's voice rose to a thin shriek. Her gaze was fixed on Hannah's face.

"Shut up, Katie," Hannah told her. "Keep your mouth shut about this. You hear?"

Katie backed against the wall, her eyes still staring at Hannah. "I won't. Honest to God, I won't, Hannah. Did that old fool beat you? It musta been you went with Jim. Oh, God!" Katie's voice dwindled to a whisper. "That's what I come over to tell you. The Boswells are sending Jim away. They're gone to town right now to see him take the train. They had an awful fight. Old lady Boswell cried and said no son of hers was gonna marry no Russian, an' old man Boswell said he guessed a Russian might be better'n some the trash Jim run around with, an' old lady Boswell said, that was right, stick up for the Russians if he wanted to but she had more pride—an' she was gonna send Jim to her uncle in the city an' he'd stay 'til school starts, an' Jim just shrugged his shoulders an' said they wasn't hurtin' him any, 'cause he liked the city better'n the country anyway, so they took him to the train." Katie stopped for breath.

"An' I never knew it was you he had went with." Katie continued to look at Hannah with envious incredulous eyes.

"I've got a splitting headache," Hannah said. Katie took the hint and left.

Hannah lay on the couch and thought of Jim. Adam *had* gone over to Boswell's last night, and now Jim was gone. Gone for all summer. But he'd be back in September. She'd have to get through the summer some way. And her father would pay for what he had said to make Jim's folks send him away.

In the field, that week, Hannah worked as slowly as she could. She put the least tax upon her strength. When Adam yelled at her she stopped still, waiting for him to strike her. When he cursed her and threatened her, she looked him in the eyes or calmly turned her back, and Adam, defeated, was forced to leave her, knowing that if he struck her she would lay down her hoe and leave.

On Saturday afternoon, after the others had gone to the field, Hannah dressed herself in a good dress, and taking Adam's car, went to Valley City.

At the beauty parlor she had her hair cut and finger-waved. "With such a natural wave in your hair," the operator remonstrated when Hannah asked for a marcel, "you should not have your hair curled with an iron but just finger-waved."

Hannah looked at her closely waved hair. She felt shorn. For a moment she wished that she had not taken this method to defy her father. Her eyes looked bigger and bluer than ever, her face longer and thinner.

"I think you cut too much off," she spoke hesitantly.

"When it's combed out, it will be lovely," the girl in the white apron reassured her.

That night, when the workers came in from the field, Hannah had supper waiting for them.

"My God! Lookit Hannah's hair!" Coonie yelled as soon as he saw Hannah.

"I don't like it! You ain't Hannah!" Chris started to cry.

Hannah gathered them in her arms laughing at them, but her laughter held a tremor.

"So-o, you cut him when I say you don't." Adam stood and looked at her, his eyes angry and blazing.

"Everybody else is getting their hair cut. I guess I want

119

to be in style. I gotta have me a new dress, too, and new high heeled slippers."

"Gott! Mein Gott im Himmel!" Adam's fists doubled and his fingers twisted.

"You hit me, and I'll do like I said," Hannah said calmly.

"Gott im Himmel! Eat der suppers!" Adam sent his fist crashing against Alec's shoulder. "What you stand gawking like chicken! Eat!" Adam slid into his chair. His shoulders slumped.

Within the next two weeks Hannah bought a new dress and slippers. She went to dances with Jake. This one gesture was the only one which met with her father's approval. But he would not have been so happy if he had known the truth.

"Jake, I'll go to dances with you, and I like you all right but you keep your hands off of me," Hannah warned Jake time and again.

"Gee, Hannah, I don't blame you for bein' hard on that old fool but you don't need to take it out on me, too. I ain't done nothin' to you. Come off your high horse." Jake grabbed her roughly to him. He slid his arms around her, his stubby fingers pressing her firm breasts, his lips bruising her lips.

Hannah slapped his face with all her strength. "Jake, you keep your filthy hands off of me!"

"God, you wildcat! You near knocked my teeth out!" Jake nursed his face. All the rest of the evening he sulked, holding her as far from himself as he could when he danced with her. After an hour of such behavior Hannah laughed.

"Jake, if you could just see yourself."

Jake didn't answer, but the next Saturday night he took her to a dance. "Got the habit," he grumbled, but he made no move to touch her.

During the summer the weather was hot and dry, but there was plenty of irrigation water. Adam rejoiced in a good stand of beets, a big alfalfa crop. "Yah, the beets is big, und the alfalfas is fine. Plenty hays I have so I feed next winter much sheeps. Yah, I make the moneys."

120

"I gotta have a new hat and some extra money," Hannah informed him.

"Gott, Hannah. Mit moneys you drive me on the poorhouse! Everythings what take moneys, you want. Und too lazy to breathe, you is. The house he is like one pig sty!"

"I get your meals, and I wash your clothes, and I take care of your kids. What more you want?" Hannah raised her eyes from the magazine she was reading. She straightened her body to a more comfortable position on the old couch.

"Hannah, mein Gott, I don't know what I do mit you. Always you lay in the bed, und the bedbugs, they eats us up, und the house, it thick mit dirt, und the clothes, they don't never get ironed, und only half washed do you make them, und big mit holes they is. Gott! Hannah, ain't you got no shame in you? Mit dirt you make us eat und sleep." Tears stood in Adam's eyes.

Looking at her father, Hannah felt shame. What he said was true. She knew that the boys and her father had worn dirty torn clothes; knew that the beds were dirty; knew that the house was like a pig pen, and that she hadn't cared. She'd taken care of Martha and herself. She'd studied her history, determined that she would pass her make-up examination in August. She had spent most of her time lying around reading love stories in the magazines which Katie Heist brought over, and had spent all her time thinking of Jim. Hour after hour she lay thinking of him. Going over in her mind that one Sunday evening, savoring its sweetness anew each time.

She kept her body clean, her hair washed and waved, her face soft with cold creams, her hands smooth, waiting for Jim to come back in the fall. She thought only of keeping herself beautiful for him. Nothing else counted or had worth except that.

"Got up, Hannah!" Adam yanked Hannah to her feet.

"Keep your hands off of me. I'll work for you, in the house and in the field, but don't you dare touch me."

Adam cursed but did not move to touch her again.

August came in hot. Hannah studied her history more

often, but tiny Martha was cranky and much trouble. As August advanced, Hannah became convinced that the baby was really sick. Her chubby little face was flushed and hot. Even her soft baby hands were hot upon Hannah's face as she walked the floor at night trying to soothe the feverish child.

"Papa, Martha's sick. We gotta take her to a doctor."

"Gott, we don't," Adam groaned. "Der moneys!"

Hannah stood Martha's crying until late afternoon, then, in spite of her father's protests, she took the baby to a doctor.

"Intestinal flu." Hannah sickened at the words of the doctor. Ochmidt's baby had died of flu. She pressed Martha's little body closer to her as she listened to the doctor's instructions.

So while examinations were held at the court house in Valley City, Hannah nursed a sick baby. Night and day she cared for Martha, rocking her, or sitting quiet, just holding her. History make-up examinations had no place in her thoughts. Not even the memory of Jim intruded upon her anguish and worry over the sick baby.

By the time Martha was well again, Hannah was haggard and thin. Some of the hard revolt of the summer seemed washed from her, leaving her more sane, more kindly.

In September Jim came home. Hannah was at the mailbox at the end of the lane getting the mail when he came from the train with his father. Hannah lifted her hand to wave but Jim was patting a huge black German police dog and did not see her.

Jim was home but he hadn't seen her.

A week dragged by with Hannah watching the Boswell house for every sight of Jim that was possible. She saw him ride by in his car going to Valley City. She caught glimpses of him playing with his big dog in the yard. She saw him running, jumping fences. But Jim did not come to see her. Did not so much as look in the direction of the Schreissmiller house.

Desperate at last, Hannah pumped Katie Heist for information.

122

Deke was the dog's name, Katie told her. "Jim's sure changed. He ain't half as friendly as he was before he went away. He never has nothin' to say to me. I guess he thinks he's smart because he's been to a city. He's always talkin' about some girl he went with back East. I guess he thinks us in the West ain't no good no more." Katie sniffed her nose and curled her lips.

It was for Hannah as if all that she had been waiting for had died. All summer she had thought of Jim, and the thought had sustained her. Now that Jim was back, he seemed farther away than ever.

Driven by her uncertain emotions, Hannah worked harder than she had all summer. Dreams did not satisfy her any more. She had no dreams, only this reality of Jim's nearness and distance.

For the first time since her mother's death Hannah cleaned the house from top to bottom. She spent hours washing every dirty and soiled piece of clothing and bedding. She even took down the faded curtains and washed them. As she hung the ragged, faded clothes on the line, shame filled her. As she dug out the dirt from the rooms, she thought of how her mother had not kept house this way. Thinking of her mother, she went into her father's room and started cleaning out the clothes closet where her mother's dresses were still hanging.

She was interrupted by the arrival of Frieda Hergenboch. "I've come to spend the afternoon with you," Frieda said cheerfully. "Fred's driving in some early lambs."

"I'm so glad you've come, Frieda. I get so lonesome." Tears came into Hannah's eyes.

"You look awful, Hannah. You're thin, and you don't look happy one bit."

"I'm all right. I'm cleanin' out Mamma's clothes. I'll give you some so you can make Freddie some pants and things."

"What you been doin'? Cleanin' house?" Frieda looked around Adam's bedroom.

"Yes, and I hate it! I hate the whole mess of keepin' house and cookin' meals. And the everlasting washing dirty dishes!"

"You gotta learn housekeepin' just like anything else."

"I'm not gonna learn it, Frieda. Next spring I'm gonna be gone. The minister's wife still wants me, and the county superintendent says I can go into high school on probation since I didn't make up history. And I'm gonna go."

Frieda put her hands on her hips and looked at Hannah. "I'm the best friend you got, Hannah, and I'm telling you true, you won't never get to high school. High school won't get you Jim Boswell nohow. You better be satisfied with Jake Heist."

"Jim Boswell don't have a thing to do with my going to high school, and that Jake Heist makes me sick with his eternal pawing!"

"But you didn't call Jim's love making—pawing," Frieda said softly.

"Jim's different." Hannah buried her head in the depths of the clothes closet.

"You might as well forget him, Hannah. Come on, poor kid, stop your crying." Frieda put her arms around Hannah. "I know you got it hard. I'll come over and help you sew and get things strung out when the beets is out." Frieda patted Hannah's shaking shoulders.

"I can't do it, Frieda. Mamma knew how but I don't. Nothin' ever goes right."

"Sure, it's hell." Frieda's voice was filled with tears. "Life's just hell."

CHAPTER V

ADAM rushed the harvesting of the sugar beets as much as possible. "Mit the lambs coming in, we got to get done the beets," he told them each morning before they left for the field.

Tabia and the younger boys were home from school for the two weeks' beet vacation in October, and afterwards Adam kept Alec and Solly home just as much as he dared without having the truant officer after him.

Still not satisfied with the amount of work accomplished, even with Jake Heist to haul beets, he hired the Goelzers with Henry and Olinda to come top the ten-acre piece.

"He's got lambs on the brain," Hannah told Jake one evening as they walked wearily from the field. It seemed to her that the days were unendingly long—from eight o'clock when she watched for Jim Boswell to go by in his coupé, until evening when he returned. He never so much as lifted his hand in greeting. There were only Jake's unwelcome attentions mingled with her father's eternal stewing about lambs coming in to be fed.

"He's never fed before and the worry gets him. I've seen these lambs make a man rich and I've seen 'em make him poor, and your old man has too. That's what worries him. You know he had to put up fifteen hundred dollars on 'em." Jake shrugged his thick shoulders.

"Where'd he get the money?" Hannah was surprised. Her father was always yelling about hard times and how poor they were.

"Oh, he had most of it saved. He told my old man he had

to put up a dollar a head and all his feed and his time and he'd get half the profits. Maybe he'll need another man to help feed." Jake grinned at her. But Hannah didn't answer. She was thinking of what Jake had said. Adam had put fifteen hundred dollars in lambs. He must have put it up last spring. She remembered Mr. Boswell coming over when they were thinning beets, and hearing them talk at the end of the beet field about buying lambs for fall delivery. And Adam had had fifteen hundred dollars. The money stuck in her mind. Adam had fooled her. He'd made her believe there'd be no money until the fifteenth of November when the first beet check was issued by the sugar factory. Well, she'd have a new dress right away. Anyway, just as soon as they'd finished topping. If she had some new clothes, maybe Jim would at least know she was on earth.

But the day after Hannah had slashed the top off the last big cream-colored sugar beet with her long hooked knife, Adam informed the family at the breakfast table that the lambs were coming in that afternoon.

"Hannah go by the field and get Olinda so she take care mit the kids. She too fat in the belly so she work nohow. You help drive lambs. I keep Alec and Solly home so they help drive but the officer say I got send them by school. Gott, such a schools! Mit craziness it fills them! Fritz, you make the sheep pens ready mit the hays so the sheeps can eat," Adam yelled as he hastily grabbed his little straight-sided black cap and followed Fritz.

Hannah took Reinie and the baby with her to the ten-acre field where the Goelzers were working.

She stood looking out over the field watching and listening to the Goelzers. Jake Heist was driving his father's big wide-bedded beet truck, loading the beets onto it with the seven-tined beet fork. One of the Goelzers' small boys was on top of the load chinking beets into every crevice. Old lady Goelzer, big-boned and fat, was standing with feet braced wide apart as she bent from the hips to hook a beet from a pile. She slashed the top off deftly, then turned to the bigger boys cursing them, yelling for them to hurry.

"Olinda, mit the laziness you drive me crazy!" Old lady

126

Goelzer caught Olinda's arm and shook her. Henry, working near, saw and came over.

"You keep your dirty filthy hands off my wife! You hear?" He cursed his mother roundly. For answer old lady Goelzer raised her knife and Henry dodged.

A contemptuous smile flitted over Hannah's face. Such a family. Olinda had certainly jumped into a mess when she married Henry. She was nothing but a weak spineless thing anyway. Just a good-for-nothing shilly-shally. Letting Henry—Hannah set her lips and shifted Martha to the other hip. Well, Olinda was getting just what she deserved. Across the rough clodded field she picked her steps. Ridges were left where the puller had loosened the huge beets.

Olinda looked up from her topping. Her face was tired and sweat-streaked.

"Gee, Hannah, I'm glad to see you. Seems like I never see you, and workin' right here, too."

"I come to see if you'd look after Reinie and the baby this afternoon while I help drive sheep."

"Gott, she don't." Old lady Goelzer's voice rose hard and determined.

"Olinda don't do much anyway. You don't want people saying how you work your daughter-in-law to death when she's big and near her time." Hannah had learned to deal with Adam through the hard summer. Old lady Goelzer was no different.

"They say that?" Old lady Goelzer lifted her fat face, her gray eyes looking intently at Hannah.

"I was just saying what they might say," Hannah started to turn away. She knew Olinda would be at the house that afternoon. A queer expression in old lady Goelzer's face stopped her.

From a pocket inside her wide black skirt, the old woman took a small penknife, and flipping the blade open she scratched her wrist until the blood spurted.

"What're you doing? Trying to kill yourself?" Hannah turned toward her startled and frightened.

"Na, na, too much der blood I have. Und I have bleed mineself. Mit a pint of blood I bleed mineself sometimes

when I is so bad. In der old country we all bleed mit ourselves when we feel funny in the head. Mit the leg we bleed
mit a glass, so." Old lady Goelzer cupped her hand on her
fat leg, to demonstrate.

Hannah looked at Olinda standing behind Mrs. Goelzer.
Olinda touched her head and made a face. "Crazy." She
formed the word with her lips.

"Yah, I'm all right now." Old lady Goelzer pinched the
cut place on her wrist, stopping the flow of blood. She
picked up her long narrow knife and went back to her work.

"Reinie, come." Hannah reached her hand to Reinie. He
made no move to go. She looked down at him. His face was
white and rigid.

Hannah set Martha quickly down in the dirt and picked
Reinie up. "Reinie, don't you make a fit! You hear?" She
shook him, but Reinie was stiffening.

With one movement of her arm, Hannah caught Martha
up, and carrying the two children, she ran for the house.
Only a warm water bath would bring Reinie out of a bad
fit. He came out of this one, crying. She dried him from
the tub. She was weak and trembling as she dressed him.
She wondered wearily if she'd ever get used to his fits. They
frightened her.

In the afternoon Olinda came to take care of the children.
While Hannah dressed herself in overalls and blue shirt, in
order to help drive the feeder lambs that were coming in,
she wondered if Jim would be helping, too. He might stay
home from school. When she saw the switch engine bringing the slatted double-decked sheep cars up the railroad
tracks, she ran down the road to the beet dump.

As she stood at one side of the long wooden incline of
the beet dump, watching the engine shunting the red sheep
cars back and forth, she looked for Jim. He wasn't there.
No one but the Boswell hired men and Mr. Boswell. Disappointed, she walked up the incline until she stood opposite
the short unloading runway which stuck out at right angles
to the main incline. She watched while the door of the first
car was finally brought even with the runway; watched while
the wide cleated board was laid across the opening from the

128

runway to the sheep car. Between the slats she could see the gray-white woolly lambs. The door of the freight car was pushed open and she saw the lambs huddled in the opening.

"Hannah, got in there und you und Fritz start 'em out!" Adam yelled. Hannah went toward the car. Fritz caught a lamb by its short ears and hauled it through the doorway. Hannah did likewise, but the lamb she seized pulled away. She drew back.

The stench inside the sheep car was almost more than she could bear.

"Hannah! Got them sheeps started," Adam shouted once more. She grabbed hold of a lamb and dragged it forward. It dodged back again.

"Here, hold on the lead sheeps. Such a dumb ox!" Adam shoved her aside and went into the car, yelling and making all the noise he could. Hannah thankfully caught hold of the rope tied to Boswell's old lead sheep.

She waited until a few of the lambs were in the runway, then she jerked the rope gently and started forward with the old lead sheep following. She kept her eyes on the lambs, walking a few steps, then waiting for them to follow.

Step by step she moved forward. Fearful, hesitating with each step, the lambs followed. Down the incline they timorously followed the lead sheep, the men shouting behind, and Shep, their own collie dog, barking and nipping the ears of laggards. Jim's big black German police dog, Deke, barked and jumped around until Mr. Boswell called him off. Adam rattled a wire hoop on which tin cans were strung. He waved it and pranced around yelling in a high piercing shriek. Mr. Boswell shouted in a deep, melodious voice that rose from a low note to a high, rose and fell as he flayed the backs of the lambs with a gunny sack. The two Boswell hired men rang cow bells and beat the floor of the incline with short-handled, ragged brooms.

Hannah waited at the foot of the beet dump while the other freight cars were shunted forward and unloaded one at a time. When the last car was emptied, Adam shouted for her to go on. Slowly, she led the old lead sheep forward along the road.

A cloud of dust rose from the lambs. It hung in the air, thick, dry and choking. Mr. Boswell's deep boom came behind her. The dogs barked. The din of the rattling tin cans and the ringing cow bells filled the afternoon air. Hannah wished the lambs would hurry faster. Timid, cowardly things they were. She wished she was in the house with Olinda.

Cars honked to get through the woolly mass. The afternoon passenger train let out a prolonged ear-splitting shriek as it thundered past. Hannah looked back, watching the lambs scrambling frantically for safety. They started milling round and round in the middle of the road. Fritz forced his way to the center of the tightly packed flock, beating to right and left with a short stick.

A car stopped. Hannah looked up to see young Jim jump out and with a loud yell plunge toward where Fritz worked.

Hannah stood waiting while Fritz and Jim gradually started the lambs forward once more. The afternoon had become bright. Now she didn't mind pulling a lead sheep. It was a glorious November afternoon. She tried to tuck her hair more becomingly at the edges of her boy's cap.

Up the lane Hannah light-heartedly led the way, into the long narrow sheep pens with their high slatted wedge-shaped hay feeders running down the center of each pen. The lambs followed with hesitating steps.

Jim helped Fritz and the Boswell hired men as they drove the sheep into the pens. He carried a galvanized coal scuttle filled with barley, and spread the grain thinly in the low wooden feed troughs which extended across one end of the feed lot. Hannah stood near him, waiting for him to notice her and say, "Hello." He paid no attention to her, and seemed not to know that she was there.

They drove the bewildered lambs in bunches of five hundred at a time in to feed. The lambs did not know what to do. A few of the wiser ones found the thinly spread barley in the neck-high troughs. Others slowly followed. Hannah worked beside Fritz trying to drive the lambs to the feed.

130

Everything was crazy confusion—the dogs barking and the men shouting.

"I don't think the dumb things will ever learn," Hannah spoke aloud in sharp exasperation as she tried to make a lamb go to the feed trough. She looked at Jim as she spoke.

"You'll be surprised." Mr. Boswell, not Jim, laughed in response. "In two weeks' time they'll be waiting at the gates ready to run for their feed as soon as you let them in."

Hannah looked doubtfully at the frightened lambs. She looked at Jim. He hadn't even glanced at her. Hadn't said a word. What was the matter with him? Well, she was going to ask him.

"Hannah! Go in house!" Adam's voice halted her. She suddenly felt conspicuous and out of place among the lambs and all the men. She turned toward the house.

Each evening at four o'clock, and every morning at seven, when she went with Fritz and Alec to feed the lambs, she looked for Jim. As she worked with the lambs, training them to come to their feed, she was filled with a kind of numb pain that was new to her. Jim hadn't even looked at her. Didn't she mean anything to him? Hadn't he ever loved her or cared a thing about her? Why hadn't he spoken to her the day the lambs came in? More and more she was coming to look back on that Sunday evening with him as a dream that had not been true. He hadn't even said "hello." He hadn't been even as courteous as his father.

Hannah looked at the lambs. She thought of Mr. Boswell's prophecy concerning them. He had been right. It was less than two weeks since the lambs had been brought in and they were already standing at the long sixteen-foot slatted gates waiting to be let into the feed pens night and morning. When the gate was swung up the lambs went running under it to the feed troughs, making a bee line for the barley spread there. Their feet, padding on the hard ground, sounded like the far off and very faint rumbling of thunder.

Hannah liked to stand at the gate and watch their ceaseless movement at the troughs and hear the soft muted champings of the many mouths. When the lambs finished feeding they crowded against the lowered gate, waiting while Fritz went along the high, slatted, wedge-shaped hay racks pulling down the alfalfa hay. With a deft motion he stuck his long hay knife between the panels and pulled the hay into the feed troughs below.

"All right," he called. Hannah lifted the gate and the lambs went running back into their long pens to feed on the hay. As she watched them go by she became aware of her ragged overalls. She thought of how she looked on the day that the lambs were unloaded. Just the same. No wonder Jim hadn't spoken to her. Adam would have to let her get a new dress. If he'd paid fifteen hundred dollars down on these lambs, he wasn't so poor, even if he did holler about going to the poorhouse.

Later that morning she sought Adam and found him on the south side of the barn chewing sunflower seeds and yelling at Mr. Boswell, "I tells you he ain't my Shep what gets your sheeps! Mit dogs everywheres you come say it my Shep!" Adam chewed vigorously and glared at Mr. Boswell.

"I'm positive it was Shep that jumped the sheep fence. He'd been in the lambs."

"Every night I lock him on the house," Adam lied.

"I'm going to call the veterinary to look him over and we'll see," Mr. Boswell said firmly, and left.

Hannah came around the corner of the barn. "Papa, I gotta have me a new dress."

"Gott, mit what you buy him?" Adam snorted. He pulled the pockets of his overalls inside out and showed her that there was nothing but sunflower seeds in them.

"I've got to have a new dress." Hannah was firm.

"I don't got no moneys!" Adam's voice rose. "Not 'til the beet check come on the fifteenth of November. Got out! Go by the house!"

"You ruined my confirmation dress. You gotta give me fifteen dollars to buy a new dress.

"Shod op! Near crazy mit sheeps I am, und you come mit moneys for one dress! Got out! I don't have no moneys!"

132

Adam jumped up and down and shook his fist in Hannah's face. Hannah moved her head, but not her body.

"You want people to say how Adam Schreissmiller is a renter and his kids go in rags?" Hannah knew that she was hurting her father in his one tender spot.

"Gott, Hannah, what I do? I no got the moneys. What I do? Mit dogs in the sheeps so I lose 'em, und Boswell a sayin' it Shep, what I do?" Adam's face was drawn and worried. He looked defeated and old. Hannah knew he spoke the truth. She'd have to wait for her dress. It was only a few days.

"When the beet check comes, I gotta have some new clothes," she said definitely and walked off toward the house. When she came into the kitchen a large black cat jumped down from a blanket-covered dishpan on which it had been lying.

"Scat! Get out of here. Layin' on my bread!" Hannah flipped the cloth cover off the partly raised dough and with it chased the cat outside. She washed her hands and began to knead the dough. It was gray and sad, without life. She lifted the great mass to her nose. It smelled sour. She'd have to bake it anyway. They could just eat it.

Toward noon Mr. Boswell and another man came into the yard. Hannah was startled to see Mr. Boswell carrying a shotgun with him. She anxiously watched them go toward the barn where Adam could be seen sitting on a bench, chewing sunflower seeds, worrying. Hannah saw the gestures of men arguing. Fritz joined the group, all four talked for a moment, and then all of them disappeared behind the barn. Hannah kneaded the bread and made it out into sour, lifeless loaves.

A shot! It was from the direction of the barn! Almost at once Mr. Boswell and the man came back to their car. Adam followed shaking his fist and muttering.

As soon as the men were gone she went outside. "What'd they do?" she asked.

"Gott, they bring the veterinary und he make Shep throw up like everythings. Sure, he throw up sheeps. Ain't he

133

been eatin' on dead sheeps what die? Gott, und he shoot him! Und I say Shep don't been in the sheeps. Mit dead sheeps he eats! Und I tell it on him, but he shoots him. What I do? What I do mitout a dog?" Adam pounded his hands together.

"We'll have to get another one," Fritz spoke up. "Goelzers have got plenty of them running around their place. We'll get one tomorrow night when we go to Olinda's baby shower dance."

That afternoon, when the bread was baked, Hannah cut off a slice. It tasted worse than it looked. They just couldn't eat it. She hid it in the bread box out of sight and baked biscuits for supper. When the family had all gone to bed she put on Fritz's sheep-lined coat and tiptoed out into the moonlight with the ten loaves of bread in her arms.

The ground was cold under her feet and the pale moonlight cast queer shadows around her. She did not know where to hide the bread. If she threw it out in the field, dogs might eat it; again, they might not. She thought of an old abandoned well down by the sheep pens and hurried in that direction. She was near the high sheep pen when a sound caused her to jump backwards.

A huge black dog leapt over the top of the solid board fence surrounding the sheep pens. Fear held Hannah motionless, but in the brief instant that the dog was in her sight he was registered indelibly upon her brain. It was Jim's dog, Deke. There was no doubt of it.

Shaken and dumbfounded, Hannah made her way to the house. She crept into bed but couldn't sleep. Jim's dog had been in her father's sheep pens, and just this morning Mr. Boswell had killed Adam's good old collie, Shep. She would have to tell Adam in the morning, but he'd ask, "What were you doing down at the sheep pens?" She couldn't answer, "Burying bread that was a failure."

Her conscience lashed her. "You've wasted ten loaves of bread; enough to last the family three whole days." It must have been the yeast, she thought. Maybe it was because the cat slept on top the cloth on the bread. But she would have to tell Adam that Jim's dog was in the lambs. At last, she fell asleep, amid a confusion of: Jim doesn't even speak to you, why should you care if his dog is a killer, you're wasteful, you must tell, maybe Jim's dog didn't kill any lambs, I'm tired, I'm tired.

CHAPTER VI

HANNAH was up early the next morning. She hurried breakfast, all the while waiting feverishly for Fritz to come in.

"Ten sheep dead," he announced briefly as he pulled a chair up to the table.

Fear filled Hannah. Ten sheep. She *had* to tell. But was it Jim's dog she'd seen last night? She watched Fritz eat and couldn't say a word.

The lamp was lighted, for it was still dark. Fritz got up early these mornings to go to the pulp pit at the sugar factory after beet pulp. He dressed warmly in extra pants, mittens, and sheep-lined coat. Adam came out of his bedroom as Fritz was pulling on his hip-high rubber boots.

"Ten sheep dead," Fritz told him without waiting to be asked.

"Ach, mein Gott im Himmel!" Adam groaned, running his hands through his tousled hair. "Mit poisons it don't done no good. Und mit killing Shep it don't done no good!" He straightened up and looked at Fritz. "Tonight, you take a gun on the barn!"

"Tonight's Olinda's baby shower dance," Fritz reminded Adam. "We'll go to the shower and come home early. You watch 'til I come home, and then I'll take your place." Fritz stolidly bundled himself up and left the house.

Hannah got breakfast for the rest of the family with her mind in confusion. She knew she ought to tell Adam about Deke, but she couldn't. It wasn't the thought of his finding out about the bread so much *now* as the fact that it was

136

Jim's dog. Anything that belonged to Jim meant something to her even if Jim hadn't come near her all fall. And again, it *might* not have been Jim's dog she'd seen.

Fritz returned at eight o'clock, his team breathing mist into the cold winter air, and the pulp juice dripping and half freezing like water from the bottom of the wagon bed. He brought into the kitchen the foul stench of fermented beets. Noodles of the white pulp lay curled upon the sides and top of the big feet of his rubber boots. He sat down at the table near the stove to warm and to drink a cup of hot coffee. Soon the kitchen was full of the stinking smell of pulp. Those whitish noodles clinging to his overall pant legs and to his boots smelt of all the rotten dead things in the world.

"Fritz, I can't stand that pulp," Hannah protested.

"I don't smell it. When you work in it, you can't smell it. It gets into you I guess. Can't go to a picture show even if you wash and scrub good with soap, without it coming out of your hide. Say, let's you and Jake and Katie and me go to the picture show before we go to the shower dance tonight. I'd just as soon call the dance short at Goelzers'. That family gives me the heeby-jeebies."

"Let's," Hannah agreed eagerly. It had been a long time since she had been anywhere.

At seven, that evening, they started out for Valley City and a picture show. Fritz and Katie rode in the front seat and Jake sat behind with Hannah.

Jake tried to put his arm around Hannah but she pushed him away. Jake always made her half-mad. He was always trying to make love to her and hug and kiss her. Tonight was the same. Most of the time it was easier to let him have his way. He was so strong and he made so much noise when she tried to make him behave. Hannah was glad when they reached Valley City.

It was warm and comfortable in the theater. Katie and Hannah slipped off their coats.

"Gee, you got a new dress," Hannah whispered.

"Yeah, an' I got me a new coat, the swellest black with black fur collar. I make the last payment on it next Saturday," Katie whispered back loudly. "Gee, it's sure swell. You oughta see it. An' I snitched a pair of old lady Boswell's chiffon stockings to wear with it."

"If I was just workin' like you," Hannah spoke enviously. "But why do you take Mrs. Boswell's stuff—"

"Gee, your old man's a renter, and he's feedin' sheep. He oughta buy you swell clothes. He—well, gee whiz, look at that old hen a turnin' around a sniffin' her old beak of a nose," Katie giggled.

Hannah sniffed. A sickening foul stench was filling the surrounding air.

"Look at 'em sniff," Jake whispered to Hannah. "I took me a bath and I scoured myself good an' put on all clean clothes, but that pulp gets into you an' when you get hot it comes out with the sweat. Look at 'em sniffin' around old Fritz!" Jake laughed. He reached across and poked Fritz in the side. He wrinkled his nose, smelling the air.

"Somethin's rotten," he said loudly. He put his hand to his nose. He turned his head and looked around as if in search of the awful smell. Fritz just sat and chuckled, watching Jake. Katie giggled loudly.

Hannah had to smile, but she wished she was out of there. Through the rest of the show she was conscious of sniffing noses, and of people getting up and moving. The only satisfaction she had was that Jake and Fritz were not the only pulp haulers in the building. She was glad when the show was over and they were outside.

"Them people know what beet pulp smells like," Jake laughed, as he got into the car beside Hannah. "Come on, Fritz, let's go where folks think pulp smells good."

They crossed the river dividing Valley City from Shag Town. Down the narrow streets Fritz drove the car at a terrific rate of speed, nearly upsetting them as he turned the corners on two wheels. Fritz always acted loud and smart when he got away from Adam. Like he was out of jail, Hannah thought.

When they got to the Goelzers' the house was lighted and through the dingy, uncurtained windows they could see people dancing. Through a litter of tin cans, buckets and

138

tubs, they made their way to the back door, where old man Goelzer met them. "Come in, come in," he called loudly. "You're late. It's way after nine."

"We come as soon as we could," Fritz told him. As they made their way through the dirty kitchen the stagnant air of the rooms was saturated with sneaking smells of dirt, sour babies, pulp. Furniture in the small dining room and living room had been moved to the side walls leaving a cleared space.

Fred Hergenboch was playing his big harpboard and one of the Ochmidt boys was playing a violin.

Hannah and Katie went to the front bedroom to remove their wraps and to leave their presents.

"What'd you get?" Katie asked.

"A hood and a pair of booties," Hannah told her.

"Gee, that's swell. I got her the swellest little dre— oh, hello, Olinda, how are you?" Katie threw her arms around Olinda.

"I don't feel so good." Olinda's face was drawn and tired.

"Well, if you're askin' me, I think this shower oughta been a long time ago." Katie primped her marcelled hair.

"But she don't been married until last May, late." Old lady Goelzer pursed her lips and put her big hands on her huge fat hips. Her brown hair straggled around her fat face, and her dress hung in dirty folds. Her enormous body gave forth the smell of stale sweat.

"Come on, let's dance." Katie caught hold of Hannah's arm and tried to pull her toward the front room.

"Go on with Mrs. Goelzer, I wanta talk to Olinda," Hannah said, pulling away.

"You look awful, Olinda. You feel bad?"

"Katie's right. This shower is almost too late but that old fool just does it to devil me. Acts like the baby ain't comin' until February sometime. She counts it up on her dirty fat fingers right in front of the whole family. An' I feel like my time was right here." Olinda started crying.

"I feel sorry for you," Hannah said gently. "But you got yourself into this mess, and what more could you expect? Stop your cryin'. It don't help none."

139

"Hannah, I want you to be godmother. Will you?"

"Oh, no, Olinda! I got too many babies now to look after. Get—"

"Hey, Olinda, you gotta dance this next one with me." Old man Heist caught Olinda's arm and pulled her roughly onto the dance floor. Hannah stood in the doorway and watched. Poor Olinda. Big as a barn and she'd have to let them haul her around dancing until midnight.

"Come on, Hannah, this is my dance." Jake laughed loudly and caught hold of her hand.

The room became hot. The smell of beet pulp filled the air. The men drifted out to the kitchen at every opportunity, and soon the stale fumes of home brew mingled with the odor of the pulp. The voices of the men became louder, some were quarrelsome. Old Heist got into an argument with old Goelzer. Goelzer stuck his bullet head deeper into his bony shoulders, his blue eyes bulged more than usual, his tow-colored hair stood up like bristles on top of his head.

It would be like old Goelzer to start a fight in his own home at Olinda's shower. Hannah wondered if he'd gotten the too pointed black oxfords at the Welfare or the Salvation Army. Why didn't he ever wash his dirty bare ankles or at least wear socks to hide the dirt? Nothing but dirt, filth and fighting. But the fight was averted by Fred Hergenboch.

"Here, you fellows, go to the kitchen and let the rest of us dance." He caught each by an arm and led them out.

When he returned he came up to Hannah. "You haven't danced with me once tonight. Of course old married men don't have a look-in with you young girls when such fellows as Jake are around." He smiled down at Hannah as they started dancing.

"Oh, but you're an old friend. You and Frieda are the oldest friends I've got. It's nice to dance with a man taller'n I am. Jake's so short. He seems just like a fat kid."

"You better not let Jake hear that," Fred laughed, swinging her easily around a tightly packed corner of older people. "How are things coming with you?"

"Everything's a mess, Fred. Papa's losing lambs. They

140

shot our Shep yesterday and last night some dog killed ten of our sheep. Fred, can you tell what a dog looks like after night? I—"

"Say, this is my dance. You gonna dance with my girl all evening?" Jake pounded Fred on the back.

At ten-thirty Olinda and Mrs. Goelzer served a lunch of hot coffee, chunks of summer sausage, huge dill pickles and thick slices of bread. Hannah looked at a slice of the bread and couldn't bring herself to bite into it.

While they were eating, Olinda brought out her presents. With all the men looking on eagerly, she opened them, and passed the numerous things around. Loud laughs and jokes filled the room. Delicate garments of pink, blue and white were dangled in rough, browned and weathered hands. As the liquor passed around more freely the jokes became shadier.

Hannah saw old Ochmidt slap Olinda smartly on the hip. "I like my womens big und fat," he laughed loudly.

"Yah, more fat out this way." Old Goelzer made an outward curving motion from his skinny stomach.

Hannah turned away disgusted. She was glad when Fritz said it was time to go home.

"Here, here, you're not goin' this early," old man Goelzer protested drunkenly.

"I promised the old man I'd get home and watch the sheep. Dogs got ten of 'em last night. Get your coat, Hannah. Hey, Katie, come on. Jake, you ready?"

Protests rose from every corner of the room but Fritz was firm. He knew that Adam would be waiting.

When they reached the Schreissmiller place Fritz let Jake and Hannah out and took Katie over to Boswells'.

"Come on, Hannah, let's go for a ride. It's early," Jake begged.

"I'm gonna change my clothes and help Fritz watch. I'd rather sit in a barn and not talk. I'm too tired to talk." Hannah walked toward the house.

"Some girl I've got. Rather go lookin' for dogs than go spoonin'," Jake snorted as he turned away.

Hannah had her clothes changed by the time Fritz got

141

back from taking Katie home. She wore her overalls and Alec's sheep-lined coat. While Fritz was getting ready, she hunted up a comfort to take along. She admitted that she didn't keep house as her mother had but at least the house didn't *stink!* Not like Goelzers'. For once Adam had been right. Goelzers were nothing but scum!

"Foolish in the head," Adam said as Hannah came into the kitchen with her comfort. "But might four eyes is better over two eyes," he grumblingly agreed.

Hannah followed Fritz to the barnloft and settled herself in the alfalfa with her comfort around her. Fritz sat hunched nearby with his shotgun across his knees. He looked grimly out the open loft door onto the lambs in their pens below. From her position Hannah also had a good view of the pens.

The moon was bright and clear, riding high in the sky. There was a bright halo spreading wide around its entire surface.

"Storm," Hannah said.

Dark shadows lay in the corners of the pens and along the off side of the high hay feeders. Five hundred lambs moved in a light gray mass within each of the three pens, set off from each other by high protecting board fences.

There was no movement on the shadowy landscape. Hannah relaxed and her thoughts were centered on Jim's dog. She remembered stories of wild dogs roaming the countryside—five and six in a pack, stories of dogs jumping the high boarded sheep pens in broad daylight, worrying and running the lambs until they milled and trampled each other to death. There was that story of old man Ochmidt, the winter he fed lambs and lost everything he had. He'd killed the boss's dog in his lambs and there'd been a fight. Ochmidt had lost his place and the boss had lost two teeth.

To the west dogs were barking. Hannah stiffened and leaned forward. Gradually the barking receded and silence settled once more over the landscape. Hannah lay back on her comfort and half-dozed. Rats or mice scampered along overhead rafters. In a corner she heard the squeals of fighting mice.

Hannah's thoughts drifted to Olinda. Her time was near;

142

old lady Goelzer had waited almost too long for the baby shower. Didn't the old fool know when the baby was expected? Surely she knew that Henry and Olinda had had to get married. Contempt filled Hannah's thoughts. Didn't they have any decency? She thought of other similar cases. They were too frequent. Olinda was spineless, always whining. All the others must have been spineless. But maybe they loved each other? No, Henry didn't love Olinda. But maybe he did? Maybe he loved her as Jim—but Jim hadn't been near all winter. Yet he'd held her in his arms, kissed her. Hannah began to remember each moment of that one ride with Jim, savoring its sweetness, the strength of Jim's arms, the clean tobacco smell, the softness of his lips. He *had* cared. In her heart she knew it. His folks were at the bottom of his not seeing her.

What was that?

A far-away rumble increased, and she recognized it as the night passenger train. A dog howled, a long-drawn-out mournful sound of agony, over in the direction of Boswells'. Once more silence settled over the countryside and Hannah relaxed, lay half asleep.

When Fritz moved she became wide awake and alert. Without moving she strained to pierce the sheep pens. Was there a movement along that field near the far corner? Her fingers dug into the hay at her side. Yes, something was moving. Two shadows moved. Now there were three. A dark form suddenly launched itself over the high broad fence.

Fritz's shotgun broke the stillness. He fired again, but the shadows had disappeared.

"Got one of them, anyway," Fritz said as he rose to his feet. "Come on, let's take a look."

Hannah followed him down the ladder and out into the sheep pens.

"Hm, fell inside," Fritz grunted. He made his way to the far corner of the sheep pen.

He turned his flashlight upon the corner. There, in its light, lay Jim's dog, Deke.

"The devil!" Fritz exclaimed. "Hell will pop for this. It's

all right for Boswell to shoot our Shep but you wait and see how Jim takes this. Come on, let's go to bed."

Adam called Mr. Boswell the next morning and soon afterwards Jim and his father came over. They walked out to the sheep pens without meeting any one. Adam was in the house at the time and Fritz had gone to the factory for pulp. Adam went outside as Jim and his father returned from their inspection of the dead dog. Hannah stood in the doorway half-fearful of what would happen.

"You dirty, damned Russian!" Jim's voice was higher than Hannah had ever heard it. He came toward Adam. His face was dark with rage.

"You think you'll get even by shooting my dog! All he was after was the leg of a dead lamb. He never killed a sheep in his life. You hear? You shot him just for spite. You shot him outside the pens and dragged him inside! That's what you did! You dragged him inside!"

"Gott im Himmel! Mit lies you feed us!" Adam shook his fist. "Hannah! Hannah! Come here und tell this good-for-nothings, he lies. Tell him he lies. Drag his dog in a sheep pen, bah! He jump himself in. Tell him."

Hannah wished she'd stayed inside the house. She wished that she was any place but where she was. But they'd seen her and she had to go out.

She walked to Adam's side and faced Jim. Mutely she begged him to understand but in his black eyes there was no sign of recognition. Hannah looked at Mr. Boswell standing quiet, his expression without judgment, and then at Jim, his face convulsed with rage.

"Say he lie! Say he lie!" Adam jumped up and down.

"Did you see Fritz kill Deke?" Mr. Boswell asked.

"Yes." Hannah could not lie to that direct gaze.

"Where was he?"

"He was jumping the high fence. There were three other—"

"You lie," Jim cried. "You lie like all the rest of your pack of dirty Russians! Nothing but a pack of damned Russians! All liars! All—"

"Jim, shut your mouth." Mr. Boswell caught Jim's arm

144

and forcefully turned him away. "You're making a fool of yourself."

Hannah stood and watched them go. Jim—dirty Russian —liar. The words sickened her. Jim thought more of a black dog than he did of her.

"You see now what he think of you?" Adam grinned into her face. "You know now what he wanted when he take you riding?" Adam's voice changed, softened. "Gott, Hannah, go by the house. Sick you look mit yourselfs. Forget him. Not worth that, he ain't." Adam snapped his gnarled fingers.

CHAPTER VII

AFTER this event Hannah went around the house with a forced expression on her face. She couldn't eat. She couldn't sleep.

That Sunday night ride passed again and again through her mind, only now there was no sweetness in it. Lust and desire stood out before her hurt eyes. Each motion, each word of Jim's, was now clear, with a new meaning. She saw herself, innocent and simple, believing that he loved her. She heard again the tones of his voice, low, half-laughing. Only time had saved her, only the fact that she had had to get back to the church by the time it was out. She was no better than Olinda. No better than all the others who had gone astray. Circumstance alone had kept her pure. Had all the others been taken in by smooth words also?

Olinda's baby, a girl, had been born just two days after the baby shower dance and Hannah went down to Shag Town to see her. She looked long at the tiny, red-faced baby. When she laid it back on the bed beside Olinda, tears stood in her eyes. Hannah caught Olinda's hand and held it tight.

"She's sweet, Olinda. I'm sorry I've been so hateful to you."

"Hannah, you'll be her godmother, and carry her to the altar and hold her to be christened," Olinda pleaded, taking advantage of Hannah's momentary weakness.

"Yes, I'll carry her," Hannah agreed.

"You're so good, Hannah. I'm goin' to call her Marie after your middle name. I want her to grow up to be a good girl."

146

Hannah stood silent, finding no words to answer. Olinda wouldn't believe her if she were to say aloud: "I am not good."

Chastising herself for her love of Jim, Hannah began to believe that every one was too good to her. Adam, when his first beet check came, gave her ten dollars with which to buy a new dress.

"Gott, you look like one sick chicken, Hannah. Buy yourselfs a dress, und got a date mit Jake. One damn' fine boy that Jake."

But Hannah didn't want Jake or any one. She didn't want to do anything. She bought a new green dress to wear to the christening. But it brought her no satisfaction.

"Gee, I'm glad it's a girl," Jake said. "Imagine me carryin' a boy down the aisle and holding it to have it sprinkled." Jake laughed loudly.

Hannah knew, as she sat beside Jake in church the Sunday before Christmas, the day Olinda's baby was christened, that people thought she and Jake were going together. It was pretty plain that Olinda thought she was encouraging a wedding when she had asked Jake to be godfather. The idea roused no emotion in Hannah. She wasn't marrying any one.

The organ rolled out the deep tones of the baptismal song. The many voices of the congregation took up the words. Olinda handed the baby to Hannah. Hannah, carrying the baby, walked slowly down the wide center aisle with Jake Heist beside her. The words of the baptismal song filled the church.

> "Blessed Jesus, here we stand.
> Met to do as Thou hast spoken.
> And this child at Thy command,
> Now we bring to Thee in token,
> That to Thee it here be given;
> For of such shall be Thy heaven."

"Of such shall be Thy heaven," Hannah repeated to herself as she looked down at the tiny baby all in white—from its soft kid shoes to the tiny hood. Poor little innocent thing.

"Dearly Beloved!" The minister was beginning. "We learn from the word of God, and know from our own experience, that all men are conceived and born in sin, and so—"

"Was every one conceived in sin?" Hannah wondered. This baby most certainly had been. Conceived in sin, yes. That was right. But was it right?

"This child, then, is also by nature sinful and corrupt—"

Was it nature to be sinful and corrupt? Hannah felt that it must be true. She had always prided herself upon being decent, but she felt now that she had only been decent because she had never been tempted. Jim could have had his way with her; could have lulled her fears; could have made her think only of her love for him. She was no better than Olinda.

"Wherefore, I beseech you, out of Christian love, to intercede for this child, to bring it to the Lord Jesus, and to implore for it the forgiveness of sin—"

But it hadn't sinned, Hannah thought. Only Henry and Olinda had sinned. But *had* they sinned? Surely. Surely, they had. But might there not be excuse for them? If every one was by nature sinful and corrupt, shouldn't they be excused? Especially if they were weaklings such as Olinda and Henry? For the first time in her life, Hannah was trying to find an excuse for another's wrong-doing. She had been taught that right was right; wrong was wrong. There was no middle path. Now she didn't know. Surely, this baby shouldn't have to suffer for its parents' sins. Hannah looked down at the tiny infant as the minister made the sign of the cross on the child's forehead and breast. She heard the words, "Receive the sign of the Holy Cross."

"Let us pray."

But she couldn't pray. Who was she to be standing here holding this little child? Only the pure in heart, the holy persons, God-fearing persons, the true believers were accepted as Sponsors in Baptism. What was she doing here when she couldn't pray? Who was she to instruct this tiny baby, to see that it learned the Ten Commandments, the Creed, and the Lord's Prayer? But these thoughts were dissi-

148

pated by hearing her voice repeating the words of prayer. Then the minister was speaking directly to her.

"Dear friends: Inasmuch as, out of Christian love, you intercede for this child, and stand in its place in this solemn act, I now ask you to answer the questions which I address to this child.

"Dost thou renounce the devil, and all his works, and all his ways?"

Automatically, Hannah answered, "Yes, I renounce." But did she?

"Dost thou believe in God, the Father Almighty, Maker of heaven and earth?"

"Yes, I believe." But do I? Am I sure?

Automatically she answered to question after question, "Yes, I believe. Yes, I believe." But active in her mind throughout were the questions: Do you believe anything? Is there anything to believe in? Is there a God?

Her mother had believed. Was her mother right? She didn't know.

She was roused from her doubts by the voice of the minister asking, "How shall this child be named?"

"Marie Lydia Goelzer," Hannah said clearly.

With outward composure she watched the minister applying the water three times to the baby's head as he pronounced each of the three names.

"Marie Lydia Goelzer, I baptize thee in the Name of the Father—and of the Son—and of the Holy Ghost—Amen."

Hannah stood mute and stiff while the minister, with his hand upon the tiny Marie's head, declaimed:

"Almighty God, the Father of our Lord Jesus Christ, Who hath begotten thee again of water and the Holy Ghost, and hath forgiven thee all thy sins, strengthen thee with His grace unto life everlasting. Amen.

"Peace be with thee.

"Let us pray."

"Peace be with thee," Hannah silently repeated again and again throughout the minister's prayer.

During the long dinner at the Goelzers' after the christening, Hannah, still repeated the words, "Peace be with thee."

All through the rough joking of the older men, during the drinking to the baby's health, through the laughter and drunken talking which followed.

She was glad when Adam insisted on going home.

She went upstairs and threw herself across the bed, believing that never again could she laugh or be happy, that her life was over. Where were her old beliefs, her old standards of honor, her old assumptions of the sweetness of life, of love that was fine and true?

Fritz, entering her bedroom unannounced, roused her from this mental strife.

"Hannah, you treat Jake like dirt. He's a good guy and he don't deserve what you give him."

"Stop trying to cram Jake down my throat," she cried.

"You'd rather lay with Jim Boswell and let him have what he wants." Fritz's voice was contemptuous.

"Oh, shut up. Leave me be!"

"Well, come on, get up. You want everybody to say you're lovesick with that Jim? Have some pride about you. Get up and come on with Jake and Katie and me." Fritz abruptly left the room.

Was it true, Hannah wondered? Yes, she knew that every German-Russian in the county knew of Adam whipping her and why. They knew that Jim had denounced her when Deke was killed. News spread by word of mouth faster than nematodes in sugar beet ground. What had her mother said? "Ach, Hannah, better we hold high mit the head und not drag ourselves deeper in der dirt. Better we make the good of a bad business."

Yes, better to make the good of a bad business.

The days passed slowly. Hannah felt a desperate need to keep busy. She cleaned the house and washed windows. But as she was digging out the dirt, the words "dirty Russian" haunted her.

Reinie needed a new pair of pants. She ripped up one of Ana's dresses. A soft blue wool. She telephoned Frieda to come spend the day, but Frieda was sick with a cold and couldn't come.

150

"Fred's going to town in the morning. I'll send the pattern over by him," she told Hannah.

Late the next morning Hannah pulled the old sewing machine out in front of the window which looked out on the main road. She saw the Boswell sedan go towards town.

The old battle started again. Over and over again she reviewed the past, as she sewed. A hard anger gradually grew inside her heart. She had been taken in by his smartness. She pedaled the machine faster and faster.

Reinie was cutting paper on the floor and Martha was crawling about trying to take the pieces of paper from him. The big heating stove was going and the room was warm and comfortable. Hannah was aware of nothing. Her thoughts were in the past.

Martha whimpered, then howled.

"Reinie, give her the paper she wants," Hannah ordered, not stopping her sewing.

Reinie offered the baby his piece of paper but she cried louder.

"Hush, hush, Martha. You're Hannah's loveling. Hush, so Hannah can get Reinie's new pants done." But Martha didn't. Hannah had to stop work and take her up on her lap. Martha immediately stopped crying.

"You little rascal." Hannah hugged her with a sudden tenderness. It seemed to her that when everything else was wrong, there was always Martha for comfort. She kissed the curly golden head, and the soft fat neck. "You're Hannah's darling. Umn, Hannah loves you." She cuddled the baby in her arms and started to rock.

Reinie got up and clung to her knee. "Me is rock. Me is darling." He stretched out his arms.

"Sure, you're a darling." Hannah helped the three-year-old up on her lap. She sat rocking the two, thinking of the words of baptism, "Of such is the kingdom of heaven." When she put the children down it was time to get dinner. She hadn't accomplished much, she thought, and started the fire.

But in the afternoon, while Reinie and Martha were napping, she sewed. She had the pockets in, the top placket finished and the narrow straps on ready for the leather belt to be run through before Tabia and the boys came home from school. The pants were all done except for sewing up the legs and hemming the bottoms.

"Tabia, go gather eggs and peel the potatoes for supper," Hannah ordered. "I wanta finish these pants—it won't take me a minute."

Hannah set the two edges of cloth together and started sewing, but something was wrong. The front part of the leg was longer than the back. She showed them to Tabia.

"Huh, they do look kinda funny," Tabia agreed. "I betcha he can't wear them crazy things when you get 'em done." Tabia giggled loudly.

"Shut up," Hannah snapped, examining the paper pattern.

"I've got the back of the pants upside down," Hannah said slowly.

"Sure, that's it. You got the pockets on the bottom of the back part of the leg piece. Oh, wait till I tell Papa and the boys." Tabia laughed loudly.

"Don't you dare, Tabia," Hannah begged, but Tabia was gone.

Hannah looked at the pants in her hand. All that work for nothing. It seemed everything went wrong. Once more she thought of her mother, who had done the planning, who prevented things like this from happening. She missed her mother more than ever. That sure serenity of her mother's had become a symbol of strength and love. Try as she might Hannah could not grasp the nature of her mother's serenity.

Adam and the smaller boys came in. The boys were grinning, but Adam's face was angry.

"Let see the pants," he ordered.

"I won't!" Hannah snatched up her sewing and fled upstairs. She threw herself upon the bed and lay there until Adam called her to come get supper.

After supper, she grimly ripped out her afternoon's work. She had to patch the cut places on the legs where she'd made the set-in pockets, and cut new slits where the pockets should go.

Adam sat at the table reading the daily paper. "Ach, der lambs he go up. Good!" He nodded and went on reading.

152

"Mit a new car I buy mineself, might, if them lambs make the money," he muttered to himself, forgetting that Hannah was sitting near.

Hannah went on sewing. It made no difference to her what Adam did. She would be gone in the spring. She looked up. Her father was sitting, not reading. He was staring off into space, a tired, despairing look upon his grim weathered features. With a jerk he set to reading once more. But for that one instant Hannah had a vision of how hard things had been for him since her mother's death. Yes, he had had to plan, to manage this new work of renting, of working without a boss. He had not had Ana to comfort him nor advise him, nor listen when he wanted to confide in someone. He was unable to bring himself to talk to even one of his children. Not even to her, though she was the head of the house in Ana's place. Hannah rolled up her sewing and stood up.

"It's time to go to bed, Papa," she said gently.

On New Year's Eve Hannah went with Jake and Fritz and Katie to Factory City in Adam's car. It was a long cool ride, but there was no snow on the ground.

Jake hummed a tune to himself as he drove with one hand. For this one time, Katie and Fritz had the back seat.

"Havin' a swell time?" Jake asked, grinning down at Hannah.

Hannah nodded, but didn't speak.

They went to a public dance hall. The large room was crowded, confetti filled the air, horns blared raucously, and there was such a din that one had to yell at the top of his voice to make a person hear.

"Ain't this swell?" Jake grinned. He bumped into couples. He became warm and the perspiration stood out on his face. With it came the stench of beet pulp. Jake just laughed and danced all the faster.

Some one backed into Hannah and squeezed her against Jake until she thought she would never breathe again. Jake laughed. She laughed. Horns shrieked and blared. Jake bought one for himself and a buzzer for her. Noise and more noise. Every one was feverishly trying to have a good time.

153

"Sure a swell dance," Jake stated as he munched pop corn.

A gong struck somewhere overhead. "One-two-three-four-five-six-seven-eight-nine-ten-eleven-twelve." The noises increased until they were indistinguishable and altogether uncontrolled.

"I'm glad the old year's gone," Hannah said soberly.

Jake tipped up her chin, smiling into her eyes. "Me too," he agreed. "I'm making plans for this year and I think you'll like 'em."

When they left the dance they hunted a hot dog stand. Sitting on a high stool eating her hot dog, Hannah grinned back at Katie. Once she laughed aloud at Jake. On the way home she relaxed in Jake's embrace and was content. She found she could smile and laugh. Jake's solid bluntness seemed, all at once, a good thing to be thankful for. And this was a new year.

"Goin' to storm," Jake said. "There's a ring around the moon."

"No, it won't," Hannah denied. "That ring don't mean a thing. I saw a ring around the moon once before, and—" She stopped. Sitting in a barnloft, she'd seen the moon—and it had had a ring around it.

CHAPTER VIII

ONE evening early in January Hannah was dumping barley from the tin coal scuttle into the long feed troughs when Mr. Boswell and Adam came into the lot.

"I tells you they lay down mit their backs und stick their feets up and bite holes mit themselves. Yah, und they pull the wools right off mit their backs so it make holes mit the skin." Adam gestured as he spoke.

"Fritz, catch me a lambs!" Adam yelled.

While Fritz held a lamb down Adam and Mr. Boswell examined it closely.

"Scab," Mr. Boswell stated briefly, rising from his stooped position.

"Ach, mein Gott im Himmel!" Adam threw up his arms with a despairing motion.

"Drive them over to the Holegate Farm," Mr. Boswell said. "Better take them in the morning. They'll have to be dipped again in another ten days so as to get all the eggs that hatch. Might as well dip the whole bunch, then you're sure you've got it all."

Adam groaned. That night Hannah heard him muttering and tossing in his sleep. The next morning he was up early ordering every one around.

Hannah planned on having the whole day to herself, but around eight o'clock Henry and Olinda drove into the yard in the old Goelzer car.

"We come to spend the day," Olinda called.

"Fine, fine! Henry, he can drive sheeps und Olinda can keep the kids so Hannah drive sheeps, too." Adam rubbed his hands together. All morning he had been groaning about how he was going to get the lambs driven over to the upper Boswell place five miles away.

"Why didn't you wait another hour, Olinda, and then they'd been gone?"

"I couldn't stand that old woman another minute. I had to get away for the day. I tell you she's crazy."

"She's certainly queer," Hannah admitted, "but she ain't no different than she always was. You just know her better, that's all."

"She makes me scour her old kitchen floor with sand! With sand!" Olinda moaned. "She thinks up work for me to do."

Hannah thought of Olinda always whining about working before she was married. Olinda never had had much ambition. She was just like her older sister, Mary. She'd have a dozen kids and always live in a dirty shack.

"Hannah! Got a move on!" Adam called from the kitchen door.

"Listen, Olinda, if Reinie has a fit while I'm gone, you know what to do, don't you? Give him a warm bath, and don't let Martha get into things. She picks things up off the floor and eats 'em. There's some cold meat in the pantry, and you can cook potatoes for your dinner. The milk's—"

"Go on, you talk like an old grandmother. You act more married than I do." Olinda pushed her toward the door.

Going along the wide dirt highway, Hannah rejoiced in her freedom. The sun—too hot for this time of year—warmed her back and she took off the light sweater that she wore. Boswell's two dogs and their own new dog trotted after the lambs with their tongues lolling out of their mouths. These dogs didn't compare with Shep who had been killed. They didn't know how to keep the lambs moving.

"This is a weather breeder," one of the Boswell hired men yelled above the barking of the dogs and the baa-ing of the lambs.

"Yah, I think we get some big storm, but not today," Henry Goelzer yelled back.

It was almost noon when they reached the Holegate Farm,

where the dipping vats were. Adam and Mr. Boswell were waiting for them, having come together in Boswell's car. The steam boiler was going, and the dipping vat, a long narrow concrete runway built in the ground, was filled with water treated with sheep dip. The smell of creosote was heavy on the air.

Part of the lambs were crowded into a pen adjoining the dipping vats. Fritz, with a stick, forced the lambs into the warm treated water. Henry stood farther along with a pronged fork pushing the lambs under the water so that their heads and backs would be soaked with the solution. The mournful baas of the lambs mingled with the yipping of the dogs and the yelling of the men.

Hannah got a rake and helped. It was fun pushing the lambs under and watching them climb up the cleated runway shaking their heads as if they were blinded. Once upon the hard ground they shook themselves. The smell of creosote rose in fumes that burned her nose.

When three-fourths of the lambs had been dipped Hannah felt a sudden cold breeze sweep along her hot body. She looked up in surprise. The wind had changed to the north. Gray clouds filled all the northern horizon.

"It's going to turn cold," Boswell shouted. "We'll have to hurry with the dipping."

"Better we stop now, und start mit home," Adam suggested fearfully.

"It won't get worse for three or four hours. The heat from the lamb's body'll dry the wool," Boswell replied. He picked up a stick and went to help hurry the lambs through the dip.

But by the time the last lamb was run through the dipping vat, the wind was colder and higher. When they were a mile on their way home, snow began to spit out of the north.

"This is just like the storm last year when we moved," Hannah said to Fritz as she came close to him.

"These lambs'll freeze," Fritz spoke grimly. "Their wool's all wet and it ain't had a chance to dry. Lambs are the

157

tenderest things on earth when they're chilled. We'll lose some of them sure if this gets any worse."

The weather did get worse. Snow came faster out of the north. The wind grew colder. The lambs wandered to the sides of the road seeking shelter from the fence posts and Russian thistles banked along the fence rows. Hannah was kept busy running after the stragglers, prodding them, making them join the main flock. She yelled until she was hoarse. It was a slow business. The wind was coming at a northwest slant against the lambs, striking them in the face. They were continually milling, trying to turn their backs to the storm.

Two miles from home the snow was banked around the fence posts and weeds. The weaker lambs were falling in the snow. Hannah kicked one of them with her foot. It rolled feebly over and got on its feet. She caught another lamb by its short ears and dragged it upright. Through her thin jersey gloves she felt the outer frozen wool crackle. Her hands were chilling. The cold swept in beneath her sweater. She tried to pull her cap down over her ears but couldn't quite cover them.

"We'll freeze," she shouted to Fritz.

"Sure, I know it! But we gotta get these lambs home. Fifteen hundred of them, Hannah. God, it makes me sick to think of it. All the money Boswell paid for 'em, and Dad has to stand half the loss. Come on, keep 'em amovin'." Fritz shouted to the dogs. He broke through the packed and milling mass; beating right and left he forced the lambs slowly forward.

Before another mile Hannah was crying bitter tears. She pounded a down sheep on the back and tried to lift it to its feet. Its wet wool frozen, it was exhausted. Hannah left it lying where it fell. Darkness was settling and it wasn't yet four o'clock. The lambs wandered to the side of the road, fell among the weeds and snow, and couldn't be found.

They prodded the main bunch onward. Hannah's hands were freezing. She saw Fritz rubbing his ears and his nose while he shouted to the poorly trained dogs. Hannah began to wonder if they, too, would perish. She saw tears fill her father's eyes.

For once in his life Adam was silent. The enormity of this

158

calamity, of this loss, was too terrible for him to voice. Grimly, he flayed the lambs on the backs, and the tears ran down his cheeks.

"Come, Adam," Boswell shouted. "It's no use trying to make these stragglers keep up. Leave Fritz to bring them in and let the others go ahead. Come on, we'll get the hay racks out and come back for them."

Adam got into Boswell's car. Henry and the Boswell hired men took the main bunch of lambs on ahead.

"Go on, Hannah," Fritz said. The wind beat upon them in freezing gusts. They were close to a farm house, and the weak lambs were milling in the shelter of the barn which was close to the road.

"I can't go another step," Hannah cried. "I'm going into that house to get warm." She ran toward the house.

Standing in the warm room, she almost cried from the pain in her hands. She dared not get too close to the heat, and so stood away from it, rubbing her hands, looking out the window.

Fritz was slapping his hands together, and pounding his arms, but never stopping his attempts to keep the lambs on their feet. When the lambs straggled away and lay down in the snow, their feet stuck straight up in the cold air. They were motionless, and seemed to be dead; then, with a convulsive shudder, they would struggle to their feet and join the small flock.

Some would lie on their sides, their feet twitching as if in the last stages of death. By the dozens they lay, mutely kicking and rolling in the snow, then get up, then fall down again. All the time, Fritz, freezing in the storm, tried to keep them moving.

Hannah was warmed; so she left the house. "Go inside, Fritz. Your ears look funny. I'll watch."

In five minutes it was as if she had never been warm. Cars whizzed honking and crowding around the lambs. Lambs got beneath the bumpers, crowded in front of the radiators. Cars had to stop while the drivers, cursing, dragged the lambs free.

Out of one of the cars stepped Jim, dressed warmly in

159

sheep-lined coat and heavy gloves. He brought forth an armful of coats.

"My God, Hannah!" he exclaimed. "Why aren't you in that house? You'll freeze to death. Get into this coat."

Jim held the sheep-lined coat for her. Hannah gratefully slipped into it. But her fingers were so numb she couldn't fasten the buttons.

Jim's strong fingers fastened it for her. His face was close to hers. "You're the pluckiest, sweetest, damned fool I've ever seen," he said. "You need somebody to look after you." He turned away and shouted to the dogs. Taking his place beside Hannah, he began slapping the lambs on the back with a gunny sack.

Fritz came from the house as the first hay rack came in sight. Hannah stood to one side, in the shelter of Jim's car, watching the men boost the lambs onto the hay racks bedded with straw. Jim worked with them. Hannah watched him. He acted as if nothing had ever happened. Did he talk to every girl he met the way he talked to her? Well, he'd find out she wasn't every girl.

When the last lamb was placed in the wagons, Jim came over to the car.

"Get in and I'll take you home," he said, and opened the car door.

"I'll ride on a hay wagon," Hannah said. But she was so nearly frozen her voice lacked force.

"Nonsense, get in this car, or I'll put you in."

Hannah got in the car and waited while Jim shouted something to the two hired men who were about to take a hay rack back along the way and pick up the lambs that had fallen along the roadside.

"This is the worst storm I've ever seen," Jim said as he got into the car. "We're going to lose lambs by the hundreds. They're all wet with dip."

"Is that heater throwing out any heat?" he asked, looking at Hannah.

Hannah didn't answer. Did he think he could call her a dirty Russian and then act as if he'd never said it?

"Dirty Russians don't feel the cold," she said.

"Hannah!" Jim's voice was sober, sincere. "Will you believe me, when I say I'm sorry? I was so mad that morning I didn't know what I was saying. I—I wish you were in town. You're too close. The folks raise Cain, and I can't see you."

"You said it," Hannah chattered. She was so cold that she couldn't keep from shaking.

"I wish I hadn't said it, Hannah. I don't know how to make you believe me."

"Oh, sure, I believe you," Hannah replied. She opened the car door as Jim stopped at the Schreissmiller gate.

"Sure, I believe it," she repeated as she left the car.

But that don't unsay it, she thought as she ran to the warm kitchen. Olinda had a fire and hot food ready.

Adam came in groaning about the dead lambs. "Gott, the ones I lose. Und all that money in them!" He sat down at the table and buried his head in his arms.

"Maybe we won't lose many. It's already stopped snowing." Hannah wanted to console him, but she knew no words would be convincing. Too many lambs were dead or dying along the roadsides.

That night the men kept the lambs moving around a huge straw stack behind the barn.

Fritz and one of the Boswell hired men took turns coming in to warm. Adam paced the floor, muttering, groaning.

Hannah curled up on the couch in the front room but didn't sleep. She was seeing Jim's dark face and hearing his words of apology. Neither brought her comfort.

She got up to make fresh coffee and prepare more sandwiches for the men. She was glad when morning came, clear and cold. It didn't seem possible that so small an amount of snow could cause such havoc.

But the day was worse than the night. The lambs died throughout the day. Fritz and the hired men were kept busy skinning the dead ones. Drying sheep pelts lay thick along the tops of the board fence surrounding the sheep pens. Mr. Boswell grew haggard and his face looked old.

When a week had passed and Adam tallied up the loss he

161

had aged ten years. In all, five hundred lambs had perished.

"Gott, mit the poorhouse I go. Debts on mine back! Gott im Himmel! Debts on mine back so I never get them off before I die," he said, bewildered.

CHAPTER IX

THE month of February was warm, though dry. Adam set Fritz to hauling sheep manure from the pens. Hannah ran the plow part of the time. Her thoughts were almost constantly of Jim Boswell. She found that she was excusing him, that the deep hurt within her was eased. She began to cherish his words, "I wish you were in town. You are too close."

The days crept by. Adam's sense of failure increased, and it weighed upon her. She found she was counting the days until Tabia would be at home to help her. She spoke to the minister about working her way through high school.

"The work will be hard," he told her. "There are the two small children and my wife isn't well."

Hannah smiled. Hard work? She knew what work was. Up in the cold early morning to start the fires, out 'tending chickens, helping harness, working in the field, managing the housework.

Tabia avoided all the work she could. "I gotta learn my catechism," she would storm. "I gotta make a story about Joseph. I gotta write it good and study my Bible. If you wasn't so mean, you'd help me instead of wanting me to work all the time. I got more'n I can do with my eighth grade exams coming an' confirmation an' everything."

Hannah thought back to the year before, when she was being confirmed. She too had argued about studying her catechism.

"I don't see how Mamma stayed so calm and sweet," she murmured.

Since his terrible loss of five hundred lambs, Adam's hair had whitened.

"Gott, what I do, Hannah?" he would ask. "On the corner last Saturday night they say how the sugar factory don't pay so much for beets this year."

Old man Heist came over one evening. They sat talking in the kitchen. Hannah was darning socks and stockings by the fire in the front room.

"I don't know if I raise beets," Adam said. "Not for one cent less over last year do I raise beets. Me, I don't sign up for none."

"Yah, und I hear how they cut the price of the beet work. Gott, Adam, what comes of things I don't know."

"Mit the poorhouse, sure," Adam groaned. "Mit five hundred lambs I am lose und the dry weathers, Gott."

"Never I seen such a dry," Heist agreed. "No snow even in the back mountains, und they say we don't got so much water in the reservoirs und the lakes. Always we have rains mit the spring und snow mit the winters."

"Gott, I don't plant one seed till we get the rain," Adam's voice was filled with despair.

"Yah, but lambs, he is high," Heist commented. "I see how they go up fifty cent on the Denver market last week und higher yet in Chicago, und Kansas City. You buy your lambs freight paid to the river, don't you, Adam?"

"Yah," Adam admitted, "but I don't send none mit the river, I ship mine mit Denver. No more feeds do I put in them."

When, several weeks later, Fred and Frieda Hergenboch came over with their children one Sunday afternoon, Hannah made it a point to ask Fred about the lambs and the beets, since there was no use asking Adam.

"Don't worry, Hannah. Even if he did lose five hundred lambs, he's not going in the hole. Lambs have shot up two dollars in the last four weeks. All he can see is what he won't make. He'll break even and be paid for his feed. Probably have to donate his time."

"Heist was talking about freight being paid to the river, Fred. What's he mean?" Hannah's voice was anxious.

164

"It just means he can ship them to any point to the Missouri River without paying freight charges—Kansas City, Omaha or Chicago. He'll sell in Denver."

"But Fred, he says the sugar company hasn't sent out the contracts yet, and the farmers are talking of not signing when they do."

"They always talk that way, Hannah. We'll raise beets just the same as usual. It's this dry weather and water shortage that is worrying more than usual. But we always get rain enough to bring the beets through the ground, then we irrigate. This won't be no different. Quit your worrying."

"It ain't me, Fred. It's Papa that near sets us crazy."

Adam went ahead and got his beet ground ready, although he swore he wouldn't sign for less than last year's price. But when the factory field man came around with the contracts at fifty cents a ton less, Adam signed and contracted to grow forty acres of sugar beets.

"I don't plant me one seed 'til we get the rain," he stubbornly declared.

Hannah saw him go over his fields day after day, stooping to sift the dry dirt through his fingers. The factory field man came out and he and Adam went out into the fields. Dust whirled around them. It was the last of April and the soil was dry as a bone.

"We start mit the planting in the morning," Adam stated briefly when he came back to the house. "But the seeds never come themselves up," he added.

The next day Hannah rode the beet drill. The wind and dust whirled around her until she could hardly see. The mountains toward the west were hidden.

Hannah planted twenty acres. She was in the far field one afternoon when clouds rolled up from the north and, before she could get to the house, the rain struck. It drenched her.

"We got the rain I guess," she laughed, as she drove the horses into the barn. "Papa ought to be happy now."

"He'll worry about something else," Fritz shouted. "It'll have to rain more'n this to do any good."

"You sound just like Papa."

It rained all afternoon. Enough for the beets that were

165

planted to come up, and for the second planting of seed after the rain also. But by the time the last ten acres in the small triangular field were planted the ground was again dry.

"You'll have to irrigate," Fritz told Adam.

"Gott, I don't!" Adam said automatically.

But two days later he decided to irrigate the ten acres. This reversal did not surprise Hannah but it suddenly occurred to her that Adam really didn't know what he wanted. He is like a bee buzzing around making a noise and watching everybody jump, she thought.

From Big Roaring Irrigation Ditch, Fritz let the water into a lateral ditch extending the length of the field. It was from this ditch that the water was turned into the rows of beets that had been planted. Adam had had foresight enough to put the ditchers on the drill, so that the ditches were already made.

Hannah put on Alec's rubber boots and went out with Fritz to irrigate. She built little dams out of wet mud at the ends of the ditches; she opened the dry ditches, and watched while the water went creeping down the dusty furrows, soaking into the earth, crawling over the entire field. It was hard, back-breaking work. Adam walked incessantly about the field.

"Gott, we don't never get a good stand mit irrigating up," he moaned. "Mit the lambs what died, und beets mit less money, und water for nothing. Gott, near crazy—"

Hannah turned on him. "Papa, if you say another word about lambs, or beets, or water, *I'll* go crazy! Go to the house, go anywhere, but leave us alone!"

"Gott im Himmel! Go on the house you tells me. You go on the house!" Adam shook his fist at her.

Hannah shouldered her shovel and started to leave the field.

"Hannah, you stop it!" Adam yelled.

"You told me to go to the house. I'm going." And in spite of Adam's threats, Hannah went.

That afternoon Hannah took Reinie and Martha with her to visit with her sister Mary.

Mary lived in a two room shack in the corner of a beet field. It was overflowing with children. There was no chance

166

to visit really, but Hannah felt that any place was better than home and Adam's nagging.

"I hear you're goin' to work for the minister," Mary said, sitting down in a battered rocking chair and preparing to feed her youngest. She pushed her bedraggled hair back from her fat face. "Some people's got all the luck," she said complacently. "I s'pose you'll work long enough to get a little money ahead and then you and Jake'll be gettin' married."

"I'm not marrying Jake or anybody," Hannah said. "You make me sick. Everybody thinks just because Fritz is sweet on Katie that I gotta marry Jake. I'm goin' to high school. That's what I'm goin' to do."

"I s'pose you'll be higher toned than Lizzie is. She don't even speak to any of us now. I met her on the street last Saturday and she just looked a hole through me and went on. All just because she married a grocery clerk."

"I'm not Lizzie," Hannah said quietly.

"You stay 'til the beets is thinned, I s'pose?"

"I'm goin' the Monday after Tabia gets through school. Papa can hire some one."

"You like to sound hard, Hannah, but you ain't. You're the softest one of all of us." Mary smiled at her sister affectionately.

On the way home Hannah was half angry, half interested. Soft, was she! Easy! Well, she wasn't. She was the only one in the family that Adam couldn't run over.

Hannah made several new housedresses and new slips for herself. She patched the boys' clothes. She knew Tabia would never do it. By the time the beets were large enough to start thinning, Hannah had the house fairly clean.

The dry weather continued. Hannah dreaded the thought of working in the beets.

Jake was helping with the work this spring. His good humor never wavered. He kidded Adam; he made the whole atmosphere on the farm lighter.

Adam would stop his horses at the end of every few rows and inspect the work of the others.

"Gott, I wish it rain," he would say. "Gott, Hannah! Mit worms they is!" Adam dug out his glasses and bent over the plants. "Gott, why don't you tell me the web worms is in 'em?" He seemed ready to strike her. She stepped slowly aside, merely looking at him.

"I'm hoeing. I wasn't watching for worms."

Adam went on a run to the house to call the factory field man. He came back to the field and closely scrutinized row after row.

"Man, you ain't got any worms to talk about!" The factory man's voice boomed loud and unworried. "There's just a few at one end of the field. You don't need to worry."

"Gott, but I do. The devil, he is after me. I got spray mit poisons."

"Oh go ahead and spray, but you'd better wait a few days. We'll watch them. If they don't get any worse, you don't have to worry. It's this dry winter that we've had that's made them come so early."

Adam cultivated a few rows that afternoon but he spent most of his time looking for worms.

The next morning he found that the worms had advanced ten feet farther into the field. He borrowed Boswell's sprayer and went to town in the car for poison. Jake and Fritz mixed Paris Green and water. They dumped the mixture into a galvanized drum which rested on the platform of a two wheeled cart.

Hannah decided to take advantage of the free day. In the morning she worked on a new dress for Martha to wear the following night at Tabia's graduation. The thought of Tabia being through school pleased Hannah. Worms in the beets, farming, nothing meant anything to her. She would be gone on Monday, and this was Thursday.

"Boo!" Hannah said to Martha toddling about from chair to chair. Martha started to run and went rolling. Hannah swept her into her arms.

"Oh, you're Hannah's girl. Hannah's great big girl. You're my darling, my loveling, that's what you are." Hannah kissed her until the baby wiggled.

"Can you love your Hannah?"

Martha threw her chubby arms around Hannah and planted an open kiss on her cheek. Hannah hugged her.

Oh, she loved this baby that she'd cared for and raised. "Sweet. Sweet enough to eat," Hannah said as she put her down.

"Hannah must hurry or she won't get your dress done, and you can't go to see Tabia graduate. Hannah's going away to town, Martha, to take care of the minister's little girl. But she won't be half as sweet as you." Hannah laughed as she treadled the sewing machine.

At noon, Tabia and the boys came home. School was over until after the graduation.

"Say, Hannah, the underneath slip to my confirmation dress is too long and if I gotta wear it tomorrow night, I gotta have it fixed." Tabia looked anxiously at Hannah.

"Go get it. I'll fix it for you if you'll stay home this afternoon and take care of Martha and Reinie. I wanta go to town."

Martha crawled about while Hannah was turning up the hem on Tabia's slip. "Stand still, Tabia. I can't get this even if you keep turning," Hannah spoke sharply.

"It's Martha," Tabia said quickly. "She keeps coming at me with her old sticky hands always a messin' up!"

Tabia gave a jerk and sent Martha sprawling.

"There, there, don't cry, Martha." Hannah picked her up. "Hannah's here. Don't you treat this baby so mean. You were a baby once."

"I'll get enough of her this summer after you are gone without starting now."

Hannah said nothing then, but that afternoon, when she went to town, she spoke severely to Tabia. "Now you watch Martha. Don't you let her get out of the yard. And if you're mean to her, I'll give you a beating. Remember what I say."

CHAPTER X

HANNAH was late starting back from town, but she was in no hurry. She had food prepared for supper. Lilacs were in bloom. The new beets, most of them as yet unthinned, stretched across the fields in narrow, green rows.

The red brick silos, almost as high as the trees which hugged the farm houses, loomed against the sky. Fields of young grain were like green carpets over the countryside. If it would only rain, Hannah thought. Adam might stop worrying if rains came. But Fritz was probably right. Her father would always worry. He still worried about the loss of the lambs, worried because he hadn't shipped part of the lambs to Chicago. Boswell had shipped two cars and had made enough to pay for the extra feed required and a neat profit besides. Now there was the worry about the beets; the worms, and the lack of water. It would be good to get away from Adam's incessant nagging. It would be heaven to have some one else do the planning. It would be play to keep a modern house clean.

Hannah blushed. She hadn't kept the house very clean this year. She began to wish that she had done so many things differently. She could have been more considerate of her father. She'd had the upper hand all summer and winter and she'd abused her power.

When she came to the field near home, she stopped the car and sat looking at Fritz and Jake operating the sprayer. Fritz stood on the platform pumping the handle of the iron pump on top of the round drum of poison. Jake leaned over looking down at the green poison as it sprayed from the nozzles onto the beets below. The horses pulled the sprayer up the field.

"Clang! Clang! Clang!" A shrill bell pealed behind Hannah. A streak of color passed by. The fire chief's special car. Hannah started her car. But maybe it wasn't a fire.

She glanced toward the house. No smoke rose from above the trees. She drove faster, for the fire chief's car had disappeared in the direction of home. When she turned in the lane, she saw the fire chief's big car and people gathered around it.

"O God!"

As she ran forward she was mystified. There was no smoke, but the fire chief had been summoned.

"What is it?" she cried, pushing her way through the crowd.

Little Martha lay on the ground. Her clothes were wet and the golden curls were soaked. The firemen were trying to revive her.

As Hannah started toward her, an arm caught her elbow and hard fingers bit into her flesh.

"Steady," came Jim's low voice.

"Why did I leave her?" Hannah cried. Tears were running down her cheeks.

Jim's fingers pressed deeper. The pain steadied her.

A choking rattle came from Martha's throat.

"She's coming around," some one said.

Martha gave a faint cry. Hannah reached out her arms but Jim's fingers held her back. Martha was wrapped in blankets and the doctor was summoned.

"Warm the blankets," he said. "Keep changing them so she doesn't get cold. She'll be all right."

The firemen and the doctor left. Martha slept as if dead. Several times Hannah thought she was, but each time the breathing could be redetected.

Adam hung over the foot of the bed. Tabia cringed in the corner out of the way. Fritz and Alec waited anxiously with Jim Boswell in the kitchen. Mrs. Boswell continued to work beside Hannah.

Four hours later Martha opened her eyes. She reached a chubby fist to Hannah.

"Nanna," she said.

"Ach, mein liebling, mein liebling," Hannah crooned, lifting the baby into her arms. She carried her to the old rocker and sat there crying. Hannah rocked the baby until she slept again. Hannah put her on the couch and lay beside her, but could not sleep.

"I'll never leave you alone again," she said softly.

The next day Martha played on the floor beside Hannah as she finished the baby's dress. Hannah watched her anxiously. She stopped work and caught the baby to her. "Mine loveling, mine loveling," she crooned.

Martha became frightened by Hannah's tight embrace. She whimpered and struggled to get away. Hannah let her go and relaxed for a moment and her gaze wandered out the window. She saw Jim polishing his car in the Boswell yard. Her lips set firmly and she went back to her sewing.

That evening she helped Tabia get dressed for the graduation exercises. She tied Adam's tie, and saw that the younger boys were clean and shining.

The whole family went together to the country school house. Hannah sat with Reinie beside her and Martha on the desk top.

Tabia was with the other graduates on the small wooden platform in front.

For the first time Hannah saw Tabia's thin pipe-stem arms, saw how spindly her legs were, how pinched her face, how small she was for her age. She saw the tired look in Tabia's eyes, the beginning of a rounding spine and a slight hump between her shoulders. She remembered that Tabia was always complaining that she was tired, and the times she had gotten white and faint in the beet field, and how Adam declared it was just Tabia's way of getting out of work. For the first time Hannah understood Tabia, understood her hatefulness, her tiredness, her impatience.

The county superintendent was giving out the diplomas. Hannah watched the serene face of the tall, middle-aged woman with white hair. She wondered how that face had reached such serenity. Not in a beet field, she thought.

At home that night, Hannah watched Tabia scuffling with Alec and Solly and wrestled with her conscience.

172

Tabia was fifteen, nearly as old as Hannah was when responsibility fell upon her. But she was little, she didn't love the baby, she fussed at Reinie, she let Martha fall in the ditch. But Hannah had a life to live, too.

All the next day, as Hannah cut the beets from the rows, the battle went on. She looked at the beets with loathing and felt that no power on earth could keep her working in the beet fields. She looked at Tabia, at Martha playing at the end of the field with Reinie. She thought of Reinie's fits.

Chop, chop, up, down, went her hoe. Her thoughts also.

I can't stay. I've got to go.

Who will take care of Reinie? You can't leave Martha.

Tabia can look after them.

You know she can't.

Chop, chop. The battle raged within while her back stiffened, her clothes became wet with sweat, and her face burned in the sun.

Four years and you'll be free.

Four years is eternity. I'll be twenty-one. Too old to go to school.

You could get a job in town and go to night school, maybe.

Twenty-one. I'll be too old! I can't do it!

You're tied. You'll never get away. Your life is beets. It will always be beets. Like your mother, you are; like her, you will work. You were born to work.

No, no. Not this kind of work. Mamma was used to it. I can't ever get used to it. I won't get used to it.

When you are old like she was, it won't matter.

Four years is eternity. They're my best years. Four years of planting, four years of thinning, four years of hoeing, four years of topping! God have mercy! I can't! I can't! Chop, chop; up, down; chop, chop.

Hannah went to bed when the others did but she couldn't sleep. Round and round the old argument chased in her mind. Finally she got up and stood looking out the window. The Boswell house showed clearly in the bright moonlight. Tall and stately, it stood for all the things which she wanted most out of life.

A car turned in the driveway and came to a stop before the

three-car garage. Jim was home. Hannah looked at the old alarm clock. Twelve o'clock. She watched until a light showed in an upstairs window.

She thought of Jim's words, "I wish you were in town. You're too close."

"I've got to go. O God, I've got to leave."

Hannah turned from the window. She felt for a match and lighted the kerosene lamp. She leaned far over the bed, holding the lamp low in her hand.

Closely she scrutinized Martha. "Such a baby, so tiny, mine loveling," Hannah whispered.

Beyond Martha lay Tabia, sprawled crosswise on the bed. Her face was pinched and thin. Her scrawny fingers clutched at her pouting mouth.

Hannah slowly turned away. She set the lamp on the dresser and stared into the wavy mirror.

"I can't, I can't," she whispered.

"Und when you no think you can stand it, Hannah, pray mit God, und he give you peace."

Hannah opened an upper drawer of the dresser. She drew forth the German Bible which her mother had given her when she was confirmed. She looked at the closed leather-bound book thinking of that Palm Sunday, of this Bible in her mother's worn hands, of her mother's calm strength, of her mother's sure words, "Treasure it well, Hannah, mein liebling. It gives you peace in time of troubles."

Hannah knelt beside the bed. "Please, dear God," she prayed, "help me to get through the next four years."

PART III
SECOND HOEING

CHAPTER I

TABIA went to work in the minister's home the day after the blocking and thinning were done. Two days later Hannah started with the second hoeing.

Through the rows of wilting beet plants Hannah walked, hoeing out the weeds and extra beets which had been missed in the first thinning. This was swifter work and not so tiring as the blocking and hand thinning, but the sun was hotter, the air more sultry and dry.

All this work, Hannah thought, in order that just one beet, the strongest and largest, might be left to grow and flourish, one beet separated by twelve inches on each side from its neighbor. Every thought, every effort, was put forth so that this one select plant should attain its greatest promise. All the plowing, the rolling, the preparation in the cold spring so that the ground would be as finely pulverized as machinery and human planning could make it, all the firming of the soil to the right degree of compactness, all the seed sowed thickly and at the right time, all the careful thinning—all in order that the strongest plant would be left. And now a second hoeing to be sure that nothing hindered this one plant.

If life were as simple as beet growing everything would be easy, Hannah thought. The weak would be hoed out, the strongest would be left to grow to their destiny. But no, the strong were taken away, and only the weak were left to worry and fret, to work their futile lives away. She thought of Olinda and Henry, weaklings; of her father, not big enough for the job he had undertaken; of Tabia, beaten before she started; of Fritz, sullenly, stubbornly fighting that which he couldn't conquer; of the younger boys, old before their time; of Reinie with his fits; of herself, beating her strength against all the forces around her. Only Ana had been sure, strong, with an inner strength.

July came in hot and dry. "It'll rain sure," Fritz grumbled. "It always rains on the Fourth when they have the celebration at Factory City."

For once Fritz was mistaken. It did not rain. Adam tried to make the family stay home to finish the last of the hoeing, but Hannah told him that all their neighbors and friends were going to Factory City. Not to be outdone, Adam stopped work for the day and celebrated.

In the town the older men stood in groups, visiting and complaining about the dry weather. They scanned the clear sky for signs of rain, shook their heads in despair.

"When we get the rain, I bet we wish we don't," old man Heist prophesied. "Too hot. It hail, I bet, like hell."

"Yah, we got to irrigate, und there don't been waters enough for all the beets," Adam said anxiously.

"Yah, next week I irrigate." Old man Heist shifted his short fat body to a shadier spot. "I use mine head. I order water when the neighbors order water. How I help if weeds und tree limbs get at der water gate so more water comes in mine ditch. Use der head, Adam."

A week later, while Hannah was out in the field helping Fritz irrigate, dark clouds rolled up from the north soon after noon. Lightning and thunder beat upon the horizon.

"We better go, Fritz," Hannah urged anxiously. "I don't like the looks of them clouds."

"Huh, you don't get much rain outta that cloud. Hail, lightning and thunder, that's all. We got to take our irrigation water when it's our turn. Rain or snow, this water's got to be used."

Hannah continued to slap wet mud into the openings of the small ditches, to open new dry ditches for the precious water. At the same time she watched the rising clouds. Every time the lightning flashed, she flinched. A few spatters of fine hail bounced around her, then suddenly stopped. From the north came a dull rumble that was not thunder. With apprehension, she looked at the white-fringed dark clouds. A cold wind swept across the heat-baked earth. The sun disappeared.

"I tell you, Fritz, we better get to the house," Hannah shouted. As she spoke a jagged streak of lightning split the clouds.

"We'll let the water run. I'll come out later an' change," Fritz shouted. He caught Hannah's arm and started to run. Hail began to beat upon the earth and them. Lightning cracked around them. Their rubber boots retarded their progress but at last they reached the house. A blinding flash of lightning, a sharper crash of thunder sent them scuttling inside.

Hannah went upstairs to put on dry clothes but she came down as quickly as possible. She was apprehensive, filled with a foreboding, unlike anything she ever experienced. To her, this was no ordinary storm.

"Yah, I say we get the hail mit all this hot weathers!" Adam groaned. "Gott, mit the hail on mine beets, what I do? What I do?"

A jagged streak of light flashed through the kitchen window. A ball of fire danced on the telephone for a second, sizzling and snapping, and Hannah screamed. Crashing thunder filled the house.

"Gott im Himmel! Mit lightnings we die!" Adam shrieked. "Run mit the feather bed under!" he shouted and dashed for his bedroom.

Hannah ran through the front room toward the stairway. The frightened screams of the smaller children halted her. Unreasoning fear filled her, yet she stopped.

"Hannah! Hannah!"

"O God, help us," Hannah breathed as the children ran to her, clinging to her skirts.

Forcing a smile to her lips, Hannah patted Coonie's shoulders and picked up Reinie. "My, my, what are you crying for? Just some old lightning that come in and hit the phone.

179

Come, come." She led the children to the old couch and there they huddled close to her.

Hannah tried to keep her body from shaking as the repeated flashes of lightning came into the room. She began repeating the Lord's prayer. Gradually she became calmer. She smoothed Reinie's hair; put her arms around the children, patting each one.

"The lightning we see can't hurt us," she told them finally, remembering her lessons in the eighth grade. She laughed, trying to reassure the little ones, but her teeth chattered.

Fritz came into the room and said quietly, "The wind's blowing it all away."

"There, stop the crying!" Hannah smiled with real relief at the frightened children. "Come to the kitchen and I'll get you each a cookie."

In twenty minutes the sun was out and the dark clouds were disappearing into the south.

Fritz went back to the field to reset his water, but Hannah stayed in the house with the children.

When all danger of storm was past, she went to the telephone. She jiggled the receiver to attract central's attention. No answer. Not even a buzz came to her ear.

"Dead," she said to Adam who was just emerging from his bedroom. She was startled by her father's whitened, fearful face. He's *afraid* of death, she thought. Suddenly the idea struck her that her father had no faith. It had been her mother's faith which had sustained them all.

"The phone's dead," she repeated. "I'll go over to Boswells' and telephone central."

"Yah, more better," Adam agreed, sitting down in a kitchen chair. "Mit hails it finishes me," he groaned, holding his grizzled head in his shaking hands.

Hannah put on a clean housedress, powdered her face, and pressed her hair into becoming waves.

She had no trouble picking her way to the back door of the Boswell house. Most of the water had run off into side ditches and had carried the white hail with it.

"Some storm!" Katie Heist laughed as she let Hannah into the bright kitchen. "I seen you out irrigatin'. I bet you

180

got soaked. Jim and Mr. Boswell come in like drownded rats, makin' all that extra work acleanin' up after 'em and me trying to get a birthday dinner. Look at Jim's birthday cake." Katie pointed to a tiered, white-frosted cake.

"Twenty-one years old today, an' we're havin' a swell party for him. Some of his high-toned friends for dinner tonight." Katie grinned and winked at Hannah standing at the telephone.

Hannah smiled as she waited for central to connect her with "repair service." Her eyes were on the inner door. She saw Jim as he came toward the kitchen. With a deep content she saw his face light up and admiration come quickly into his eyes.

She reported their phone out of order and hung up.

The telephone rang immediately. Katie sprang to answer it.

Jim came toward Hannah. "How are you?" he asked, his voice low, beneath Katie's shouting.

"Fine. I—"

"Oh, my God! Oh, my God! Oh, my God!" Katie's voice rose to a hysterical shriek. She fell to the floor, put her hands over her face and moaned. Her whole body shook with loud sobs.

Hannah and Jim knelt down. Mrs. Boswell came running into the kitchen.

"What's the matter, Katie? What's the matter?" Hannah kept repeating.

"Oh, it was the shovel what killed him. He's *dead!*"

"Who's dead?" Hannah shook Katie roughly to make her stop her hysterical crying.

"Papa's killed. The lightning struck him. His shovel on his shoulder. It struck his shovel. His shovel! Ooh! Ooh!"

"Jim, you must take her home," Mrs. Boswell directed.

Hannah and Mrs. Boswell went to Katie's room in the basement and gathered together the clothes she would need. Hannah stood awkwardly around. Old man Heist dead. Fat, laughing George Heist. It didn't seem possible. She stood on the Boswell back steps watching Jim's car disappear.

"I can't believe it," she repeated slowly. "Old man Heist

dead with an irrigating shovel on his shoulder. I seen him just last Sunday."

"Hannah."

Mrs. Boswell's voice brought Hannah back to the present. "Hannah, could you possibly help me this afternoon? My son is having a birthday dinner this evening and I can't get everything done without help."

"Oh, no, Mrs. Boswell, I couldn't. I can't leave the kids."

"Can't you leave them with an older sister, or some one?"

"I s'pose Olinda could take care of 'em," Hannah admitted. "I'll phone her an' find out."

Hannah turned from the telephone.

"She'll come."

"Please hurry, Hannah. Come back right away."

Hannah found Adam out by the barn. "Old man Heist's dead," she stated.

"Gott, crazy mit the head, is you?" Adam looked searchingly into her face.

"The lightning struck him. He was carrying a shovel. Irrigating."

"Mein Gott im Himmel! Mein Gott im Himmel!" Adam sat down on the wagon tongue, and buried his face in his hands. He began to cry.

"Mit Heist I come from Russia," he cried brokenly. "Troubles. Troubles. Nothings but troubles on mine head. Everybodys he die. What I do?"

Hannah patted his shaking shoulders. At last she said, "Mrs. Boswell wants me to come over and help her cook Jim's birthday dinner since Katie can't help."

"Ach, you have to go," Adam agreed, and got stiffly to his feet.

CHAPTER II

HANNAH ran upstairs to her room. Once more she powdered her face and combed her hair. She looked at herself in the mirror and tremors of excitement ran through her body. Going to Boswells' to Jim's birthday party! She couldn't believe it. Jim would be there. Jim. Maybe she'd better put on a good dress. No, there'd be work to do this afternoon. She could come back just before the supper—no, Mrs. Boswell had called it dinner—well, dinner then. She'd come home and put on her new green dress. It was the finest dress she had.

She almost skipped as she went toward the Boswell house. Her heart was singing. She smiled at Mrs. Boswell as she entered the kitchen.

"Goodness, Hannah, I thought you were *never* coming. We will have to hurry. There's everything to do."

Hannah looked around the shining kitchen. She felt Mrs. Boswell's hurried anxiety, the sharpness of her tone, but she couldn't see anything to worry about.

"Thank goodness Katie has the chicken all ready to fry. Hannah, you get these potatoes ready." Mrs. Boswell pushed a pan of small new potatoes toward Hannah and hurriedly left the kitchen.

Hannah picked up the paring knife. Slowly, carefully, she started peeling the potatoes. She wondered why the Boswells, who were supposed to be so well fixed, couldn't afford potatoes that were potatoes instead of little knots. Hannah decided to ask Jim.

"*Hannah!* What *are* you doing? *Never* peel new potatoes.

Scrape them. Like this. They must be just as round and perfect as possible. Now hurry, please. And when you are finished you can mold the cheese balls. Ten of them. One for each salad plate."

Hannah heaved a deep sigh. Who ever heard of potatoes being round and perfect? She looked at the dish of yellow cheese. Cheese balls. What were cheese balls? She turned to ask Mrs. Boswell, but she was gone again.

Uncertainly, she picked up a tablespoon. She looked at the yellow cream cheese. Cheese balls. Were cheese balls as big as baseballs? She didn't know.

"Hannah, hurry, *please.*"

Quickly, Hannah put a gob of cheese in the palm of her wet hand. Round and round she rolled it.

"Hannah, *not* that way. Small balls, the size of this. Now roll each ball in these chopped nuts. Put them on this plate and set them in the refrigerator. And wash your hands and *dry* them well before you begin." Mrs. Boswell's deep exasperated sigh filled Hannah with greater uncertainty.

"Listen, Hannah, I want you to cut these melon balls. Put the muskmelon balls on this plate, the watermelon ones in this one. Now watch me closely. See. Cut them out smoothly, and perfectly round like this. Do you understand?"

Hannah nodded her head dumbly. Gingerly, she picked up the metal cutter, carefully she scooped out a ball. It was ragged along one edge. She looked at the ball Mrs. Boswell had made. Smooth and round. She could never do it. Why *had* she come over here to help? She bit her lip and dug desperately into the thick yellow flesh of the muskmelon.

Mrs. Boswell stayed in the kitchen after this, washing lettuce, mixing salad dressing, breaking apart little sprigs of feathery green stuff. Part of the time she talked aloud concerning her dinner. "Watermelon and cantaloupe balls with Melbourne sherbet—new potatoes with parsley butter—chicken all ready to fry—cheese balls ready to go with the molded salad—goodness, Hannah, don't watch every move I make. Keep your eyes on your work. You're making those melon balls so ragged I don't know whether I can use them."

Hannah's body quivered at Mrs. Boswell's sharp, nervous

tones. Her hands were trembling so she *couldn't* make the melon balls round. What was the use of being so particular anyway? She bit her lip.

"Oh, the rose leaves for my rose molds!" Mrs. Boswell exclaimed. "Hannah, take the scissors. Cut a small spray about this long from that climbing rose under the window. Cut ten of them."

It was a relief to Hannah to get outside. A rose spray. Whoever heard of eating rose leaves. Green ones?

"Hurry, Hannah."

"Not the *middle* of the stem. A *spray*, Hannah. Can't you do anything? Not a thing?"

Hannah set her face in an unemotional, expressionless mask; but her hands were shaking as she lifted them to her hair.

"Take this dust cloth, Hannah. Dust the dining room and the living room. Polish the furniture until it shines."

Hannah gratefully accepted the dust cloth. Dusting was something she could do. She rubbed the legs of the dining table. With all her strength she went at the buffet and chairs. None of this furniture looked as if it needed polishing, but Mrs. Boswell had said, *polish*.

"Hannah! What are you doing? You must not rub the furniture so hard."

"Do you want the windows dusted?" Hannah looked at the ivory curtains, their folds touching the floor.

"Windows? No, just the furniture. And hurry, please." Mrs. Boswell hastily placed ivory white vases filled with roses and blue larkspur at each end of the dark buffet.

"Hannah, see what time it is, and you haven't even put the potatoes on to cook!"

"But, Mrs. Boswell, I don't know how to start the stove," Hannah admitted, her voice breaking slightly.

"Just turn the switch. This is an electric." Exasperation deadened Mrs. Boswell's voice. "Come, Hannah, we must set the table. I'll help you."

I'm just too dumb to even set a table, Hannah thought bitterly as she followed Mrs. Boswell into the dining room.

She helped place the silken cloth with wonder. She held

185

her end of the ivory damask tablecloth with the broad band of silvery lavender color through the center. With stolid outward calm she helped place the sparkling goblets of palest lavender, their silver bands gleaming in the late sunlight. She quietly helped place the rows of silver forks, knives and spoons. The further the table setting progressed the more panic-stricken she became. She wanted to tell Mrs. Boswell that she could not possibly help. She felt desperate when Mrs. Boswell tried one of Katie Heist's white aprons upon her.

"It will have to do. Come, Hannah, I'll tell you how to serve. The melon balls will be on the table. I'll help you place them. You will fill the water glasses after we are seated. I'll prepare the plates for the second course while you are removing the first. The salad will be served as a separate course. You will bring the cake to the table when the dessert is served. Place it in front of my son so that he can cut the first piece. We'll cut and serve it at the table. You can serve the coffee from the side table—no, you had better serve it from the kitchen."

The longer Mrs. Boswell talked, the drier Hannah's mouth became.

"And remember, Hannah, you serve from the left. Fill the water glasses from the right. Do you know which is the left—my left? I'll sit here at the table. Now you are serving me the hot rolls. Oh, no, Hannah, you serve from *my* left, so that I can take the roll with my right hand. That's right. Are you sure you remember?"

Hannah nodded her head. Back in the kitchen she felt as if she wanted to run out the back door. As she was carrying a sherbet glass from the refrigerator it slipped but didn't fall. Quivering from head to foot, she carried two Melbourne sherbets, each on its lavender glass plate, to the gleaming table. The fragrant sweet peas in their silver dish on the oval mirror in the center of the table held no beauty for her. The correctly set table only added to her panic. She cringed when she heard the first light voices of arriving guests. With silver ice tongs she clumsily lifted ice cube after ice cube and dropped them into lavender goblets. Her

186

knees were shaking. She was putting ice into the last glass as the guests came to the dining room.

She stopped, still holding her ice bucket. She smiled an uncertain smile. What was she supposed to do?

She nodded her head and spoke: "How do you do, everybody."

Eyebrows lifted. Smiles quirked the corners of young mouths. Hannah saw Mrs. Boswell's frown. Jim's eyes betrayed no sign. She fled to the kitchen. She wouldn't go back in that dining room for one hundred dollars. She couldn't go. Nobody could make her go. Not even Mrs. Boswell. She took a step toward the kitchen door to escape. Her glance rested upon a sparkling water pitcher.

"As soon as we are seated, pour the water, Hannah," Mrs. Boswell had said. Forcing herself, Hannah lifted the pitcher and went back to the dining room. Her shaking hand made the water splash in the pitcher. She steadied it with her left hand.

Serve to the right, remove from the left? Serve to the left, remove from the right? God, which was right? Which was left? Which?

Was this the right? O God, no. She couldn't reach across the plate. It had to be the other side. She tripped over a chair leg. She almost fell.

"Remove the plates from the right," Mrs. Boswell whispered, then excused herself and went into the kitchen.

The right. Hannah looked at that table, at that sea of laughing smirking young faces, and she knew that she didn't know which was right. Her brain was as if it were dead. She hesitated. She had to take the plates off. Grimly she began. In her shaking hands the glass sherbets rattled against the glass plates.

The girl next to Jim snickered as Hannah took her plate. She heard Jim say, "Sh."

Time stood still and became a dragging hell of rattling dishes, trembling fingers, knees shaking.

At last came the dessert—molded ice cream roses of palest lavender and of delicate pink, each rose resting on its spray of rose leaves. As Hannah reached Jim she stubbed

187

her toe against a chair. She stopped dead still, watching a pale lavender rose go skittering across the dark carpet. She heard the suppressed mirth from the table. Then came Jim's low voice at her elbow.

"Steady, Hannah."

Hannah picked up the fallen rose. In the kitchen, she leaned her head against the door jamb, shaking.

Mrs. Boswell's bell recalled her to her duties. Hannah quickly placed a fresh rose upon the plate and took it to Jim. With more calm than at any time during the entire dinner, she served the coffee, yet she could hear the coffee cups rattling against the saucers as she carried them.

She was still trembling when she reached home. She had washed and dried every fragile glass and plate.

Tears wet her pillow. Why couldn't the Boswells eat a meal like ordinary folks? Just pass the food to each other? Or better yet do as she'd heard her mother tell about in old Russia—put a kettle of food in the center of the table and let all dip in, each with his own wooden spoon. Then Hannah giggled. A crowd of college juniors eating as the German-Russians ate in old Russia!

CHAPTER III

EARLY one morning in the middle of July Hannah looked up from her preparation of breakfast to see Fritz come into the kitchen with a bundle in his arms.

"Well, Hannah, I'm leavin'." Stolid, stubborn resolve emanated from his thickset body.

"Oh, Fritz, not now! With all this dry weather and extra irrigating, and alfalfa, and everything?"

"I'm twenty-one today. I told you a year ago I was leavin'. I've give him eight good years in the field. He ain't got no business howlin'."

"But, Fritz, we can't get the work done without you," Hannah pleaded. "You're not—" She stopped. Fritz *was* fair. He was right. It was right that he should go. Yes, she realized, seeing the bitterness and defeat in his eyes, he should have gone long ago. He had a right to live his own life.

"You better tell Papa."

"Nope. Just be a fight. I'm ridin' in town with the milk man. Bye, Sis. You're a damned fool, just like I been. You won't get no thanks for stayin' home an' workin' your life away." Tears of emotion filled Fritz's eyes as he turned away.

Hannah went to the window and saw the milk man swing the ten-gallon milk can onto his truck. Then Fritz climbed into the cab of the truck.

It seemed to her that the last prop was taken from her. She had come to lean on Fritz, to enjoy working with him in the field. She thought of her father, of this latest trouble for him to face, and he with no patience or strength with which to face trouble. She wished Ana was there to tell him instead of herself.

"Fritz is gone," Hannah said simply when her father came from his bedroom a half hour later.

Adam halted, dumbfounded, in his doorway. "Gott im Himmel! Mit worthless—"

Hannah stopped his torrent of curses with an upraised hand.

"Better you don't say it, Papa. He's got the right. He's twenty-one."

"Gott, und I feed him, und buy him good clothes, und I gives him mine car to drive, und he leaves me flat! Gott—"

"But you never paid him. He didn't even have spending money without asking you. He worked hard. If you'd paid him a little money, I think he woulda stayed."

"Gott, pay mine own kids so they work! I don't! In Russia the kids work mitout pay, and the old mans don't never work. Pay mine kids! Gott im Himmel! Mine own father, he don't work one lick in Russia. Und us kids is work. Gott, I tells you we is work. Like hell, we work mit the field und the old man rides his buggy in und out, und he whips us mit the black whip, und he lays mit the shade, und us kids work! Pay mine kids! Crazy mit the head, you think I been! Gott, I die before I pay mine kids!"

"But this ain't Russia."

"Gott, more better it was if it been Russia. Better I save mine moneys und gone back mit Russia. Like one lord, I could live mit Russia. Old Reuben Liepner was smart mit the head. He save his moneys und gone back. Five thousand dollar, he save but he have ten boys so they work beets und they don't leave mit twenty-one years. Gott, what I do? What I do?"

"We'll have to hire somebody."

"Yah, und all that moneys. Moneys! Moneys! Moneys! So I go mit the poorhouse!"

Adam got in the car and left the place as soon as breakfast

190

was over. He returned at noon with a self-satisfied expression on his face.

"I hire Jake Heist, und you see you treat him good, Hannah. Might he stay und work mit the rest of mine life."

Hannah didn't answer.

As she worked in the garden, hoeing and planting, as she irrigated, as she helped put up hay and do other work in the field, she thought of the Boswell house and of Jim's birthday dinner. Each piece of furniture, every detail of decoration in the immaculate interior remained in her memory. More and more the Boswell house became to her a symbol of the better things of life. When she came to her own dingy kitchen at the close of each day's hard work she looked at it with newly seeing eyes.

The woodwork had been washed with lye until it had reached a tint of a mangy yellow and brown. The wallpaper was chipped and dirty. She remembered running her hand along the smooth ivory cream of the woodwork in the Boswell dining room. It had been like no woodwork she had ever seen. She remembered the smooth dark walnut buffet, the oval dining table, the chairs with dull gold and blue cloth-covered seats. No scratches, no mar on any piece. The whole dinner party kept coming back. It still had the power to send a wave of trembling through her.

She thought of Mr. Boswell's promise to furnish paint and paper for their own dingy house. She would ask him to supply the materials, she decided. If she was going to remain for four more years, at least they would *live* during those four years. But in summer there was not time to do more than keep the worst of the dirt down.

Dressed in her oldest overalls, a kerchief around her throat, gloves on her hands, and a big hat on her head, Hannah took her turn at the hand pump. Paris green bubbled out and caked around the pump. The two-wheeled cart jiggled and wabbled. A breeze came up and blew the fine poison spray back upon Hannah. It stung her flesh. She was thankful that only the small ten-acre field needed spraying. At the end of the field she got down and looked at the lush, growing beet plants. White webs covered the crown of the beet. Great holes gaped in the broad beet leaves where the ravenous worms had fed.

Hannah went for a swim in the ditch as soon as she finished spraying but her skin still felt dry and burning.

After supper she took another dip in the irrigation ditch. As she lazily paddled in the water she saw her father walking along the ditch bank going toward the upper end of the field with a shovel over his shoulder.

The water must have broken out, she thought, and hurried to dress. Jake wanted her to go to the Lake. "Band concert tonight," he had said. "Come on, let's go. We'll dance a little and come home early."

Hannah no longer objected to Jake's cheerful plans. It would be good to go to the Lake, hear some music and dance.

But her enjoyment of the lights rippling across the waters of the lake, the lively music, and the sight of the strolling couples, was spoiled when Jim's big coupé drove into a vacant space next to Jake's rattly little roadster.

She could have reached out and touched Jim. She was close enough to see that he had with him the same girl who had sat next to him at his birthday dinner—the very girl who had snickered when Hannah had sent the molded rose skittering across the carpet.

Not wishing to be seen, Hannah shrank against Jake, trying to make herself as inconspicuous as possible.

"Shall we go, Jim?" The girl's voice was imperious, certain of her power to possess.

"O. K., Eileen."

Eileen! The name wound in and out among her thoughts as she danced with Jake. Eileen! It kept her awake when she tried to go to sleep hours later.

Hannah was in the back yard hanging up clothes the next morning when Mr. Boswell appeared and said to Adam: "I tell you this water is breaking out too often, Schreissmiller. That headgate gets clogged too easy. I'm getting tired of it. I'm warning you."

192

"Gott, Boswell," Adam said, "I don't know is the water out. Mit the bed I go. How I know the water is out?" Adam spread wide his knotty cracked hands, and appeared unconcerned.

Hannah knew that her father lied. He'd gone up to the ditch the night before with a shovel on his shoulder.

"Don't let it happen again," Boswell said brusquely.

But the next week, when a farmer farther down the ditch had water, Adam ordered water also and set the smaller children to watching while he diverted more than his share of the water into the rows of his own wilting beets. When the farmer came striding across the fields, or came more speedily around by the road in his car, to see what had happened at the headgate, the proper amount of water was serenely going the way it should go. But when the farmer's back was turned, or he had set his water and gone to other chores, extra water once more wandered down Adam's rows of beets.

Coonie, Solly and Chris thought it funny to watch and report the movements of the farmer.

"That's not right. It's not honest. That farmer pays for his water. You're no better than thieves," Hannah said one evening at supper.

Adam winked at the boys, slapped his knees and grinned at Hannah.

The continued lack of rain made the irrigation water more precious and scarce. Lack of sufficient irrigation water caused farmers to fight. Just the day before Kniemer and Ochmidt had had a fight at the ditch. Kniemer had thrown his shovel at Ochmidt, grazing the latter's head. Ten stitches had to be taken. If Boswell learned that Adam was diverting the water he would certainly evict him and possibly send Adam to jail. Hannah mentioned this.

"Gott, Hannah, the gate gets stopped mit tree limbs und weeds. How it my fault if the water come down mine own ditches?"

"You know it just don't happen by itself."

"Yah, but who say for sure it don't?"

"You're doing just like old man Heist was telling on the Fourth of July. You're stealing it."

"Ach, Gott! und Heist he is dead," Adam groaned.

Hannah watched her father more closely. He ordered water when Boswell ordered. Day and night, Hannah, Jake and Alec took turns setting the water, seeing that it stayed in the rows between the beets. Five irrigations. Still there was no rain.

One night Hannah was sitting in the front room sewing a patch on Solly's overalls after all the others had gone to bed. She heard the kitchen door open and close and then her father's bedroom door close after him. *She had thought Adam was in bed.* She stopped her sewing. She was sure that part of Boswell's water was running down into their beet rows. She determined that she would see with her own eyes.

She rose quietly, went to the kitchen, stealthily slipped on Alec's rubber boots and left the house. She got a shovel from the woodshed and made her way up the field to the headgate.

"Dog eat dog," she whispered, thinking of her father. "He acts with everybody like he had to fight always for his very life; had to fight to be able to live at all." Had it been that way in old Russia, she wondered? Was that where Adam had learned to consider no one but himself? Grab. Grab. Cheat the other fellow. Take all you could get and give nothing.

Slosh, slosh, went her boots in water. Suck, suck, in mud. Water was running here more swiftly than it should. Water running down many open beet rows.

Shadows hung thick around the cottonwoods growing along the ditch bank near the Schreissmiller headgate. Low bushes hugged the sides of the ditch. The sound of the falling water came musically through the half-darkness. When she came up Hannah saw instantly that the gate was standing higher than it should. She continued on beyond until she reached the Boswell headgate. There Hannah found what she was looking for. At the small box-like gate lay a branching tree

194

limb and many weeds, so choking the outlet that most of the water ran past and found its way through Adam's open headgate into the open ditches on the Schreissmiller place.

Hannah tried to push the obstructing mass away with her shovel. She dug harder and almost lost her balance. She settled her foot more firmly and dug again at the limb. She tried to lift it by using a small branch and getting the right leverage. The dead branch broke with a snap. The noise startled her. She stood still, listening. Only the sound of the dashing of the falling water came to her ears. She began using her shovel once more. Then, suddenly, and for no reason of which she was aware, she knew she was not alone. She tried to pierce the shadows with her eyes. A rooster crowed from their own chicken house. A sleepy bird called from a far tree. An owl nearby let forth a long mournful hoot. Hannah jumped. "You're crazy," she said to herself. "Jumpy. It's all in your head." She set savagely to work prodding at the sodden weeds and tree limb.

"So that's the way the gate gets choked!"

Hannah dropped her shovel and it went sailing down the stream of water.

"I thought you were honest." Jim's voice came from out the shadows with withering contempt.

Hannah stood dumb before that cold judging voice.

"God, I thought *you* were honest!" Jim reached out with his shovel, knocking at the debris with swift savage strokes.

"Now you go home and tell that thieving father of yours that if I catch him stealing any more water I'll fill him with buckshot. Tell him that!" With these words Jim disappeared into the darkness.

The next morning Hannah faced her family at the breakfast table. Her face was white and drawn, her eyes heavy from loss of sleep, but her voice was calm and hard.

"Papa, if you steal another drop of water from Mr. Boswell or from anybody, I'm going to call the sheriff. Last night Mr. Boswell found out you was stealing his water and he said he'd fill you with buckshot." Hannah's hands gripped the pancake turner she held until the knuckles stood out

195

white. "Thieves! Liars! That's what we all are. Not honest. Not even *honest!* You make even the little boys thieves."

"Gott, Hannah, der beets, they dry up—"

"Better the beets dry up than for us to be thieves. If we can't buy more water, better the beets to dry up."

CHAPTER IV

THE dry August was followed by a drier September, but Adam stole no more water. Mr. Boswell had come over the morning after Jim found Hannah at the headgate. What he threatened, Hannah did not know. Whatever it was, was sufficient to scare her father.

Hannah continued to hope that she would see Jim. She framed excuses, adequate cutting remarks in response to anything he might have to say to her. But she did not see him.

One day Hannah missed seeing Jim's big coupé go along the road. She watched for it the next day, and the next.

"Well, Jim's gone," Katie Heist told her. "Gone East to finish his school. Valley City ain't good enough for him. And I'm leavin', too. Fritz's got a job heavin' feed at the mill, and I'm gonna clerk in at Gundstroms'. Can you imagine me clerkin' at Gundstroms'? Swell, ain't it? When you want to buy some new clothes I'll see you get the swellest dresses and swell stockings and pants like old lady Boswell wears." Katie lifted her dress.

"Katie! That's not right! That's stealing!"

"Oh, gosh, no! Mrs. Boswell'll never miss 'em. She's got scads! Dozens! I snitched these last summer an' she never even knew it. I got me some other things laid away, too. I guess I want nice things when I go out with Fritz, don't I?"

"I s'pose you an' Fritz will be gettin' married right away?" Hannah changed the subject.

"God, no. Fritz wants to save some money, an' I'm gonna save my money to buy some swell furniture. And believe me

197

I'm gonna have some swell stuff just like the Boswells, too."

"I s'pose Mrs. Boswell's got another girl?"

"Nope, she says she don't need one now that Jim's gone. Only once in awhile when she gives a party or has to have somebody help her clean house extra. Well, I gotta be goin'. Be seein' you."

Hannah continued to think of Mrs. Boswell. She might be able to help Mrs. Boswell part time. But when she thought of helping to serve another party, the idea lost its attraction.

Nevertheless, two days after Katie left, Hannah went to see Mrs. Boswell.

"I thought, maybe, if you needed some one just once in awhile I could help, maybe. I—I—I'd be willing to work for less than Katie if you'd just show me how to do things. I— I ain't never had no chance to learn nothin'—an' I thought— I thought I might learn how—"

"Why, I think that would be lovely, Hannah. So handy for me. I can telephone you whenever I need you." Mrs. Boswell smiled reassuringly at her.

"I couldn't come when we was in the beets, but other times I could."

"That will be convenient. I'll telephone you when I need you."

Although Hannah feared the prospect of another dinner party, she was determined. Dinner party or not, she was going to learn. There was no one but Mrs. Boswell to teach her.

When she told Adam that she would work spare time for Mrs. Boswell, he rejoiced loudly.

"Gott, such a luck. Mit the beets adrying out, und lambs what I lose last year, und the worms eating, we need the moneys. How much she pay you, Hannah?"

"I don't know. I didn't ask her."

"Gott, such a dumb ox! Mit the moneys you ask her first!"

Hannah pressed her lips tightly. No use telling Adam that it was not a question of money with her. No use telling him that she wanted to learn.

The first time Mrs. Boswell telephoned, it was for Hannah to help clean house. Hannah went with relief. Gradually her fears began to diminish, and during that fall Hannah's work at the Boswell house was the one bright spot in her life.

Adam continued to worry from morning until night. "Gott, mit the poorhouse I go. Mit lambs, I don't feed. Und the beets they little like turnips in der big field. Gott, five tons mit the acre. Gott, und I should have fourteen, eighteen ton on him. Ach, Gott, near crazy, I go mit the head."

"We'll get along some way." Hannah tried to console him, but he would have none of her reassurance.

"He'd worry if he made a million dollars," Jake told Hannah.

"But we don't really have the money." Hannah was serious. "I'm making the milk money and the eggs buy our groceries. Money don't go far. And Tabia's always wanting money for something in high school. It's awful how high school costs."

"She gets paid at the minister's, don't she?" Jake's tone was hard and condemning.

"Yes, but that just buys her books and things. She don't have nothing for clothes."

"She looks swell enough to me. Forget about her, Hannah. Tabia'll look out for herself."

"Oh, I don't worry about her. It's Papa. He looks so old and we don't have money to get along."

"Yep, beets are out. My work's over. I guess I'll have to hunt another job. Hannah, I got some money saved. What you say we get married? I'll stay here an' work 'til spring, an' help the old man out. You won't have to work outside, then."

Hannah looked at Jake's serious face. "I'm sorry, Jake. I just can't. I can't, that's all."

"Hannah, it kills me to see you workin' like you do. I wanta do things for you." Jake caught Hannah in his strong arms. "God, Hannah, I love you. Don't you know it?" His lips pressed roughly against hers.

"Ho, ho, Jake's kissin' Hannah," Chris yelled from the doorway.

"Say, you brat, get outa here before I knock you out," Jake yelled and turned on Chris, who was making a dash for the door. He stubbed his toe and Jake picked Chris up by the overalls and tumbled him outside.

Hannah had to laugh. "That's what you get for being so smart," she laughed.

"Next time, I get you where there ain't no kids," Jake grinned. "I meant what I said, anyway."

"And I say, no." Hannah tempered her refusal with a friendly smile.

Jake's proposal stuck in her mind. But no, she couldn't stand Jake. Jim would be home in the spring—to stay.

When the first beet check was issued Adam came home with ten one-hundred-pound sacks of flour.

"Yah, we have flour und we have potatoes from our own field, und beans from the field. Und a hog in the pen. I guess we eat if we don't have no moneys." For once his leathery face was wreathed in smiles.

"I buy the flours cheap, Hannah. They have worms in them but we can sift the worms out."

Yes, they most certainly had worms in them, Hannah agreed when she opened the first sack. The crawling woolly things sickened her. She felt she *couldn't* use the flour, nevertheless she had to.

She sifted part of the flour from the sack into her big dishpan and set the sifted flour in the oven. Maybe the heat would kill any eggs or worms that she had missed. When she felt that the flour had been heated thoroughly, she sifted it again before putting it into the big flour bin.

That winter she had to force down every bit of bread that she ate. Many a meal she left the bread plate untouched. Ten sacks.

Mr. Boswell put lambs in the Schreissmiller pens and hired Adam by the month to feed them. He bought Adam's alfalfa hay, also. Hannah knew that these transactions meant that her father had money again, but there was no change in her father's conversation. "We go mit the poorhouse." It was his only phrase.

During beet harvest Hannah and the boys had been compelled by Adam to pick up the fallen beets along the ends of the field and along the roadsides. Early each morning,

200

Adam sent the boys to the railroad tracks with gunnysacks to pick up the huge beets that had fallen from the passing beet cars. These beets they had stacked in the cellar, and Hannah was kept busy washing them in her washtub and running them through the big kraut cutter. Then she dumped the clean shredded beets into the washboiler and cooked them until they were soft.

Adam made a homemade press by boring holes inside a small box built in the center of a ten-foot board. He filled the box with cooked beets and pressed out their juice. The next day Hannah would boil the syrup down. When the huge boiler of syrup foamed over the edge she took it off and put the syrup away in jugs and jars.

The children and Adam liked to eat it on pancakes and on bread. It saved sugar, but for Hannah it was too strong and black.

Adam was openly proud. "Ach, the sugars it saves und the good syrup it makes. Like the old country it is."

He talked more and more of the old country. "We make the hog up in summer sausages just like the old country," he argued as he cut up the butchered meat. "Mit garlic und peppers we make it full."

"Oh, but I don't want garlic," Hannah objected. "We *don't* put garlic in all of it." She had her way.

On the first of January, Mr. Boswell shipped his first lambs. Because the Chicago market was higher, he did not sell them this year in Denver. During the week that Mr. Boswell was gone to Chicago, Adam butchered a lamb. He brought it to the house one evening, skinned and ready to cut up.

"Hannah, you put him in cans tomorrow und cook him so we have him."

"Did you pay Mr. Boswell for that lamb?" Hannah put her hands on her hips and looked Adam in the eye.

"Gott, no, he die. Like anythings, he die."

"I told you what I'd do if you stole another thing from anybody, didn't I?"

"Gott, Hannah mit the poorh—"

"Didn't I tell you what I'd do?"

"Hannah, mit all them lambs in the pens, they don't can miss one lamb. What you think you do? Tell *me* what you do? Gott, mit the head I knock you! Gott—"

"You've got your choice. I call the sheriff or you pay Mr. Boswell for that lamb. I'm sick and tired of people calling us thieves!"

"Thiefs! *me,* a thiefs! Who say Adam Schreissmiller is a thiefs? Who call *me* one thiefs?"

"I call you a thief. And if I call the sheriff, he'll call you a thief, and he'll put you in jail."

"Gott im Himmel! Mein Gott im Himmel! Call the sheriff. Call him. I don't pay for no lamb!" Adam shook his fist in Hannah's face. "Let Boswell look out for his stuff. Me, I watch mine own. Good business, it—"

"It ain't good business. It's stealing!"

Adam pointed to the telephone. "Go call mit the sheriff," he screeched.

Hannah hesitated. She couldn't call the sheriff. She couldn't have Adam taken into town and thrown in jail. Yet—"I thought *you* were honest." The recollection of Jim's words decided her. She walked grimly to the telephone. She took the telephone directory off its hook, and, without looking at Adam, who was still daring her to call the sheriff, she looked up the number.

Hannah took the receiver off the hook. Her voice did not tremble as she gave the number.

"Could I speak to the sheriff?" she said loudly.

"Gott, Hannah! *Hannah! Hannah! Stop it!*" Adam tried to yank the receiver from Hannah's hand.

"Gott, Hannah, I pay for him. I pay for him."

Hannah put the receiver back. "Give me the money," she said firmly. "I'll pay for it."

"I pay him mineself. Gott, such a—" But Adam brought forth his long money pocket and counted the bills into Hannah's outstretched hand.

"We don't have to steal to live, Papa," she said quietly. "I'd rather live on wormy bread and beet molasses than eat stuff that you stole. Some way, we gotta pay for what we get."

"Gott, Hannah, mit the poorhouse—"

"We won't go to the poorhouse. You're gettin' paid every month, and next year is a new year. Maybe we'll have lots of rain. We've already had snow, and we'll get more. We'll have beets twenty ton to the acre. Sure, we can pay our way. Does Adam Schreissmiller, the renter, have to steal lambs to eat? No, we hold high our head, Papa."

"Gott, sure I done him, Hannah. Next year we raise the big beets." Adam brightened. The worried lines lifted for a moment from his face.

As Hannah went over to the Boswells' she thought of what she would say to Mrs. Boswell. It seemed to her that stealing must be a common trait among her people. She thought of Katie Heist, of stories told by Kniemer, Ochmidt and others, of bills beaten, of sharp deals, of small appropriations made from the boss's supplies. "Not honest." Jim was right.

"We want to buy one of Mr. Boswell's lambs so we can butcher it," she said to Mrs. Boswell.

"You'll have to wait until Mr. Boswell gets home." Mrs. Boswell's voice was kindly.

"We—we need the meat right now. Today, even. You think this will be money enough? If it ain't, we'll pay more." Hannah couldn't meet Mrs. Boswell's searching gaze. "This is money for just one lamb. We gotta have the lamb." Hannah raised her glance, mutely begging Mrs. Boswell to accept the money.

"If that's the case, certainly, kill one." Mrs. Boswell's perplexed tone revealed her doubt.

CHAPTER V

THE month of January continued cold. The thermometer dropped to zero, went ten below, twenty below, thirty, then to thirty-eight. For weeks it stayed below zero. The ice on the lakes and on the irrigation ditches grew thick and hard as glass. There was deep snow in the higher back mountains.

Skating parties were organized. Jake took Hannah to the lake in Valley City, where they skated under electric lights. Fritz and Katie often went with them.

"This lake's all right but we used to have more fun down on the old irrigation ditch," Fritz grumbled one evening as a cold wind swept the lake. "The high banks kept off this damned wind. And I like an open fire to warm by."

"Well, what say we have a party?" Jake cried. "We'll have roast weiners and we'll build a fire. The ice is swell on the Big Irrigation Ditch back of Schreissmillers. What say?"

"Swell!" Katie agreed.

"The old man'll kick me off the place," Fritz growled.

"He won't, Fritz, you come and see," Hannah urged.

On the afternoon of the skating party Hannah said to Adam, "Fritz is coming tonight to skate."

"Gott, he don't!" Adam pounded his knee with his fist. "He don't come inside mine house! He no son of mine!"

"Papa, Fritz has helped you good. Think of all the years he worked and helped you."

"He no son of mine."

"All right, then. He's my brother. I want him to come here."

"I say he don't come. Shod op! Shod op!" Adam pounded his fist on the table.

Hannah wished that she knew how to say the right thing. Her mother had known how to manage her father. What was her secret?

"If Mamma was here," Hannah said suddenly, "it would hurt her if you said Fritz was no son of yours or of hers."

"I no can do it. Not even for her what is dead. I love mit your mother, Hannah, but that Fritz, I spit in his face if he comes in the house." Adam got up from his chair and started pulling on his coat.

"Papa, you want people to say how Fritz works for you 'til he's twenty-one and you never pay him and then you kick him out of your house and don't speak to him? You want people to say how Adam Schreissmiller has a little soul that can't forgive his son? Adam Schreissmiller, who goes every Sunday to church, forgives not his own son? You think the minister will think high on you?" In her earnestness Hannah dropped back into some of the crudeness of her mother's speech.

"Hannah, they say that?" Adam stopped with one arm in his coat.

"They will say it, Papa, if you don't treat Fritz decent. You know how they all turn up their lips when Lizzie's name is mentioned. How she don't speak to her own people."

"Gott, Hannah, I don't know how I speak mit Fritz. I don't can do it."

"Sure, you can. All you got to say is, 'Hello.' That's all. Sure, you're the big renter. You can afford to forgive Fritz. He works only in a feed mill."

"Yah, sure, me, I'm the renter." Adam complacently smoothed his mustache.

When Fritz did later edge into the kitchen at the rear of the laughing crowd, Adam was reading at the table. He raised his graying head and spoke, "Come in. Set yourselves. Shut the door, Fritz." Then he set to reading once more, as if unconcerned.

Carrying her skates in one arm, Hannah stopped near her father. She patted his shoulder and whispered, "Good."

The crowd of young people trooped outside and tramped across the fields to the ditch. A bonfire was soon going briskly. "All here except Tabia," Katie Heist observed.

"Tabia? Is she comin'?" Hannah was surprised.

"Sure, I told her an' she said she'd come."

An hour later Tabia arrived in a sleek roadster with a sleeker looking young man. She barely spoke to the skaters. Going to the fire, she sat on a log while her companion put her skates on her.

"Thinks she's smart, too good for us," Jake Heist grumbled.

Hannah wouldn't admit to Jake that Tabia worried her. Always wanting money, always making up excuses so she wouldn't have to come home even to visit—she acted just like their older married sister, Lizzie, as though she was ashamed of them all.

Thereafter Hannah skated by herself or with some of the other boys. Out into the darker end of the ditch she skated with the Kniemer boys and with the Ochmidts. When they tried to put their arms around her, she skated back into the light of the fire, laughing.

Tabia caught up with her once as she was skating alone. "Say, Hannah, I gotta have two dollars. I just gotta have it."

"But, Tabia, I just gave you a dollar last week. We had to do without some things for me to do it. Part of it I'd saved for some new stockings for myself."

"You don't need no stockings. Where do you go? Jake Heist'd think you was swell if you didn't have nothin' on." Tabia giggled, and then wheedled. "Come on, Hannah. Be a good sport. I gotta have the money. Honest to God, I have."

"I don't have two dollars, Tabia. I only have a dollar, and we need that."

"Listen, let me have the dollar and I'll pay you back when

I get paid by the minister. Please, Hannah." Tabia clutched Hannah's arm with her thin fingers.

It seemed to Hannah that Tabia never came home unless she wanted some money. Tabia never asked Adam. She knew she wouldn't get anything but a curse.

"Tabia, I don't have no money. Papa uses my money that I get from Mrs. Boswell and when I do have some extra the boys or Martha need so many things. You ought to be more careful."

"Aw, please, Hannah, let me have the dollar. Please. I tell you, I gotta have it. I'm desperate. I just gotta have it."

"Don't hang on me so, Tabia. I'm tired. Go get my dollar bill. It's upstairs in my top dresser drawer folded up in my Bible."

"Gee, you're swell, Hannah." Tabia went skating away and she and her escort left without so much as saying good-by.

Hannah saw Jake from a distance starting toward her. She pretended not to have noticed and skated off down the ditch into the darkness. She wanted to get away and think about Tabia.

"Say, Hannah Schreissmiller." Katie Heist caught up with her and grabbed her arm. "I'm gettin' sick and tired of the way you treat my brother Jake. Just like dirt under your feet. I seen you treat him like mud tonight, and I'm tired of it."

"Oh, lay off, Katie. I like Jake but I ain't fallin' on his neck. I got enough troubles without any more."

"Yeah, I s'pose you'd fall on Jim Boswell's neck an' like it! You been treatin' Jake like dirt ever since you had that date with Jim a year ago when your old man licked you. If you wasn't to blame, why'd he whip you, and why'd the Boswells send Jim away? I'm goin' to tell you somethin'. You won't like it but I'm gonna tell you. Jim wouldn't wipe his feet on you. He never went with you only when he had a fight with his girl. And God, the girls he's had! And I'll tell you something else. He's gonna marry that Eileen he's been going with for the last year."

"He's been gone for the last six months," Hannah reminded her sarcastically.

"Dumbbell! He writes to her. I know Rachel who works for Eileen's folks and she says Eileen gets letters from him all the time, and Rachel reads them whenever she gets a chance and they're plenty hot, believe me. I seen one of them an' I know. And Eileen told her folks she was announcing her engagement to Jim this spring, and another thing, Jim ain't comin' home no more. He's gonna get a job. So now, what you got to moon over?"

"I'm not mooning."

"No? Well, what you wipin' your feet on my brother Jake for? Thought you was goin' to hook a swell with lotsa money, didn't you? You make me sick. Jim wouldn't wipe his feet on you."

"Oh, shut up about feet!" Hannah cried. "Better you look to your own. They're not so clean. If us Schreissmillers are such dirt, what you goin' with Fritz for?"

"You shut up about Fritz—"

"Shut up about my business, then!" Hannah was angry. "I don't need you to run my business for me."

She left Katie and skated farther and farther down the ditch. Jim was engaged, Jim not coming home, she'd never see him again. Clearly, she had been very foolish to count the days until Jim should come home. It was true that Mrs. Boswell hadn't said a thing about Jim not coming home. But then, Mrs. Boswell never mentioned Jim to Hannah. Could Katie be wrong? Katie was seldom wrong in her gossip. She had had her ear attuned to every breath of scandal since she worked in at Gundstroms'.

"Hannah! Yoo hoo! Hannah!" Jake's voice broke in upon her thoughts.

"Say, kid, what's the trouble? Tell it to old Jake." Jake slipped one hand around her waist.

"Things never seem to go right," she said humbly.

"Sure, it's hell. If you was to try thinkin' of yourself once in a while, Hannah, you'd have more fun."

"I feel like an old woman."

208

"Well, you don't look like one. You look mighty damned sweet to me, Hannah. I think you're pretty swell."

Hannah didn't push him away. His thick-set shoulder felt comforting. His arms gave her a sense of security. For the first time his lips were gently tender and sweet to her.

CHAPTER VI

DURING the cold winter weather Hannah pulled the torn dirty wallpaper from the kitchen and front room walls. She scoured the woodwork until most of the paint disappeared.

From Mrs. Boswell she obtained paper and ivory paint with which to redecorate the two rooms. She consulted Mrs. Boswell about the best way to paint the woodwork, and was gratified when the older woman became interested to the extent of explaining the procedure, and lending her books on painting and interior decorating for her to study.

Hannah set energetically to work. She sandpapered the woodwork according to instructions. But when the soft paint was dry it failed to measure up to the hard finish of the Boswell woodwork.

Hannah asked Mrs. Boswell why.

"Oh, but Hannah, our woodwork has the highest grade of enamel on it. Yours is just flat paint."

"I wanted it to look like yours," Hannah spoke slowly. "Do you suppose if I was to do extra work for you, like your washing and ironing, maybe, that Mr. Boswell would buy me some enamel?"

"Why do you want to do that, Hannah?" Mrs. Boswell's voice was gentle. Like Jim's, Hannah thought.

"Well, I gotta live there for four years, and it seems easier to do the right thing if you live in a clean decent place with nice things. We don't have any pretty things in our house like you. It's all dirty browns, and dingy colors all faded—" Hannah stopped. What was the use of telling

210

Mrs. Boswell that the dun-colored house and the dun-colored interior filled her with despair?

"You shall have the enamel, Hannah. And, if you want them, I have my old curtains from the front room. I folded them and put them away last year. They seemed too good to throw away."

"Oh, Mrs. Boswell, you're swell."

"Hannah, the word 'swell' is not one of the best in the English language." Mrs. Boswell smiled as she spoke.

"That's what Mamma always said," Hannah spoke softly. "I appreciate your telling me, Mrs. Boswell. Thanks."

As Hannah enameled the woodwork in the Schreissmiller front room she thought of Ana, whose voice was gentler than Mrs. Boswell's, whose dignity was greater. Yes, her mother, dressed in wide gathered skirt almost sweeping the ground, in black lace head shawl framing a weathered, wind-beaten face, had been as much a lady as Mrs. Boswell who dressed in the finest of stylish clothes and who lived in a bright, clean house. But her mother had lived in a clean house. She had not been dirty, ever.

"Ach, Hannah, better no paint *als* dirt." Hannah smiled as she thought of her mother's words. Tears dimmed her eyes.

"I'm going to keep house, now, Mamma," she whispered aloud.

When the painting was finished Hannah attempted the papering of the kitchen. She had helped her mother paper the rooms in Shag Town.

She waited until Saturday when Alec was home, for she knew there was no use asking her father to help.

Standing on top of the kitchen table, Hannah held the strip of pasted ceiling paper above her head.

"Hold it straight behind me, Alec," she said, and tried to press the strip of paper straight across the ceiling.

"Alec, I gotta take it off. It's crooked."

"Aw, it's all right. Leave it be. You're too finicky. It looks better'n the dirty stuff that's on there."

"But I want it to look right." Deliberately, Hannah loosened

211

the strip. Once more she endeavored to paste the paper as it should go.

Her arms ached in their sockets. The back of her neck was like a coal of fire. She felt that she would scream if she held her arms aloft another second.

Alec fidgeted, moved sideways. Hannah felt the pull of the paper, heard the tearing sound.

"Alec, you've torn it! Why can't you stand still?"

"Aw, I'm done. My arms ache till I could yell. I'm through. You can put your old paper on by yourself." Alec dashed the paper to the table top and jumped to the floor. He grabbed his cap and coat and ran outside.

How was she going to paper the kitchen by herself? She couldn't. She had to. The kitchen was going to get papered. Grimly she set to work pasting a new strip of ceiling paper.

Once more she stepped upon the table. Once more she held the strip aloft. Doggedly she attempted to set one end of the strip in a straight line.

"Good night! What do you think you're doing?" Frieda Hergenboch's cheerful voice startled Hannah.

"I'm tryin' to paper and I can't do it," Hannah admitted, and she lowered the strip of paper to the table.

"Well, I should say not. Fred's going into town. I'll stay and help you paper." Frieda started taking off her coat and hat.

"Fred, you go on. I'll help Hannah." Frieda spoke to her husband as he came to the door.

"I'm a champeen paper hanger. Give me a pair of overalls to cover my suit and I'll help put the ceiling on." The cheerful voice ironed the tiredness from Hannah's face and body.

Fred's firm, sure fingers set the strips evenly while Hannah held the paper upward behind his broad shoulders. With Frieda pasting new strips, the ceiling was put on in short order.

Adam came in from the barn. He sniffed his nose, twisted his mustache. "Foolishness! Crazy mit the head!" he snorted. "That's woman's work, Fred. What you do it for?"

Fred laughed. "It's a man-sized job, Adam. Come up here and try it."

"Bah! I don't!" Adam spat in the coal bucket.

"Say, you better go to town with me. I'm going to see about taking out my first naturalization papers. You better become an American, too."

"Gott, crazy mit the head, Fred. Me, I don't take no papers. Mit American I don't—"

"You'll never go back to Russia no more than I will. I'm buying my own place, and I don't ever intend to leave this country, so I'm becoming a citizen. I went to school here, and here's my home." Fred's voice was sober and sincere. "Why would I want to go back to Russia? Why would any one? You can have no property there. I saw Reuben Liepner last Saturday night—"

"*Liepner!*" Adam shouted.

"Yes, he's been in Kansas two years, he said, since he got back from Russia. He got in the old country just as the war broke out, and they took all his money and sent him and his family into Siberia. He got away and came out—by way of Siberia. Some of his boys starved to death. The whole family came down with smallpox, and the rest of the boys died except his youngest one. You ought to see him, Adam. Blind in one eye, face all pock-marked. Seeing Liepner and talking to him was one of the reasons I made up my mind to take out my papers."

"Gott! Liepner! He took five thousand dollar mit him." Adam shook his head as if in disbelief.

"Sure. You're better off here. Didn't you read that letter in the Omaha paper telling how there was not an animal in Russia? Not even rats or mice, or cats. All had been eaten up."

"Yah," Adam agreed. "Might you is right, Fred. Might, I better take out mine papers here. Wait, I go mit you."

During the argument Hannah had not said a word. Now while Adam dressed in his bedroom she smiled at Fred. "Fred, you're a peach. You know just what to say to him."

"I spoke only the truth, Hannah. Your father knows when a man speaks truth."

After the men had left, Hannah and Frieda put on the side wall paper.

"How long you think this'll stay clean with all the kids running around?" Frieda asked.

"It's going to stay clean—if I have to skin them a—" Hannah stopped. She sounded like her father.

In a quieter tone, she added, "The children like clean things as well as I do."

"Yeah, but too many kids is sure a curse. I bawled all the time I was carrying this last one of mine, but when they brought it to me, I loved it. And when it died, only two days old, I bawled my eyes out. That's the kind of a fool I am. But I don't want no more. Wait till you marry Jake and have to live in a shack with a kid coming every year or two."

"Frieda, don't. When you say things like that it hurts. Fred's good to you!"

"Fred's the swellest guy on earth, even if he is my own husband. I was talking about babies, not husbands. Jake's a good kid, Hannah. He's as good as any of them, I guess. You set the date yet?"

"Oh, Frieda, no! I don't want to marry him! Sometimes I like him all right. Other times I just can't stand him! Everybody keeps throwing us together. It makes me sick!"

Frieda nodded her head. "I thought not. You ain't got over that Boswell yet."

Hannah remained silent. It was true, she knew. She never would get over Jim. She'd tried, but it was no use. Every time she went over to help Mrs. Boswell she looked at Jim's pictures. Jim, in his car; Jim, half smiling from the mantel above the fireplace in the living room; Jim, in profile, sitting on the piano; Jim, laughing on his mother's dresser upstairs. How could she forget him, when each week she saw his face looking at her—that half laughing glance in a still face.

"You *better* forget him." Frieda's voice brought Hannah back to the present.

"I won't marry Jake!" Hannah flung the words out defiantly. "I've got to put in these four years, and then I'm goin' to get away. I gotta have some freedom, Frieda."

"What you workin' yourself to death on this old house for, then?"

"I don't know, Frieda. Inside of me, I gotta be something. I gotta do it. I won't get no more schooling, but I gotta learn how to live. I gotta live like I was somebody and I'm going to!"

"Don't shout. I'm not deaf."

"That's what I mean, Frieda. Mamma was a perfect lady. I never heard her shout in my life. Mrs. Boswell, even, when she gets the maddest, don't—doesn't ever raise her voice. Sometimes I think there's not one bit of Mamma in me. I'm just like Papa. I can hear my voice raising to a shriek just like his, and it's easier for me to yell and pound my fists than it is to speak like a respectable person."

"You make me laugh, Hannah. You ain't like old Adam. You're just like your mother. You even talk like her. Your voice sounds just the same lots of times, low, sweet, like music. You're just trying to find fault with yourself."

Frieda's words brought Hannah some comfort. *Was* she like her mother? Did she have her mother's voice? But she wasn't calm as her mother had been. In bed she prayed silently, "O God, I gotta be a lady. Help me to be calm and not get mad. If I could be just like Jim's mother—or Mamma, even."

CHAPTER VII

WHEN Hannah had finished painting the boys' room up-stairs she called to them. "Coonie, Solly, Chris, look at your room. Ain't—isn't it sw—fine?"

"Gee, it's swell, Hannah. You can almost skate on the floor, it's so slick."

"Don't let me catch one of you skating on this varnished floor, and don't let me catch you setting on the bed in your dirty clothes, nor with your feet on the bed either."

"Aw, gee, Hannah, I guess we like pretty clean things as well as you do."

Hannah felt ashamed. In a more friendly tone she asked them what they thought of her own room. They all seemed genuinely pleased.

That evening Hannah sat at the old organ after supper and played by ear—songs that her mother used to like, hymns from the hymnal, and even popular music.

Adam came to the organ and actually sang—singing in a deep melodious voice. The younger boys called for "Three Blind Mice." Hannah pumped the old organ and joined the children. She laughed. This was the way life should be—clean, joyous, full of laughter.

But the next day, when she was taking a bath in the old washtub in the middle of the kitchen, she lost her temper when Coonie came dashing in unannounced. There was no lock on the door. She finally propped a chair against the door knob. There was no privacy anywhere and her bedroom was too cold to bathe in.

"Gott, mit baths all the time!" Adam stamped his feet and
216

shook his fist as he saw her emptying the tub. "Baths! Baths! Baths! Gott, you use all the waters! Mit waters fifty cents for one load you use it all for baths! On Saturday nights is all we take baths! You hear me good, Hannah!"

Mrs. Boswell had said a person should take a bath every day. Well, Hannah vowed, she was going to take a bath every day, water or no water.

In a magazine which Mrs. Boswell had given her she found an article on voice culture and how to lower the speaking voice. Hannah read it thoroughly. She thought of how loud and shrill her own tones were at times. Especially when she got mad at the boys. She waited to practice until she was in the house alone one Saturday. The children were down in the field playing.

"Pick a good easy chair," Hannah read. She promptly sat in Adam's brown leather rocker.

"Relax and breathe deeply."

Relax? How did a person relax?

"Sink down in your chair. Breathe deeply." Hannah sank and breathed until she could hear her breath whistle.

"Now you are ready to use your voice. Repeat something from memory which you like."

What did she like? A prayer—yes—

"Our Father, Who art in heaven—" Her voice sounded funny and she felt foolish. She looked around to be sure that she was alone in the house. Maybe she'd better try the words of a song.

"Thou art my portion, O my God—" It didn't sound any better. No matter, it had to be said. Grimly, she quoted from memory:

> "O save Thy servant, Lord!
> Thou art my Shield, my Hiding-Place;
> My hope is Thy word."

Now what came next? She looked at the magazine.

"Relax. Press the soft spot below your breast bone. Pant like a dog."

Hannah panted. Just like old Shep, she thought, and this

made her think of Deke, and of Jim. "Not honest." Hannah straightened her shoulders. She *was* honest. And when he came home in the spring she'd tell him so—tell him in a sweet, low, serene voice.

Reading the instructions, she placed her hand on her stomach and said, "Ha! He! Hi! Ho! Hoo! Who *are* you? Who are *you?*"

Hannah exulted in making her voice ring more deeply in the silent room.

"Ha He!—" A loud jeering came from the kitchen door.

"Ho, ho! Hannah's holdin' her stomick and talkin' to herself," Alec yelled. "Come see her. Go on, Hannah! Keep it up! We wanta watch you some more." Reinie, Chris, Coonie, Solly, and little Martha crowded around Alec in the doorway.

Hannah looked at their grinning, mischievous faces, and felt as if she could cry.

"You kids get outa here. You're always a sneakin' around the house. I can't take a bath. I can't do nothin'. Get out!"

"Want sumpum to eat," Reinie pleaded with a sober face.

"Get out! You don't get nothing to eat!" Hannah threw the magazine at Alec. He dodged and herded the children out of the doorway, laughing loudly.

Hannah followed them to the door. "And don't you come—" she stopped her shrill shouting. Standing motionless, she looked at the magazine on the floor.

Like her father, she had yelled. She knew all at once that not all the voice lessons in the world could ever change her loud strident tones when she got mad. Slowly she picked up the magazine and closed the door. Her mother or Mrs. Boswell would never have spoken so, no matter how angry or upset they became. Voice lessons had not made their low, serene tones. Clearly, and for the first time, Hannah sensed that it was an inner grace which prompted the serene calm of those she admired and loved. An inner peace—"Pray mit God und He give you peace, Hannah, mein liebling."

Hannah laid down the magazine and went upstairs and hunted for her Bible. She took it downstairs, and, sitting at the kitchen table, slowly turned the thin pages, reading the words, hunting for guidance.

At last words with definite meaning for her alone stood out before her.

"Though I speak with the tongues of men and of angels, and have not charity, I am become as sounding brass, or a tinkling cymbal—"

Charity meant love. She had no charity, no love. If one spoke with love in her voice, Hannah thought, then that person could not speak in a hard, high voice.

"And though I bestow all my goods to feed the poor—and have not charity, it profiteth me nothing."

Hannah knew she worked for her family. She'd fed them, but she hadn't loved them, none except Martha.

"Charity suffereth long and is kind."

She had suffered but she hadn't been kind.

"Doth not behave itself unseemly, seeketh not her own, is not easily provoked, thinketh no evil."

Clearly, Hannah had had only the thought of herself. Was a Christian life just loving others, doing for them with love in your heart? That had been her mother's way. Her own life verse came into her mind:

> *"Rejoicing in hope,*
> *Patient in tribulation,*
> *Continuing instant in Prayer."*

She *had* coveted happiness only for herself. She *hadn't* rejoiced in hope, not since she had been confirmed. She had *not* been patient, neither had she continued to pray. Only when in deep need for herself had she ever prayed.

"Ach, Hannah, der most beautiful verse in der Bible, you have," her mother had told her.

At last Hannah rose and laid the book on the stand table in the front room.

"Reinie, Chris. All you boys. Cookies!" Hannah sent a calm, serene voice echoing across the back yard.

CHAPTER VIII

JIM BOSWELL did not come home with Mr. and Mrs. Boswell, although they had gone East for his graduation expecting him to return with them. On their return, without Jim, Hannah, cleaning the Boswell house, heard Mrs. Boswell, talking on the telephone, say: "Jim's going to New York for the summer. He has the promise of a job there. If it doesn't materialize, he will be home. Probably in July or August."

A job in the East! Hannah found herself hoping that Jim wouldn't find work. She was cleaning the clothes closet in Mrs. Boswell's room and she stopped before the dark eyes of the picture on the dresser. At least he wasn't marrying that Eileen Grandon.

All through the second hoeing Hannah continued to think of him. In the evenings she cleaned her house, or sewed on new cotton dresses for herself and Martha, and she was kept too busy patching, cooking, washing, to think very much of herself. But as July merged into August the thought of him dominated her. She had not heard a word about him spoken in the Boswell house.

One day, she had seen a letter with the New York postmark and Jim's name in the corner of the envelope. Mrs. Boswell was outdoors saying good-by to a friend. Hannah knew that she could read the opened letter undetected. She extended her hand toward the white envelope—and stopped. "Not honest," had been the last thing Jim had said to her. Leaving the letter untouched, Hannah turned away.

The next day, as she washed clothes out under the big cottonwood tree in the Schreissmiller back yard, she thought of how Katie Heist read other people's mail, as did Rachel, who worked for Eileen Grandon's parents. Was Jim right? Not honest. Hannah rubbed a pair of overalls more vigorously.

"Hannah, look at my rock. Ain't it perty?" Reinie held up an ordinary rock for Hannah to inspect.

"*Isn't* it pretty. You must not say 'ain't,' Reinie." Hannah smiled at him as he sat on the ground pouring rocks from one tin can to another.

"Pitty?" Martha, now past two years, held up a rock.

"Yes, pretty," Hannah laughed.

She wrung the suds from one of the boys' shirts and looked at her hands. They were red, and wrinkled from the hot water and soap, with holes worn through the skin on the first knuckles. They did not look like a lady's hands. *But my clothes are clean.* She looked at, and exulted in the lines of clean white sheets and bright colored garments. No holes in her clothes these days! Neat patches adorned the boys' shirts and overalls. And—*my hands look much nicer in the winter when I have more time to take care of them.* Such reflections as these were interrupted by the mailman stopping at the Schreissmiller box. Hannah went to get the mail at once.

Walking back up the lane, slowly, she glanced through The Valley City News, and opened the paper to the society page. There, staring out at her, was Eileen Grandon's picture— Jim's Eileen. And she *was* Jim's Eileen, for, underneath the picture, was the statement that the parents of Miss Eileen Grandon had announced her engagement to Mr. James Boswell at a dinner given to friends of the two families.

Hannah stood still in the center of the dusty lane. She felt sick, beaten and old. Slowly she read the account of the dinner party, hearing the laughter, seeing the happiness on Eileen's thin face, the lovely clothes, the smooth hands, the well-cared-for faces and bodies.

"Mr. Boswell has accepted a position in the East." The words seared themselves in Hannah's mind. "No date has been set for the wedding." There was no comfort for Hannah in that.

Hannah went wearily into the back yard and sat down on the back steps, still holding the paper, but her eyes looked past the printed page into a future without Jim—Jim, with his laughing black eyes, his black hair, his thin face, his lips.

"Lookit the perty rock, Hannah! Hannah! *Hannah!*" Reinie offered Hannah a rock but she did not see him.

"Pitty." Martha clung to Hannah's knee but Hannah saw only Jim's laughing eyes.

Adam, coming from the barn, wiping sweat from his weathered face with one horny hand, jarred Hannah from her thoughts by sitting down beside her and groaning as if in mortal agony.

"Are you sick, Papa?" she asked. His face was a sickly yellow; his hand trembled as he wiped his face.

"Where do you hurt?" Hannah shook his arm, trying to make him answer, but he only groaned louder. "Do you want me to call the doctor?" She got up.

"Gott, Hannah, sick mit mineself; sick so I die," Adam moaned. "Look by this. *Look! Look by him!*" He held aloft a small, sickly looking, cream-colored sugar beet.

"Like a turnip, he is. Gott, Hannah, what I do? What I do?"

"Give it time, and it'll grow as big as the rest," Hannah said listlessly. Crying over a sugar beet! What if the whole prop of his life had been removed as hers had been? Once more she sat down on the step.

"Gott, Hannah, he don't grow! *Nematode! Yah! Nematode!*" Adam shrieked and waved the small beet in the air.

At the word *nematode* Hannah was shaken alert. That word was dreaded by all beet growers.

"*Nematode!* Papa, are you sure?" Hannah took the small beet and, looking at it intently, saw what looked like white mold.

"Yah, nematode, he is. The factory field man say that ten acre is nematode. I don't get two ton mit the acre off him. Turnips, that's what. Turnips! The field man, he pull one beet, und two beet und three beet. Here he pull, und there he pull, all over he is pull, und the beet he is all the same! Mit little white worms like threads so fine they look like mold

222

oncet, und the beets they don't grow. Gott, Hannah, what I do? What I do?"

"I don't know. I don't know what you'll do."

"Seven year I don't can raise beets on them ten acre," Adam moaned the words. "Just once in them seven year do I get to raise beet on him. The factory man say so. Ach, mein Gott im Himmel!" Adam covered his face with his hands.

"You'll have to plant corn, or alfalfa, or barley, or wheat," Hannah said without conviction.

"Yah, but Hannah, waters, he is high und no moneys is in them crops. No moneys like sugar beets. Everything, he go backways, never do he go forways. Always backways. Und the work, he is so hard! Everything, he is hard."

Everything *is* hard, Hannah thought as she rose wearily to hang up her clothes. Everything took too much work, no matter what it was. Papering a room, seeding a lawn, making a dress, working beets, or even just taking a bath in a galvanized washtub. It was easier to be dirty, easier to be lazy, easier to never try to do anything. What was the use when everything always went backwards?

Morning, noon and night, Adam worried about the nematode beets. The children seemed noisier than ever. The house seemed harder to keep clean. Hannah felt tired all the time. The joy of living was gone. At times she felt that she could not stand another day of the same round of ceaseless duties.

Finally she took the car and drove down to see Olinda. If Olinda and Henry would move into the Schreissmiller house, Henry could work for Adam and Olinda could keep house.

The front yard of the Goelzer place was cluttered with all kinds of junk. Hannah picked her way to the back yard and to Olinda's one-room, tar-paper shack. The yard in front of the shack was not even swept; boxes and tin cans littered the doorway; slop and refuse were dumped near by. Scrawny chickens picked near the door.

Hannah knocked at the open door. No answer. She looked in.

On the floor, on a sheep-lined coat, lay Olinda. Her mouth

223

was open and she was breathing loudly, fast asleep. The table was littered with dirty plates, saucerless cups and half-filled dishes of food. Flies swarmed over everything. Olinda was too lazy to mend the screen door and keep it shut. The floor was spattered with grease and mud was ground into the splintery boards until it had caked. The room stank of soured milk and dirty diapers. The windows were fly specked; fifty-pound lard cans contained soaking diapers; the top of the stove was caked with burned grease; ashes had been sifted out onto the floor; the oilcloth on the table encrusted with old food and weeks of dirt; dirty bedding covered the one bed in the corner where small Marie lay sleeping beside the new baby. Olinda was having babies just about as fast as possible, Hannah thought, and turned her gaze again upon her slovenly, dirty sister.

Olinda opened sleepy eyes. "Oh, hello, Hannah," she said, and sat up. "Gee, it seems good to see you."

"Are you sick?" Hannah asked.

"No, I ain't sick. I was just tired so I laid down for a nap. I don't never feel real good, but I ain't no sicker than usual."

"If you'd clean up this house, you'd feel better, Olinda. It's filthy. You weren't raised in dirt. Mamma was clean."

"Yeah, an' she died. Well, I aim to live awhile and not work myself to death like she done."

"You're not living. Mamma lived. She didn't lay in filth and laziness. Her life meant something."

"That's right. Jaw. You don't have to live in no one-room shack. You got that old lady Boswell wrapped around your thumb so she gives you paint and varnish, and even puts a lawn in front of your house so you can set on it. You've got plenty of room. But I don't see you ever inviting us to come live with you."

"Part of the paint I worked for. Part of it was given because they knew I'd keep it clean. It takes work to keep a house clean, Olinda. A clean house doesn't just happen. You gotta wash dishes when you feel like you're too tired to move your arm. You gotta scrub floors when your back aches so

224

you can't bear to bend it and your knees are so stiff you can't stoop even. That's what keeping house means."

"Well, I can't do it," Olinda whined. "I ain't strong like you are. If we could move in with you, I could help you and we both wouldn't have much work to do."

This was what Hannah had come for. But now she shook her head. "There's no room, Olinda. If you'll heat some water, I'll help you clean this house."

"Forget the dirt. Dirt'll be here after you're dead and gone. Let's visit. I see by the paper where Jim Boswell's going to get married. I s'pose you and Jake'll be the next on the list. If you take my advice, you won't never get married. Kids comin' every year and a mother-in-law snoopin' all the time. That old fool near drives me crazy. I know she's—"

Hannah left as soon as she could. There was no use letting Olinda and Henry move into Adam's clean house. They'd last just long enough to get everything battered, torn and filthy like a pig pen. Then Adam would kick them out and Hannah would have to come home to clean things up again. Better never to leave.

Adam still worried about his nematode beets. "What I do, Hannah?" he kept asking her.

"Let's go out and look at them," Hannah finally said.

They went through the rows of beets, stooping now and again to pull a beet. A few of the beets were large, but most were small, covered with the white, fine threadlike nematodes. Here were the best of the beets, the big beets, and now their strength was sapped! Could so small a thing as this fine mold sap the strength from these beets? It most certainly could.

"You might as well stop worrying. Next year you'll have to plant something else on this piece of ground," Hannah said at last.

"Yah, that's what Boswell and the factory field man say. Gott, Hannah. Everythings, he go wrong."

On Sunday Jake Heist took Hannah to the evening services at the church. He did not take her straight home, but stopped his car on a side road.

"Well, Hannah, everybody's gettin' married. What say we

225

do the same?" He put his arm around her and tried to draw her closer to him.

"Everybody's got us married now. We might as well stop their worrying. Katie and Fritz are gettin' married and I seen by the paper where Jim Boswell's takin' the leap. Say, what's the matter? I ain't poison!"

"You make me tired, Jake. I'm sick and tired of every one saying, 'I suppose you and Jake'll be getting married.' I'm not ever going to get married. All I'll do is stay home and keep house for Papa and grow old and ugly. That's all."

"Listen, let's get married and we'll live with the old man. I'll—"

"Keep your hands off of me, Jake. I hate to be mauled and pawed. I like you but I want you to keep your hands off of me."

"You don't think much of me, Hannah, if you don't ever want me to touch you. Sometimes you act like you loved me and other times you act like you hated me. When you love a guy you want him to put his hands on you. You want him to pet and kiss you. I bet you never told Jim Boswell to keep his hands off of you the night he took you riding. I know Jim Boswell and—"

"Please leave Jim Boswell's name out of this and *please* take me home," Hannah said desperately. "I guess I don't love you, Jake. You better get a girl that likes to have you touch her."

"Them's my sentiments too, Miss Schreissmiller. I can tell you there's plenty of girls in this world beside you. Maybe they ain't so swell lookin'. Maybe they don't have great big blue eyes and hair like gold, nor swell clothes like you been wearin' lately, but they ain't no icicle that freezes in a feller's arms."

"Take me home."

"Okay, Miss High-uppity. Now that your fancy Jim Boswell's getting married, just who do you think you'll find that's good enough for you? You make me sick."

"It's mutual," Hannah said quietly.

"Mutual?" Jake snorted. "Huh, that's old lady Boswell's

pet word. That's what you been doin'. Trying to live like the Boswells. Too good for decent guys."

Hannah remained silent. She knew she didn't consider herself too good for Jake. She wanted only one man near her.

"Get you another girl, Jake. There's no use waiting for me. I couldn't get married if I wanted to."

"I think I'll take your advice. It listens good."

CHAPTER IX

TABIA was in her second year of high school, but she was no longer at the minister's. One year had been enough for the minister's wife, as well as Tabia.

"I got a swell place this year. A professor's home. Everything is just swell, but I need some money," Tabia announced.

Hannah reluctantly complied and told her to be more saving.

When the beets were pulled, topped and hauled to the sugar factory, winter settled down in earnest.

Alec would graduate from the eighth grade and was to be confirmed at Easter. Hannah helped him in the evenings with his catechism and Bible lessons. Studies were not too easy for Alec, but when he once learned a thing, he did not forget it. Night after night Hannah sat with him while he recited the Ten Commandments and their meaning, the Creed, and the Lord's Prayer.

Hannah sat sewing with Alec's catechism open on the table near her. "Give the first commandment, Alec."

Alec laboriously recited the words.

"Give the meaning." Hannah set a neat patch on Reinie's overalls.

"We should fear, love and trust in God above all things." Alec grinned with satisfaction. He knew that one.

"The second commandment," Hannah prompted. "Its meaning?"

"We should so fear and love God as not to curse, swear, conjure, lie or deceive, by His Name, but call upon Him in
228

every time of need, and worship Him with prayer, praise and thanksgiving."

"Alec, you'd better think about that particular commandment when you are swearing."

"Gee, Hannah, the old man swears every day of the week, and on Sundays, too. I guess he don't swear in church, but that's about the only time. He—"

"That's enough, Alec. Go on."

When Alec had finished with the tenth commandment, he sat a moment. "I never thought of it before, but I guess the old man busts a lot of them commandments, don't he?"

"That's no way to talk about Papa. He's an old man, Alec, and he never has had the chance you've had. He never had a chance to go to school as you are doing. Maybe he doesn't know any better. You do know better. More shame to you if you don't do what is right."

"Gee, I know, Hannah. I was just thinkin' about how he used to swipe water until you sat down on him."

"Don't let me hear of you doing anything like that. With your schooling you know better."

"Say, Hannah, do you suppose he'll let me go on to high school like Tabia?"

"I don't know, Alec. High school costs a lot. Tabia's got two more years, and she's always wanting money."

"All she does is chase around. Me, I want to study. And I'm big. I betcha I could play football. Gee, wouldn't that be swell, Hannah. Just think, me aplayin' football. Oh, gee whiz. Just see what a muscle I got, Hannah."

Hannah felt Alec's flexed arm and smiled. "Time to get to work on your catechism. Everybody else is in bed."

"But, Hannah."

"I'll talk to him, Alec. Don't you say a thing about high school. I'll ask him."

Alec was confirmed and graduated from the eighth grade; the beets were planted, thinned, and hoed through the second time, and Hannah had found no occasion to speak to Adam about Alec going to high school. She suspected that all she could say would do no good. When she watched Alec, standing so tall and broad shouldered, she knew that his very bigness was his undoing. Adam would never part with such a stalwart worker.

"Hannah, have you asked the old man, yet?" Alec would ask.

"I'll talk to him this evening, Alec."

She did when the others were in bed.

"Alec wants to go to high school."

"Gott, he don't!" Adam was emphatic.

"He's smart, Papa. He'd make us proud of him."

"Yah, proud mit himself like Tabia what speaks to no one so good is she. Und so smart she makes herself on the street. Bah, high school, he is foolish."

"The youngest Kniemer boy went to high school this last winter, and one of the Ochmidt boys will go next year."

"Alec don't go." Adam removed his shoes and took off his work socks.

"But, Papa, you're starting to become American. All the Americans send their children to high school. You want to be like the Americans now that you are becoming American."

"Gott im Himmel! Hannah, I don't can done it. Last winter I buy mineself one new car, und I buy you mit good clothes, und Alec he is confirm this last year und new clothes it take, und I no can hire no more help. Gott, I don't can done it. Foolish mit the head it is anyways. That Tabia, it is money thrown away mit her. Better she be mit home scrubbing und cooking und helping mit you. She go und got married when she is done mit school und that is that. School, he is foolish. Und Alec, he big so he help. He work by me 'til he twenty-one. You hear? Und I don't want no more talk mit it."

The next morning Hannah told Alec as he was getting ready to go swimming with the other boys.

"I'm sorry, Alec. If you were little and puny, I might make him let you go, but you are big for your age and he needs your help."

"What do I care?" Alec said unexpectedly. "I don't want to go to school anyway. Cooped up in a little old desk. Gee, what do I care if I never see an old school again. Swell! Swell!"

Hannah, going down to the garden for vegetables, saw him

an hour later sitting with his back to a tree out of sight of the ditch where the others were swimming. He sat hunched over, his knees drawn up, his head on his arms. She wanted to go to him and comfort him. Long ago she had fought the same battle. It must be fought alone, she knew.

As the days shortened into winter, Hannah saw silence settle upon Alec as it had done upon Fritz. In the once laughing eyes a stubborn revolt smoldered.

Why was it, Hannah wondered, with some of the same revolt, that the healthy, robust and sturdy body which housed the good spirit, the brilliant brain, should be yoked to the soil to work until twenty-one years had passed? Worked until the spirit broke and the good years were gone? The whole scheme of life was wrong when such a thing was possible. If Adam had been an American, and Alec had been the son of an American father, high school would have been a matter of course. Would Adam change when he received his final papers and really became an American? Hannah doubted it.

"Papa, are you sure you don't have to learn anything in order to get your final papers?" Hannah asked him.

"Gott, Hannah, such foolish questions, they ask. Is I married? How many kids do I have? When do I come into this country? Do I own mine own farm? Do I think America is the good country? Gott, such a simple questions they ask. Sure, I answer them all."

"But Fred Hergenboch says you have to study civil government," Hannah protested.

"Gott, Fred, he crazy mit the head." Adam stamped out of the house.

When January came and the Naturalization Court met, Adam, taking Mr. Boswell with him as one witness, went into town.

"I'd like to go with you," Hannah suggested.

"Gott, I don't have no womans mit me!"

Through the cold forenoon Hannah waited anxiously. She telephoned Frieda to see if Fred had gone into town to the court.

"Fred's sick in bed with the flu, and is he mad!" Frieda

groaned. "He says he's studied for two years and now he can't get in to town to get his papers. He'll just have to wait until next January. Did Adam go? Let me know how he gets along."

When Adam came into the house Hannah knew by his face and the dejected slump of his scrawny body that something had gone wrong.

"Let's see your papers," she laughed, trying to appear unconcerned.

"Gott, Hannah, I don't get him. Such questions, they ask." Adam sat down at the table. "Crazy mit the head, they is," he mumbled. "Who is Lincoln? What is legislature? Who a representative? What is a law, and how you make him? Mein Gott im Himmel!"

"By next January you'll know all those questions," Hannah said reassuringly. "You wait and see. We'll get a civil government book and we'll learn them. Fred Hergenboch was sick today so he'll be getting his papers next January. You can go to the court together. That'll be lots better."

The next day she asked Mrs. Boswell about the naturalization questions.

"Mr. Boswell says that he'll have to learn civil government. I don't know, Hannah, whether he can ever learn so much. It's hard on these older men."

"If I just had a civil government book," Hannah murmured.

"Jim used to have one. I'll look in the basement. It may be among his books."

Hannah went home with something of Jim's. His name was in the front of the book. There were notes throughout the book in his handwriting.

Employing all her knowledge of her father, Hannah set about to teach him civil government. It was hard, despairing work. At times it seemed that Adam could never learn how the United States Government was organized and operated.

One evening while Adam was studying Coonie stuck his head in the door and exclaimed: "Hey, Lizzie's comin'."

"Gott im Himmel!" Adam exploded. "That Lizzie, mit her

232

snooty ways, und her long nose stuck in everybody's business!"

Hannah agreed with her father but gave no sign and went to welcome her sister.

"What you doin'?" Lizzie casually asked. "Studying civil government? About time. I hear you flunked out last January. You might as well give it up. An old man like you can't learn such stuff. Too old."

"Mein Gott im Himmel! Old! Me? Mit one foots in the grave! Gott! I work mineself harder than your old man und you put together oncet! Bah!" Adam got up from the table and stamped outside.

"Lizzie!" Hannah cried. "You have no business talking to Papa that way. Why throw it into his face that he is old? He has enough to worry about without you making him worry about dying."

"Oh, lay off! Lay off! Get that kid away from me. Looks like you'd keep the brat clean!" Lizzie pushed Martha roughly away from her.

"I do keep her clean. Sticky fingers aren't a sign that she's dirty."

"Say, what's happened to you and Jake Heist? Did he throw you over? You was sure dumb, Hannah, to let that guy get away from you. Well, I gotta be goin'. I'm going out to see if Mary can help me clean house next week. So long."

"Boy, I'm glad that old hen's gone." Chris thumbed his nose at the departing Lizzie.

"Chris, you must not do that!"

"Huh, you don't like her no better'n the rest of us do. Boy, I'd hate to have to live with her. She'd shake your socks off and knock your teeth out!"

Hannah and Frieda Hergenboch went with Adam and Fred when they tried for their final papers.

It was a warm January day and the district court room was close, with the sun streaming through the long windows. The judge sat at his desk on the raised platform looking down upon the six men sitting in a single row within the enclosed railing. His face was calm and kindly. The examiner from Denver was sharp, crisp and very business-like.

The first man to be questioned mumbled his answers. The questions were hard, Hannah admitted.

"Fred's sure been studying, and he had all this when he took the eighth grade," Frieda whispered. "Do you suppose Adam'll make it this year?" Hannah pressed Frieda's hand. She was afraid. The questions were exactly the same as the ones in which she had drilled upon many, many times.

"Fred Hergenboch, bring your witnesses." The judge rapped his gavel on the desk.

"Hold up your right hand. Do you solemnly swear, to the ever living God, that the testimony you give before this district court is the truth and nothing but the truth?"

"Yes, sir."

Hannah sat erect while the judge questioned Fred's two witnesses. Fred stood tall and strong in his brown suit. His dark brown hair was smoothly combed back. He held himself proudly and answered the examiner's questions with sure, quiet dignity.

"Fred Hergenboch, how old were you when you came to this country from Russia?"

"Eight years old."

"Are you married?"

Frieda pressed Hannah's fingers when Fred said yes.

"How many children have you? Were they born in this country?"

"Two, all born in this country."

"How old are you?"

"Thirty-three."

"You live on a farm? How far from town is it? Do you own the place?"

"Yes, I am buying the place."

"Do you take newspapers? What are they?"

"Gee, he must think we're plain dumb," Frieda whispered. "He talks like we was just numbskulls."

"It's just a form they have to go through," Hannah whispered. "The judge told Papa what they would ask. It don't— doesn't mean anything."

234

The questions continued with Fred answering clearly. "Do you read English? Can your wife read?"

Frieda snorted.

But the smile was wiped off of Frieda's face when the examiner started firing questions on civil government. They were hard, but Fred answered most of them easily, briefly.

"Who is Congressman from this district? What is the highest court of the United States? Tell how a bill becomes a law. Who is the Chief Justice? How do the judges of the supreme court get their offices? For how long are they appointed? Who is the Governor, the Senators, the Representatives of Colorado?"

"Lord, I'm glad I'm not up there," Frieda whispered.

"Papa will never get his papers," Hannah said. "He can never answer such questions as that man is asking Fred." If her father didn't get his papers this time, she knew, he would never try again. He was too old.

Hannah looked at Adam's thin and bony back in its best black suit, at his thin gray hair, his wrinkled neck. He would come next after Fred. Even now the examiner from Denver was asking Fred a final question.

"Do you believe that this is a better government than the Russian government?"

"I do."

"That is all." The judge motioned Fred to take a chair at one side.

The judge called Adam's name and told him to bring his witnesses. Adam seemed frail and small to Hannah as he stood with uplifted hand. She relaxed when Adam sat down while the judge questioned the two witnesses, Mr. Boswell and Mr. Gundstrom, from Gundstroms' Dry Goods Store.

"Are you a citizen of the United States?" Hannah smiled at such a question being addressed to Mr. Boswell.

"Do you know the applicant? How long? To your knowledge has he ever been arrested? Is he a desirable citizen? Has he lived for eight years in this state?"

When the witnesses were dismissed the examiner picked up a sheet of paper. He read the regular routine questions that Fred Hergenboch had answered. But Adam was hesitant. He did not answer instantly, as had Fred. The examiner's voice rose a trifle.

"Talk a little louder please," he kept insisting.

"How many houses are there in the state legislature?"

Adam was confused. Hannah knew by the droop of his shoulders that he didn't know, even though she had told him the answer only yesterday. Her whole body ached as, mentally, she stood with her father.

"Answer the question," the examiner cried.

Hannah looked at the judge, who sat with his head tilted on one side, his hand over his mouth, a white cuff showing. His hand moved from his mouth. Kindly, friendly words came from the thin lips.

"Think a moment, Mr. Schreissmiller. Are there two bodies of men in the state legislature? Or three? Or four?"

Adam's shoulder straightened. He smiled at the judge and answered immediately: "Two."

The judge covered his lips with his hand and sat back in his chair. The examiner sharply fired the next questions at Adam. Hannah had begun to hate this smooth-faced young man from Denver, but all at once she realized she was misjudging him. She analyzed the questions and knew that these questions were not the hard technical ones that had been asked Fred.

"Who is the President of the United States? Who makes the laws? What is this court you are in now? Who comes around and fixes the valuation of your property?"

Hannah saw her father hesitate. He didn't know.

The judge spoke once more. "Who comes around in the spring to assess taxes on what you own?"

Adam nodded his head. Sure, the assessor.

Hannah was glad when the questioning was ended with: "Do you expect to live here the rest of your life? Do you believe that this is a better government than the Russian government?"

"Yah, sure."

While the remaining applicants were questioned Hannah leaned back in her seat and thought of their own home, clean inside, painted white outside. If her father received his final

236

papers, he would be American not Russian. If he got his naturalization papers he would be proud and could hold high his head. Maybe he wouldn't worry so much. He looked so old.

The last applicant took his seat. Then the judge said: "You are all admitted to citizenship this morning."

A dapper clerk stepped forward, called each applicant by name and read from a paper so fast that Hannah could catch only a few phrases.

"And renounce all allegiance and fidelity to Russia—heretofore been subject—bear true allegiance to America—so help you God."

As each man stepped forward to take the oath, the clerk handed him a paper.

"Well, that's over, thank the Lord," Frieda whispered.

But it wasn't quite over. A woman walked forward with a bundle of folded American flags.

"In the name of the Daughters of the American Revolution," she said in a formal voice, "I want to extend you a welcome to this country. I want to congratulate all of you. I am asked to present to each of you a flag of our nation. I hope that you may be good citizens of the United States."

"Fred Hergenboch. . . .

"Adam Schreissmiller. . . ."

Once more the judge spoke. "You may retire to the clerk's office and sign the papers there."

While Adam and Fred were signing the papers, Frieda and Hannah waited in the dim halls.

"You know," Hannah said, "this is a big day in our lives. It means we've severed the last link with old Russia. We are truly American families. No one can ever throw up to us the fact that we are Russian and not American." Had not Jim once called her father and herself "dirty Russian"?

While she had been speaking to Frieda, and while her thoughts had turned back to Jim, she had been half aware of a conversation going on behind her. The name "Eileen" had been spoken by a young man's voice. Suddenly Hannah heard with overwhelming clearness the young man say "—yes, she's

237

married, and not to Jimmy Boswell. What do you think of that? Well, I'll be seeing you soon." Hannah faced around but saw no one she recognized. She saw two young men shake hands and start off in different directions down the corridor.

CHAPTER X

JIM BOSWELL came home the spring that Tabia graduated from high school. Mrs. Boswell telephoned Hannah to
come help her clean house.

"We'll clean my son's room. He'll be home next week."
Mrs. Boswell laughed happily.

Hannah showed no emotion, but her heart started to sing.
Jim was coming home. Jim wasn't married. Jim. Jim.

Happier than she had been for months, yes, for years, she
made the work fly. *She* was cleaning Jim's room, getting it
ready for him, making his bed, cleaning the shelves in his
clothes' closet.

Would he look the same?

During the days that followed Hannah lived in a kind of
upheaval. She cleaned her own house. She groomed herself.
She washed her hair and had it finger-waved. She scrutinized
her face each day, looking for flaw or blemish. Clear com-
plexioned, delicately modeled, her face looked gravely back
at her. Her eyes, blue as ever, shone. So did her golden hair.
She had to smile. She tried on a new print dress, and was
glad she was so slender. She wasn't two pounds heavier than
she had been the night of the ride with Jim. And now Jim
was twenty-five. Twenty-five—*a man.* Hannah smiled at the
recollection of having said she was old. She was only twenty-
one—*only* twenty-one.

The day that Jim was expected home Hannah could not
work and kept glancing up the road.

"Gott, Hannah, we never gets the work done," Adam
stormed when he came to the house. "You go mit the field

und run the harrow oncet. Got a move! What you stand for?"

Standing on the harrow, dressed in her work overalls, Hannah went back and forth across the field. And Jim came home while she worked in the dust and dirt.

That evening Hannah saw Jim walk with his father and mother to the big red barns, get in the car with them and start off toward Valley City.

In the days that followed she kept track of his every movement. She saw him when he came home driving his new coupé, long, low, maroon. It became a habit to watch for its coming and going.

"Gott, Boswell make the moneys!" Adam grumbled, his voice filled with envy. "Twenty thousand sheeps he is going to feed next winter. Twenty thousand. Gott!"

But Hannah was not interested in sheep. Boswell hired Adam to feed some of the lambs on the Schreissmiller place. Jim would *have* to come over once in awhile to see about the feeding. But that would be next winter, not now, and this was spring.

And then Mrs. Boswell telephoned and asked her to help her serve a dinner in Jim's honor.

In spotless white apron Hannah went to the Boswell house. Easily, confidently, she cooked the dinner, set the table, saw to it that everything was perfect. Four years of training in the Boswell home had made her sure of herself.

She served the dinner quietly and efficiently. These guests were older friends of Mr. and Mrs. Boswell with only a few of Jim's friends. These were not snickering kids laughing at a green girl serving her first dinner.

As she served the dinner short, keen, appraising glances toward Jim told her that he was older, not quite so slender. His hair was the same glossy black, his lips the same—no, they weren't the same. The smile was gone from his lips.

Once he looked up and their eyes met. His black eyes were sober, shrewd, impersonal—looking at a stranger.

Jim was home, but he was not the same. The youth of him was gone. And he had looked at her as at a stranger.

Hannah washed the dishes, polished the glassware until it sparkled. But there was no sparkle in her.

240

It was a seasonal spring. The beet work was early, and as Hannah went hoeing and thinning through the rows of beets, she tried to answer the question she was afraid to have answered. Why hadn't even a little recognition come into his eyes? Was it because he felt that it was not the proper time to recognize a neighbor—a neighbor who worked in the capacity of hired girl? Hannah looked up at their own neat white house with its green lawn and well-kept fences. She was no hired girl, she felt, and she knew that Mrs. Boswell didn't think of her so.

One evening after Hannah had come from the field, bathed, combed her hair and was busily getting supper, he came to the door.

"Is your father here?" he asked impersonally.

"He's in town," Hannah answered, looking directly into his eyes. *Now* he would smile. She started to smile before she realized he was turning away. So that was that. Jim would have none of her. Dirt beneath his feet? Not honest? A dirty Russian? In mute and profound misery she watched him get into his new car. Then, in the empty kitchen, Hannah felt suffocated and hemmed in. She went out on the back porch and stood with the soft spring breeze blowing upon her hot face. She looked down at her immaculate house dress, her neat shoes. She looked at the hands she tried to cream each night and protect with gloves by day.

Now she *must* go away. It seemed to her that she could not wait until Tabia graduated. The first week in June—two weeks. It seemed an eternity.

During the next few days, as Hannah swung her hoe, she made her plans for leaving. On Saturday afternoon, she went to the minister's to see about working. Yes, they did need a girl. She could come the Monday after Tabia's school was through. The minister and his wife had not liked Tabia overly well, but then nobody had cared to retain Tabia for more than the one year. This last year Tabia had worked in three different places.

Tabia came home the day before the commencement exercises, dressed in a new frilly print. She lounged into the kitchen while Hannah was getting supper.

241

"You ain't coming in to see me graduate, are you?" she asked.

"Certainly, we are. We're all proud of you—the first Schreissmiller to graduate from high school."

"Oh, lay off. Say, what's the matter with you? Been to a funeral or something?"

"I've been working. I'm trying to leave everything clean for you. The house is more pleasant and all the boys will be in school next winter. Martha is five. I wouldn't send her to school until she's six. She'll be company for you." Hannah went on with her supper preparations as she talked.

"Oh, Lord, Hannah, I don't know how I'm gonna stand it. Papa gives me the willies with his shrieking and yelling."

"He's not so bad, Tabia. His bark is worse than his bite."

"Oh, I don't know. He beat you once, and you say now he's not so bad. You sound like Mamma. You talk just like her sometimes. Well, I gotta be goin'. Did you get my silk slip made? I need it, and say, have you got a couple of dollars you can let me have?"

"Tabia—"

"If I gotta stay here and work on this farm for the rest of my life, you might at least let me have a little fun the last day of my freedom. And say, if it's all the same to you—I'd just as soon none of you come in to see me graduate. I don't much fancy that string of kids in the auditorium and the old man with his old-fashioned clothes."

"*Tabia!* Papa dresses as well as any American. He is an American now, and the boys—"

"Well, if you and the old man have to come, all right. But you can't bring the kids. I got just two tickets, and you got to have a ticket to get in." Tabia slammed two tickets on the table and picked up her silk slip and Hannah's two dollars.

At supper Hannah told the boys, "Just the parents are allowed to attend the graduation exercises. Tabia brought just two tickets. But Sunday afternoon I'll let Alec take all of you to the show. It's a western. Won't that be fine?"

"Gott, der money!" Adam exploded.

"Huh, I guess it wouldn't a hurt her to sneaked a few extra tickets," Alec said, a wise look on his face.

242

"Alec, you'll have to get along with Tabia. I'm going to the minister's on Sunday evening."

"Gott, I don't like it, Hannah," Adam groaned. "That Tabia, I don't like her much good. No good mit the work. Bah! I think I hire Jake Heist again. He back from Nebraska. That Tabia, she no good." Adam shook his head as he pushed himself away from the table. "I don't see why you go, Hannah. I give you more moneys. I let you keep all of Mrs. Boswell's money she pay if you stay by me."

Hannah looked at her father. He was pleading for her to stay, offering inducements. She was touched, he seemed so old and pathetic. She pictured him with the hard brittle Tabia, but she shook her head.

"I've got to go, Papa. I've waited all these years. I—" She stopped. She couldn't tell him that she had to get away because she couldn't live here and see Jim every day.

"When Tabia is used to things," she said gently, "you will like her all right."

"Aw," Coonie shook his head, "she don't look no good to me."

Tabia didn't come home from the commencement exercises with Adam and Hannah.

"Listen, Hannah, I got a date for tonight, and I just gotta go. I'll come home tomorrow afternoon or evening. Honest to God. You don't know how important it is for me to stay in town tonight. Please, Hannah."

"You'll be out home, surely, tomorrow?" Hannah looked searchingly into Tabia's face.

"I'll be there."

When Hannah told Adam that Tabia would come home the next day, he snorted. "Gott im Himmel! Smart mit the head she is. Yah, stay mit town 'til the beets is all thin. Lazy like nothings! Gott, she no good, Hannah. I think on how I no can stand her. Hannah, if you stay, I buy you one new coat und dresses. More you make over staying mit town."

"I can't, Papa. I can't tell you but I have to go."

The next day Hannah met Jim and his father as she came in from the field. They were standing near the empty sheep pens, gesturing.

243

"Good evening, Hannah." Mr. Boswell spoke in his genial voice.

Hannah smiled at him. But Jim stood with his arms on the wooden gate of the sheep pen, nodded and touched his hand to his straw hat. Disappointed, Hannah went on toward the house.

She felt grimy and smoothed back her sweat-dampened hair with one hand, holding her gloves and hoe in the other. Her overalls were streaked with dirt and in the protecting canvases on the knees there were holes.

At the back gate stood a coupé. Some one had brought Tabia home. When she went into the kitchen Tabia was standing near the table. There was no one else in the room, only Tabia, dressed in the smartest of tweed suits. Brown gloves to match and a brown purse with a fine linen handkerchief beside it were on the table. Covering her newly marcelled hair was a new spring hat.

Hannah was acutely conscious of how bedraggled and dirty she herself must look.

"Whose car did you drive home?" Hannah asked as she went toward the stove to start the fire. Her bread was risen to bake. She would have to hurry. "You better change your clothes."

Tabia didn't speak.

"Why don't you answer me?" Hannah said sharply. "What are you just standing there for? Haven't you come home to stay? If you just came out for some money, say so. I've only two dollars, if that will do you any good. Goodness knows, Tabia, what you do with all your money." Hannah touched a match to the paper in the stove.

"What's the matter with you?" She looked sharply at Tabia who still stood silent.

"I don't know how to tell you," Tabia said at last.

Hannah slowly fitted the stove lifter into the stove lid. Keeping her eyes on the stove lid she carefully set it in place.

"What do you mean?" Hannah said.

"I mean I'm not coming home!" Tabia cried. "I'm never going to need more money. I'm married. I was married this afternoon."

244

Hannah braced her hands against the railing of the stove, her back to Tabia. "God help me, God help me," she thought. After a moment she turned around.

"Who is he?" she asked quietly.

"He's an American. His folks have got oodles of money. We're going to live with them. You can have all your money for yourself now, Hannah. You don't need ever to worry or think of me no more." Tabia's voice was high and brittle.

"You promised me, Tabia, four years ago, that if I let you go to high school, you would come home so that I could leave."

"Oh, for goodness sake! You give me the creeps. You stand there with your face a blank and talk to me about promises. You was a fool if you ever thought I'd come home here and look after a bunch of kids and an old fool who yells his head off all the time."

"If you could have given me just a few months of freedom, Tabia, I think I could have forgiven you."

"What do you want to get away for? You ain't had no other life. You don't know what you're missing. If I was to come home and stay, I'd a had to stay always. I wasn't going to do it. You can marry Jake Heist. Jake'll come here to live and everything will be swell. You shoulda married Jake a long time ago." Tabia shrugged her shoulders and picked up her purse and gloves.

Hannah watched Tabia for a moment. At last she spoke. "There are worse men than Jake Heist," she said. "Jake is honest, and fair and square. I can at least depend upon his word."

That night she told Jake she would marry him the next fall, as soon as the beets were out.

PART IV

HARVEST

CHAPTER I

HANNAH drove the hooked end of her narrow beet knife into a large, fat cream-colored sugar beet. With a deft motion she grasped the root with her left hand and quickly slashed off the green top. She mechanically tossed the beet into the topped pile and was about to bend forward to sink her knife into another untopped one, but stopped.

Adam was driving a team hitched to the puller up the field (the prongs of the puller dug beneath the soil loosening one row of huge beets at a time). The ground was hard this year and as Adam went up the rows of green-topped beets, Hannah could see his skinny, shriveled figure bouncing up and down on the iron seat with each motion of the puller. When he reached the end of the row his eye caught sight of her.

"Hannah! Got to work!" Adam yelled as he started his horses back up the field.

Hannah sank her knife into a beet and with a sure motion severed its green top.

Beet topping was drudging work. The beets were loosened by the puller. Then Hannah and the older boys pulled them from the ground by their green tops, knocked the dirt from the huge roots by striking two beets together, and tossed them onto the strip of ground made smooth by means of what the beet growers call the A frame. From these piles Hannah and the children topped the beets. They tossed the roots into new piles which Jake Heist later loaded onto the truck and took to the beet dump.

Hannah worked steadily but, from time to time, across the road, she could see Jim Boswell riding a beet puller on the

Boswell place. During the entire summer Jim had remained the same courteous stranger. He was always pleasant, spoke when she came within speaking distance. But—he was not interested in her.

Many times Hannah had felt she couldn't stand it.

Hannah sank her beet knife into another beet. She was foolish to let Jim intrude upon her thoughts. He meant nothing to her. Why should she be eternally thinking of him? Why should she expect him to look at her differently than he looked at her father, or Alec, or Solly? But she *did* expect it. Long ago Jim had kissed her and held her in his arms.

Near her Alec and Henry Goelzer worked. They swung their narrow hooked knives as if they were mechanical machines. Swiftly, surely, apparently untiring, moved their knives, their hands, their bodies. The flashing of their knives in the sun was like the winking of the electric sign in front of Gundstroms' in Valley City. The knife went down, came up with the beet fastened securely on the hook at the end. A quick jerk of the left hand caught the root of the beet and the knife in the right hand flashed downward, slashing the top of the beet from the root. The beet was tossed to the pile and the knife struck down again.

Hannah couldn't hope to keep up with them. Fourteen-year-old Solly and she worked better together. Solly was a thin, slight boy with a delicate face. He talked to her in his low, reserved voice as he would not to the others.

"Hannah, I've made the highest average in the room so far," he confided to her. "I'll be able to stay ahead if Papa doesn't keep me out after beet vacation."

"He won't keep you home, Solly. Don't worry." Hannah looked toward her father as he drove the puller. She saw him yell and yank at the horses. He jumped off the seat and bent down to look at the prongs in the ground. Hannah could hear him cursing clear across the field. When he came around to where Hannah and Solly were working he shouted: "Mein Gott im Himmel! The ground hard like one rock und the puller point, he is busted. Gott, I have go by town." He drove his team and the puller to the fence and tied the horses there.

250

A few minutes later Hannah saw him go tearing along the road in his sedan, headed for Valley City.

Hannah pulled her hat down lower over her face and went on topping. The sun was tanning her skin, but what difference did it make? Jim would not know whether she was tanned or white. And Jake Heist wouldn't notice.

"Hannah! Hannah! Come! Come!" A scream from the end of the field caused Hannah to drop her knife. Martha, she thought in panic, had Martha hurt herself?

"Which one? Which one?" she cried.

"Reinie's cut his knee. Reinie's bleedin' to death! He's cut his knee with the beet knife."

Hannah picked him up. He was screaming and holding his knee. Blood oozed out between his dirty fingers.

As she ran toward the house Hannah could feel Reinie's body stiffening. He had become blue around his nose.

"Oh, Reinie, don't. Please, don't. O dear God, don't let him have a fit." Hannah blew her breath upon the whitening face.

At the house she poured iodine on the cut knee and bound clean muslin around it. Then she washed Reinie's face with a cold washcloth until he came out of his fit. When his eyes opened and saw the rapidly darkening bandage he started to howl with fear.

"I'll have to take you to a doctor, Reinie. He'll wrap it up so it won't bleed." Hannah's voice was calm, but she was wondering frantically what she would do. Had Reinie cut an artery? She didn't know. It was bleeding more than it should and the cut was a long, deep one. She *had* to take him to town. But Adam had taken the car. Mrs. Boswell? She would take Reinie into town.

But no one answered at the Boswell house. Hannah thought of Jim riding the puller. His car was home, because she'd seen him washing it at noon. Thinking now only of Reinie, Hannah ran out of the house and down the road.

Jim! Oh, Jim! Stop, please! Jim!" Oh, couldn't he hear her? Yes, he was stopping his horses.

"Jim, Reinie's cut his knee, terribly. Will you take us into town? Oh, please."

"Sure thing!" Jim turned his horses toward the fence.

By the time Jim reached his car, Hannah had carried Reinie over from home. All the way into Valley City she held him in her arms.

While the doctor and the nurse took the necessary stitches and bandaged the cut, Jim stood beside Hannah. Relieved at having the doctor in command, Hannah became aware of Jim near her. She remembered the time Martha had almost drowned and Jim had held her arm and told her to be steady. Now, calmly, quietly, she stood, waiting, and Jim stood beside her, not touching her.

Jim drove his car to the back gate of the Schreissmiller yard. He lifted Reinie from Hannah's lap and carried the boy into the house and put him on the old green couch.

"Well, I expect you'll be right there for several days. But you'll be all right." Jim smiled at Reinie.

Reinie smiled back at Jim.

The smile faded from Jim's face as he turned to Hannah. His eyes looked into hers. "If there's anything more that I can do, don't hesitate to call me," he said. His voice had the same, quiet impersonal tone as usual, but his eyes were no longer so cold. Hannah felt he was aware of her hair, her face, her overall-clad figure. She was suddenly glad that Jake's engagement ring was in a teacup in the cupboard. She never wore it in the field.

"Still carrying the burdens of your family, aren't you?" he asked.

"I could do no different," Hannah answered.

"I hope the boy gets along all right." Jim went toward his car.

He hadn't said much, Hannah thought, as she went back to the field, but there had been a difference. When she went back to the field the beets seemed lighter to lift, easier to top.

Hannah continued to top beets each day. She kept Martha at the house to keep Reinie company, but Martha liked to go over to the big Boswell house whenever she found an opportunity.

Two days after Reinie had cut his knee, when Hannah

went to the house to get supper she found Martha rocking in her little rocker, Reinie lying on the couch.

Hannah smiled and went to the bread box and got some cookies. As she handed them to Martha she noticed a pin fastened to the front of her dress.

"Martha, where did you get that pin?"

Martha stopped rocking. She put her small hand over the pin. She looked at Hannah with wide eyes.

"I finds him, Hannah. I finds him right in the road."

Hannah looked at the golden, curly hair and large blue eyes. "Let me see the pin." Hannah held out her hand.

It was a gold tie pin containing one diamond. Hannah knew it well. She had seen Jim wearing it. She had seen it upon the dresser in his room when she had helped Mrs. Boswell clean house.

"Martha, you disobeyed me. Why did you go over to Mrs. Boswell's?"

"No, I didn't, Hannah." Martha rocked faster than ever. "I finds him, Hannah."

"She did too go . . ." Reinie started to speak but Hannah shook her head at him.

"Where did you find it, Martha?"

"I jus' finds him."

"Just where, honey?"

"Jus' any place."

Hannah stopped her questioning, defeated.

"Martha, come here." She gathered Martha into her arms and silently rocked her for a moment.

"Martha, Hannah loves her little girl. She wants her little girl to grow into a lovely lady like Mrs. Boswell. And Martha, lovely young ladies don't ever tell stories. They never take things which do not belong to them. Did you want a shiny pin so very much, Martha?"

"Yes! I want him *so* bad."

"Then, Martha, you must earn the money to buy one. You might gather eggs for me. You could feed the chickens for me, and you could save the pennies that Mrs. Boswell gives you once in awhile. When you have saved enough money, you can go to the fifteen cent store and buy a pin of your very own. We must pay for everything we get, Martha. Everything must be paid for. Don't you think that Mr. Jim will feel sorry when he finds his pin is gone? He probably worked hard to earn the money for his pin."

Martha started to slide down from Hannah's lap. Her face was sober. "I takes him back, Hannah. But he was layin' so easy like on top of the dresser." Martha touched the pin.

"That's a good girl. I'll walk over with you."

Hannah hurriedly started her supper to cooking, then she washed her face and brushed her hair until it shone. As she put on a clean dress and powdered her face she was suddenly tired. She wished she knew how to rear and teach Martha. She was so little. Should she have spanked her and told her she was a thief? But Martha wasn't a thief! People shouldn't leave things lying around for children to pick up. Did all little children steal?

Taking Martha's small hand, Hannah went across the road with her. "You must tell Mrs. Boswell you are sorry and that you won't ever take anything from her house again."

"Yes."

Mrs. Boswell was getting supper. She smiled at Hannah and Martha. "How's the sick boy?" she inquired happily.

"Just fine. Martha came over to see you," Hannah said quietly.

Martha soberly went toward Mrs. Boswell holding Jim's pin in her hand.

"I finds him upstairs—I won't take no more pins—not anything—"

"Thank you, Martha." Mrs. Boswell took the pin and looked at Hannah. "Thank you," she said. "I have a cookie for a good—"

"No, she must not be paid for being honest." Hannah's firm voice stopped Mrs. Boswell. She smiled at the older woman. "Thanks."

"Of course you are right, Hannah. Come see me again, Martha."

That evening, after supper, Adam went to town with Kniemer. The boys had gone off to play. Reinie and Martha were in bed. Hannah was alone in the kitchen stirring a cake.

A knock at the door surprised her. She opened the door to see Jim Boswell holding a pair of crutches under one arm.

"I brought Reinie a pair of crutches. I think they'll fit him. I broke my leg when I was about his age."

"Oh, thank you." Hannah took the two small crutches.

"I want to thank you for returning my pin."

Hannah could find no words to answer him. She could only look at him as he stood leaning against the side of the door frame. Her heart was pounding, the old breathless feeling gripped her as she looked into his black eyes.

"Hello, Jim." Jake Heist, coming onto the back porch, shattered the quiet moment with his loud voice.

"Hello, Jake," Jim said without looking around. "I hope the crutches fit. If they don't, maybe we can adjust them," he said and left.

"Say, is that guy over here makin' eyes at you again?" Jake demanded, shutting the kitchen door.

"He brought these crutches over for Reinie."

"Oh, yeah?" Jake caught Hannah by the shoulders. "Hannah, you and me's got to have a show-down. When that Jim was here before you couldn't see nobody but him. When he was gone, I said it was good riddance of bad rubbish. You're wearing my ring now. You're engaged to me. I don't want you making no eyes at him. You hear?"

"You're talking nonsense, Jake. Jim just came over to bring these crutches to Reinie."

"I seen him lookin' at you. I know him, he runs after everything that wears skirts."

"That's insulting, Jake."

"Well, he ain't asked you to marry him, and he never will. His kind don't marry your kind. Listen here, Hannah, you're my girl. You're engaged to marry me. I don't want no other guy even lookin' at you." He roughly pulled her to him. He kissed her again and again.

Hannah was still, letting him kiss her. Quietly, without emotion, she let him hold her. At last Jake released her and looked at her. "So-o, that's that. I guess I know how you feel. I might as well been kissing a store dummy for all the—gee,

255

Hannah—I'm sorry—but you used to like me." Jake's voice was choked and bitter.

"Jake, I do like you—but not that way. You better take your ring back." Hannah slipped the ring off her finger.

"Hannah, I wish he was in hell and burning. He won't marry you."

"You wouldn't want me, anyway, Jake, if I couldn't love you."

"No, I guess I wouldn't." Jake went outside into the cold darkness. Hannah heard his car roaring out of the yard.

Adam came home a few seconds later. "Crutches!" he exclaimed. "Where they come from?"

"Jim brought them over."

"Jim! Huh? Him! Hannah, I tells you—"

"Don't tell me anything, Papa. I'm twenty-one." Hannah's voice was calm, final.

CHAPTER II

JAKE did not come home that night. The next morning the Schreissmillers went to the field without him. Adam snorted and swore.

"Alec, you have to shovel beets," he commanded. "Und when I see that Jake I fire him. Gott, the good-for-nothings!"

Shoveling beets was a severe tax upon Alec's strength. The fewer number of toppers could not keep up. Adam was forced to hire one of the Kniemer boys to shovel.

The day after Jake Heist left, some of the Boswell lambs came in. They were turned into a field from which all the beets had been topped to eat upon the shriveling, browned beet tops.

Overnight, the weather changed to winter.

Working in the field became almost unendurable. Hannah's hands became chilled from handling the frozen, sleet-caked beets. Mud caked her heavy shoes. Mud stuck to the roots of the beets no matter how hard she cracked the roots against each other. A cold, rainy mist stung her face and chilled her body. The other workers were suffering as much as she.

Adam sat hunched down in the seat of the puller. Across the road Jim sat on a similar puller, his sheep-lined coat collar turned up around his ears.

"Gott, the beets freeze mit the ground," Adam yelled.

"It's too cold to work," Alec replied.

"God, I never seen such weather," Kniemer grumbled, beating his hands against his shoulders.

"Solly, you stay away from school und top beets," Adam ordered.

Solly looked at Hannah.

"Solly worked during the entire two weeks' beet vacation. He has to go to school." Hannah's voice was firm.

"Gott, he don't—"

"He's too little and puny to do much work." Hannah looked reassuringly at Solly. Solly's lack of ability to do work was the only argument that Adam could understand or would consider.

"Gott, such a troubles!" Adam did not argue further.

Hour after hour Hannah worked in the bad weather. At night all the topped beets left in piles in the field had to be covered with the green beet tops to keep them from freezing. In the morning the tops had to be removed before the beets could be hauled to the beet dump.

Hannah rose long before daylight, but even before she left her bed she heard the trucks and wagons going along the road to the beet dump. In the darkness of early morning she could see the glow of a fire near the Boswell Dump. In the light of the flames the dark figures of the haulers moved around like black shadows. Through the chill darkness came their boisterous voices. One morning Hannah heard Jake's voice above the other voices. She missed him. *Could it be?* Yes, she found she was wondering where he had gone.

"Gott, the dirt on the beets!" Adam groaned. "Mit dirt they run the tare up high like one cat. Mein Gott im Himmel!"

Adam wasn't the only farmer groaning about tare, and arguments were not unusual. One morning Hannah saw drivers jump off their wagons and go running toward the scale house. A crowd gathered.

"Some fight," Alec laughed when he came rattling back to the field in his empty beet wagon.

"What was the matter, Alec?"

"Ochmidt sailed into the weigher at the scale house and like to a give him the beating of his life. Said the weigher was docking him too much for mud. They been running the

258

tare higher every day, and Ochmidt said he knew he didn't have that much dirt on his beets. The factory sure think they're the king of the earth. Think they can do just as they please. If a few more of them would tie into a weigher, maybe he'd be a little careful how he socked the tare on the beets." Alec drove his wagon down the field to load up.

Hannah looked at the muddy beet in her hand. She knew that the weigher at the scale house took a sample of beets from each load to test for the amount of dirt and this percent of dirt was deducted from the weight of the load of beets. This was spoken of as tare. Every fall the farmers grumbled about excessive tare. Even Jim and Mr. Boswell grumbled.

"I'll tell you, Adam, the Farmer's Beet Association is the only thing," Mr. Boswell said. "The farmers have to stick together, and when they finally do stick together, the beet business will make them some money, and not be a hand-to-mouth enterprise as it is now." Mr. Boswell's voice was more emphatic than Hannah had ever heard it. He continued: "It's fellows like you, Adam, that make it hard for the rest of us. If you'd join and stick with us, we'd get a better contract from the sugar company in the spring, and we'd get a better deal all the way around. Think it over."

"Yah, that Boswell!" Adam said as soon as he was gone. "Just because he's president of the Farmer's Association, he think he know what everybodies should done. I don't see they get no bigger price for our beets for all the Association talk so big mit itself."

"Maybe that's the reason. If all the farmers joined as Mr. Boswell said, maybe it would be better for all of you."

"Gott, I don't. I don't have nobodies telling me if I plant beets or if I don't plant beets. I do like I think I do. Worries I got mitout no associations. Gott, Hannah, mit this cold weathers, the beets freeze themselves in the ground sure. Ach, mein Gott!"

Adam was right. In spite of working in cold, sleety weather. In spite of long hours that chilled the body to the bone, the beets froze.

"Gott, three acre I don't get out the ground," Adam moaned.

"Mr. Boswell had fifteen," Hannah reminded him.

"How you know it?" Her father looked up with interest.

"Jim told me when he came over to feed the lambs this morning."

"Gott, Hannah, you don't done yourself no good mit that Jim."

"I'll have to judge that for myself," Hannah told him gently. No use telling her father that Jim was never more than pleasant to her. Hannah knew she was living from one contact with Jim to the next.

Adam looked keenly at Hannah.

"You have a fight mit Jake?" he asked.

Hannah didn't answer.

"Gott, Hannah, you crazy mit the head if you turn Jake Heist down. That boy, he smart in the head."

On Sunday morning, Katie Heist telephoned Hannah. Her voice was high and excited.

"Say, Hannah, have you heard the news?"

"No."

"Jake's married! Been married for several days I guess. He just come in with his wife last night and told Mamma they was married. Just like that. He went to a dance at Factory City last week and they was married that night! Gee, who ever heard of such a crazy thing! Ain't you surprised? And boy, does she dress. And she paints like everything. Jake sure can pick 'em. See you at church."

Hannah turned from the telephone. Jake married! Married for spite to a girl from Factory City.

CHAPTER III

IN JANUARY Tabia came home bringing her month-old baby boy.

"Tabia, you shouldn't be out in this cold weather with that tiny baby," Hannah reproved her, taking the child from her sister's arms.

"I've come home to stay. I'm through with that lousy bunch. I can't do anything to please 'em so I got out."

"Tabia!"

"Well, it's the truth. They watch every move I make. You'd think I was something the cat drug in. I'm lazy! I'm good-for-nothin'. They raise their eyebrows nearly off their heads whenever I open my mouth."

"Tabia! Stop!" Hannah unwrapped the baby and Tabia sank into a chair.

"It's the truth, Hannah, so help me God! I'm through with 'em. Frank's no better than his mother, and that's sayin' something. She's the worst old crank that ever walked. And Frank, he sides in with her. He don't have a mind of his own. Just a nit-wit, that's what he is! He threw it up to me just this morning that I was a Russian! A *Russian!* I slapped his face and I left!"

"Tabia, you better go back and get things straightened out. You've got to think of this baby."

"I don't go back. I'm home to stay until I get my strength back and then I'm goin' to get a job. Believe me, I'm not goin' back there and have that old hen look down her nose and tell me what to do."

"You've had life entirely too easy, Tabia."

Tabia stretched herself in her chair.

"Life's been too easy for you, Tabia," Hannah persisted. "The more I think of the way we did without things here at home so you could go to high school, the more I know that I made a mistake. You should have come home in the summer time and worked here on the farm."

"Oh, I don't know. I'm still alive and as soon as I get my strength and my figure back, I'm getting a job."

"Tabia, you're going back to Frank. Marriage means more than just a whim. Go back and do what they want you to do. Make yourself what they wish. Watch the ways of Frank's people. His people must be your people."

"I can't, Hannah. You don't know all of it." Tabia sat sullen and stubborn. "I'm not going back. I'm suing for divorce, and you nor nobody else can stop me. Frank can pay alimony to keep the baby and I'll get a job. But they don't get my kid. I don't wanta do any more talking about it."

Hannah had to admit that she could do nothing about Tabia. When the men were in the house, Tabia had nothing to say, but when she and Hannah were alone, she talked incessantly in a resentful, nagging monologue.

"You're better off not married, Hannah. Men are all alike. All they want is some one to lay with, and have their kids, and get three meals a day. Drudge, drudge, drudge, all they want is just some one to fill their bellies, that's all."

"Tabia, stop it!"

"Stop it! That's all you can say. You've been shielded here at home all your life. You don't know nothin' about men. Take my advice and don't get married, but if you are crazy enough to marry, don't live with your husband's mother. You'd better be in your grave. You'll wish you was dead more'n once if you get in a mess like I was in."

Hannah continued to work to the accompaniment of Tabia's wrangling voice. Sometimes it seemed to her that she would scream if Tabia didn't stop talking. She stayed outside the house as much as possible. There was peace in the barn milking a cow.

Being outdoors so much, Hannah was constantly coming in

contact with Jim Boswell for fifteen hundred of the Boswell lambs were being fed in the Schreissmiller sheep pens and Hannah often encountered Jim. They would speak for a few moments about impersonal things. "The lamb market doesn't look good," Jim said one day. "The market is dropping every day."

When Hannah went in the house, Tabia looked at her sharply. "Was that Jim Boswell you was visiting with?"

"He came over to look at the lambs. They are going to sort sheep tomorrow." Hannah took off her coat, unconcerned.

"Well, if you want my advice, you better stay away from that Jim Boswell. You'd better be dead than marry an American. I know. I been married to one."

"Don't start in on that, Tabia."

"It won't work, Hannah. These Americans think they're kings of the earth. We're just Russian; just beet-workers. Not good enough for them to wipe their feet on."

"You're not Russian. Neither am I Russian. We were born in this country."

"Yeah, but our folks come from Russia. The old man's Russian and all the Americans call us Russian. I guess even Jim Boswell called you a Russian once when he got mad at you when Fritz killed his dog, didn't he? And ain't that lousy Frank called me a Russian? Just wait, I'll get even with him and he'll pay through the nose."

"Tabia."

"Don't yell 'Tabia' at me. If you marry that Jim Boswell, if he ever asks you, which he won't, you'll see.

"I don't set down to suit Frank's mother. I don't talk to suit her. She don't like the way I wash my face, even. Said my neck wasn't clean, just powdered over the dirt. Oh, Lord."

Hannah found herself inwardly sympathizing with Frank's mother. Tabia most certainly wasn't clean. She left her clothes just where she stepped out of them. She was undeniably sloppy and lazy. Wearily, Hannah wondered how long Tabia was going to stay.

"What do you do, live outside all the time?" Jim asked her one morning.

"My sister's home. I don't need to be in the house so much."

Jim's eyes twinkled with understanding. "You're more conservative than your brother, Chris. He was visiting with me last night. He said, 'You know that Tabia, she just turns her mouth on and then goes off and forgets it. She talks 'til a fellow's head buzzes. I'd rather hear the lambs baa and the chickens cackle than her voice.'"

Hannah laughed. "I'm afraid that I agree with Chris."

"Not *your* voice. It's like music, Hannah." For an instant, there was a fleeting tenderness in Jim's eyes.

Hannah sang at her work paying no attention to Tabia.

"Hannah, what's the matter with that Martha? She's coughing so funny." Tabia asked.

"She's had a cold. She had the measles a month ago, and she hasn't been real well since. It's just a cold."

But it wasn't a cold. Hannah was up with Martha most of the night. The next morning she called the doctor.

"Whooping cough," the doctor pronounced.

"She's just had the measles," Hannah told him.

"Then you must take specially good care of her. Whooping cough and measles are never a good combination."

"Lord, I'm getting out of here," Tabia said as soon as the doctor left. "I'm takin' my kid and going to town. I'll go stay with Lizzie or somebody."

As Hannah cared for the whooping Martha, she felt that the only redeeming feature of this sickness was the fact that it had caused Tabia to leave. The silence of the house seemed wonderful after Tabia's garrulous jangling.

Martha's throat, weakened from the measles, closed when she was taken with a spell of coughing. Her face became blue, and her breath refused to come. Hannah, many times during the day, would catch her up in her arms, run with her to the door and frantically blow upon her livid face, or try to open her throat with her forefinger.

"What's the matter?" Jim came walking swiftly to the back

264

steps one of the mornings when she was working over Martha.

"She'll never come out of this one," Hannah sobbed.

Jim took Martha from her arms, held her face down and slapped her on the back. Martha came out of her choking with a strangling gurgle and a swift intake of breath.

"Kids are certainly a curse sometimes," Jim said. "How often does she have these?"

"I can't keep track of them."

"You look worn out. You're too thin."

"You don't look so well yourself," Hannah said and smiled.

"I'll look worse when these lambs are all marketed. We're taking a licking on them." Jim ran his hands through his hair. "You ought to have some fun once in awhile, Hannah. Sometimes you act as if you're married to these children."

"I've raised Martha."

During the following weeks Hannah sometimes thought Jim looked at her as if he cared. At other times she thought he seemed just as impersonal as when he first came home. He never so much as touched her hand. He never asked her to go for even a ride in his car. Sometimes Hannah told herself that he cared nothing for her.

"Ha, I guess that Boswell don't hold his head so high," Adam exclaimed one night. "Gott, twenty thousand lamb und they go down, down." His voice conveyed a gloating satisfaction.

"I don't think it's a thing to rejoice over," Hannah said.

"Gott, it done me good to see him lose der moneys. Yah, I guess he don't been so smart mit der head. Him, mit his associations und everythings."

"You'd better join the association. Fred Hergenboch is joining. He says it's the only way to get a fair price for your beets. Already the sugar factory is talking of a cut in price. Jim says you beet growers should join before the contracts come out. It's the association that will see that the farmer gets a decent contract."

265

"You talk like old Boswell. Gott, Hannah, we don't can raise beets for one cent less."

"You'd better join the association."

"Yah, might, I better done it. I think on him awhile," Adam agreed.

CHAPTER IV

AFTER the spring work started Hannah saw very little of Jim. The lambs were shipped and he had no occasion to come to the Schreissmiller place. Hannah was busy in the field. This year Adam said they would get the ground ready and plant the beets themselves, then he would hire contract beet-workers to work twenty acres. This left only ten acres for the children and Hannah to work, since ten acres of beet ground was nematode and would be planted to green beans and cucumbers, to be sold to the canning factories in Valley City. There was the usual talk of the farmers not signing the beet contracts sent out by the sugar factory, but the talk died down and the contracts were signed.

When the beets were ready to thin, Mr. Boswell came over and looked at Adam's fields of beets. He walked past where Hannah was hoeing beets with Alec.

"This is the best field of beets on your place or mine. The factory's got a new-fangled beet blocker, mechanical blocker, they call it, and they want to try it out on a good stand of beets, and then on a poorer stand to test it. Better let them test it on these beets."

"Yah, good beets I raise." Adam expanded under Boswell's praise.

The next morning the factory field man and several executives from the sugar factory came out with the government man, who was conducting the tests.

Fred Hergenboch and Frieda came over as well as several neighbors. Hannah went with Frieda to the field to watch the work.

The blocker was nothing more than the ordinary beet cultivator, but with the knives set so that six inches of beets were cut out and four-inch blocks of beets were left in the row.

Hannah listened to the comments of the farmers.

"You can't tell me that thing'll work on a poor stand of beets."

"Yeah, it's all right for a good stand."

"You can't get away from the hand thinning. This does the blocking but you got to thin by hand."

"What about in the fall? You have to top and pile by hand."

"Yah, I do mine mit mine kids," Adam agreed with the other farmers.

"It looks good to me," Jim Boswell spoke up.

"What you do when the rains don't come right und the beets is thin mit the row?" Adam argued.

"I don't think it will take many more beets out."

"Gott, you don't never thin no beets!" Adam snorted. "How that machine leave a beet closer mit the end of a vacant space. It don't. It cut out the beet. He don't have no eye in him. Gott! No machine work like a beet-worker."

"Machinery is coming. It's only a question of a few years until hand labor will be gone."

"That's right," Fred Hergenboch agreed. "I was talking to the government man who is doing this experimenting. He says they have a beet topper that pulls the beets, tops them and piles them. He's going to try it out on my place in the fall."

"Bah, crazy mit der head!" Adam snorted.

For several moments Hannah stood watching the cultivator work, then she turned to walk the half mile to the house.

"Going home?" Jim asked.

"Yes."

"I'll take you. My car's right here.

"What do you do? Stay at home all the time?" Jim asked as they walked toward his car.

"Most of the time," Hannah admitted.

268

"I have to go to Factory City tomorrow afternoon. Can you get away to go with me?" Jim smiled as he stepped on the starter.

"I don't know. I'll try. I'm supposed to be thinning beets. But we have only ten acres to work."

The next morning when she announced her intention Adam said:

"Gott, you don't go mit no Jim Boswell. You work mit the field."

"We'll get the beets thinned. Alec and Solly can hoe, while Coonie and Chris thin. Reinie and Martha can help, too." Hannah was undisturbed.

"Hannah, I tells you he mean you no good."

"Papa, let's not go over that. I'm twenty-two years old." Defeated, Adam went to the field to ride his cultivator.

It was a glorious day in early June. For a long time Jim didn't speak. But it was enough to be sitting beside him going places.

"Happy?" he suddenly asked.

"Happier than ever before in my life," Hannah said simply. "I used to think freedom was getting away from what you hated. Now, I know it's conquering what we don't like."

"Where did you learn that?" Jim asked and slipped his arm around Hannah's shoulder.

"You'd be surprised, Jim. Some day maybe I'll tell you." Hannah's voice was low and serious.

There was a long silence which was broken when Jim said, "A penny for your thoughts."

"I was thinking how much nicer you are now that you are older." Hannah stared at the road ahead.

Immediately the car began to slow until it came to a stop. "For that—" Jim held her close to him and kissed her. Briefly, tenderly, then he smiled into Hannah's eyes. "You're not the same girl I knew a long time ago, either. Much finer." Jim kissed her again.

Hannah sat silent as the miles flew by. She should have been thrilled at Jim's caress, but she felt more alone than ever. Jim had kissed her, but the passion of long ago was gone from his lips. Why was she disappointed? For months she had yearned for Jim's arms, for his lips. Why wasn't she happier? Oh, she was happy.

During the rest of the summer Hannah went riding with Jim at frequent intervals. As Hannah's trips with Jim increased, Mrs. Boswell's demand for Hannah's help decreased. Hannah sensed the increasing reserve of the older woman. No more did she laugh and visit with Hannah as they cleaned house.

"Hannah, I'm going to get a girl to work all the time, so I won't be needing you any more," Mrs. Boswell said one evening as Hannah finished ironing.

Walking slowly home, Hannah thought bitterly that Mrs. Boswell had nothing to worry about. Jim took her places, and kissed her, but his kisses didn't mean a thing.

That fall Adam let Solly start to high school. "Me, American. I guess mine kids just so good as that Boswell what lose so much moneys mit his sheeps last winter. Solly, he smart mit the head. Solly, you like go mit high school?"

Solly, sitting at the supper table, looked up. "Aw, naw. What's the use. I don't get to go."

"Yah, I say you go. Kniemer, he sends his boy und he stop by for you." Adam glowed with generosity. "Und Alec, he go mit you."

"Me, go to high school? I'm too old." Alec went on eating. "All I want is a job so I can have my own money."

"Gott, you don't! You work by me 'til you twenty-one!" Adam roared.

"I'm working, ain't I? What you hollering about?" Alec's voice was sullen.

In the fall, Jake Heist came to haul beets for Adam. For, although Adam contracted most of his beets, he had to hire the hauling done. Jake worked in silence.

Hannah missed Jake's old good humor and boisterous laughter. One evening he walked along with Hannah toward the house.

"How are you, Jake?"

"Not so good, Hannah."

270

"I'm sorry."

"She's no good, Hannah. I was a fool. I was mad. I got drunk, thought I didn't care for nothin' and this is the way it ended."

Hannah was silent. At this moment she felt more friendly toward Jake than ever. He personified for her all the people she knew who were fighting against circumstances they themselves could not change.

"Has that Jim asked you to marry him yet, Hannah?"

"You've not the right to ask, Jake."

"Lord, don't I know it," Jake cried. "But I know. He ain't.

"If I'd waited, Hannah, you'd a married me," Jake continued. "I know it. I was a fool. I'll never love any one else, Hannah. I never loved her. I never will love her. Sometimes I think I hate her. It'll always be you. Till the day I die, it'll be you." Jake's voice was tired and helpless.

"Perhaps that's the trouble, Jake. Women feel whether there's love or not. If there isn't love our lives are hopeless. Since you've married her, you should try to love her. Go out of your way to please her, to pet her."

"I can't, Hannah. I look at her and think of you."

Was that what Jim did, Hannah wondered? Did Jim look at her and think of Eileen? Hannah found herself feeling pity for Jake's wife.

"Jake, you've *got* to love her. Make believe if you don't. A person can do anything if he makes up his mind to do it. I know."

But as Hannah rode to town with her father and the children that Saturday night, she was not sure of anything.

"Another week, we go loose," Adam chuckled, as he drove past the sugar factory. "One week you see plenty beet cars go over the high line." He pointed to the high trestles.

Hannah heard the clanking of the metal as the bottoms of the cars opened, letting the beets fall.

In another week there would be the rush to get the beets out of the ground as fast as they could. Hannah looked at the many windows of the red brick sugar factory as they went past. Lights streamed out into the darkness. There was

271

a cloying sweetness in the air near the factory—a nauseating, smothering sweetness. It made her think of a field of seed beets in blossom.

"The pulp will soon be stinking," Hannah said.

"Yah, the beet pulp, he good," Adam agreed.

"I don't like the smell of it."

"Gott, he smell good, Hannah. The sheeps got fat on him. Boswell, he feed again this winter. Go more in the hole I betcha. Debts he got on his back so he don't never come out. So many names he have on his beet check this fall he don't have room so he write his own," Adam chuckled.

"What do you mean so many names?"

"Everything, he is mortgage. He mortgage his beets for everything. The bank, the machineries company, the feed company for corn und last year's hay, oncet. Gott, he owe everythings."

Hannah was in town on the fifteenth of November, beet pay day. Cars crowded the curbs, filled the center parking spaces of the streets and extended down side streets. Adam had gotten out at the bank and left Hannah to park the car.

Men stood on the street corners in bunches talking. Farmers thronged the streets. Every bank in town was overflowing with beet growers cashing their beet checks, or, as was more frequently the case, going to the bank to get what was left of their mortgaged beet checks.

Hannah went into the bank to hunt Adam. She had to have some money to get Martha some stockings. She could hardly make her way through the throng to her father. She noticed the quiet tenseness of the men, waiting. The grim, serious look upon faces, the anxious questioning in eyes as they talked to each other or to officers of the bank. Behind the railing at the back of the bank Hannah saw Mr. Boswell and Jim sitting and talking to the banker. Mr. Boswell looked very old. His hair was almost white, his smooth face had fine lines etched upon it. His loss on lambs had told upon him.

"Gott, Hannah, what you want?" Adam looked sharply at her.

"I have to have two dollars."

272

"Gott, I don't get mine check yet. Go mit the grocery store und wait."

As Hannah went toward the side door of the bank to leave, Jim glanced up, looked directly at her, nodded briefly then glanced quickly down at the paper spread before him on the desk.

He, too, looked old, Hannah thought, as she stepped into the fresh air outside.

CHAPTER V

THE price of feeder lambs did not come back that winter and spring, as many of the farmers hoped. They barely got their money back plus payment for their feed. The lucky ones got a very small amount for labor. Foodstuffs were down. The bottom had dropped out of the price of wheat and corn. Only the price of sugar beets held up. Last year there had been money in beets when there had been money in nothing else. During all the talk of surplus crop production the sugar beet farmers had stood secure.

In the spring there were serious rumors of price reduction in the beet contracts to be put out by the sugar factory.

"Gott, I don't grow beets for one cent less," Adam declared, as always. "They say they pay according to how much sugar is in the beet along with so much a ton. Gott, I don't like him."

Even Fred Hergenboch was worried. "It looks like we won't get much for our beets. If the farmers would stick together, we might get a fair contract, but they won't stick."

"This is only January, Fred. Plenty of time for the contracts to come out."

In February there was still talk of a cut in the price of beets. Farmers discussed the new contract. Officers of the Farmer's Association met with the sugar factory officials to discuss the terms of the coming year's beet contract. The association published long statements. The factory officials remained silent.

In March, when the contracts usually were issued by the

sugar factory, notice was sent out by the factory of their new price: a two dollar cut.

The association said, "No. Farmers can't grow beets for that price. No contracts will be signed."

"Gott, what I do, Hannah?" Adam moaned. "The association say we don't can sign the contract. Und the field man he was around mit the contracts today. He say the factory don't change mit its price. What I do? I got raise beets. Beets is where the money is. Gott, what I do?"

"You belong to the association. You can't sign a contract until the association releases you." Hannah was firm.

April came. Time to plant beet seed. Still no contract. Adam walked the fields by day, and paced the floor at night.

"The beets, they got been planted. Mine ground, he is ready und I no can plant beets. That Boswell und his beet association, he make me sick mit mine belly. That association, he worth that." Adam snapped his gnarled fingers in Hannah's face.

"I tells you I plant beets. When I am come to this country they raise beets for three dollar under what the price the sugar factory offer this year und we make moneys!"

"You worked beets by contract then. You didn't grow them," Hannah reminded him.

"Gott, Hannah, we got raise beets. Me, I take two dollar cut mit the sliding scale of sugar content. The beet help, he is cut, too. Gott, Hannah—"

Hannah tried to see Mr. Boswell to talk to him, but he was always away. The whole country was in a fever. The very livelihood of northern Colorado depended upon the growing of beets. It was the paramount issue in every one's mind.

At the supper table one night, Adam sat silent for a long time. At last he spoke without the usual moan to his voice.

"The farmers what don't join that association is the smart ones. Old Ochmidt, already he has all his beets planted. Already, a long time ago, he sign his contract. Yah, smart mit the head, he is, when he don't join Boswell's association."

"It's not Mr. Boswell's association," Hannah objected.

275

"It's a nationwide association. At least wherever sugar beets are grown."

"Yah, might, but Boswell, he is at the head of it. But I know how to fix him." Adam nodded his head. Slyly, he grinned at Alec. "Old Kniemer tell me what he do. Yah, und I done him like Kniemer."

"You better not listen to Kniemer—"

"Yah, Kniemer smart mit der head. He belong mit the association but his boys don't belong mit the association—so, his boys sign the contract so they grow beets."

"Papa, you can't do that."

"Gott, sure I done him. In the morning, Alec, und you, Solly. You go by the sugar factory und sign the contract und we get our seed so we plant beets."

"Papa, you're in the association. You can't do that unless they say you can. You can't break away."

Adam smiled knowingly. "Kniemer gets around the association. I is in the association, but Alec he is not, und Solly he is not, so I puts the crop in their name. They sign the contract, not me. Me, I don't grow no beets. Me, I belong mit the association." Adam smiled and licked his lips.

"But, Papa, you can't do that. That's not honest!"

"Gott, Hannah, we got raise beets. How we live if we don't raise beets? The association, he don't hold together nohow."

"Certainly, it won't hold together when you do as you are planning to do. Certainly, it can't do anything if all the farmers turn against it. You told Mr. Boswell you'd stick."

"Yah, und I am stuck. I don't raise no beets. Not a beet do I raise in mine own name. Me, I stick mit the association."

"There's no difference. You're not honest." Hannah thought of her father clogging the weir. Jim had blamed her for that. Probably he still blamed her. Did he still think of the time that he'd told her she wasn't honest? And here was her father planning to be dishonest again. Nothing she could say to her father would change him this time. He had learned of a legal technicality that he could use to beat the association. He was within the law, but he wasn't honest.

276

Others besides herself would say that he was dishonest. For her father's own sake he must not do what he planned. As she washed the supper dishes, her mind was in a turmoil. What would Mr. Boswell say? What would the other farmers in the association say? What would Jim say? Jim was the important one. More and more, he was managing the farm, taking his father's work over. Not honest. Not honest.

Hannah looked at her father sitting near the table reading the daily paper. He was old and shriveled. There seemed no strength in him; yet he was crafty, crooked. No, not crooked. Beets were his life. He'd sacrifice anything to maintain his standing as a farmer. Beets meant more money than any other crop, therefore he would plant beets, honestly, or dishonestly. Didn't he know that people would not think well of him if he did not stick to the association?

As she worked, she watched Alec, Solly and Coonie. They sat lounging around the table in the kitchen. Solly was getting his lessons. Alec sat looking into space, smoking one cigarette after another. Coonie was building a fence with matches. Adam was immersed in his paper.

If she went to the telephone hanging on the wall, they would hear her. But she had to tell Jim. She couldn't let her father and the boys go through with their plans. There was no use waiting until they went to bed. Adam would hear her telephoning even after he went to bed.

Hannah went into the front room. Aimlessly, she picked up some of Martha's toys. At last she went upstairs. Standing at the window in her bedroom, she looked across at the Boswell house. There was a light in the living room. No use going over there. She couldn't tell Mr. Boswell that she wanted to see Jim, and she felt that she couldn't confide her fears to Jim's father. Neither could she tell Mrs. Boswell. Jim's mother was more than cool towards her.

Hannah straightened and peered more closely out of the window. She saw lights flash on in the Boswell three-car garage. The Boswell sedan slowly backed out into the driveway. Possibly Mr. and Mrs. Boswell were going into Valley City. It wouldn't be Jim taking the sedan. He always drove his own coupé.

Hastily, Hannah brushed her hair, and prepared to leave. Quietly, she went through the front room to the front porch.

"Hannah, where you go?" Adam called.

"I'm going out in the yard. Just walking around," Hannah answered, her voice steady.

She made her way to the shadows of the big lilac bush at the gate. When she knew that she was hidden from the house by the bushes, she ran across the road and into the Boswell yard. If she went to the front door of the Boswell house, no one from home could see her. Maybe Jim's mother hadn't gone to town. Hannah went up the steps and stood looking at the door for a moment before she knocked. What if Jim's mother answered? What would she say to her?

It was Jim who opened the door. His shirt was open at the throat, his sleeves were rolled to the elbow, a black pipe was in his hand.

"Jim, I've got to talk to you." There was a catch in her voice.

"Hannah! Come in." Jim led her into the large comfortable living room. He placed a pillow for her on the big couch. He sat down in a deep chair facing her, and inquiringly he looked at her, waiting for her to speak.

"Jim, Papa's going to break over." Hannah looked down at her neat oxford. "He's going to have Alec and Solly sign the contract in the morning." Why didn't Jim speak? Why didn't he say something? Hannah looked up. Jim was smiling at her. An amused, tender smile.

"Why did you come over to tell me, Hannah?"

"It's not honest, Jim. It's not right. But I couldn't make him change his mind. He must not do it. I wanted you to talk to him. Maybe, he'll listen to you."

"You can't change these old men, Hannah. I've been expecting your father to break away. There's more than one doing as he's doing. The association can't hold them. They've always raised beets. They're used to taking whatever price the sugar company offers them. You can't blame them too much." Jim's voice was business-like, brusque.

Hannah rose to go. Her trip had been for nothing. Jim wasn't even interested.

278

Jim was looking at her intently. He rose. Laid his pipe upon a small table. He came close to Hannah, tipped up her chin with his strong fingers. "Look at me, Hannah. A long time ago, I told you that you weren't honest. I want to take that back, along with a lot of other things I said. I was just a hot-headed kid with too much temper." Jim smiled, and love and tenderness was in it. Hannah felt her throat tighten. Tears filled her eyes.

"Jim," she whispered, "that means more to me than anything else in the world."

And then Jim was kissing her. Demanding, passionate kisses without any thought or reason.

"Jim, you love me, sure?" Hannah cupped his face in her hands and looked searchingly into his eyes.

"What do you think?"

"I think—it's—heaven."

CHAPTER VI

THROUGH the summer and fall Hannah worked with a lighter heart than at any time in her life. Jim took her riding in the evenings whenever possible. On Sunday afternoons they often drove to a distant city, or through the lower mountain roads.

When irrigation work was heavy she did not see so much of him. Again in the fall, when the harvesting of the sugar beets was in full swing, there were few opportunities to be together.

Frieda Hergenboch, with her four months' old baby girl, came over to spend the day a week after the last of the beets were out of the ground.

"Hannah, I never saw you look so happy in all your life. It's just like a light was shining in you. Are you really going to marry him, Hannah?"

Hannah smiled as she took Frieda's stylish coat. She nodded. "That's our plan."

"Where's your ring?" Frieda caught Hannah's left hand, turning the slender fingers in her own more stubby palm.

"Times are hard, Frieda." Hannah wasn't going to let Frieda know that an engagement ring was the dearest wish of her heart.

"Not so hard for the Boswells that Jim can't buy you a ring, Hannah." Frieda's glance was shrewd.

"I'll have a ring, Frieda. Isn't it enough to be so happy you could cry? I wake up in the night, praying that nothing will happen. I'm so happy I can't believe it's really true." Hannah's eyes filled with tears.

"That's just the way I felt when Fred and me were first

married. You get over it after the first year or two and begin to worry about having a baby every time you turn around. Hannah, I swear to God, I don't have no more kids!"

"Frieda!"

"Hannah, Mamma had fourteen. I'm just like her. Already I've had four. We can't take care of no more. Fred's paying for his place and we want to send these three that's living through high school and give them a better chance than we've had. You'll realize all this after you're married. Do Jim's folks like the idea of his getting married?"

"Jim's mother doesn't approve. She never has me help her any more, and she just barely speaks when she meets me on the street in town. As long as Jim was in the East she liked me and helped me but sometimes I feel as if she almost hated me now."

"Well, one consolation, you ain't marryin' his folks. You're just marryin' Jim. You ain't gonna live with his folks, are you?"

"I don't know. Jim's never said."

"You don't know much of anything, do you, Hannah?"

"Yes, I know the most important thing of all, Frieda. I know that Jim loves me. He looks at me as if he thought I was the most wonderful person on earth." Hannah smiled. "If I never have more than that, Frieda, I've had more than Olinda, more than Katie Heist, or Mary, or Lizzie. For even though they married, I never saw one of their men look at them the way Jim looks at me. There's a lot of difference between passion and love, Frieda. They let passion get the best of them, then they have to marry to give the baby a name. They have to stay married because more babies come, and marriage becomes a habit. I want my life to be different than that. Anybody can marry and have a family. Not every one can have love such as I have."

"You're living in a fool's heaven, but here's more power to you, and I hope you don't hit the earth."

In May, just before the thinning of the beets started, Jim asked Hannah to go to the hills with him to spend the entire day. "Let's go early next Sunday morning and spend the

281

day. We'll hike, have our lunch, and—" He smiled, leaving the sentence in mid-air.

When Adam heard of it he pounded on the table. "Gott, Hannah! Mit church you leave so you ride mit that Jim! Gott! No good he does you, Hannah! It not right!"

"Frieda said she would teach my class." Hannah calmly pulled on a pair of hiking boots.

"Mit boys' pants you wear und boys' shirt! Gott, Hannah! Sunday is made for church und not for such business."

When she and Jim were in the car she kept her eyes straight ahead on the mountains in the distance. The far peaks were snow covered and reared their gaunt heads high into the blue sky. The closer mountains were black purple; the foothills a brownish green. Trees were coming into first leaf.

When Jim stopped he said: "I'm going to take you up on a hill so you can see the valley, then we'll come back to the car and go farther on to eat lunch. I know just the spot."

Pine needles, browned from the winter snows, lay thick under their feet. The old pines brushed their faces, caught at them, as they climbed. Hannah wasn't used to climbing. At last she had to stop.

"Jim, my shoes hurt. I can hardly walk."

Jim stopped immediately. "Get up on that rock. Let me look at those feet." Jim expertly loosened the laces.

"I'll have to train you better than this, Hannah." He laughed up at her, his eyes loving.

They climbed through the pines and came to a steeper incline of pure rock. Jim went ahead and reached back to take her hand.

"Well, here we are on the hogback." Jim stopped and faced toward the east. They were standing on the bare rocky summit of a peak. Below them lay the lower foothills, beyond lay the valley.

"There's the beet country of Northern Colorado." Jim extended his arm in a sweeping motion.

Dozens of lakes shone in the morning sun. The roads were like tiny threads criss-crossing the entire valley. Gradually,

282

toward the east, the trees grew fewer, and the plains of the dry lands stretched to the haze of the horizon.

They began pointing out landmarks to each other—in Factory City and in Valley City. They could not see their own homes. As always when human beings catch a broader glimpse of the world, they were awed.

"Beet growing's the best game on earth," Jim said suddenly.

"The beet country is entirely different to me," Hannah said softly. "I've seen only the growing of sugar beets. The planting, thinning, second hoeing, and the harvest. My hands have been in the dirt, grubbing out the extra plants so that one beet could grow. Everything for one beet—the strongest, the finest. It hasn't been a game. It's been hard back-breaking work. I used to hate the beets. Now I don't know what I think about them."

"And only a road has separated us." Jim put his arm around her. "From now on you'll see the landowner's viewpoint, not the beetworker's," he said protectingly. "Come on. I'm starved and I want to drive thirty miles before we stop for lunch. Love me?" Jim took her face in his hands.

"What do you think?"

"This—and this—and this."

Thirty miles farther up the canyon Jim stopped again. "We'll pack our stuff up that gulch. Just around the bend. The nicest little stream runs there, and the grassiest little nook in which to eat our lunch and spend the afternoon."

From the back of his coupé Jim took pillows, a blanket and a hamper of food. "Two baskets of lunch!" he said happily. "Let's stay for supper." He looked at Hannah for an answer.

"Let's." Hannah took a basket and a pillow.

"And this is the way to start a fire." Jim pushed twigs and dried grass between upright stones. "Barbecued steak is the best food there is. Ever eat any, Hannah?"

They had some and Hannah liked it. When they had finished lunch and were lying on the blankets, Hannah spoke of her debt to Jim's mother and of how she had once thought that if she could be like Mrs. Boswell she would be satisfied.

"I like you best just as you are." Jim reached out and drew Hannah down next to him. "I like the gold of your hair. I love the blue of your eyes. I love that little dimple there." Jim touched her hair, kissed the dimple. "Hannah, I love you."

Now it no longer mattered to Hannah what happened. She scarcely listened to Jim (what did anything matter except his love and his caress?), who was whispering, "It's true, Hannah, and it's for always." He took her left hand. Suddenly Hannah realized he had put a ring on her finger.

"Jim! Oh, Jim!" Hannah cried.

"I had to wait until everything was settled," Jim said quickly. "Mother and Dad have decided to move to Valley City to the town house. I'm to run the old home place. But they can't get possession of the place in town until the first of November. Let's make our wedding day the first day of November. Hannah, look at *me*, and not at that ring. I'll be thinking you are marrying me for my money and not for myself." Jim laughed.

"Jim! You know better than that." Hannah scarcely knew what she was saying. It had come true, *it had come true.*

"We're busted now, Hannah, but lambs will come back and so will the price of sugar beets. We've hit the ups and downs before. We'll ride them this time. It's hard on the old men, but the world always belongs to the young."

"Jim, I wish your mother liked me better," Hannah said idly.

"She likes you, Hannah. She'd be the same no matter whom I married. But she'll make a good grandmother."

"Jim!"

"I think we'll have two; a girl and a boy," he said with growing intensity. "I like girls best but I suppose we'll have to have a boy to carry on the Boswell name." Suddenly, he crushed Hannah against him. "God, Hannah, I can't wait until November. Don't make us wait, Hannah."

Hannah couldn't resist, but only murmured, "Jim, Jim, you're hurting me."

284

"Let's get married right away, Hannah." Jim's arms loosened their demanding hold upon her. "I know where I can get a license at a town that doesn't have a newspaper, so no one will know. I'll get it in the morning. Tomorrow evening, we'll be married. We don't need to announce it until November."

"I hate to sneak," Hannah whispered. "We're so happy."

"If you loved me, Hannah, you'd say yes—"

"I do. I love you better than anyone else in the world. I—"

"Tomorrow it is then. I'll come for you at eight o'clock."

It was nine o'clock when they reached home.

"Tomorrow night," Jim said as he kissed her good-night.

"Yes," Hannah agreed.

CHAPTER VII

ADAM met Hannah when she entered the kitchen. "Gott, Hannah, why don't you come home, oncet? Mit the mountains you go! Gott im Himmel! You lay—"

"No." Hannah's stern voice stopped her father.

"Gott, mit worry near crazy I make mineself. Frieda, she is in the hospital, und Fred, he calls und says will you come stay mit his kids. Gott! Und you is in the mountains!" Adam shook his fist as he shouted.

"Frieda! Why, she was all right yesterday."

"Yah, but today she don't teach mit the Sunday School class. She goes mit the hospital this morning, und you is gone! Get a move. We go mit Fred's house."

Hannah hurriedly changed her clothes. What had happened? Frieda had been all right the day before. She'd looked tired, but nothing out of the way.

"What's the matter with Frieda?" Hannah asked on the way to Fred's place.

"Gott! Fred, he don't say. He just say his mother und father is in Nebraska und no one is there to stay mit his kids. Und for you to come mit his house."

A neighbor, with Frieda's baby in her arms, was impatiently waiting for them. "I thought you never would come," she said. "I've got to get home to my own family."

Hannah took the baby from the neighbor's arms and went into the kitchen. Fred's oldest boy was downcast; the second boy was crying.

"Come!" Hannah said cheerfully, cuddling the baby in her arms. "It's time boys were in bed."

286

"Hannah, is Mamma gonna die?" twelve-year-old David asked.

"People don't die just because they go to the hospital, Davey. They go there to get well. Your father will be home soon. Everything will be all right." Hannah patted his head. After the boys were in bed, she fed the baby and tucked her in for the night.

In the quiet of the kitchen Hannah washed the dishes, mopped the floor, and set everything in order. She kept watching the clock. Why didn't Fred come? She picked up a magazine and sat down to read. It was no use. She looked at the ring on her finger. Tomorrow night she would be Mrs. James Boswell. It didn't seem right to be secretly married— it always looked suspicious when the wedding was finally announced. Not honest, exactly. They were both old enough, they didn't need to ask any one, but then, Jim's argument was sound. If they announced their marriage now, she'd have to move in with his folks. Jim couldn't stay at the Schreissmillers. It was better that no one knew they were married. What if— Hannah did not finish the thought. She looked at the clock. Twelve o'clock. She might as well go to bed.

The next morning she rose early. There were the cows to milk, pigs to slop, chickens to feed and water, breakfast and the boys' lunches. The baby was fussy. The boys didn't want to go to school.

"If your mother gets worse or anything happens I'll come get you," Hannah promised them.

They left reluctantly. Hannah took care of the baby, baked bread, darned socks, and sewed on a dress for the baby which Frieda had started. She telephoned Adam and was relieved when he said that Olinda had come to spend the day.

In the afternoon, Lizzie came to see Hannah. "Thought I'd just come out. Heard how Frieda is?"

"I called the hospital but I couldn't learn anything. They always say a patient is getting along as well as can be expected. If we just knew what they expected, it would be all right."

287

"Well, I always said that Frieda was too smart for her own good." Lizzie nodded her head and pursed her thin lips. "What is the matter with her?"

"Lord, don't you know?" Lizzie's features were sharper and more pinched than ever. Hannah shook her head.

"Well, if you don't know, I'm not the one to tell you. Say, where'd you get that ring?" She caught hold of Hannah's hand. "Hmm. So Jim Boswell really means it, huh? It won't work, Hannah. You're marryin' out of your class, but then I guess the Boswells lost plenty on sheep. They're not so high and mighty as they used to be. But it won't work. Mark my word. Tabia's didn't work. But of course she had to get married. She told me she did it on purpose."

"Lizzie, I'm not Tabia, and I don't want to hear anything about her."

"All right! All right! I was just tellin' you. You might as well kiss your relations good-by when you marry Jim. He won't stand for none of your family bein' around him. Imagine Papa sittin' at the Boswell table eatin' with his knife and wipin' his mouth on his shirt sleeve. A year from now you'll be singin' a different tune. Say, who is goin' to keep house for Papa and the kids?"

"Housekeepers *can* be hired, Lizzie." Hannah's voice was hard. "If you are going past home, I'll ride that far with you. I want to get some things. One of the boys can bring me back."

"Sure, come along."

At home Hannah took a bath and put on her very nicest clothes. She wrapped her best dress in a neat paper bundle. This night was her wedding night.

"Jim's coming over this evening," she told Solly. "Tell him that I am at Fred's. Tell him to come over there. Don't forget, Solly."

"Sure. I'll tell him," Solly promised, his thin face lighting with affection.

Solly took Hannah and Frieda's baby back to Fred's. She picked up Fred's two boys at the schoolhouse.

Lizzie's visit had tired Hannah, and she was worried

288

about Frieda, but the great emotional upheaval within herself was caused by doubts of the secret marriage she and Jim had planned.

After supper that evening Katie and Fritz stopped in. "Have you heard how Frieda is?" Katie asked anxiously.

Hannah shook her head.

"It's too bad. She'd better had that kid than to lose her life. She ain't so smart."

"Katie! Is it true?"

"Oh, sure. She always said she wouldn't have no dozen kids. Well, she won't, not if she dies."

"Katie! Are you sure? This baby's not a year old."

"Yeah, but it's the truth just the same."

After Katie left Hannah put the baby to bed, then sat in Frieda's low, armless rocker, waiting. Fred's mother was coming to spend the night.

Slow dragging steps came up on the porch. Hannah hadn't heard a car drive in. It must be Fred. "No. No, it must not be," Hannah whispered the words.

The door opened and Fred stood framed there. His face was gray. He closed the door and stood leaning against it.

Hannah sat still. She knew that Frieda was dead.

Fred sat heavily down on the wooden stool beside Hannah's chair, and laid his head in her lap.

Hannah looked down upon Fred's bent head. She smoothed the brown hair, laid her hand on his shoulder. Heavy broad shoulders thickened by hoeing, strong shoulders that had known work in the beets for all his life, shook now with grief. It is a terrible thing to see a strong man cry, and tears dripped from Hannah's cheeks upon his head. She had loved Frieda, too. Now Fred had lost Frieda. He was not old—thirty-six. Alone with three children to look after, one of them a nine-months-old baby.

At last Fred became quiet. Hannah spoke to him then.

"Fred, have you had anything to eat these last few days?"

At her words, Fred raised his head.

"It was so needless, Hannah. It was my fault."

"I don't know, Fred," Hannah said gently. "I don't think so. I used to think that Papa was to blame for Mamma's death, but I'm not so sure, now. Frieda loved you, Fred. She told me so, not long ago."

"I should have stayed away from her."

"If Frieda loved you as I love Jim, you are not to blame. Come, I'm going to get you something to eat."

Hannah sat across from Fred as he started to eat the supper she prepared. He took one bite and stopped.

"It's no use, Hannah. I'm not hungry."

"Fred, your mother and father will be here to stay with you tonight." Hannah rested her hand on his shoulder. He caught her hand, pressed it. He turned her hand over.

"I see you have your ring. If my wishes are any good to you, I wish only that you will be as happy as Frieda and I have been."

At that moment the door opened and Fred's mother and father came in. Simultaneously an auto horn sounded.

"Jim Boswell waits for you," Mrs. Hergenboch said heavily.

Without speaking, Hannah got into the seat beside Jim.

"We're off for Valley City and the minister," Jim whispered.

"Jim, we can't. Frieda died this evening. We can't be married tonight."

"Hannah, don't cry. I'm sorry."

"Jim, it's terrible when anything happens to a married couple who love each other like Fred and Frieda. Jim, I just kept thinking if anything were to happen to you, I'd feel just like Fred. I'd want to die, too."

"You're tired, Hannah. Nothing's going to happen to me. Come, let's be married tonight as we planned."

"I can't, Jim. I just can't. We'll just have to wait until fall. I didn't feel right about us sneaking about getting married, anyway."

"You don't love me, or you'd forget—"

"Jim, I do! I do!" Hannah pressed Jim's face to hers. "We've got to start our marriage right. We're too old to do such unreasoning things." Wearily, she wondered at Jim's insistence. Was he afraid to marry her openly? No. Not that!

290

CHAPTER VIII

HANNAH worked as usual through the second hoeing, blocking and thinning, helping irrigate, and in the fall she took her place in the field to do her full share of the pulling and topping. Solly was home this year. Hannah had hated to see him miss this year of high school but there was no other way. Adam was failing and could no longer work as he had in the past. And there was no money. Even the landowners' children were being kept out of high school and college. When there was no money, there was none, that was all. Hannah tried to soften Solly's disappointment.

"Papa's sick, Solly. You're young, and there's always another year."

Hannah stopped topping for a moment to look across the road. As usual Jim was riding the puller. Just a few weeks now. Not more than three or four at the most. Sometimes, Hannah felt that it must be a dream. At night she turned her ring in the darkness and felt that she shouldn't be so happy. At other times she was almost panicky. Something would happen! But Jim always laughed at her.

"It don't been right," Adam grumbled. Lizzie openly snorted. Even Mary shook her head.

Mamma would have been happy about it, Hannah thought. *She* used to pray for my happiness.

On Sunday morning, as Hannah stood in the choir singing her mother's favorite hymn, she looked down upon the congregation and saw Fred holding his baby in his lap. His two boys were beside him, their backs prim and straight. Hannah's voice faltered as she looked at them. Old grandmother Ochmidt kept house for Fred now, but Fred said it wasn't the same. He dreaded Sundays, for that day she spent with her daughters. Hannah decided to have Fred and the children for dinner at Adam's.

Her father was sitting apart from the other men on the right side of the church. He sat staring straight ahead, his thin old work-worn hands folded in his lap. He looked so alone. Hannah realized he had indeed been alone these last eight years. He sat there quiet, lifeless, motionless. Hannah thought of Jim standing on a mountain top exulting in the battle of the beet country, the constant struggle. How ironical, how immemorially ironical!

After church she slipped her hand under Adam's arm and said, "Papa, shall I ask Fred and the children to come to dinner?"

"Ach, yes, Hannah. Fred, he look bad mit himself. It not good to been alone."

At dinner she watched over her table. Fred was relaxing, was eating, and the sadness was lifting from his face. But Adam wasn't eating—her father, who always gulped his coffee and wolfed his food. Hannah watched him anxiously. She saw him go outside with Fred. The two of them sat on the bench under the old cottonwood and talked. Fred held his baby in his lap.

A little later Fred brought his baby into the kitchen. "She's sound asleep, Hannah. Where do I put her?"

Hannah led the way into the bedroom and threw back the spread.

"Hannah, she won't even remember her mother. It's been pretty bad since Frieda's gone."

"I know, Fred. Sometimes life hits us so hard we think we never can get up and go on, but we can, we have to. I'm worried about Papa."

"He looks sick, Hannah."

"Hannah, Jim's coming," Martha's shrill voice cried. Hannah and Fred walked out into the kitchen.

"Jim, listen, if you take Hannah riding, can I go along?" Martha was begging.

"Not much. Little sisters don't go riding with big sisters. Do you want to go for a ride, Hannah?"

"I'd love to. I'll hurry." Hannah ran into the house for her coat and bumped into Martha.

"Go play, Martha."

"You promised you'd take me riding this afternoon," Martha whimpered.

Hannah stopped. She looked at Martha, and then she looked at Jim. "I did promise her, Jim. I told her if she'd help me I'd take her somewhere this afternoon."

"You'll have to take her some other time."

"I promised her, Jim. Can't we take her with us?"

Jim's face clouded. Hannah could see that he did not like to take Martha, but he nodded his head finally, and Martha went streaking into the house for her coat.

Jim drove slowly along a country road, watching the fields. He stopped his car suddenly and motioned for silence. He picked up his gun from the shelf behind the seat and sighted it. There along the ditch walked a stately old pheasant.

Jim was just ready to press the trigger when Martha shouted, "Oh, Jim, there's another one!" She grabbed his arm just as Jim shot. The pheasant went whirring into the air and disappeared.

Jim put his gun away and looked at Hannah.

He turned the car around and started back toward home. He kept both hands on the steering wheel. Hannah found that she couldn't think of a thing to say.

At home, he let Martha out. She pouted, but Hannah was firm. Then he and Hannah rode away.

"Kids are all right," Jim said, "but I don't want them around when I have my best girl with me."

On Monday Adam did not eat any breakfast, but went to the field as usual. He jolted up and down the field on the puller until eleven o'clock; then he called Alec to take his place. He walked down the field and came to where Hannah worked, and staggered as he walked. When he came even with Hannah, she asked anxiously, "Papa, what's the matter?"

"Gott, Hannah. I sick so I die. I go call mit a doctor."

"I'll take you in to town." Hannah took his arm.

"I don't can ride mit town," Adam murmured. As soon as they got into the house Adam went to bed. Hannah telephoned for the doctor.

"What I do? What I do?" Adam moaned. "Sure, I die."

"The doctor will be right out. He'll fix you up so that you'll be feeling fine." Hannah smoothed her father's bony hand, straightened his pillow.

"We'll have you up and around in a day or two," the doctor said cheerfully, as he measured out medicine. But to Hannah, as he was leaving, he was not so optimistic. "He hasn't any vitality. He's apt to go any time. There's nothing I can do."

Hannah watched the doctor drive away. *Her* father dying? It was not possible. For years he'd been thin and shriveled. He had always groaned about aches and pains. This was no different. She went back to his bedroom. He lay like some little shriveled gnome. His gimlet eyes stared with a feverish brightness. He *was* sick.

"Hannah, I die!" Stark fear was in his voice. "Don't you leave me, Hannah."

"I'll not leave you." Gradually the medicine took effect and he became quiet.

The boys and Martha came in for dinner.

"Is he really sick, Hannah?" Alec asked.

Hannah nodded her head and put her fingers to her lips for silence. As she did so an old and shrieking voice came from the next room.

"Hannah! Make them kids go mit the field! We never gets the beets out the ground! Gott, und they freeze, sure!"

Hannah went to him. "They're going back to the field," she told him.

"Call Ochmidt. Call Kniemer so they come stay mit me, und you go mit the field, Hannah. We got get the beets out."

"Kniemer and Ochmidt are both working in their own beets. I'll call them tonight." Adam became quiet. Through the afternoon he seemed to sleep, but toward evening he became anxious and fearful.

294

"Hannah, I think I die. I feel it, Hannah. I no can die, Hannah!" His voice rose to a shriek.

"Papa, you must not excite yourself. I've called Mary and Lizzie to come so they can be with you. And Fritz and Tabia are coming this evening. The minister is coming right after supper. He would be here now but his wife says he is out of town."

"I don't can die, Hannah. I don't can die!" He clung to her and tears ran down his cheeks.

The terrible fear of death was in her father's face. Always, he had feared death, Hannah knew. Now this reality as she faced his panic unnerved her. She had to comfort him. Her mother had not feared to die. Only of others had she ever thought. Her faith had sustained her at the last moment. All his life her father had gone to church, yet he feared death.

"Papa, it is not death to die," Hannah said desperately. "Papa, remember the words, 'I am the resurrection and the life: he that believeth in Me, though he were dead, yet shall he live: and whosoever liveth and believeth in Me shall never die.'"

"I don't know if I believe. Gott, what I believe?"

"Mamma believed in God. Remember how strong and sure she always was."

"Ach, Gott, I miss her. Hannah, you sure she believe?"

"Yes, I'm sure. She was never afraid."

"Hannah, you believe?" Feverishly Adam clung to her hand.

"Yes, I believe." Hannah's voice was firm and sure.

"You would not tell me wrong, Hannah?"

"I believe in God the Father and in Jesus Christ, Our Lord."

"Yah, sure. Mit Gott, I no been afraid." Adam was comforted.

Ochmidts came, and Kniemers. The Schreissmiller children all gathered at home that evening. For once Lizzie's sharp tongue was stilled. Mary cried loudly. Fritz stood stolidly, his back against the wall. When the minister came he said upon entering the door:

"Peace be to this house, and to all that dwell therein."

295

Lizzie cried; tears streamed down Tabia's face; old lady Ochmidt and old lady Kniemer sat inscrutable in their black lace head shawls, their wide fat bodies dressed in black waists and wide gathered skirts, their flat feet planted firmly on the floor in front of their chairs. Hannah stood among them all in that kitchen. They were her people.

CHAPTER IX

HANNAH was working in the beet field, helping to finish the topping. Only for the day of her father's funeral had the work stopped in the field. The Goelzers had come to help top.

A flock of young lambs was coming up the road. A small boy came first, pulling an old goat by a short length of rope. Hannah saw that it was Fred Hergenboch's oldest boy. Dust rose from the main body of the flock. Hannah could hear the shrill shouts of a woman, the barking of dogs, the guttural orders of men. As the lambs came even with the field where Hannah worked, she saw old lady Hergenboch, Fred's mother, short and fat, with a white kerchief tied over her head. She beat her way energetically among the lambs, driving them before her.

"Hello, Hannah!" she shouted, not stopping to say more.

Fred Hergenboch brought up the rear and came to the fence to speak to Hannah.

"How's things going?" he asked quietly.

"As well as possible, I guess. We've got to get the beets out of the ground. We'll finish this week."

"I see by the paper you're having the sale the seventeenth of November."

"Yes, two days after the first beet check comes out. People ought to have some money, then."

"I suppose the older married ones will take the younger children. Deaths are hard on children. They can't defend themselves like older people."

"I know. They are all coming next Sunday afternoon to

talk over what's to be done with the boys and Martha. Everythings seems such a jumble, Fred."

"I know. I'm lost without Frieda. Grandmother Ochmidt does well enough for us, but it's not home. She's old and slow, and the children bother her. I must be going. If you need any help, let me know." With a smile, Fred left her and went striding down the road to catch up with his slow moving flock.

Hannah went back to her topping. As soon as the beets were out, she decided, she'd have to start packing things. There was the fruit in jars in the cellar. She supposed that would have to be divided up among the other children, but she'd done the work, had even picked the fruit. No matter. Jim would have no need of the fruit. What he wanted he could afford to buy. It would seem queer to be able to have things without skimping and saving for months and years. When the younger children were divided among the older children and the sale was over and everything settled, she and Jim would be married. The thought eased the hurt in Hannah's heart. She had not realized before just how much of her days Adam had occupied.

They finished the beets on a Friday and on Sunday the family met at the old home to decide about the children. The sale was to be held ten days later.

Fritz was the first to push himself back from the table.

"Well," he said, "we might as well get busy and get this deciding done. No use putting it off."

Hannah followed his glance around the table. There was Mary, fat and shapeless, hushing her baby on her lap; Lizzie, angular and straight, with her mouth pursed in a disapproving line; Olinda, her round face lined with complaint; Tabia, getting fat like Mary and trying to hide it by expert dressing. She had obtained her divorce and had married a Russian several months before; Fritz, getting slovenly, with a bad hump between his shoulders from too much hoeing when he was small.

At one end of the table lounged the boys—Alec, Solly, Coonie, Chris and Reinie. Martha was out playing with Mary's girls.

Hannah looked at all of her sisters and saw their defenses go up. She knew that an argument was bound to come. Alec stood up and faced the group.

"I'm leaving," he said, almost defiantly. "Probably won't see you again. I start work tomorrow. I've got a job by the month. You don't have to do any worrying about me." He strode out.

Alec was nineteen. Hannah did not blame him.

Solly, thin, with sensitive lips, stood up also. His voice was lower than Alec's. He did not have Alec's defiant frustration. "I have a job, too," he said. "I'm going to work my way through high school. I have the chance."

"You're a fool," Lizzie told him. "What good did high school do Tabia?"

Solly left the room without answering. Only the older married ones and Hannah were left to decide.

"Well, who's goin' to take who?" Fritz again spoke to them. He cleared his throat and looked around. "I might as well tell you that Katie an' me's expectin' one of our own before long and we can't take any of them, us only havin' two rooms as it is."

"I don't see how we can take any unless it is Martha," whined Olinda. "I'm sick all the time. She'd be big enough to help me some. I couldn't wait on another boy."

"Hm, you would want somebody to work to death. Well, I'll tell you if I take any it'll be Martha." Lizzie's tone was high and sharp. "Goodness knows how we will manage but I told my husband we'd take Martha since we have to take one of them, I suppose."

There was silence. Hannah saw Mary lean over to Katie and heard her say, "I'd rather see one of my girls in her coffin than livin' with that Lizzie."

"What's that?" Lizzie glared at Mary.

"I didn't say nothin'," Mary answered.

"This ain't gettin' us nowhere, an' I got to get home in time to milk," Fritz insisted.

There was silence.

Hannah saw she would have to take charge. "There's Coonie, he's fourteen. Who will take him?"

"If we was contractin' instead of workin' by the month he could help us a lot but as it is—well, I guess one more to feed don't make no difference. We could take him," Mary said.

"Lizzie will take Martha. Mary will take Coonie. There's Chris, he's twelve." Hannah looked around the group again.

"Well, I suppose if we hafto, we hafto," Olinda said. "We might as well take him, hadn't we, Henry?"

Henry nodded.

"Then there's Reinie. He's ten." Hannah's voice ended in a silence. Stolid faces greeted her.

"Tabia, could you take him?"

"No, I can't."

"Somebody's got to take him," Hannah said.

"Well, I won't take him," Tabia snapped. "I think you got your nerve askin' any of us to take him, with his fits and everything. Why don't you take him? You're gettin' married; you can take him."

"If some of you would just take him for this first year—" Hannah looked at them. She knew that Jim would not approve of her taking Reinie. He had never liked Reinie. She knew they should have this first year to themselves. The others had had their lives.

"I think he ought to be sent to a home for the feeble-minded," Lizzie said.

"Reinie's not feeble-minded. Just because he has fits once in awhile is no sign he's crazy." Hannah was angry.

"Well, you don't want him. Neither do we want him."

"I didn't say I didn't want him. I love Reinie. He's a good boy and he's a worker. I've cared for him ever since he was born, but I think Jim and I should have our first year alone."

"I think Hannah's right." Katie stood up for Hannah. "Some of you kids can take Reinie. It won't hurt you."

Lizzie pursed her lips into a straighter line. She was set like solid granite. "It's all right for you to talk. I don't see you taking none of the kids."

Mary looked troubled, but Hannah could see that she wouldn't take Reinie. Fritz was sullen and obstinate. He

300

would not change. Tabia glared. She dared any one to suggest Reinie to her.

Hannah looked at them. "You think it over," she said, "and we'll decide after the sale."

They all looked relieved. "I think that's a good idea," Lizzie agreed.

"Yeah," Tabia whined. "They might as well stay here till the sale's over."

"I do think, though, Hannah, we might as well decide about dividing up some of Papa's things." Lizzie rose from the table with a determined expression on her thin face. "I'll take that pink wool blanket on Hannah's bed, the rest of you can have all the other bedding. That's all I want." Lizzie started toward the stairs.

"That pink blanket belongs to me, Lizzie." Hannah's quiet voice stopped her sister.

"To you! You don't own nothin' in this house, Hannah. Papa bought all of it with his own money. And I guess we come in for our share of it."

"No, Lizzie. These last years I've kept the money I earned from working for Mrs. Boswell. Papa gave me extra money for staying here and keeping house. I bought that blanket with my own money."

"That's a lie, Hannah. Papa never give a dime to one of his kids. He worked them to death, but he never give them nothin'."

"None of you stayed after you were twenty-one. I did," Hannah insisted calmly. "Papa wasn't so bad. He was pretty decent when you understood him."

"Oh, quit your fighting!" Olinda whined. "I want to take some of the fruit down cellar. I can use it."

"Yes, we might as well divide the fruit," Hannah agreed. But down in the cellar, the sisters almost came to blows.

"I wish you'd leave a half dozen cans of fruit for us to eat this week," Hannah suggested.

Reluctantly, each girl returned one can of food.

"You'll have to wait to divide the bedding," Hannah told Olinda, who was folding a comfort off Adam's bed. "When

301

you decide definitely about the children you can divide things, then."

Wearily, Hannah watched them leave. None of them wanted the children, but they wanted everything else that was of value. Even her very own things. And nobody wanted Reinie.

CHAPTER X

HANNAH told Jim her troubles that night. "Jim, they want to send Reinie to a home for the feeble-minded. Lizzie suggested it. And she wants to take Martha. She'll whip her, Jim, and she'll be mean to her. There's no goodness nor charity in Lizzie."

"Nobody wants extra children, Hannah. You can't blame them too much." Jim's voice was unconcerned.

"But, Jim, Reinie isn't crazy. He'd go crazy, though, if they put him in a home. Just because he has a fit once in awhile is no sign he can't feel, and can't understand."

"He's a problem, Hannah. Personally, I can't stand him. Those big eyes of his give me the creeps."

"Jim, it hurts when you say things like that. You mean you'd even let him be sent to a home?"

"We can't take him, if that's what you're hinting at, Hannah." Jim stopped his car at the side of the road and turned and faced her.

"Look here, Hannah, quit worrying about those kids. You've looked after that family for eight years, and that's enough. You've worked in the field! You've slaved for them. It's the place of your older brothers and sisters to worry about the younger ones, not you."

"But, Jim—"

"Listen, Hannah. You and I are going on a long honeymoon. We're going to be gone most of the winter. Mother and Dad are going to stay on the place this winter while we are gone. I'm going to make you forget your family. You're going to forget you've ever had a responsibility.

Smile, Hannah. You're going to have the time of your life. I'm going to have more fun buying you the kind of clothes that will make your hair more golden and your eyes blue as the sky." Jim kissed her.

"You know I love you, Jim. I do. But Jim, I couldn't be happy if I knew that Reinie was in a home, and Lizzie might get mad and hurt Martha." Hannah felt Jim stiffen.

"Hannah, you've got to choose right now," he said hotly. "I can see you want to keep Reinie and Martha. Hannah, they can't live with us. That's final. If you care more for those two kids than you do for me, now's the time to decide."

"Jim, you don't love me when you talk like that."

"I do love you, Hannah, but I don't love your brothers and sisters. I'm marrying you, not your family."

"I don't ask you to, Jim, but Reinie and Martha are like my own. I've looked after them ever since they were born. Mamma asked me to care for them."

"What do you think I am? Marry you and bring two half-grown kids into our house? Not a minute's privacy. Always underfoot. It's enough that—" Jim's voice stopped, choked with anger.

"Go on and say it," Hannah said quietly. "Say it's bad enough that you are marrying me without my family thrown in."

"I didn't say it, Hannah. But since you've said it, I agree with you. I'm marrying you, not your family. You'll have to decide. It's either me, or Reinie and Martha. It can't be both." Jim was hard, cold, angry.

"I can't decide now. Take me home, Jim."

"God, Hannah, do you mean to sit there and quibble over two kids? If that's how you feel, you don't love me."

"Jim, you've never faced anything in your life. Love has nothing to do with it. Take me home. Maybe you'd better take your ring."

"I don't want your ring." Jim angrily started the car.

Hannah did not sleep that night. She knew that Jim wanted only her. The day she married Jim she would have to part with her family. Lizzie had said, "Jim won't have nothing to do with your family." Well, who would want Lizzie around? Who would want Olinda? But they were her sisters. Mary and Fritz were beetworkers, crude, unpolished, but were they not her people? Solly, with his sensitive face, working, going on to high school—should he not be helped? Alec, Coonie and Chris? But none meant as much to her as Reinie and Martha did. She *couldn't* let Lizzie have Martha, she *couldn't* let them send Reinie away. Reinie wasn't crazy.

"Gott, Hannah, it don't can work," Adam had told her again and again.

Perhaps it wouldn't, Hannah thought. Jim already was talking of taking her away for the winter. Away from what? Away from her own people, or away from his own parents' disapproval or both?

"You're a fool, Hannah, if you ever marry an American," Tabia had said. "He'll always throw it up to you that you're a Russian."

A Russian, yes. Would his friends be like his parents and object to a Russian?

"You're living in a fool's heaven," Frieda had said. "I hope you don't hit the earth."

A fool's heaven alone with Jim—no friends, no family. Round and round in her head went the argument.

"Come, breakfast," Hannah called the next morning. She made pancakes at the stove and served the children at the table. She looked at Martha. Her eyes were as blue as Hannah's own. The delicate-featured face, the sensitive lips, the merry laughing eyes, etched themselves indelibly upon Hannah's mind. Hannah thought of Lizzie's sharp tongue. Then she watched Reinie. He was all arms and legs, big for his age. But he was willing to work. It was Reinie who kept her woodbox filled, carried in the coal, ran the errands. And his fits were further apart. He didn't have them nearly so often. The doctor said he would outgrow them. Send him to a feeble-minded home? No!

All that day Hannah expected Jim, but he did not come. He didn't come that night.

The next day was the same.

After a week Hannah was angry. Did she mean so little to him that he would not patch up a quarrel, that he never wanted to see her again?

The children did not add to her peace of mind. As the day of the sale drew near they talked more and more of whom they would live with.

"I wouldn't want to live with that old Lizzie," Coonie said. "I like Mary better."

"Who did you say was going to take me?" Reinie raised his glance from his plate.

"I don't know, Reinie. We haven't decided yet."

"Hannah, take me to live with you," Martha begged.

Fred Hergenboch and Fritz came to help get the farm machinery lined up at the side of the barnlot so that it would be in a position to be sold easily.

"Well, Hannah, has everything been settled?" Fred asked.

"Fred, no one wants Reinie. They want to send him to a home. And Lizzie wants Martha."

"It's a bad business, Hannah."

"I don't know what I'm going to do, Fred."

"You marrying Jim as soon as the sale is over?"

"I don't know, Fred. If I marry Jim, I give up my family, my people, my friends, my church. I give up everything that is German-Russian."

Fred nodded.

The morning before the sale, Jim came over. Hannah was coming from the barn after having fed the chickens. Jim's big coupé drew up beside her.

"Get in, Hannah. I want to talk to you." He held the door open for her, but Hannah made no move to get in.

"Hannah, I've gone through hell this last week. I'm willing to pay some of the others to keep the kids for this winter at least." Jim's eyes were sober.

Hannah slowly took Jim's ring off her finger. "I love you more this minute than ever before in my life," she said slowly, "but it won't do. It wouldn't work."

"Hannah! You don't know what you are saying!"

"Yes, I do. I've thought of nothing else this whole week."

306

"Just how do you think you're going to look after those two children?"

"I can work."

"Hannah, you can't do that! Marry me, and forget the children."

Hannah backed away, leaving Jim's ring lying on the seat beside him. "I know what I'm doing. You can be happy without me. Good-by, Jim." Hannah bit her lip and looked into his eyes, at his lips. She turned and went toward the house.

"What are you crying for?" Lizzie's voice was sharp. "Huh, so he threw you over, did he?" Lizzie's voice rose as she looked at Hannah's ringless hand. "I told you it would never work."

Hannah went silently through the rest of the day. With relief she watched her sisters drive away in the evening. After supper, with the children in bed, she sat alone at the kitchen table. She had to plan what to do.

She looked at her hand, which now had no ring. It was a beetworker's hand. What was she fitted to do? She could work as a hired girl—Jim's mother had taught her. Jim. Jim.

A knock at the kitchen door roused her. "Come in," she said listlessly.

It was Fred Hergenboch—tall, broad-shouldered, his kindly face showing new lines since Frieda's death.

Fred sat down at the cleared table. "What are you going to do, Hannah? Tomorrow is the sale."

"I don't know, Fred. I can't think."

"I heard that Jim—"

"Yes, I've known it wouldn't work, but I loved him, Fred. I'll never love another man like that. Part of me is gone."

"Yet you sent him away."

"I could do no different. Lizzie wants Martha. They want to send Reinie to a home. They are like my own. You know that."

"You're paying too high a price, Hannah. Jim loves you."

"Fred, I've argued for a week with myself. But it wouldn't work. Jim's mother doesn't want him to marry me. His father doesn't say anything, but he's not satisfied. And Jim has a hot

307

temper. Some day, he'd throw it up to me that I was a Russian."

"Hannah!"

"I know it, Fred. As surely as I sit here. But I love him. I don't see how I can live without him. But I've got to."

"I know how it is, Hannah. With Frieda gone, I am lost. There is one love, and nothing is ever like that again."

"I know, Fred. I'll miss him all my life, but I've got to look after Reinie and Martha."

"It won't be easy, Hannah." Fred rose and stood looking down at her.

"You've decided for certain that you will not marry Jim?"

"I can do no different," she said sadly.

There was silence for a long time. Then Fred spoke. "Hannah, my baby needs a mother. My two boys cannot look after themselves. Coonie and Chris are too young to shift for themselves, and you say you cannot leave Martha and Reinie. Marry me, Hannah."

Fred's words jarred upon Hannah's grief. She got up from her chair.

"You mean you'll take the four younger children?"

"I need help in my beets. The three boys can work. I'm paying for my place. It will mean hard work for the next two or three years."

Hannah looked at Fred.

"I do not offer you love, Hannah. Neither do I ask it. But I respect you as no other woman I know. I ask you as a friend that I admire above all others. I shall try to never let you be sorry that you married me."

His eyes were both sad and kind. Fred was of her own people. Her best friend. He would be good to her, kind to the children—a strength in time of trouble.

"Fred, you've always been near in time of need. You've always been near when I've needed help. I'm tired."

Her head bent forward and touched his arm.

Hannah lifted her beet knife and sent it through the huge beet she held in her left hand. Across the field was the new white house that had been Frieda's, and was now hers. She saw Fred's two boys working with Chris, Coonie and Reinie, and Fred bending his strong back. At the end of the field Martha played with Fred's youngest child. Nearby was a baby carriage. In it was Hannah's own son.